WALKING WITH NOTHING

Lindsey-Anne Pontes

WALKING WITH NOTHING

Front and back cover design by Jasmine Keats (@jasminekeatstattoo)
Formatting by Indie Publishing Group Inc

ISBN: 978-1-9992421-2-1 (paperback)
ISBN: 978-1-9992421-3-8 (ebook)

ACKNOWLEDGMENTS

Café O Roaster & Bakery: Big thank you to Irina, and all the lovely ladies (Brooke, Brianna, Emily, Kadence, Abigail, Sarah, Stacie, Miranda, Macy, Susan, and others), who've made my exclusive café days ones to remember. I've loved becoming a regular, where my order is started almost immediately as I walk through the door while having you all ask me about my new book and writing journey on a regular basis. Getting to know each one of you has been a life-changing experience, one I'll carry with me forever. Cheers to continued friendships and future partnerships.

Catherine Muss: As always, you continue to amaze me on just how good you are, both as an editor and as a friend. I enjoy the friendship we've developed over this writing partnership and can't believe I got so lucky to find someone like you. From editor Catherine to reader Catherine, I've loved both sets of comments and feedback. Again, without your help, this self-pub book wouldn't be what it is today. I look forward to working with you in the future, even if it's not with a new manuscript, and can't wait to be a beta reader for your future release!

Telma Rocha: Oh boy, where to start. Telma, you've always been my sensei when it comes to writing, editing, and self-publishing. I appreciate all the hard work and time you've put into me and my writing over these last few years. You always present me with challenges to improve my writing and/or story, and I can't thank you enough. You're a fantastic author and editor, and I can't wait for your next work to be released.

Amanda Pagliaro: You are my number one fan for this book, by far. I loved how excited you got when I asked you to be a beta reader and how quickly you dived into the story after it was handed to you. The excitement you conveyed about the characters, giving me detailed feedback on each individual one, was beyond helpful. I also love how attached you've become to the story, wanting to know the feedback from other beta readers and willing to go to war for the characters you adore most. I'm grateful to have you in my life, especially during this process. Thank you.

Melissa Frattolin: Thank you for taking time out of your busy schedule to be a beta reader and proofreader for me, yet again. Your edits are extremely helpful, as you tend to have an eye for things most people overlook. I appreciate all your time and help in making both my books bookstore ready. You've been a great friend and resource!

Samantha Jennings: Thank you for being a beta reader for not only this book but also my first. Although we have very different viewpoints when it comes to developing characters, you have been a big supporter of my writing from day one. You pushed me to finish my first book, and now here I am, releasing my second! Thank you for all your help.

Jasmine Keats: Above all, I must give you a GREAT BIG thank you for your amazing cover design. After all the compliments I received from your first work on *Let Me Save You*, I just knew I needed to have you work on the cover for my second book, too. Thank you for taking the time to work on something beyond tattooing, something neither of us knew much about, to create art in a new way. You've been a pleasure to work with, and I heavily apologize for all my annoying antics during this partnership. Thank you, thank you, thank you!

Doug Wicken: Never would I have thought that we'd become good friends, connected by writing, based on our age difference—but here we are. Thank you so much for helping me proofread this book and getting it that much closer to being print ready. It's been a pleasure helping you along your own writing journey, while bonding over our favourite place, Café O.

Julie Johnson: Thank you so much for taking on a proofreading role. You and your keen eye were a tremendous help in finding those little things that many have overlooked. I'm so glad you agreed to help me with this lengthy project. You went above and beyond my expectations! I have Frank Bianchi to thank for our fated encounter (shh, don't tell him I said that).

DISCLAIMER

This book uses harsh language and discusses topics much darker than my first book, **Let Me Save You**. Please be advised that some may feel triggered by scenes and find it hard to read about certain subjects of death, drug and alcohol abuse, and child abuse and neglect present in the story. This book is recommended for mature readers.

For those less experienced with Japanese formalities, I have kept the usage of honorifics, such as -kun, -chan, -san, etc., limited. These are traditionally used when addressing an unfamiliar individual out of respect. For instance, the last name of a person is typically used when speaking to someone with whom you do not have a close relationship. In most cases, it isn't until a rapport is formed that the first name will be used in everyday conversation. I have chosen to write in such a manner so I could incorporate a passion of mine, while introducing a culture other than my own, to those willing to read something different. In no way, shape, or form, am I an expert on Japan or Japanese culture. I apologize if I have used anything incorrectly. The story is a standalone fiction, and is to be treated as such.

Without further ado, please enjoy!

Thank you,
Lindsey-Anne Pontes

Part One:

NOTHING

Chapter One

*T*HE FRONT DOOR *slammed shut, sending an echo throughout the small, one-bedroom apartment.*

Lifting my head from where I laid, I rubbed the sleep from my eyes. "Hmm . . .? Mommy?"

Rising to my feet, I slowly walked out into the narrow hallway hoping that my mother had finally returned. Looking down the hall, I saw her figure standing in the doorway, along with a man I had never seen. Locking eyes with me, my mother clicked her tongue.

"What the fuck, I didn't know you had a kid?" said the man.

She clicked her tongue again, then faced him. "Don't worry 'bout him. He won't say nothin'," she answered with irritation before turning back to me. "Why're you awake?"

"U-um . . . I was sleeping, Mommy, b-but then I heard the door and thought—"

"Go back to sleep," she demanded, just before passing me.

She walked into the bathroom, signaling the strange man to follow. He did as he was directed, and I did as I was told. I walked back to the corner of the multipurpose living area, where my tattered blanket remained, and tried my best to wrap myself in it to keep out of sight—the way my mother liked me to be. At this point, my mother had shut the bathroom

door after the man squeezed in behind her. With the small apartment, and the paper-thin walls, I could hear everything they were saying.

"How old's the kid?"

"I dunno, like five or somethin'. Don't bother concernin' yourself with him, Daigo. He'll keep quiet."

"'Ya sure? Kids are always spittin' out the truth to anyone who'll listen."

"He won't. He knows better."

"If you say so."

Not knowing what was going on behind the door, but understanding enough, I covered my ears and tried with all my might to fall back asleep.

⁂

"-ku! Riku! Hey, Riku!"

"Hmm . . .?" Flipping to the other side of the pillow, I peered up with sleep-deprived eyes. Standing beside my bed was a fully clothed woman.

"I'm leaving now, just thought you'd like to know. I know you don't like girls who linger," she giggled to herself. "Last night was fun. Call me anytime."

Normally, I wouldn't have been pleased about being woken up so early in the morning for something so trivial, but the memory I was reliving in my sleep wasn't that pleasant, either.

I got off my stomach and turned over in bed to face the off-white wall, then shut my eyes. I heard the dying sound of feet tapping against the wooden floor. Seconds after, the front door opened.

"What the fuck? Riku, you left the door unlocked all night! What if someone entered while we were sleeping?"

My eyes rolled in their sockets. "So?"

"So? What do you mean, 'so'?" she exclaimed angrily from the entryway. "Someone could have killed us in our sleep!"

"They would've been doing me a favour," I declared over my shoulder.

"Stop joking! I can't believe you're not even fazed by this."

Refusing to turn around and look at the woman whose name I couldn't remember, I let out a sigh. "The way I choose to live is none of your concern. Besides, we barely did any *sleeping* last night. Now, get out and go bother your husband or something."

"You're such a little shit!" she shouted, just before slamming the door as hard as she possibly could.

The angry clicking of her high heels faded into the abyss, so I attempted sleep once more. Though, sleep eluded me as I heard a knock on the door shortly after.

"Riii-ku! It's me, I'm coming in!"

Recognizing the bothersome voice that sang my name, I opened my eyes and flipped back over, dragging the single bed sheet along with me to cocoon myself. Peering down the short, narrow hallway of my small studio apartment, I stared at the door. Like a gust of wind, it flung open, and another troublesome person appeared.

"Oh good, you're awake," he stated, eagerly. Taking off his shoes, he lined them up at the raised entryway.

"Not really," I muttered, covering my face with the sheet. "Go away."

"I saw that woman leave your apartment, again," he continued, ignoring my plea. "That's twice this week. She seemed pretty upset today, though. What did she call you this time? Wait, wait, let me guess . . . 'Shit face'? 'Asshole'? 'Dickwad'?"

"'Little shit,'" I replied from underneath the covers.

Hearing laughter emerge from my friend, I felt a weight descend on me.

"Meh, close enough."

Removing the sheet from my head, I could see that he had made himself comfortable on my bed, practically on top of me.

"Oi, Makoto, get off."

"Come on, Riku. You can't miss school today. I covered for you yesterday, as well as the day before, and *all* those other days, too," he dragged. "Kobayashi-sensei was really pissed off and chewed me out yesterday because you didn't show up. He treats me as if I'm your caretaker or something! You're older than me, so why am I the one looking after you?"

"Ugh! I got off a shift just a few hours ago. Why won't anyone let me sleep?" I sobbed into my pillow.

"Stop complaining; that's no one's fault but your own," he said, smacking the back of my head. "Uncle Ito already said that you don't have to pay rent, but you still insist on working like a maniac."

Continuing to hide my face, I mumbled into the pillow, "Your family's done a lot for me already. I can't freeload forever."

"Riku, you're like a brother to me. No one in my family thinks you're a freeloader."

Lifting my head, I turned back to face him with a warning look.

"Fiiine. Continue being a stubborn pain in the ass," he said, as he rolled his eyes. "Do you work today?"

Makoto Fujimoto was a glasses-wearing virgin with an impeccable sense of style. He cared a lot about his appearance and presently rocked one of those quiff haircuts that required a ton of maintenance.

I let my black hair do its own thing. It was too short to tie back, but long enough to annoyingly get into my eyes. For P.E., I'd often push it back with a headband so I could see what the hell I was doing.

Getting up, I unraveled my cocoon and swung my feet out of bed to place them firmly on the floor, then stretched my arms in the air. "Nah, today's one of the few days I have off."

"I know," he said smugly, just before twisting his face and gawking at me. "GAH! Put some damn clothes on, you perverted flasher!"

Peering down, I forgot I was naked. "Touché," I said, as I found the boxer briefs I had discarded lustfully earlier this morning and got myself decent.

"Anyway," Makoto said, clearing his throat and uncovering his eyes, "it was a trick question. I always take a picture of your schedule, remember? I'm the one who must keep on top of you or else you'll NEVER show up at school. Why else do you think I'm here?"

Raising my leg, I kicked Makoto off the end of the bed. As he hit the floor, he made an exaggerated, high-pitched scream.

"AHH! You're going to break my glasses, you *little shit!*" He threw my school uniform at me. "You know, you should really hang up your uniform. Principal Koga, and all the teachers who see you, are going to give you shit for how wrinkled it is."

"I lost the hanger."

"Liar!" he shouted. "It's right here!"

Throwing the hanger in my direction, he missed me completely and hit the lamp sitting on the side table, causing it to fall on the floor and shatter. For a moment, we both froze, staring at all the pieces.

"You idiot."

With one hand cupped over his mouth, as if to hide his shock, he wailed, "Bro, I'm so sorry! I'll replace it!"

"You better. I might get this apartment at a discounted price, but the furniture didn't come with it."

"I will, promise!"

Giving up on the idea of sleep, I got ready for school. After brushing my teeth, I put on my navy-blue school pants and slipped on a plain, black undershirt before buttoning up my white, short-sleeve uniform shirt over top. Leaving the last two buttons undone, I loosely added the green school necktie to complete the regulated attire.

Each grade had a designated colour to display which year a student was from; third years wore green. We also had two different uniform sets: summer and winter. The winter uniform entailed a long-sleeve dress shirt, a vest, and a blazer. We weren't required to wear all the pieces of the full winter uniform unless it was a special occasion.

Makoto, being the doting housewife that he secretly was, opened my chest-high refrigerator and bent to see the contents inside while I searched for my schoolbag.

"Man, Riku, are you eating properly? There's barely anything in here. All you have is a bunch of beer," I could almost hear his eyes rolling by his tone, "and canned coffee." Reaching for a can of coffee, he frowned sourly. "I don't know how you can even drink this stuff black—cold no less. Yuck." He gagged for emphasis.

Turning away from him, I shook my head reflexively and began sorting through the mess on my floor. Pretending to focus on the task, I shouted over my shoulder. "I usually eat at my part-time jobs or bring home leftovers from work. I don't keep much food in the fridge. It goes bad faster than I can eat it. As for the beer and coffee," I said, shifting to look at Makoto, who was staring at me, "one, I get my older coworkers to buy the beer, and two, coffee's the only thing that keeps me going. Coffee's gotta be cold in the summer and warm in the winter. Both drinks quench the thirst just right."

"Isn't that what water's for?"

"Water? Never heard of it."

"You're hopeless," he said, as he massaged his temples.

"But you love me."

"Shut up, you manwhore."

Before going back to my search, I hollered, "Actually, bring me that can, wouldja babe?" Then, I blew him a kiss and winked.

"Did you suddenly turn stupid, or what?"

Slamming the refrigerator door closed, he hurled the coffee can at me. I dropped everything to catch the can before it bounced and exploded. Radiating stress and irritation, Makoto reluctantly came to help me find my magically misplaced schoolbag.

"Why'd you throw it if you were gonna come here, anyway?"

"Because," he said, puffing out his cheeks as he bent down, "you're so goddamn annoying that I had hoped it would have smoked you in that dumb, pretty-boy face of yours."

"Jeez, aren't you just a breath of fresh air," I said, haggardly.

"Don't pepper me with compliments."

While we bickered, Makoto found my schoolbag and threw some stuff into it. Irritated, he chucked the bag at me, then shot back up and walked swiftly to the entrance to put his shoes on. "Come on, we're going to be late, jerkface."

"All right, all right. I'm coming."

⁂

Distancing ourselves from the apartment complex, we headed to Shibuya Station. The busy streets of Tokyo could be alarming for visitors, but everything was easily accessible. Vehicles zoomed past us as we continued along the paved sidewalks to the underground Metro. My apartment was a few, painfully long stops away from our school.

Even though my place was in the opposite direction from Makoto's, making his commute to school twice as long, he often woke up extra early to come by and guilt me into attending school on the days I didn't have work. Not knowing how Makoto had the patience to put up with my sorry, delinquent ass, I accepted his helicopter friendship since I knew he had my best interests in mind. Makoto also often made second copies of his school notes and would leave them at my door so I could use them to study for tests and exams. He was a diligent notetaker, so even an idiot like me could understand the material enough to get a passing grade. Most of the time.

It brought me great joy tormenting Makoto with my bromantic affection because I loved watching him squirm with embarrassment. We had been best friends since elementary school. That's when Makoto and his family entered my life and saved me.

Thanks to the relentless kindness of the Fujimoto family, Makoto's uncle allowed me to rent one of his units. Uncle Ito was probably the coolest person I had ever met. The title of 'uncle' didn't suit him whatsoever. He was much more of a cool, older brother than an uncle. Though he wasn't my actual uncle, he made me call him as such.

It was forbidden for minors to live on their own, but Uncle Ito overlooked my age as long as I stayed out of trouble; although, trouble seemed to find me.

It was difficult to find one's way and make a decent living in a gigantic, expensive city like Tokyo. However, with a population of over thirteen million, it had its perks, like no one knew who you were, and people left you alone. Unless you had overly caring people in your life, like the Fujimotos.

We were in our final, and most crucial, year of senior high school. This year, Makoto became the student council vice-president, stating his involvement looked better on university applications. But it sounded like a lot of unnecessary work. Makoto, being the genius that he was, wanted to become a doctor who specialized in treating children with life-threatening conditions. We weren't even done high school yet and this guy had already planned to add another hundred years of school onto his workload. I've never met anyone more genuine, caring, or dedicated.

I, on the other hand, have always sunk to the bottom ten in student rankings.

School was never important to me. So, after passing the high school entrance exam, naïve me thought I had triumphed over the ultimate hurdle. Little did I realize that I needed to maintain my efforts so I could advance to the following year; I wouldn't be free from homework and tests until graduation. I had no desire to further my education by attending college or university, so high school just felt unnecessary and repetitive. But I made a promise to Makoto's parents. A promise I intended to keep.

After one transfer and four stops later, we got off the subway and headed up to the street. Walking along, Makoto and I continued in meaningless conversation until the school building was in sight.

"MAKO-KUN!"

As we approached the school gates, Makoto, who walked beside me, vanished. Almost dropping my can of coffee, I saw Makoto struggling to remain standing as one of our classmates attacked him from behind by jumping onto his back.

"AHH! Sakura, what the hell are you doing?" Makoto questioned, as he pushed her off. Bashfully, he adjusted his glasses and fixed his hair.

"A surprise attack, duh!" she said, sticking out her tongue. "You're so fun to sneak up on; you scare so easily."

Makoto blushed. "That's . . . not true."

Makoto had secretly liked our petite classmate, Sakura Sato, since our first year of high school. Sakura was one of the shortest girls in our year, giving her the 'cute and innocent' look, but appearances could sometimes be deceiving.

In first-year, Sakura was a well-behaved student who abided by all the rules. Nowadays, she hiked up her navy-blue plaid uniform skirt, sloppily tied her uniform bowtie, wore make-up, painted her nails, and even dyed her hair inappropriate colours. Presently, her long hair was a reoccurring light pink, complimenting her name.

Makoto still hadn't confessed his feelings to Sakura, even though he made it so obvious to everyone. Everyone except the person herself. Sakura was a natural airhead; her head was full of nothing but friends, fashion, and boy bands, so she was completely oblivious to Makoto's pathetically pure feelings. No matter how hard I've pushed Makoto into confessing, he was too much of a wuss to act upon it.

"Wow, look who it is! Riku! You finally decided to show up, eh?" she said, shoving me playfully. "I almost forgot what you looked like."

"I thought I should grace you with my presence every once in a while."

"BAKA!" Sakura shouted, pulling down on her lower right eyelid and sticking out her tongue once more. Somehow, this had become her trademark.

"Come on you two, we're going to be late. I'm sick of getting lectured by Kobayashi-sensei. Today, I refuse to get shit on because of you guys!" Makoto stressed.

"Yes, Mako-senpai," we said simultaneously, teasing the goody-two-shoes.

"Oh, shut up!" he hissed.

Entering the school, I tossed my empty can into the trash at the entrance before stopping by the shoe lockers to swap my outside shoes for the regulated indoor slippers. The multi-level school building made navigating it a pain in the ass for us third years. The fourth floor was our home, meaning we had to climb a thousand set of stairs just to get to homeroom.

Makoto and Sakura walked ahead of me up the stairway to our class. They began chatting about the week, things I had no idea about or input on. When I reached the first landing, I gazed out the huge window at the school's outdoor soccer field where a few members from the soccer club were kicking the ball around.

"What are you looking at?" Makoto asked, throwing an arm around my shoulder. "Oh, the soccer club, huh? That brings back some fond memories."

"Y'know, you could've continued playing with them into third year. You shouldn't have let me stop you."

"I know, but I have to study hard this year. With cram school, and being on the student council, there's just no time for sports." Makoto smiled timidly, letting go of my shoulder. "Besides, it wasn't any fun without you."

I nodded disappointedly.

The three of us climbed the remainder of the stairs and walked down the hall, passing some third-year classrooms until we got to ours: 3-5. Like all others, our classroom had two doors: one at the front and one at the back, and we entered through the back. I made my way to my usual seat near the back window only to find an unfamiliar girl sitting at my desk.

"Ah, Riku, I forgot to tell you," Makoto said, rushing over to me. "We had a new seating arrangement recently. Kobayashi-sensei moved you to the front."

"The front!" I exclaimed, accidentally raising my voice. *That demon!*

"Sorry, man. I don't know what to tell you," Makoto said, shrugging his shoulders.

With all the commotion, the unfamiliar girl turned to face us.

"Sorry for disturbing you first thing in the morning, Tachibana," Makoto apologized, bowing his head. Standing upright, he feathered a hand in my direction. "This is Riku Nakajima. Please get along with him, as he's also a part of our class."

Tachibana looked me up and down, her eyes on guard. She answered somberly, "I'll be in your care."

The way she looked at me was cold and standoffish. I was caught off-guard; speechless.

Tachibana was formidably beautiful.

Her eyes were like no others I had ever seen. Two colours: one dark brown, almost black, while the other a light hazel. Two beauty marks rested side-by-side, right under her left eye. Her earlobes were double pierced, but she wore no earrings, as per the school rules. Did this mean she was a strict rule follower, or did she simply want to blend in with the crowd?

She had brown hair that just passed her shoulders, accompanied by bangs that feathered into the layers of her hair. It had a reddish undertone, which seemed natural. Lowering my gaze, I couldn't help but examine her chest: average, but anything bigger wouldn't suit her. She was slim, but not too thin for her height. Her legs appeared long, even though she kept them tucked under the desk.

When my eyes finally made it back up to hers, she redirected her attention to her desk, as though I was no longer there.

My body felt like it was on fire. I kind of liked it.

Fumbling over my words, I answered, "Ye-yeah . . . likewise."

Just then, the school chimes rang, and Kobayashi-sensei walked in through the front door of the classroom.

"All right, everyone to their seats," he commanded as he entered. "Come on, let's go."

Focusing on the items he was holding, he eventually looked up to face the class and locked eyes with me. His eyebrows quickly narrowed.

"Ah, Mr. Nakajima, so nice to see you present in my class. I saved you a special spot, right here at the front." He walked to my newly assigned desk and slammed his hand down on it, making sure to point out the specific seat.

Although Kobayashi-sensei was smiling, his face was twitching, and his voice was sharp.

He was a human-shaped headache—and a demonic asshole—but also one of the younger, more popular teachers at our school. Since he refused to tell the students his age, everyone estimated him to be in his mid to late twenties. Like usual, he wore a well-fitted, subtlety flashy suit with a tie, and complimentary dress shoes. His jaw was chiseled, and his hair was always on point; groomed, parted, and slicked over to the side.

As much as I hated to admit it, he had style. Maybe if he wasn't such a demon, he might deserve such a compliment to his stupid face.

"I had no other choice," I said with an insinuating smile. "I heard rumours you missed me." I made my way to my seat with the class laughing behind me.

Summer break was nearing, which to me meant more time for fooling around and earning money at my part-time jobs. Jobs that I had to lie about my age to get. The first semester started in April, and it was currently the middle of June, but I had only attended a handful of days. I completely missed out on sports day and the class trip, as I had worked instead. So, to me, this school year was flying.

"Is that so?" he replied, still showcasing a fake, disarming smile. "Well, you heard correctly. I missed you so much that I planned on inviting you to spend today's lunch with me, just to catch up."

Taking a seat, I looked up at him and matched his irritable smile. "Oh, how thoughtful of you. But I think I'll pass."

Leaning in close, his face inches from mine, he replied with, "It's non-negotiable."

Breaking eye contact, I clicked my tongue in defeat, then leaned back in my chair.

"Now then," Kobayashi-sensei said, heading back to the front in triumph, "let's begin homeroom." He picked up the attendance book. "We'll commence roll call."

I crossed my arms and sulked in my seat. *Stupid, bitch-ass, Kobayashi.*

Going in alphabetical order, Kobayashi-sensei eventually stopped at Sakura.

"Sakura Sato."

"Here, Sensei!"

With a frustrated sigh, and a flash of disappointment in his eyes, Kobayashi-sensei groaned and pinched the bridge of his nose. "How did I get stuck teaching a class full of delinquents?" He put the attendance book down before leaning on his desk and clearing his throat. "Miss Sato, are you trying to identify as a delinquent?"

"What?" Sakura said, feigning innocence.

"Your hair," he said, with a clipped voice, "why is it pink, again?"

"Sensei, come on! You're too strict. Loosen up a little."

The whole class laughed. Not having attended many days, it was still easy to understand that this type of conversation happened often.

"How many apology letters must you write before you finally obey the school rules?"

"I'll write them until I graduate," she said with an untamable smile.

"I see," he said, giving up on the hopeless dispute, while the rest of the class continued its laughter. "I expect a letter on my desk by lunch."

"Sure thing, Sensei," Sakura said, in singsong.

Shaking his head, he picked up the book once more. "Let's get this over with." After reading off two more names, he reached Tachibana's. "Hinata Tachibana."

"Here," Tachibana answered.

Turning to face the back of the class, down the row of desks behind me, my eyes sought her.

'Hinata,' huh?

Chapter Two

THE FIRST CLASS of the day was physical education, and unfortunately the demon, Kobayashi-sensei, was also our teacher. At the end of homeroom, I ventured to Makoto's desk, which had been relocated far, far away from mine.

"Yo, Makoto, what's the deal with Tachibana?"

Makoto looked up at me from his seat as he continued collecting and organizing his things. "What do you mean?"

"Liiike, who is she? When'd she transfer here? Annnd, how come you didn't tell me that a total babe transferred into our class?"

"She transferred at the end of May. You'd know if you showed up," he jabbed.

"Point taken," I said, grinning in defeat.

Makoto shook his head and stifled his laughter. "Basically, her family moves around a lot because of her father's work. From what I've heard from Sakura, this is Tachibana's fourth high school. Her grades are impeccable though; she's already made it into the top three of our year. But, according to everyone, she's a bit hard to approach. She's friendly, but cold. Not sure if it's intentional. That's all I really know about her." Makoto stood up with his P.E. uniform in hand.

I shut my eyes and sighed heavily, as

Kobayashi-sensei's stupid, haughty face appeared in my mind. "Vice-Prez . . . I forgot my P.E. clothes," I whined, opening my eyes.

"No, you didn't. I packed them in your schoolbag. Check near the bottom. I couldn't find the drawstring bag you usually use for P.E., so I shoved them in your bag with the rest of your stuff."

Going back to check, I grabbed my schoolbag off the hook attached to the side of my desk and unbuckled the clips. Digging through it until I reached the bottom, I looked back at Makoto with relief. "I love you, Mako-kun!" I shouted across the room.

The class went dead silent as an iciness clawed the air.

Makoto shot me something just short of a death glare, and I couldn't help but crack a playful smile. He marched over and punched my arm violently.

With a flushed face, he whispered loudly, "Shut up, you prick! Stop spewing nonsense; you're embarrassing!" A coldhearted glimmer flashed in his eyes as he grew even more irritated by me. "Hurry and get changed or else we'll both get in trouble by Sensei."

I scanned the classroom as I came back to my senses and took note that Kobayashi-sensei, and all the girls, had already left. "Oh, are we changing in here today?"

"Duh," he said, flicking my temple. "The girls went to go change in the changing room."

"Okay, jeez." I rubbed my temple. "No need to flick me so hard."

As the rest of the guys in class finished changing into their P.E. uniforms, they folded their regular uniforms neatly and placed them on top of their desks. About to leave my uniform in an unkept mess on mine, Makoto rolled his eyes in frustration before ripping my clothes out of my hands and folding them.

Laughing, I shook my head. "Mother Makoto, just leave it."

"Man, Riku, you sit in the front now. If Sensei sees this, he'll throw a fit."

"He's always throwing a fit. That stupid Kobayashi's gonna go bald. Or worse, he'll die young and alone with the amount of stress he puts himself under."

"He accumulates it all from you, you blockheaded idiot! Between you and Sakura, he has his hands full."

We both laughed as we headed out of the classroom behind some of our other male classmates, making our way to the gym. Travelling to the first floor, Makoto picked up our conversation from before.

"Why did you ask about Tachibana?"

"Why wouldn't I?" I raised my brow mischievously. "She's hot; definitely my type."

Again, Makoto rolled his eyes. "Your type is anyone of the opposite sex who's willing."

I laughed gratifyingly. "You aren't wrong."

"I don't know, man. I don't think she'll give you what you want. She doesn't seem to pay much attention to the guys in our class."

"Yeah, but she only met me today. I'll get her to pay attention."

"Riku, that side of you is no good. Girls aren't just playthings you can toss away when you're done. When will you understand that?"

I once heard and found humour in the comparison between a cigarette and a woman. You crave a cigarette knowing it's bad for you, but you get your fill of it anyway until it eventually disappears, leaving you with a bitter aftertaste—just like a woman.

I laughed under my breath, dismissing Makoto's advice. "Women are fickle creatures, bro. They're just objects of desire, nothing more. If they can't give me what I want, then they're useless to me. It works both ways. We all die sooner or later, right? So, to hell with it."

Makoto stopped in his tracks. "Riku!" he hissed. "Sleeping around can't be your cure for being lonely. You know that, right? It's not healthy."

Walking in front of him, I spoke over my shoulder. "Makoto, you, outta all people, should know how I am. Now, let's go. You don't want your precious Kobayashi-sensei to get mad, do you?"

I heard Makoto's footsteps pick up again as he walked cautiously behind me.

⁂

Lunch was finally upon us. I sprinted to the door of the classroom, desperate to skip out on my forced date with Kobayashi-sensei.

"Going somewhere, Mr. Nakajima?"

I instantly froze. To my right was Kobayashi-sensei. He had his arms crossed as he leaned and mounted one foot against the wall. With a sickening smile, he tilted his head.

"I was just about to make my way to the teacher's lounge to see if you were ready for our 'lunch date,' Sensei," I said, with an exaggerated smile.

"Hmm, I see," he said with doubt, one eyebrow extending upward. "Looked as if you were headed out in quite a hurry."

It's impossible to escape this crazy asshole! Doesn't he teach another class before lunch or something? Did he let his students out early just to come back here and hunt me down before I could run off? Demon . . ..

"I didn't wanna be late, of course."

"Of course," he challenged, as he stood up straight. "Shall we?"

"Haiii," I moaned, dragging my feet behind him.

Approaching the teacher's lounge, Kobayashi-sensei slid the door open, guiding me to enter ahead of him. I stepped inside and waited by the door. Immediately, all the teachers looked my way, then drifted back to focus on what they were doing once they saw Kobayashi-sensei behind me.

"My desk is over here," Kobayashi-sensei said, directing me.

I know. Stupid, Kobayashi. I should have my own goddamn desk in this place with the number of times I've been in here.

We arrived at his unorganized, cramped desk near the back.

"Sit."

Obeying, I sat in a chair that he pulled out for me as he took a seat at his desk, facing me. Kobayashi-sensei exhaled deeply.

"It was nice of you to show up today, Riku, considering the numerous important days you have missed."

Don't address me by my first name like we're friends, asshole.

"Let's see now," he went on, using his fingers to count, "the class trip to Kyoto, sports day, student-teacher meetings . . ." He purposefully, but in a know-it-all attitude, listed off each and every event I intentionally missed. "All jokes aside, do you understand why I asked you to meet with me?"

Not sure if a sarcastic comment would be appreciated, I sat in silence.

Kobayashi-sensei leaned back in his chair, stressed. "Riku, I'm only trying to help you. I'm on your side. You know that, don't you?"

Still choosing to remain silent, I avoided eye contact.

"Riku, after these past couple of years together, come on, work with me here. I know your home situation isn't ideal—"

"What home?" I barked.

With the way his eyes widened, I could tell he had been caught off-guard. "In all honesty, I can't even begin to imagine the kind of hardships you have had to endure while growing up. I have a suspicion that you live alone and are working multiple jobs during school hours just to support yourself. Which, as I'm sure you know, isn't allowed, but that is beside the point." He paused to take a breath. "Please, Riku, believe me when I say that I'm here to help you, and so is Fujimoto. We both care for you and your well-being. Riku, you're only seventeen, you have your whole life ahead of you. Don't throw away your future just to settle for the bare minimum from the crappy hand you were dealt."

Kobayashi-sensei's words sent a jolt through me; a twist of rage started to build inside. Irritated, I glanced at him and calmly spoke my mind. "Sensei, with all due respect," I said, my tone clipped, "you know nothing about *me* or *my* life. And as for Makoto, he should learn not to run his damn mouth."

"None of this is Fujimoto's fault. I pressured him into telling me what was going on with you."

"Sensei, you're meddling in unnecessary things . . .."

"I don't believe I am," he answered, flatly.

Squinting my eyes, I remained quiet and listened as he explained his bold statement.

"Riku," he said, leaning on his knees informally, "you are *my* student; therefore, *I* am responsible for you. I'm trying my best to help in whatever way I can. Although you may not know this, I have covered for you many times when it has come to Principal Koga."

"Principal Koga?"

"Yes. Principal Koga has approached me many times about your attendance record and grades. Each year, your attendance and grades worsen. I tell him that 'I'm working on it,' when in fact, I have made less progress than the time before. You are at risk of not graduating, Riku. And, if you keep this up, you're going to be stuck here with me during summer break for supplementary lessons." He sat upright, crossing one leg over the other.

"Tuition is expensive, and you're so close to graduating. Are you really okay with throwing it all down the drain?"

My eyes shot open. '*Not . . . graduating*?' "Sensei, I gotta graduate. I don't *need* the highest marks, but I *NEED* to graduate."

Kobayashi-sensei tilted his head. "Why the strong need?"

Not wanting to open up to him, I leaned back in my chair and gripped the back of my neck, tugging on it aggressively as I looked up at the ceiling.

"Riku."

Continuing to gaze up at the ceiling, avoiding his intense stare, I couldn't fight my hesitation. "I just . . . can't fail. Not at this."

"Is this because Fujimoto's family paid for your high school tuition?"

I flung myself forward, locking eyes with him against my will.

"From your reaction, I assume I'm correct?"

"How . . .? Was it Makoto? Did he—"

He shook his head. "It wasn't Fujimoto. I checked the school's records and found out that your tuition had been paid for by the Fujimoto family. The school's records also had your address listed at the same residence as 'Makoto Fujimoto,' but like I said, I don't truly believe that you're *actually* living there. If you were, I think that you would be made to attend school a lot more regularly than you currently are."

At a time when I wasn't sure if I had enough money to attend a low-grade high school, Makoto brought up the issue to his parents, and the next thing I knew, I received a congratulatory letter of acceptance for the same high school as Makoto. From there, I got my first ever part-time job to begin paying back the Fujimoto's generosity.

So, no. He wasn't wrong. He was a sneaky-ass bastard, but a right one. *Typical of a demon.*

"What then? You gonna report me to Principal Koga?"

"Riku, is that why you think I brought you here?"

"Dunno, maybe? You aren't giving me much to go on."

Shaking his head in disappointment, he leaned forward and put a hand on my shoulder. "I want to help you, Riku, but *you* have to let me. I can't keep covering for you without knowing what's really going on in your life outside of school."

Not sure how I felt about Kobayashi-sensei's heartfelt sentiment, or his hand on my shoulder, I could feel my heart pricking destructively within my chest.

"Sorry to interrupt, Kobayashi-sensei," Endo-sensei informed, poking her head around the corner and bowing, "but there is a phone call for you on line three."

Standing abruptly, I shook off Kobayashi-sensei's hand. He broke eye contact with me in order to acknowledge the other teacher. "Thank you, Endo-sensei. I'll just be a minute."

"Of course," Endo-sensei replied, before leaving us.

Taking the opportunity to flee, I turned on my heel, but was quickly caught again by the arm.

"This interruption might have saved you this time, Riku, but don't think I'll let you evade this conversation forever. I'd like to pick this back up after school today. Understood?" he said, letting me go.

Knowing I couldn't escape him, I lowered my head and accepted my fate. "Yes, sir."

Chapter Three

NEEDING TO COOL off, I took a walk through the sheltered passage that connected the main building to the second one. Coming across the music wing, I heard the sonorous sound of a piano. Even having no musical talent, I could understand that whoever was playing knew what they were doing. The tone of the song seemed dark, as if the person playing it was troubled. I found myself moving toward the music room at the end of the hallway.

Right before I could get a glimpse of who was playing, the school chimes rang, indicating lunch was over. With that, the piano playing also stopped. Snapping back to my senses, I gunned it to class.

It was better not to add another *late* to the demon's list of *don'ts*.

***

I anxiously looked at my wristwatch, counting the time left before I had to meet with Kobayashi-sensei again. I slammed my head down on my desk.

Why does that demon even care? Why can't he just be like every other damn teacher and not give a shit? I can't fuckin' understand him. What does he gain from this?

By the end of fifth period, I had renewed rage for Kobayashi-sensei. I decided to grab another canned coffee from a vending machine before heading to the roof to skip the next class—because fuck that demon. With easy access from the fourth floor, I climbed up the stairwell to the roof and reached for the door's handle. Often, the faculty would forget to lock it, so there was a fifty-fifty percent chance that the door was unlocked.

Trying my luck, I turned the handle and exhaled thankfully. *Perfect.*

I walked straight to the guardrail, cracked open the coffee, took a sip, then placed it on the ground so I could pull out a lighter and a pack of cigarettes from my pocket. Leaning over the railing with my forearms, I took out a cigarette, put it in between my lips, and lit it. Inhaling and exhaling the first puff, I chuckled at the thought that crossed my mind.

I wonder how long it will take before Makoto sends me a LINE message asking me where the hell I went.

As I stood looking out over the school grounds, I heard a rustling noise from behind me. Quickly, I put out the cigarette and held it in my palm to hide the evidence, not wanting to get caught smoking by a teacher. Turning around, to my surprise, it wasn't a teacher.

"Tachibana?"

Sitting against the wall was Tachibana, holding a book. She placed the book to the side and stood to walk toward me. Keeping some distance between us, she leaned her forearms over the railing, as I had done, and fixed her gaze out at the open sky.

I couldn't help but blatantly stare. The way her body moved as she came up beside me was something I felt I needed to watch closely. The admiration I'd had for her long legs when they were tucked under her desk didn't compare to what I experienced now. Tachibana's face, and body, were out of this world; it was hard not to imagine what she'd look like naked. Everything about this new girl was interesting, exciting. I hadn't figured her out yet, but with time, I would.

She remained silent for a few beats as we stood next to each other.

She spoke first. "Don't let me stop you from smoking. I won't tell. Despite the fact that it's a disgusting habit."

Intrigued by her willingness to start a conversation, I had no issue engaging. "Don't mind if I do." I took the lighter back out of my pocket and relit the cigarette hidden in my palm, then bent down to grab my coffee.

Leaning against the railing once again, I took a sip and looked to my left where she stood. "So," I pressed, trying to further our conversation, "was the door to the roof unlocked when you came up here?"

"No," she answered, without looking at me.

"How'd you get up here, then?"

"I stole the key from the teacher's lounge."

Astounded by the rebellious actions of a top-ranked student, I burst out laughing. "Oh, you did, did you?"

Hooking her chin on her shoulder, she turned her head to look at me. "Does that amuse you?"

Shaking off the laughter, I replied, "Very much so."

She held my stare as I looked directly into her eyes. *Her eyes are cold, but sharp; like they're piercing my soul. She's beautiful as hell.*

"I heard that you're at the top of our year. What's a super smart girl like you doing stealing keys and skipping class?"

"If I'm as smart as you say, then what's the point of me wasting my time by attending every single class?"

Each time she spoke, I couldn't help but laugh at how her true character was reshaping my image of her. She piqued my interest; I couldn't wait to discover more.

"I've also heard a few interesting things about you, *Riku Nakajima.*"

"You remembered my name. I'm flattered." I smiled. "What've you heard?"

"Hmm, where to begin," she said, looking out into the distance in thought. "That you're a smooth-talking playboy who likes to sleep around. That you have either *gone* out with, or *slept* with, half of the girls in our school, even senpais who have graduated to college and university. That you're popular amongst your peers, but oddly don't attend many days of school or group outings with classmates. One rumour even suggested that you were a male escort in the red-light district, while another stated that you were part of the Yakuza. Let's see, what else . . .."

Taking a drag from my cigarette, I was choked by laughter at her quick ability to list off all the things she'd heard about me. "That's all extremely fascinating. I just learned a few things about myself."

She glanced back at me. "How much would you say is true?"

"Just one. *Definitely* the rumour about me being a male escort in the red-light district."

She refocused her attention out beyond the schoolyard. "Thought so."

Laughing under my breath, I caught her doing the same. "Ah! So, she does know how to laugh."

She side-eyed me with a brief smile. And what an attractive smile it was. Her lips were full and naturally pink in colour, as if she had applied a light layer of lipstick or lip gloss. But I was fairly certain she didn't have an ounce of makeup on. I knew of girls who would be jealous of Tachibana's natural beauty, probably kill to have just one of her alluring features. I felt privileged just being able to witness it all firsthand.

"Can I ask you something?" she said, pulling me from my trance.

"Sure."

"How come you haven't been to school at all this past month?"

Trying to think back to the last time I attended a full day, I corrected her. "More like three weeks."

From the way her eyes flashed, I could tell my answer didn't suffice as a response to her serious question. We hadn't met before today, so I couldn't figure out why she seemed bothered by what I had said.

Turning the question back onto her, I asked, "Why d'you care?"

"Frankly, I don't care about your attendance," she said strictly. "I just found Kobayashi-sensei's interaction with you this morning entertaining. He seems to treat you differently from the rest of the class, so I was curious as to what the reason was."

"You're the first I've heard who doesn't care about my attendance record. Apparently, it's a hot topic right now."

"Why do you do that?"

Thrown off by her question, and her lack of appreciation for my sarcastic comeback, I raised a brow. "Do what?"

"Avoid the questions I ask."

"I don't."

"You do."

Staring at her, I wondered what her intentions were with my answers. As I was about to reply with another quip, my phone vibrated. Thankful for the interruption, as she was beginning to knock me off balance, I placed my coffee down to pull out my phone. I had a message from Makoto.

> [LINE Makoto Fujimoto]: Bro, where are you?! You come to school like ONCE a month! What makes you think you can afford to skip a single class? Get your ass back here, dipshit!!!

Laughing out loud at Makoto's message, I finished smoking the last of my cigarette, then dropped it on the ground to step on it.

I could've sworn it was three weeks, but maybe it really was a month?

Shrugging my shoulders at the thought, I picked up the remainder of my coffee. Makoto was always looking after me, bettering me. He had the decency to come over to wake me up and drag my sorry ass to school. Though I was enjoying my unplanned time alone with Tachibana, the least I could do was attend class to keep Makoto happy.

I looked at Tachibana. "Well, it's been fun, Tachibana, but my in-school guardian is impatiently awaiting my return. Later."

As I walked away from her and toward the door, she made sure I caught her reply.

"Until next time, Nakajima."

"Hmm," I hummed, taking in the emphasis of her reply. "Don't fantasize about me too much in my absence."

"I'll try to keep a handle on my thoughts."

Smirking over my shoulder, I shook my head, then made my way inside.

Finishing my coffee on the way back to the class I had hoped to skip, I thought more about my encounter with Tachibana. She was a force to be reckoned with; a beauty with quick-wit, and I couldn't wait to stumble upon more of those enticing moments. In the middle of remembering Tachibana, the promise I made to Kobayashi-sensei popped into my head. Sighing with annoyance, I went back to staring at my watch and counting down the time left until our next scheduled interrogation session.

Entering through the front door of the classroom, I apologized for being late. Not only did I get scolded by Endo-sensei for my tardiness, but as I casually walked to my desk, I looked over at Makoto and saw his eyes stab me with kunai. Just as I took my seat, the door at the back of the classroom opened abruptly. Tachibana was the one who disrupted the lesson this time. Whispers began forming rumours from those in the class.

"Do you think Tachibana was with Nakajima?"

"Oh no! Did our new school beauty also succumb to Riku's charms?"

"Man, Nakajima sure works fast. Think they've done it already?"

"I heard that the few times Tachibana has skipped class, she's been making out with guys from other classes. Even our kōhai!"

Hearing the idiots in our class badmouthing Tachibana pissed me off. Turning around in my seat, I raised my voice. "Hey! D'you guys come to school to talk shit or learn?"

Instantly, the class hushed with deafening silence. I wasn't one to speak out in anger, since I usually drove on cruise control at school and limited myself to playful jabs, but for some reason when it came to Tachibana, I didn't want her name dirtied.

Everyone's confused eyes had remained on me until Endo-sensei stepped in.

"That's enough everyone. Now, for those who have just joined us, we are at the top of page one hundred and fourteen in the textbook. Mr. Nakajima, you may continue from there."

Though Endo-sensei was much nicer than Kobayashi-sensei, she hated lateness and made sure to punish you by making you the centre of attention. As I finished reading my section, she picked on Tachibana next.

"Miss Tachibana, please read the next part. Continue from where Mr. Nakajima left off."

Tachibana was quiet for a moment, then stood emptyhanded. "Sensei, to be honest with you, I did not plan on attending your class today, so I do not have my textbook."

I looked back and forth between the bold Tachibana and the shocked Endo-sensei. *Ohhh, shit!*

The girl beside Tachibana slapped her textbook down on Tachibana's desk.

"Thank you, Miss Ueda," Endo-sensei applauded with words. "Miss Tachibana, I will overlook your disruption today, but I do hope that you are better prepared next time."

"Yes, Sensei."

Smiling in disbelief, I turned to face the front. *Tachibana sure has guts. Man, it's moments like these where I'm thankful to have Makoto, my guardian angel.*

⁂

After school, I went to the teacher's lounge to meet with the demon, as promised. A teacher informed me that Kobayashi-sensei left urgently and would have to reschedule our meeting. Relieved, I made my way back to the classroom to collect my things.

"Riku!" Sakura came flying at me like a ball of energy, stopping inches from my face. "I thought you had to meet up with Kobayashi-sensei?"

"I was supposed to, but that demon left early and had to reschedule."

"Perfect!" Sakura squealed excitedly. "Now you can come to the karaoke mixer."

"Mixer? Now?"

"Yeah!"

I had nothing better to do, and it's not like I was going to study, so meh, what the hell. "Sure, why not. But I'm not footing the bill this time, 'ya hear me?"

"Yes!" she exclaimed, with an overflowing amount of excitement.

"Calm down. You're waaay too loud," I said, covering my ears to protect them from the shrieking banshee before me. "What about Makoto?"

"Mako-kun has a student council meeting. He was going to wait for you to tell you, but then he remembered you had to stay late because of Kobayashi-sensei, anyway. Plus, you know him, he never comes out to have fun. He's so serious."

"True. It's rare for Makoto to attend these types of things."

"It's rare for you, too," she added. "You're never around."

"Yeah, yeah."

Latching on to my arm, a little closer than I would have liked, she dragged me out the door along with some of our classmates. As I was forcefully led, my eyes searched for someone specific near the back of the room, but that person was nowhere to be found.

I wonder if she's gone home already.

"Is Tachibana going?" I couldn't help but ask.

"Tachibana?" Sakura questioned, hesitantly. "No . . . She's turned down the last few we invited her to, so we didn't bother asking this time."

"Hmm, I see."

Chapter Four

ON THE SUBWAY, Sakura informed me that there would be others from neighbouring high schools joining us at the karaoke bar in Shibuya. Honestly, I didn't really care who was coming, as long as I could find someone to mess around with and waste some time.

Shibuya was one of the special wards in Tokyo where I spent most of my time. I lived, worked, and went to school in Shibuya. But I didn't always reside here. I grew up in the ward of Shinjuku, in the Kabukichō district. I didn't go back to visit often, but when I did, I never left feeling good. Shinjuku didn't hold many fond memories for me.

Leaving the station, I walked with Sakura and the others until we pulled up at the karaoke bar.

"Sakura, you're gonna be my wing-girl, right?" I asked, leaning into her.

"Wing-girl?"

"Yeah, y'know, you'll look out for me by seeing which girls are interested in messing around, won'tcha?"

Sakura went uncharacteristically quiet. "Yeah . . . sure thing."

Her response to my joking request seemed hesitant, so I wanted to make sure she was okay before we got involved with everyone at the mixer. "Hey, you good?"

"Yo, Nakajima! Save some of the girls for us too, okay?"

"Yeah, man! Don't hog all the cute ones to yourself just because you're a good-looking ikemen!"

Two guys from our class, Akira Yamada and Kurosaki Ono, came up from behind me and threw their arms around my shoulders, interrupting my conversation with Sakura. They were harmless, but extremely awkward when it came to engaging with girls.

With all their bodyweight on me, I almost toppled over as I watched Sakura walk on ahead. "Guess you guys are just gonna have to try harder," I teased, slipping through their grasp. Straightening myself out, I sneak attacked Yamada and put him in a headlock. "C'mon, I'm one guy. How hard can it be to score with at least one of the ladies tonight?"

Yamada, dramatically gasping for air, was at a loss for words. Ono, who stood idly by and made no attempts to help his buddy, answered, "Well, Riku, we've tried, but we just aren't as good as you."

It never took me long to get well acquainted with those around me. Since entering high school, I've kept things light and fun in front of my peers and co-workers, creating a fake persona where everything in my life was okay, average, normal. It's what I wanted them to see.

I've had guys idolize me, yearning to either be me or have my life, as some have admitted to my face. I guess the persona I fabricated was working. Most people knew little to nothing about me, but still, they called me their 'friend,' and I let them. If they truly knew who I was, or the fucked-up life I've lived, they'd rethink their idolization and probably discard the strange power they bestowed upon me.

I kept most people at a distance, allowing only a select few in, like Makoto and his family. The more people you involve yourself with, the more problems you acquire.

Watching Ono's soul get crushed by his own words, I released Yamada. Having them stand beside each other, reunited, I laughed passively. "Guys, believe me, you don't wanna be anything like me." With those words, I turned around and headed into the karaoke bar.

Once inside, I made my way to the reserved karaoke room for our group. The room selected for our party was larger than average. This was probably one of the biggest mixers I had ever attended.

My eyes scanned the room for Sakura. I needed to follow up with her to make sure she was okay. Sakura being at this mixer probably meant that she had intentions of finding herself a boyfriend, which didn't look good for the absent Makoto. By the time I found Sakura, she was already chatting away with someone.

I don't recognize that guy. I looked him over. *What's up with his fake-ass blond hair?* I laughed to myself at how ridiculous the colour was. *She seems to be fine now. Guess I'll check-in with her later.*

As people were finding their seats, and selecting which songs they wanted to sing, I took a good look around the overcrowded room. I ended up sitting beside a cute girl I had never met before. Coincidentally, she also had pink hair. A different shade from Sakura's, though. She was conversing with another girl, but I wasted no time in making my presence known.

"Hey, I don't think we've met before," I said, with a crooked smile. "I'm Riku Nakajima."

The pink-haired girl paused the conversation she was having with her friend and turned to me, giggling. "I know who you are. Why do you think I came tonight?"

With a wide eye, I watched the girl reveal a mischievous grin.

"Really? Funny," I chuckled, "I only decided on coming last minute."

"Word travels fast amongst us girls," she giggled again. "Anytime your name is mentioned, you can almost guarantee girls will follow." She excused herself from the conversation she was having with the other girl and moved in closer to me. "I'm Miyu Iwasaki."

Smiling, I greeted her properly. "Hello, Miyu Iwasaki. Can I grab you something to drink?"

Returning my playful smile, she bent over and reached a hand into a purse resting on the floor against her leg. "I've got us covered."

She pulled out a bottle of alcohol, something minors weren't allowed to consume—legally. I indulged in a cold beer frequently enough to get me through a rough night or two, although I knew Makoto didn't approve. But life was less complicated for Makoto; he had a loving family waiting for him at home.

"Perfect," I said, as I grabbed two empty glasses from the far end of the table meant for water. I placed a cup in front of Iwasaki, and then one for myself. I watched her sneakily pour the alcohol into both glasses, then I raised mine to her. "Cheers."

"Cheers," she said carelessly, clinking our glasses together.

The night carried on with Iwasaki, and so did the drinks. It got harder and harder to focus and make sense of my surroundings as I downed the next drink. In time, I ended up making out with Iwasaki, and quite possibly a few other girls. I was, what some might say, 'sloppy.' It was all fun and games, until my world was draped in black, and I was piss drunk.

I struggled to open my eyes to the blaring sun shining through the sliding back door. Sitting up in bed, my hand was instantly drawn to my forehead to try and soothe the pounding headache about to explode my brain. Looking around groggily, I was happy to see that I managed to find my way back to my apartment. That was one thing I was at least good at doing while drunk, making it back home. Searching for my cellphone, I found it beside me on the mattress. The time read: 7:42 a.m. *So much for sleeping in.* Dropping my phone, I rubbed my temples for some relief. Just then, I heard a moan next to me.

Ah, so I must've had a good time last night. That explains why I'm naked. Wonder if I ended up spending the night with that Iwasaki girl? Man, she sure gave me some strong stuff to drink. I can't remember shit.

Looking over to see who I had shared my small, single bed with, my heart sank in my chest and dropped into the pit of my stomach.

"Sakura . . .?"

Rolling over to look at me, the hair that swept across her face was definitely the wrong shade of pink.

"Mmm, good morning, Riku."

Chapter Five

ENTERING THE APARTMENT, *there was a pair of shoes next to my mother's that I didn't recognize. I had just finished the walk home from elementary school, alone. The apartment was quiet, but I knew there must have been people inside. Scared to announce my arrival, I eventually mustered up the courage to do so.*

"Mommy . . . I'm home."

Things were silent. All the lights were off, and from what I could see, the tattered curtains had never been open; the apartment was pitch black. Slipping out of my sneakers, I quietly walked down the short hallway until I reached our multipurpose living area where I found my mother, stretched out on my tattered futon with a somewhat familiar, but strange man.

Kneeling next to her, I poked her shoulder. "Mommy, I'm home." With no response or movement from her, I began to worry. "Mommy! Are you okay? MOMMY!"

"Relax, kid."

Shuddering, I looked to the half-naked man sitting beside my mother's lifeless body.

"She's soarin' right now," he slurred, laughing to himself. "She's doin' greaaat."

From what I could see in the dark, the man had a weird rubber band wrapped around his arm. He stared at it for a moment, then took a needle and stabbed it into his arm. He seemed to enjoy watching the injection he was giving himself; he smiled the entire time while doing it. Terrified, I backed away from the futon. Just as I was about to stand, something grabbed my wrist.

"AHH!"

"Riku . . . is that you, baby?"

It was my mother who had grabbed me and stopped me from leaving. Peering down at her, she seemed weak and looked pale, like the blood had completely drained from her. The arm that reached out for me had many scabs and bruises. She was wearing a tank top and shorts, but having only seen her bare arms a handful of times, it looked scary.

"Riku . . .," she spoke, somewhat out of breath, "y'know . . . Mommy loves you, right? Be a good boy . . . go play outside . . . 'kay?"

"But Mommy—"

She tightened her hold on my wrist. "I SAID, GO PLAY OUTSIDE!"

Avoiding the pain from my wrist, my brain shut off. After my mother raised her voice, I shook her off, ran to the door, stepped back into my sneakers, and fled the apartment.

⁂

In the past, I had thought trouble sought me out. But now, I'd learnt that I was the trouble I was running away from. White noise enveloped me; the only thing I could hear was the sound of my breathing. Everything from my mind had been wiped as I stared at the mistake lying next to me.

"Riku?"

Hearing my name leave Sakura's lips made me want to rip my ears off. She eventually sat up, exposing her naked body for what felt like the first time; I was seconds away from gouging out my eyes.

What the—WHAT THE FUCK HAVE I DONE?

"Riku," she repeated, concern trapped in her eyes, "what's wrong?"

Snapping back into an unbelievable reality, I jumped out of bed. "'What's wrong'? Are you fuckin' kidding me right now?" I exclaimed, my voice elevated.

Taken aback, she grabbed the sheet off my bed to cover herself. "Riku, stop yelling."

Bringing my hands to my pounding forehead, I slowly ran my fingers through my hair, pushing back my bangs. "This, this was a mistake."

Shaking her head repeatedly, she wrapped the sheet around her torso and rose onto her knees on the bed. Her eyes brimmed with tears. "Don't say that!"

"Sakura," I said, her name getting stuck in my throat, "you need to go."

I veered my eyes from her and desperately searched for my boxer briefs in the haphazard pile of clothing on the floor. I couldn't help but shake my head in disgust at what I had done. Finding pieces of her clothing, I tossed them aimlessly at her.

"Riku! Stop for a sec!" She got out of bed with the sheet still wrapped around her. "Can we talk about this?"

Finding my underwear, I stopped to put them on, then walked to where she stood. "Sakura, there's nothing to talk about. This NEVER happened, understood?"

She reached out to touch my shirtless chest, but I grabbed her wrist and redirected it. Assertively holding her, I forced her to look at me. A single tear scaled down her cheek.

"Riku, please . . . I, I love you."

The grip I had on her loosened; I was shocked at her declaration.

"I've always loved you, ever since our junior year. This wasn't a mistake for me, so please, stop saying it was."

Releasing her, I dropped my head. I had never wished I was dead more than I did at that moment. I didn't love Sakura, nor did I harbour any romantic or lustful feelings toward her. Ever since I found out Makoto liked her, I had been careful not to make any passes at her or lead her on. I never hung out with her one-on-one, mainly so that something like this wouldn't happen. But, despite all my efforts, I still fucked up and ruined everything.

"Riku, say something."

"Get out."

"Ri—"

"This isn't right, and you know it, Sakura. You need to go. NOW!"

"Why? Why can't this be right?"

"Because!"

"Because, why?"

"BECAUSE, it should have been Makoto!"

She paused. With distraught eyes, she asked, "Mako-kun? What does he have to do with this?"

Aggravated by her refusal to leave, I couldn't help but grovel. "Sakura, please, I'm begging you."

"NO! Tell me what Mako-kun has to do with this?"

"God, you're so fuckin' dense! Makoto likes you, okay? Get it now?"

She took a step back. Without a word, she gathered the remainder of her clothes and got dressed. While she got ready, I sat on the edge of my bed. Hunched over, I used my knees as support for my elbows before bringing my hands to my face. I needed time to collect my thoughts and mull over what to do.

How could I be so fuckin' stupid? HOW DID THIS HAPPEN? When did I even begin talking to Sakura? I thought I was having drinks with that bimbo, Iwasaki!

Sakura rushed down the narrow hallway to the door. Slipping on her shoes, I could vividly see the tears continuing to pour from her eyes. As she reached for the handle, I had to make one final thing clear.

"Sakura."

With her hand resting on the doorknob, she waited.

"Don't tell Makoto."

"I won't!" she said loudly, shaking her head.

"Promise me."

Silence filled the apartment.

"Promise me!" I repeated, frantically.

"Why should I?"

I attempted to swallow the saliva stuck at the back of my throat. "Please, Sakura . . . He's all I have left."

Without another word, Sakura was gone.

All I could do was pray and wait to see what would happen. I fell back on my bed to rest my eyes. Sprawled out in complete silence, I prayed this was all some awful nightmare.

Not being able to concentrate, let alone function, I called in sick to work at my convenience store job. Thinking long and hard on what to do, I decided to go to school to see what rumours the others from the mixer had spread. I needed to figure out what really happened before word got back to Makoto.

I made it in time to catch the end of second period. Stopping by the shoe lockers at school, I swapped my shoes, then bolted it up the stairs. Making it to the classroom, I was about to enter through the back door until I remembered my new assigned seat was at the front.

Fuck me.

Sliding the front door open, I took a step into the room as the teacher was at the chalkboard writing out math equations. Turning to the doorway, he paused his lesson to acknowledge my abrupt entrance.

"Mr. Nakajima, you're late."

"Sorry, Sensei," I bowed. "My alarm didn't go off."

With the laughter of my classmates to back me, I stood tall and walked behind the teacher toward my desk. Taking my seat, I hung my schoolbag on the hook attached to my desk. The teacher shook his head in disappointment before returning to the chalkboard to carry on with the lecture.

Leaving home in such a hurry, I realized I had none of my textbooks. All I had in my bag was a random notebook and a few writing utensils. Pulling those out, I pretended to pay attention to the math lesson taking place. Not even a minute later, the cellphone in my pocket vibrated. As the teacher's back faced me, I took out my phone to see who had messaged me.

> [LINE Makoto Fujimoto]: Two days in a row? Who is this new and improved Riku? Haha! Didn't you have work today?

Turning around in my seat, I caught Makoto smiling at me. Not sure how to react, I tried my best to smile back normally. Drifting away from Makoto, I shifted my gaze a few rows down to where another set of eyes were fixed on me. As soon as our eyes met, Sakura shifted her attention to the front.

Fuck! Sakura came to school, too? Why'd I just assume that she wouldn't come today?

Dying for this period to end, I looked back at Sakura every so often.

I need to catch her in between classes to talk to her. Who knows if she'll tell one of the other girls in class, if she hasn't already. Girls are always gossiping and absorbed in everyone's business but their own. I absolutely CAN'T let Makoto find out.

After class, I slung my schoolbag over my shoulder and hurried to try and catch Sakura. In the process, Makoto approached me, blocking me from reaching her.

"Yo, Riku! I can't believe you came, man. This is definitely a new record for third year. I think the last time you came to school two consecutive days was probably like, what, middle of last year?" he said, laughing.

Not having time to deal with Makoto's vapid conversation, I remained still and looked past him at Sakura. I watched as Sakura left the class with some of the girls. Panicking, I desperately tried to remember the variety of classes that occurred throughout a normal school day when it came to electives.

Fuck! What does Sakura have next? Uh . . . P.E.? No, that can't be right, she was in my P.E. class yesterday. Science or home EC., then? Shit! I gotta try and catch her!

"Sorry, Makoto, I'd love to shoot the shit, but I gotta go."

"Go?" Makoto questioned with a raised brow. "Go where?"

"Go . . . to . . . speak with Sensei," I lied miserably, not even sure which Sensei I was referring to.

"Sensei? Oh, you mean Kobayashi-sensei? Yeah, he was looking for you this morning. He was pretty pissed that you missed out on homeroom."

My eyes widened. Frigid with nerves, this time Makoto had my full attention.

Fuuuck me. That stupid Kobayashi—I completely forgot about him! Now, I gotta try and avoid him while catching up to Sakura.

"Yeah . . .."

Makoto smacked my back and laughed as he passed me. "Good luck, bro."

My eyes followed Makoto as he also exited the classroom.

Existing is exhausting. Shit like this is a prime reason why school is a fuckin' annoyance. If I hadn't come yesterday, none of this would've happened.

Chapter Six

TRYING TO FIND Sakura, I ran up and down the halls like a madman. Wanting to avoid the teacher's lounge like the plague, I made sure to check each corner before turning down the corresponding hallway.

If I run into that stupid demon now, I'll miss my chance.

Turning the corner of the next hallway, I recognized the back of Yamada's head. He was walking alone, so I ran up to him.

"Yo, Yamada, hold up!"

Startled, his shoulders tensed as he turned around. "Hey, Nakajima. Jeez, man, you scared the shit out of me. What's up?"

"D'you know where Sakura is?" I blurted out irritably.

"Sato? Uh," he pondered, "I'm not sure which class she has next, but I did see her downstairs with a bunch of girls heading toward the second building."

"Thanks, man," I said, patting his shoulder before taking off.

"So, you and Sato, eh?"

Stopping in my tracks, my stomach dropped. Looking over my shoulder, Yamada was winking at me as if he knew something.

"What . . . did you say?"

"It's all good, man. No need to hide it. Ono and I saw you two leave together last night. You were drunk out of your mind, and Sato seemed a bit tipsy. You were both late today, too," he said suggestively, wiggling his eyebrows up and down. "Is Fujimoto over her, then? Didn't he have like a major crush on her or something?"

My chest inflated and I succumbed to rage. Instinctively, I grabbed Yamada by his uniform shirt and pinned him up against the wall. As I did, the books he was carrying fell to the floor.

"Ow, Nakajima," he said, the back of his head hitting the wall. "What the hell, man?"

Feeling the rush of adrenaline, I lost all control as I held Yamada by his collar and pressed into him with my forearms. "You better shut your fuckin' mouth if y'know what's good for you," I demanded, desperation apparent in my voice.

Struggling to break free, Yamada grabbed my wrists and tried pulling them away. "Nakajima, I don't know why you're so pissed," he cried. "Everyone knows that you're a player. It's not like you've ever tried to hide it."

He was laying harsh truths on me, and it pissed me off even more. Everything he said was true. But he was wrong about me and Sakura. I wasn't a guy who backstabbed his friends, or at least I thought I wasn't.

Clenching my fists tighter, I brought my face closer to his. "Like I said, shut your fuckin' mouth. You dunno anything and you *saw* nothing."

Tossing Yamada to the side, he fell to the floor gasping for air.

"You're fucking crazy, Nakajima."

"Yeah," I confirmed, staring at him fixedly from above. "Make sure you relay the message to Ono, as well."

The air around me grew thicker, poisoning each breath I took as I walked away. With the hotheaded mood I was in, finding Sakura now would only make things worse. I would surely lose it on her again.

I redirected myself to the roof instead.

Itching for a cigarette to take the edge off, I couldn't wait to get outside. Stepping onto the landing of the stairwell, I grabbed the handle of the roof's door and turned it. Again, it was unlocked.

No way . . ..

Just the possibility of seeing a specific someone somehow made everything better. My head felt clearer, and my mood subsided. But why, why did I feel like that? Did I have the *right* to feel like that?

I opened the door and turned my head right, then left. The eagerness that bubbled inside me settled comfortably once I saw her. Sitting in the corner against the wall, reading a book and eating a pudding cup, was Tachibana.

Smiling to myself, I walked straight to the other end of the rooftop like last time. At the guardrail, I pulled out my pack of cigarettes and grabbed one. Putting it between my lips, I lit the cigarette and leaned over the railing. I heard the sound of a hardcover book being closed and soon her footsteps approached me from behind.

"May I have one?" Tachibana asked, pulling up beside me.

Huh? "Thought you said it was a 'disgusting habit'?"

"It is. Doesn't mean I won't partake in it."

Grinning, I held out the pack of cigarettes and lifted one up with my thumb for her. She took the cigarette from me elegantly and placed it between her lips. Holding out my lighter, I struck it as she leaned into the flame. Pinching the cigarette with her index and middle finger, she inhaled the smoke, then pulled the cigarette away from her mouth to exhale—like an experienced smoker. Her delicate movements sent a shiver up my spine and shot goosebumps down my arms. She was impossible to figure out.

"What happened to your hand?"

Pulling my head out of the clouds, I followed her gaze and looked at my right hand. My knuckles were all cut up and bruised, but I had no memory of recently being in a fight or even getting hurt. I had that mere tiff with Yamada, but I hadn't hit him?

As I made a fist, there was a hint of pain that shot up my hand and past my wrist. I hadn't it noticed until now. Peering up at her, I shrugged. "Good question."

Tachibana tilted her head and squinted her eyes as if to study my weak response. Her judgmental silence didn't last very long as she shifted straight into another topic.

"Two days in a row; this must be a new record for you."

"You're not the first to remind me," I chuckled. "I like to keep the teachers and my peers in suspense of my arrival."

"Quite the narcissist, aren't you?"

"Me?" I joked defensively, laying a hand over my chest.

"Mhm," she replied, simply.

Turning to her, I took in her stoic expression as she looked out calmly over the schoolyard. Nothing I did or said seemed to faze her. She was indeed beautiful, but she had a sharp tongue, matching her ice queen appearance perfectly.

Like Makoto pointed out, I hadn't seen her interact with many people in class; her presence inside the classroom was almost lost. Although, she had no problem starting or engaging in conversations with me up here on the roof.

Did that mean something? Did I have some sort of effect on her? There was more doubt than possibility in those questions. Maybe all of it was just wishful thinking on my part. She would be my hardest challenge yet.

What the fuck am I thinking? I don't have time to pursue Tachibana! I gotta figure shit out with Sakura before getting involved with anyone else.

"What's your home like?"

Shaken by her abrupt question, I stared at her for a beat, then looked away. Taking a drag from my cigarette, I exhaled the smoke and watched it fade in the air. "What's it to you?"

"Just curious, is all. You don't have to tell me, but I'd like it if you did."

Cocking an eyebrow, I glared at her with caution. *What's her game?*

Though I had only met her yesterday, it felt incredibly difficult to brush off her questions. A part of me wanted to change the subject, to talk about anything other than myself, while the other part wanted to challenge myself through her.

Not sure if I was falling into a trap, one I'd regret later, I took the chance and played along. "Empty."

I could tell I piqued her interest with how her eyes shifted. "Empty?"

"Yeah."

"I see. Well, in that, we are alike," she said, flicking the ash from her cigarette over the railing.

Catching her in a lie, I pridefully corrected her. "You've got parents at home. It's not empty."

Staring into my eyes with her guarded ones, she smiled distantly. "Just because there are people at home, doesn't make it full. I also have two younger brothers—twins. Go figure, right?"

Perplexed by this information she willingly gave me, I was left wanting to discover more, though I knew I shouldn't. "How old are your brothers?"

Fuck.

"Six. They're at a really fun age right now." She smiled again, though it was still faint. "They're also too smart for their own good."

She says her home life feels 'empty,' but the way she goes on about her brothers says otherwise. "Six-year-old twins, huh? Guess we know who the mistakes were," I said, a sad attempt at a joke.

"They weren't mistakes, they were blessings," she stated, firmly. "My parents were told they couldn't have children."

Confused, I asked the obvious. "But they had you?"

With a smug look on her face, she evaded my eyes. "They didn't. They adopted me."

My heartstrings snagged. I was starting to feel the regret I feared from before. How'd we get into the topic of family so deeply so fast? I had so many questions, but I knew the details of her life were none of my business. I didn't want them to be. I had enough hardships and burdens of my own to deal with, so why did hers suddenly interest me?

Stop it, Riku! Cut the crap. No strings, no attachments.

"Tachibana," I said, shaking my head, "you don't gotta tell me about such personal matters. You hardly know me."

"On the contrary, Riku," she started, using my first name flawlessly as she pushed away from the railing. Standing tall, with the cigarette between her fingers, she faced me confidently. "I may have only met you yesterday, but I'm oddly drawn to you, and I can't help but want to tell you stuff about me. Why is that?"

My dick throbbed. *Why, indeed.*

Everything she said resonated with me, but I didn't want it to. It—this—wasn't allowed. While not knowing the answer, I somehow understood completely what she was asking. For the last two days, I've caught myself looking for her multiple times, seeking her out.

Again, not allowed.

Dropping my half-smoked cigarette, I snuffed it out with the toe of my school slipper. "Honestly, Tachibana, I have no idea."

With my eyes on the ground, I saw her feet move toward me. Looking up,

I noticed that her eyes were almost level with mine. Though she was on the taller side for a girl, she was still a head shorter than me.

I was in trouble.

"Can I try something?" she asked, as she rose to her tippytoes. She was close enough that I could feel her breath on my face.

I had a good feeling I knew what she was getting at. I responded with a warning, "If you try it, you better not be disappointed with the outcome."

"That's for me to decide."

"I may not be able to give you what you're looking for," I advised, usually knowing myself, but in this moment, I wasn't too sure that I did.

"But Riku, I don't know what I'm looking for."

Gazing into her eyes, I grabbed her chin and tilted her head upward. Taking my thumb, I traced her bottom lip. With her free hand, the one without the burning cigarette, she gently reached down for my other hand and guided it up to her cheek.

If I did this, I would only be complicating my life further. But with her so close, literally in the palm of my hand, the will to resist was fleeing.

Of their own accord, my fingers tucked the loose strands of hair behind her ear, and I placed a kiss on her inviting lips. Asking for trouble, she stuck her tongue into my mouth, almost daring me to go further. She tasted like strawberries and cigarettes; sweet, but also bitter.

FUUUCK!

With embarrassing speed, I grabbed her by the waist and lifted her into my arms. As I did this, she dropped the cigarette and wrapped her legs around me, then began ruffling my hair in a way that drove me crazy. A twinge of desire grew inside me, and travelled all the way down into my pants, each time her hand passed through my hair.

Holding her in my arms, I walked us toward the wall where she had been reading and pinned her against it, refusing to break the connection of our lips. In the heat of the moment, all I wanted to do was strip Tachibana and have my way with her. Readjusting my footing, I felt my foot bump into something. With a quick side-glance down, I saw Tachibana's book. Taking it as a sign, I immediately came to my senses. Knowing this wasn't something I wanted to be doing with her at school, or possibly at all, I lowered Tachibana to the ground and regretfully pulled away from her lips. With my blood scorching, I rested my forehead against hers as we both gasped for air.

"So," I began to ask, breathing heavily, "did you find it?"

"Hmm?"

"What you were looking for."

"I'm not sure," she said, her eyes glowing with a passion that darkened the dual colour of her irises. She tried to regain her composure. "But I wasn't disappointed with my search."

Fuck. Fuck. Fuck.

Fighting the desire to pull her back to me, I backed away from her. After straightening my necktie, I turned my back to her and went over to the cigarette she dropped to put it out. Stepping on it, I drew in a deep breath before speaking over my shoulder. "You dunno what you're getting yourself into, Tachibana." *Look who's talking.*

"Hinata."

I looked back at her. "Huh?"

"I want you to call me Hinata."

With a smirk, I walked back toward her to retie the uniform bowtie that had come undone around her neck. "Make sure you look half-decent before going back to class, *Hinata*. We don't want our classmates to spread more rumours."

"It's okay, I don't mind if they do."

"Aren't you bothered by what others say?"

"Not really."

"Well, you should be," I said, just as I finished adjusting her bowtie. "You don't want them to start calling you a slut or something."

Puzzled, she tilted her head. "How can I be labelled as a 'slut' when I've never kissed anyone other than you?"

Dumbstruck, I removed my hands from her. "What?"

"You are the only person I've ever kissed. How does that make me a slut?"

Listening to her words, I couldn't begin to process them. "You're joking . . .."

"Am not," she said, reassuringly.

Frozen, my jaw dropped. *She's messing with me, right? I can't believe she's that inexperienced based on the passionate moment we just shared. But what reason would she have to lie?*

"Riku, I may be a lot of things, but when it comes to matters such as these, I'm not a liar."

Trying to wrap my head around yet another confusing situation, I brought my lips together and stared at her absentmindedly.

"Riku?"

Thinking about how much experience I had in comparison to her gave me a whole new set of conflicting feelings. She was so mysterious. What kind of innocent fantasy world did this girl come from?

"I believe you. I'm just trying to figure out why you'd wanna try something like this with me."

"I'm not sure. It just felt right."

"Felt . . . right?" *What?*

"Yes," she said, as she backed away from me to pick up the empty pudding cup and hardcover. Taking a better look, I noticed the book she had been reading had to do with music. Once she collected all her belongings, she made her way to the door, then stopped. "I quite enjoy our secret rendezvous, Riku." She smiled playfully. "Until next time."

I was dying to continue this conversation, to dive deeper into who Hinata Tachibana truly was, but it seemed she was done with our time together. "Yeah," I responded, unexpectedly dumbfounded. "Until next time."

And like that, she was gone.

Next time? Who the hell is this girl? WHAT THE FUCK HAVE I GOTTA MYSELF INTO?

Before leaving the roof, my phone vibrated in my pocket. Appearing on the lock screen was a message from Sakura. Setting aside my thoughts of Tachibana, I felt fear consume me.

[LINE Sakura Sato]: I don't care what you say, but we desperately need to talk. Meet me after school at the storage shed behind the school.

[LINE Riku Nakajima]: I'll be there.

Chapter Seven

WHEN I *DID* attend school, I'd eat and hang out with Makoto and others from our grade, but today was different. Within the last twenty-four hours, I had accumulated many secrets and experienced uncharted territories. All while needing to hide from Kobayashi-sensei.

It would be easier to simply end my life at this point. I was a self-inflicted, ticking time bomb.

I went down to the first floor and ventured off to the second building to clear my head of Tachibana and get rid of the lust ready to explode inside me. Walking past the music wing, I heard the familiar sound of a piano. Just like last time, the tone of the song was heavy, and before I knew it, my feet were carrying me toward the music room with long strides.

Peeking through the window of the door, I was gifted with yet another surprise, one much more satisfying. The one playing the depressing tune was Tachibana. Though I had just *seen* her, I hadn't *seen* her like this. Her back was pin straight, and her eyes were closed, as she touched each one of the keys gracefully; she was in a world of her own.

I quietly took a seat on the floor next to the door. Resting my head against the wall, I shut my eyes. I wanted to see if I could briefly enter and comprehend Tachibana's world. I cut out all the background noise, focusing solely on the sound of the piano. Suddenly, the sad tune Tachibana had been playing changed tempo. The notes were no longer slow and steady, but upbeat and harsh. It sounded as if Tachibana was screaming through her music; it was aggressive, and I loved every second of it.

There was so much I didn't know about Tachibana. She had so many layers, like an onion, and I wanted to peel back and discover all of them. Who was 'Hinata Tachibana'? What made her happy? What made her sad? What made her tick? *Who* made her feel all those things?

Man, what the hell am I doing?

"There you are!"

Alarmed, I nearly jumped out of my skin. My eyes grew wide as I turned to face the loud and distracting voice coming from down the hall. Closing in on my right was an angry Kobayashi-sensei.

Fuck.

"Mr. Nakajima, I've been looking everywhere for you! I know you've been avoiding me," Kobayashi-sensei stated, approaching me in a fast-paced walk.

I sprang to my feet to try and silence him. "Sensei, shh! Okay, okay, I'll go with you," I said, directing him away from the music room.

Gawking at my acceptance, Kobayashi-sensei stopped. "Well, that was easy . . . A little too easy if you ask me."

With all the commotion, the piano playing stopped.

"Gah!" I gasped. Taking a quick peek over my shoulder, I stared at the door of the music room. Wanting to put distance between myself and Tachibana, so that she wouldn't discover me in this situation, I grabbed Kobayashi-sensei's arm and ran, dragging him along.

Maneuvering us through the halls in panic, it wasn't until we were back at the entrance of the second building that I was able to catch my breath.

"Ri—Mr. Nakajima! What do you think you're doing?" Kobayashi-sensei demanded, also out of breath.

"You came at a bad time, Sensei. You almost blew my cover."

With that twitch of his brow, he glared, then smacked me over the head. "You know you're talking to a teacher, right? Show some respect."

"Ow! What the—You can't go around hitting students!"

Shaking his head, he straightened his tie. "Teacher's lounge. Now."

"Haaai."

I diligently followed Kobayashi-sensei into the teacher's lounge back inside the main building. Kobayashi-sensei cleared a few things off his desk and opened a drawer, pulling out a large, bloated file. Dropping the file on his desk, he turned to face me, then dropped into his chair and leaned back casually.

"How come you skipped out on homeroom and first period this morning? I heard you came right at the end of second period, disrupting the class with your entrance—typical."

Also leaning back in my chair, I crossed my hands over my stomach. "I slept in."

"Riku."

"It's true. Why don't 'ya believe me?"

Arching his brow, he admitted defeat with a sigh. "You're mentally exhausting, you know that?" He slid the file closer to me. "Last time we spoke, I had only briefly looked into your academic career. This time, I did my proper research."

I sat up straighter. "What're you talking about?"

Looking into my eyes, he sat in a more lax position. "Riku, I read your file."

"File?"

"Yes. The school keeps files on all its students. It states the names of the schools you have attended, your attendance record, your grades, suspensions and fights you have been involved in, who paid for the tuition and by which method, and your family situation growing up. After reviewing it, I have made note of a few things, some expected and some *un*expected. Now," he paused for a quick breath, "family situations are only recorded if specific incidents occur and if outside services are involved."

Furious by Kobayashi-sensei's overbearing step into my private life, my face grew hot. At times, it felt like I was living in a fragile, glass box where my life was on display for those in power to see and comb through. Trying to break free was futile. I would always be dragged back by those trying their best to 'help' structure me, keeping me on a tight leash. Practically imprisoned.

Curling my hands into fists, I crossed my arms and remained silent.

He continued. "Riku, I'm sorry if me prying into your life has upset you. But I did this so I could better understand you. I want to help you achieve success and graduate. I bear no ill intentions."

Not knowing what to make of this situation, of him, I had to ask, "Why?"

"I explained why."

"No. Why me? Why're you only harassing me, Sensei?"

"'Harassing'?" Sighing with uncertainty, he spent a moment formulating his response. "You know, Riku . . . I used to teach elementary school."

Not sure where he was going with this senseless change in conversation, I played along. "Okay . . .?"

"It was my first teaching position; I was there for about three years."

"I see," I said, wishing he would hurry on with his predictable 'teaching moment.'

"In my final year of teaching elementary, something traumatic happened that almost made me quit teaching altogether."

Suddenly intrigued, I tried to anticipate what the next part could entail. "What happened?"

"Well, in the middle of the year, I noticed one of my female students had randomly acquired very suspicious bruises. Although she tried to hide them, they were clearly visible whenever she wore dresses or skirts, and also on the back of her neck if she wore her hair up. At first, I noticed her mood started to change. She used to be a very bright and bubbly girl with a big personality, but suddenly, she was dejected and scared of getting in the slightest bit of trouble. For the life of me, I could not understand what could have caused her to change so drastically, until it hit me—she was being abused at home. Looking into family matters, I learned that her mother had recently been divorced and had found a new boyfriend." He turned his head. "I was advised by my superiors to contact child services."

Kobayashi-sensei's eyes glistened as he told his story. I easily related to the story, and he knew it.

Turning my gaze downward, I became invested. "What happened to the little girl?"

"After child services got involved, she was removed from the home."

"Did she ever reunite with her mom?"

Observing Kobayashi-sensei's feet, he uncrossed his legs and placed his feet firmly on the floor. With the jittery movement of his leg, I could see the sole of his fancy dress shoe flexing up and down.

"No."

Even though I had guessed his answer, my heart still tightened. Suddenly, breathing became difficult. Finding the words lodged in my throat, I had one more question to ask. "Where's the little girl now?"

An unusual silence lingered in our corner of the teacher's lounge. Needing to know the answer, I quickly brought my gaze up to meet his. Catching his eyes, Kobayashi-sensei was already staring at me attentively.

"Where's the little girl now, Sensei?" I repeated.

"She was removed from my class and forced to transfer schools. I lost all means of contact with her after that." Kobayashi-sensei's throat rolled as he swallowed. "Later that year, I was informed that she had died by suicide. She was ten years old."

Unable to catch up with my feelings, it was as if my boiling blood had turned to ice. I vacantly stared at Kobayashi-sensei. With a hammering chest, I mourned for this little girl who I had never met.

Why's he telling me this? Does he think I'll off myself like she did? "Did you tell me this story because you wanna redeem yourself by using me? To make yourself feel better about the past?"

"Riku . . . that's not the case." He stilled. "Well, to be honest, maybe it is," he sighed heavily. "To this day, I have no idea if what I did was the right thing. I wonder now if I should have checked in on the girl at her new school, or if I should have just left the entire situation alone. Maybe, if I had ignored the signs of abuse, she would still be alive. But it's too late for what-ifs. I failed her."

I respected Kobayashi-sensei's honesty. Usually, he was just a giant pain in the ass to deal with, but in this moment, I couldn't let him drown in self-pity.

"Sensei, you didn't fail her. It's the system that failed her. The system is flawed."

With a tilt of his head, Kobayashi-sensei seemed confused by what I had said. "The system?"

"Yeah, the child protection system and their Child Guidance Centres.

They're shit. The word 'protection' is literally what they claim to stand for, but it does everything EXCEPT protect kids."

Taken aback by my words, Kobayashi-sensei's head dropped. "Riku, I'm sorry you've had to live such a difficult life. Nobody, especially a child, should be tossed around in a system controlled by strangers who aren't providing the proper care." Lifting his head, he opened the file and took out some of its contents, then laid them out on the desk. "In your file, it's documented that you were placed into temporary custody and shuffled through a few different Child Guidance Centres but were then moved into foster care. Why?"

I was not prepared to deal with this walk down memory lane, and with Kobayashi-sensei no less. From a young age, I knew my life was screwed-up. I knew my mother was different than other kids'. I knew my home life wasn't like others in my class, and that I was considered poor and unfortunate. These were all aspects of my life that had been pointed out to me by others, leaving me to shine in a targeted spotlight. Those who didn't want to get involved with me, mostly teachers and parents of other kids in class, made it clear that I wasn't worth their time. Just because you cry, doesn't mean someone will come and save you.

At first glance, adults could easily tell I had it rough, but to a kid who knew no better, I was the same as them. Until second grade, everything was fine, normal. It wasn't until I was taken away from home for the first time and placed into foster care that things started to change. I quickly began to understand my situation. Things were no longer 'normal.' Technically, they never were.

With tight shoulders, I leaned over to take a better look at the papers he pulled out from the file. There was quite a stack of documents, most of them stamped by the Shinjuku CGC. Glancing at the paperwork from a distance, I read some familiar names that I had wished to forget.

"Riku?"

Knowing Kobayashi-sensei would not rest until I explained parts of my past, I decided to cut my hostility so we could get this over with. He didn't need to know everything. He just needed enough to satisfy his new obsession—me.

"Okay, Sensei, you win. I'll tell you." Taking a deep breath, I went off. "After being in and outta the CGC back in Shinjuku, I was first moved into foster care when I was seven. From there, I was placed in a handful of different homes over the years because my abusive, cracked-out mom couldn't get her shit together enough to keep custody of me. The woman society deems as 'my mother,' trades her body for drugs and money. Often, my mom would come home with a new guy, one who could help feed and maintain her addiction. There'd been times that I'd come back from a full day of school, just to find her high and passed out on the floor of our apartment."

Listening attentively, Kobayashi-sensei didn't miss a word.

Right after I finished, he asked another question. "What about grandparents or other family members? Was going to live with one of them not an option?"

Shaking my head, I answered. "The CGC officer's told me they exhausted all family options. I dunno anything about my extended family. I've only ever known my pathetic excuse of a mom, who I haven't lived with in years."

Trying to avoid Kobayashi-sensei's distressed eyes, I heard his voice cracking as he continued with his interrogation. "S-so, you were in and out of foster care?"

Taking another deep breath, I rolled my eyes. "Like you, an elementary school teacher noticed how neglected I was because I'd come to school beaten black and blue, without a lunch, wearing the same dirty fuckin' clothes for weeks on end. The Shinjuku CGC placed me with my first foster family in Edogawa to distance me from my unsafe surroundings, also transferring my case."

Overlooking my inappropriate word choices, Kobayashi-sensei went silent for a moment, then proceeded to ask, "After everything, how did you settle in Shibuya?"

"My last foster family lived in Shibuya," I continued. "They didn't wanna have to pick me up and drive me to a school that was outta the way for them, so I was made to transfer. I was ten at the time, and it was at my new school in Shibuya that I met Makoto. Makoto and I hit it off, so much so that I spent many nights at his place because my piece of shit foster family didn't give a damn about me. From there, a lot of shit went down, and soon after, Makoto's family got involved and took custody of me as my legal guardians until I turn eighteen."

"Ah, so you and Fujimoto have been friends for quite some time. I'm glad you were able to meet a person who could help you, Riku."

"Makoto's life has always been well put together, while mine was destined to fall apart. In normal circumstances, we would've never become friends," I said, feeling the need to clarify the difference in mine and Makoto's social standings.

"Why do you say that? I think the way you two became friends is perfectly normal," he rebutted.

Thinking back to last night, and how I betrayed such an important person in my life, I chose not to comment.

"Have you seen your mother since you were permanently removed from home?"

Something snapped in my head, triggering my brain to take a step back and reevaluate what the hell was going on. I was falling right into his trap; he had me baring my truths out in the open, willingly, as if I was being interviewed for a biography. How could I be so fucking oblivious?

"Riku?" he said, squinting his eyes, as if trying to get a read on me. It was then that he realized I had caught on to him.

Seeing the pity plastered on Kobayashi-sensei's pathetic face made me want to punch it.

"You're a cunning man, Sensei," I snorted, shaking my head.

"Riku, it's not what you think. I'm just trying to get to know you better. I want to help—"

Silencing whatever excuse he was crafting; I lifted my hand with an open palm. "No matter who says they're trying to 'help,' at the end of the day, everyone's only looking out for themselves. I'm not a charity case, okay?"

His eyebrows knitted into one. "That's not true, Riku. I am, without a doubt, looking out for you. And what about the Fuji—"

"Sensei," I cut in, lunging forward, "at the beginning of this conversation you admitted to not knowing if you were using me to make yourself feel better, remember?"

"Riku, that's—"

Just as Kobayashi-sensei was about to reply to my accusation, the bell chimed, signifying lunch was over.

I could not wait to get the hell out of the teacher's lounge and away from him. As I stood and turned to leave, Kobayashi-sensei grabbed my arm, just like before.

"Ri—"

"Sensei," I said, cutting him off again, "this is the last time I wanna discuss this. I understand that you wanna *help* me, but I'm past the point of being helped. If you're afraid that I'll kill myself, just like your past student, then don't. I'm not afraid of dying, but I don't hate my life *that* much. I'll try my best to attend more days of school. That's all I can offer. As for post-graduation, I won't be attending any college or university. Just like my career survey states, I plan on going straight into the workforce to start an independent life."

Kobayashi-sensei released me from his clutches. For once, he was speechless.

I made it out of the teacher's lounge in one piece, physically. But mentally, I was in shambles.

I wanted nothing more than to skip the rest of the day and head straight home to sleep off my problems. But then, I remembered. I still needed to meet with Sakura after school.

This is the longest fuckin' day of my life.

Chapter Eight

WHILE MY MOTHER was occupied in the bathroom, I grabbed her purse and hid in the corner of our small kitchen. Crouching, I placed the purse on the floor and scavenged through it, desperately searching for whatever money I could get my hands on. I dreamt of the convenience store dinner I would buy, an upgrade from the dumpsters I had completely picked over the past week.

Not wanting to waste the little time I had, I decided it would be faster to flip the purse over and shake everything out. With all its contents poured out, I frantically examined the floor for dropped cash. After placing a few undesired items back into the purse to clear up the space in front of me, I came across a white, powdered substance within a clear plastic baggie. Holding it up to get a better look, my eyes widened as they met with something beyond terrifying. My mother stood over me, smiling cynically. Bending down to my level, she ripped the small baggie from my hand.

"Riku, baby, what're 'ya doin'?"

Frightened from being caught, I froze. I had no idea what her scary smile entailed. "Um, I was just—It's not what it—"

"ENOUGH!" she screamed with a raspy voice. Correcting her face, the smile returned, and she laughed hysterically—like someone unhinged.

Adjusting her tone, she tilted her chin down and lowered her glare, then smirked. "You're too young to get your nose into this shit."

Not knowing what she meant, I remained quiet out of fear.

Yanking her purse out of my hands, she stood. "C'mon, stand up." Tugging on my arm, she involuntarily brought me to my feet. "Lift up your shirt and turn around. Y'know what happens when 'ya steal from me."

"Mommy, I'm sorry! Please, no!" I begged, hopelessly trying to glue my shirt to my body. "I didn't take anything! I promise, I won't do it again!"

"Stop your whinin'! I'm sick and tired of hearin' your annoyin' ass voice."

Dragging me into the hallway, she forced me to face the wall and removed my shirt from my unwilling grasp. Pulling out a lighter and a pack of cigarettes from her purse, she took out one cigarette and flicked on the lighter. As the cigarette caught fire, she brought it closer to me and pinned me against the wall with her arm.

"Hold still."

With the burning end of the cigarette, she pressed it into my bare back.

"NOOO! MOMMY, PLEASE!" In between each plea, I gasped for air, as if my lungs were full of water.

When she was done, she put the cigarette in her mouth and walked toward the multipurpose living area. "Serves 'ya right, damn brat."

Falling to my knees, I curled up into a ball and inaudibly cried in the hallway until the pain slowly diminished.

⁂

My mind wandered through the rest of my afternoon classes. Trying to prevent my brain from entering a dark place, I spent most of the time with my head down on my desk. When the final set of chimes rang, I shot up from my chair and threw my stuff into my schoolbag. Looking to the back of the room, I saw Sakura also gathering her things in a hurry. Not wanting to leave at the exact same time, I waited for Sakura to exit the classroom first.

Leaving from the back door, Sakura turned the corner and merged into the bustling hallway. Slowly, I made my way to the front door, hopefully giving her enough time and distance. As I was about to leave, my name was called.

"Yo, Riku!" Makoto shouted. "Rushing to one of your part-time's?"

I had forgotten that Makoto was also in our last class. Stepping aside, I allowed other classmates to leave ahead of me before glancing back at him. Makoto was at his desk preparing his bag.

Drawing in a deep breath, I went to speak with him. "Uh, yeah . . . I have work today, but uh . . . first I gotta meet up with Kobayashi-sensei."

I lied.

"Again? Man, Sensei's really on your case, huh? I almost feel sorry for you," he teased.

"Yeah, he's getting super annoying."

"I bet," he grinned, putting the straps of his bag over his shoulder. "Oh, hey. Listen, before you go, can I ask you something?"

Unsure of what it was that he wanted to ask, my heart nearly stopped. "Ye-yeah, what's up?"

"It's to do with Sakura."

My eyes almost popped out of their sockets. *Holy fuck . . . Did Yamada say something? That bastard! I fuckin' told him to keep his damn mouth shut!*

"Have you noticed that she's a bit weird today?"

Listening to the way Makoto asked his question, he seemed more concerned than upset. Wondering what he knew, I chose to feel out the situation.

"What d'you mean?"

"I don't know, it's hard to explain. I kind of feel like she's avoiding me," he said, dejected.

That airheaded idiot. Is she purposely avoiding Makoto because of what I said this morning?

"Sorry, Makoto. I haven't noticed anything outta the usual."

"Ah, no worries," he chuckled loosely under his breath. "Maybe it's all in my head."

"Maybe . . . .."

I had become a good liar, but I knew this wasn't a skill to be proud of.

"I plan on confessing to her soon," he abruptly declared.

My chest stiffened. "Why?"

"What do you mean 'why'?" His eyebrow raised. "You know I've been planning to do so ever since first-year. You harass me all the time about it."

Gutted, I stared blankly at Makoto. "I know."

"Then, what's the problem?"

Panic coursed through me as I searched for the right thing to say. I had backed myself into an invisible corner. "You're right . . . Go for it, bro." Acid climbed the walls of my throat as those words left my lips. *Could I be any more of a shittier person? Shittier friend?*

With a comforted smile, Makoto threw his arm around my shoulder. "Thanks, man. I'm going to need all the support I can get."

"Right . . . When d'you plan on confessing?" I asked, trying to gauge how the near future would pan out.

Removing his arm from my shoulder, he tried to cover his flushed face with both hands. "Not sure," he said, talking through his fingers. "Maybe next week . . . or the week after."

Good ol' Makoto; still as indecisive and shy as ever. Gaining energy from Makoto's wavering response, I knew this gave me more time to figure things out.

"I wish you luck, bro," I said in a lifeless voice, tagged with a fake smile. *The answer was 'yes,' I could be shittier.*

"Thanks, Riku."

"I'll catch you later," I said, heading for the door.

"Oh, hey, are you coming to school tomorrow, too?"

Pulled back once more, I answered, "Nah, I work." *Granted, I did tell that stupid demon I'd make more of an effort to attend school. But I can't afford to keep calling in.*

"Too bad. I was getting used to having you around again."

With mountains of guilt eating away at me, I was finding it harder to look Makoto in the eye. The more I looked at him, the more I felt sick to my stomach. Keeping up the façade, I smiled in acknowledgment as I walked out the door.

Racing down the stairs, I ran to the shoe lockers to exchange my footwear before meeting up with Sakura. With Makoto nowhere in sight, I bolted outside.

Wrapping around the school building, I headed for the storage shed at the very back corner of the school grounds. As I approached, Sakura was leaning up against the shed, scrolling on her phone. At first, she didn't notice me, but after my feet appeared in her line of vision, her head jerked up.

"Ri-Riku!"

Staring at Sakura, I could see that her eyes were red and puffy. Suddenly aware of how terrible her face must've looked during class, I felt the guilt pile on.

"Have you been crying?"

Even though her mouth was closed, I could tell she was gritting her teeth by the way her jaw tensed. "What do you think?"

Shaking off her snarky comment, I pressed forward with what I had come to ask. "Are you avoiding Makoto?"

She pursed her lips and turned her head. "I don't know how I should act around him, now that I know he likes me."

"Sakura, you're being unfair to him. He's already noticed that you're acting weird."

"What are you implying? That I'm solely to blame for this?" she snapped, taking a defensive step toward me with sharp eyes.

Frustration accumulated under my skin. "We're both equally at fault, Sakura. I'm not implying anything. But to be honest, I still don't understand how any of this shit happened. I have no recollection of even speaking to you during the mixer. What happened last night?"

She hung her head. "What's the last thing you *do* remember?"

"Having drinks with that one Iwasaki girl."

"That's it . . .?"

Unable to recall most of the night, I admitted it honestly. "Yeah, that's the last thing I can remember."

"BAKA! BAKA! BAKA!"

My body jolted back from her outburst. As she profusely called me an idiot, she looked up. I could see the tears welling in her eyes.

"UGGGH! Why did I fall for a JERK like you? Why couldn't I have just fallen for Mako-kun instead?" As she spat out rhetorical questions, the tears that had gathered now fell from her eyes. "Why, Riku? Don't you feel *anything* for me? Even if it's just a little . . . I'd take just a little."

Listening to her spill her heart out, regarding the feelings she had hidden for so long, was troublesome. There was a heat growing inside me, causing my hands to tense and clam up. Thoughts were racing through my head so fast that I couldn't even think straight. How did I miss all the signs?

At this point, I knew there was nothing I could do or say that wouldn't hurt her. We were in this mess too deep. Conscious of how emotional she was, I needed to organize my shit so I could give her a fair response. I needed to own up to my actions, being drunk was no excuse.

"Sakura, I'm sorry."

"I don't want to hear that you're *sorry*! I just want to hear you say you love me!"

I tensed. Love was a foreign concept to me. It was something I've heard casually spoken, or used in bribe, but never understood. This time was no different. Sakura was trying to force her feelings on me. She wanted me to do something I feared I wasn't emotionally capable of doing, especially with her. I can't even remember the last time I told someone I loved them.

How could she feel so strongly for me? For anyone?

I couldn't make sense of it.

"Sakura, I can't love you. I don't think I'm capable of it, of love. And even if I was, or knew how, I wouldn't."

Wiping her tears as they fell, she asked in a hushed voice, "Because of Mako-kun?"

I sighed. "Makoto fell in love with you—almost at first sight—and ever since then, I never once dared to think of you in a romantic or lustful way."

Her tear-stained cheeks grew red from her consistent wiping. She drew in a shaky breath and upturned her chin to the sky, then jabbed her palms into her eyes and rubbed them.

"Want to know something, Riku?" She sucked in a deep breath. "I changed my image for you, hoping that one day you'd notice me. I thought that if I changed my prim and proper style, and became like the other girls, you might take interest in me." She removed her hands and brought her gaze down. "Foolish, right?" She wore a broken smile.

"What happened last night?" I repeated, uncomfortably. "Don't make me ask again."

"You're not even going to acknowledge my confession? I'm putting my heart on the line here," she hissed.

"Sakura, stop making this harder than it needs to be. I already told you; I can't return your feelings."

"You *can't* or you *won't*?"

"Both."

Her bottom lip quivered as I boldly made my statement. She broke our eye contact by turning her head, tears continuing to cut down her cheeks.

She was putting me in a difficult spot. "Sakura . . .."

"You saved me."

Not sure if I had heard her correctly, I sought out clarification. "Saved you?"

"Yes."

"From what?"

"The guy I spent most of the night talking to."

"You mean the guy with the stupid bleached hair?"

"Yeah, him."

"What about him?"

Still avoiding eye contact, she dug her shoe into the dirt under her feet. "He wasn't the type of person he made himself out to be."

Encouraging her to elaborate, I quirked a brow. "Which was . . .?"

"Well, at first, he was very nice and exciting to talk to; he made it easy to keep a conversation going. He seemed respectful of me and the others around us." She paused to take a full breath. "Once people moved away from our corner, or became distracted by the karaoke, he placed his hand on my thigh and inched closer to the edge of my skirt. Things became super uncomfortable, but I didn't want to cause a scene. I didn't want to be *that* girl. So, I didn't say anything. But inside, I was freaking out."

"The hell, Sakura? You should've told him to fuck off and got the hell outta there!"

"I didn't have to. You did it for me."

I felt my face twist. "What d'you mean?"

She shot a look up at me. "As soon as it happened, you came to my rescue."

Trying everything in my power to remember, my mind drew a blank. It was as if my memory had been completely wiped. "I don't . . ."

"You came running toward us, grabbed his hand, and twisted it so far back that I thought you had broken it," she said, filling in for my lack of response. "Right after that, you said: *Don't touch her with your disgusting hands, you piece of shit!* Then, you punched him in the face, took my hand, and led me out of the karaoke bar. Once we were outside, you gave me shit for apparently allowing guys to do as they pleased with my body. But the funny part was, you never asked me if I had *wanted* him to touch me. You just assumed I didn't like it."

I had no memory of this. Zero.

I was angry with myself for not remembering something so important. How could I not recall a single detail of how the night played out? Especially when these details led into a night I could never take back.

Well, that explains why my hand is so fucked up. One mystery solved.

My mind shifted and fixated on the end of Sakura's story; I was hung up on the last few words. "The hell? Why would I waste my time asking you if you wanted him to touch you when you just admitted you didn't like it?"

"I did just now, yes, but not yesterday. You made that assumption all on your own."

The fuck? What's up with this weird ass, back and forth bullshit she's pulling? Isn't it normal to wanna help a FRIEND if they look uncomfortable in a situation? Did she expect me to look the other way while that asshole touched her inappropriately? In public, no less? Obviously drunk me ain't that much of an idiot. Why's she pinning this 'assumption' bullshit on me? Get fucked.

"Well, sooorry. I guess I didn't want someone touching my best friend's girl," I said with the slip of the tongue, immediately regretting my choice of words.

"I'M NOT MAKO-KUN'S GIRL!" she exclaimed at the top of her lungs. "And you obviously didn't care that much about whose girl I was, because you slept with me in the end!"

Words were trapped in my throat. Dropping my head, I stared absently at the scuffs of dirt on the edges of my worn-out runners. Thinking about the unfortunate words I'd chosen, I realized, who was I really trying to fool? Myself? I was exactly the type of guy I tried to save Sakura from.

Disgusted with what I had done, and who I was becoming, the air around me turned thick. Down to my core, I knew I was nothing more than the piece of shit I described.

"You're absolutely right. You're not Makoto's girl, and in that moment, I obviously didn't care that he liked you. I have no idea what possessed me into taking you back to my place and sleeping with you. I have no explanation for my actions," I admitted, glancing up at her. "I know it means nothing now, but Sakura, I'm truly sorry. You're a dear friend to me, but that's all. I have no idea how we got here, where we'll go from here, or how we can recover this friendship. All I know is that it was a grave mistake and I regret what I did."

Shaking her head repeatedly, she clenched her fists. This time, instead of lashing out at me, she kept quiet.

Needing to know one crucial detail, I asked, "Did I . . . take your virginity?"

Continuing to shake her head, she answered, "No. I lost it in second year because I thought you wouldn't like me if you knew I was inexperienced."

Having started to calm down, her revelation made me see red once more. *The fuck . . . because of me? She thought I'd like her if she had experience? WHAT?*

"WHAT THE FUCK, SAKURA?" I blurted out, practically seething. "Have you lost all sense of dignity? Do you really base yourself on those bullshit standards? How could you be so fuckin' stupid?"

How could she lower herself, her value, for a dumb guy like me?

"Why does that make me stupid?" she asked, desperately seeking an answer. "It's no secret that you sleep around, so it's obvious that you prefer girls with experience."

'Obvious'? Yo, what the actual fuck.

I lost it. "FUUUCK!"

I thought Sakura was smarter than this. Right now, standing in front of me, was someone I felt I knew little to nothing about.

Any future apologies died on my tongue. If I could take back what I felt guilty about just moments ago, I would. This wasn't supposed to be about me. It was supposed to be about Makoto. How experienced I was with women wasn't relevant to Makoto's feelings for her.

My blood had reached its boiling point.

In an unforgiving rage, I marched up to her. Startled, Sakura walked backwards until her back collided with the shed, leaving her no room to escape. My body was on fire; I became scared of the thoughts I had of bringing her harm. Searing with anger, I tried to remain in control but fell short and slammed my hand against the shed, inches from her head.

"Don't pin this all on me! You *obviously* dunno SHIT, so don't pretend like you do." Tilting back, I removed my hand and laughed mirthlessly under my breath. "Y'know something, Makoto's too good for you. You're not as innocent and harmless as you tricked us into believing you were. I'm glad I got to finally see you for who you really are. You're just a manipulative bitch, and your personality is obnoxiously ugly."

Sakura slid down the shed and fell to her knees in shock, as I turned around and walked off.

Chapter Nine

I T WAS NEARING the end of June, and I didn't bother with school. I already knew I would have to attend supplementary lessons during the summer break, so what was the point?

The promise I made to Kobayashi-sensei went down the drain, along with my faith in people keeping their mouths shut about Sakura and me. My chest would stiffen each time I received an incoming LINE message, especially from Makoto, as I expected each one to finally reveal that he had learned the truth. It killed me to think about Makoto finding out that I had slept with Sakura. Although I no longer approved of him and Sakura becoming an item, I couldn't handle the thought of being an even bigger disappointment to him than I already was. The fact that Makoto hadn't mentioned Sakura in any of our messages also meant that he hadn't confessed yet.

The days blended altogether. I'd leave one job and go straight to the other, picking up as many shifts as I could. Anything to keep myself busy. After every evening or night shift there would almost always be some sort of bag leaning against my front door. Most of the time, the bag contained school notes and handouts from Makoto, but every so often, there would also be a home-cooked meal from Mrs. Fujimoto.

Finishing my dayshift at the convenience store, I went home to shower before starting my next shift at the restaurant. Climbing up the sheltered, outdoor stairway to my apartment, which was at the top floor of the complex, I turned the corner and expected to see another bag at my door. To my surprise, there was nothing. Finding it unusual, I checked the time on my watch.

Ah, I guess school just ended. Maybe Makoto hasn't come by yet.

Entering my apartment, I dropped my backpack by the entrance, then kicked off my sneakers before stepping up onto the small, raised entryway. Stripping off my clothes, I tossed them on the floor near my bed, then went into the bathroom to turn on the shower. When the water ran hot, I stepped inside. Closing my eyes, I faced the showerhead and placed both hands on the wall, letting the water pour onto my head and run down my body. Exhausted, I could have easily fallen asleep if I wasn't careful, so I washed myself quickly.

Reflecting upon the situation involving Makoto and Sakura, I kind of wished Makoto knew already, just so I could stop living in a constant state of uneasiness. I had many opportunities to tell him, but I was too much of a coward to do it.

When the water turned cold, I got out of the shower and reached for the only towel I owned. First, I shook my head with it to quickly dry my hair, then wrapped it around my lower half. As I was drying off, there was a knock at the front door, so I poked my head into the hallway and stared at the entrance.

Shit, it's probably Makoto.

I remained silent to see if he would drop off the stuff and leave. Not hearing any commotion, I dipped back into the bathroom. Continuing to dry off quietly, I heard another knock at the door.

He sure is persistent. Does he always knock and wait to see if I'll answer when I'm not around? Whatever, I'll just open it and face him. I doubt he knows anything yet. Right . . .?

Walking toward the door with the towel around my waist, I stepped down into the entryway and reached for the handle. "Yo man, you could've left—" I finished opening the door to find out that the determined knocker was, in fact, not Makoto. "Haaah, Tachibana?"

"Hello, Riku," she greeted, with a small, slightly awkward wave.

In awe, I gawked at Tachibana as I rested one hand against the door frame. "What're you doing here?"

"I'm here to drop off today's school notes and worksheets," she said, handing me a bag.

I slowly grabbed the bag from her. "Thanks . . . but why're you dropping these off? Usually, Makoto's the one who does this."

She looked me up and down, then brought her eyes back to mine. "Would you prefer to continue this conversation inside?"

Following her eyes, I looked down. Forgetting I was half-naked, I laughed. "Might be best." I raised an eyebrow. "But are you sure you wanna come into a guy's apartment, alone?"

Without batting an eye, she answered, "I'm sure."

Continuing to be blown away by Tachibana, I stepped aside and allowed her to enter. She waited at the entrance with her shoes on as I shut the door and walked past her. Going into the multipurpose living area, I threw the bag onto my bed. Glancing over my shoulder, I could see Tachibana standing with her schoolbag dangling in front of her, in the same respectful stance; she hadn't moved an inch.

"Are you gonna awkwardly stand there the entire time? Should I speak up so you can hear me better?" I teased, slightly raising my voice.

"I wasn't sure if you wanted to put on some clothes before conversing." Her eyes darted away from me.

"All right, all right. I'll get dressed in the bathroom," I said, as I began looking for clean clothes. "It's fine, come in."

"In that case, pardon my intrusion," she said, bowing before removing her loafers and setting her schoolbag on the floor.

I watched as she bent down and collected her shoes with one hand, carefully tucking her uniform skirt under her butt. She then turned her loafers around to face the front door and lined them up at the edge of the raised entryway.

Hmm . . . Is she here to address our time up on the roof? If she doesn't mention it, then, should I? Or do I pretend like nothing ever happened? Shit, why the fuck am I so antsy about this?

Finding a pair of black jeans, a black t-shirt, and a fresh pair of black boxer briefs, I headed to the bathroom to throw them on. My go-to was black; black on black was my favourite look. Black was mysterious and quiet; colour didn't suit me.

"Give me two seconds while I put these on. In the meantime, make yourself comfortable."

After dressing in the bathroom, and hanging the wet towel, I stepped back into the hallway and looked toward my bed. Tachibana had taken a seat on the floor on one of the zabuton cushions at my chabudai table in the middle of the room. With a perfectly straight back, just like the time she was playing the piano, she sat in seiza, as if she were a model right out of a proper etiquette textbook.

I crossed my arms as I leaned against the edge of the hallway wall. "So, before I offer you something to drink, care to explain why you're here?"

"You don't have much furniture," she avoided, rotating her head to look around the studio apartment.

Not including the items that came with the apartment, I had minimal furniture: a single bed, a small side table, the chabudai table with some zabuton cushions, and a small dresser to store clothes—sometimes. Every piece of furniture I owned was second hand.

The less shit you owned, the easier it was to move. I came to learn that early on as a child.

After my mother had a handful of failed attempts at landing a decent apartment, leaving us to spend many nights out on the streets, I promised myself I would never live like that ever again. So, when Uncle Ito offered me his smallest unit, I jumped at the opportunity.

My current apartment resembled the one I grew up in, back when I lived with my piece of shit mother, just a slightly different layout. The entryway was small, the kitchen was small, the bathroom was small. Small was the theme of affordable housing in Tokyo. But, for one person, it was more than enough.

For a while now, it had just been me, a pack of cigarettes, a lighter, and a can of black coffee. Those were the only things I made sure I always kept in stock; other worldly possessions were pointless to hold on to. When you came from nothing, it was easy to have nothing.

I raised an eyebrow. "I don't need much."

"There's a faint smell of cigarettes in here," she commented, sniffing the air.

"Sometimes I smoke inside. Does the smell bother you?"

"Not really. Just an observation," she said moving on, examining the space further. "Do you live alone?"

"Yes," I answered, skeptically.

"Is that what you meant by 'empty'?"

Recalling our conversation on the rooftop, I replied, "In a way."

"I see," she said, almost in a whisper.

"Any other questions, or are you gonna finally answer mine?"

Facing me, she remained seated. "I asked Fujimoto why you hadn't been attending school lately, and he replied: *'Riku is like that sometimes. He'll show up once, or twice, and then go missing for a couple of weeks.'*"

Laughing at the way she mimicked Makoto, I smiled. "Sounds like something he'd say."

"Afterwards, I requested your home address from Fujimoto. He asked if I had plans on paying you a visit, and after confirming that I did, he asked if I could drop off some school notes and worksheets in his place," she explained, taking in a breath. "It was hard to find your apartment; there isn't a visible nameplate."

"I don't have a nameplate," I stated dismissively. "And jeez, is he just giving out my address to anyone who asks? I wonder how many other girls know where I live." I shuddered. "Creepy."

"I'm not sure."

I took a moment to regard her. "Y'know, Tachibana—"

"Hinata."

Focusing on her, she returned my stare. Her two-coloured eyes were sucking me in; I couldn't help but gaze into them. With each encounter, I grew more and more conscious of her. "Y'know, *Hinata*, you don't have to be so formal all the time."

"I don't mean to," she said, dejected.

She was so earnest; I couldn't help but be entertained. I laughed again. "Why did you wanna know where I lived?"

"Well, you were absent from school . . . .."

"Aww, Hinata, were you worried about me?"

Her eyes glistened in realization. "I guess I was."

Not expecting her to be so upfront and honest, I was rendered speechless.

Uncrossing my arms, I walked toward her and bent down to her level. Leaning into her, I stared at her with the intent to intimidate. She was getting closer and closer to me, and not just in a physical aspect. She was putting in all this effort, and for what? What did she want from me?

"Why?"

Hinata held her ground. "I'm not quite sure myself."

Her eyes, which had once been guarded, seemed clear and almost welcoming. They lured me in; I could feel myself being drawn toward her. And like before, I wasn't sure what to make of her responses.

Fuck, I'm in deep trouble with this one.

Needing to back away from temptation, I broke eye contact and rose to my feet. Clicking my tongue, I turned my back toward her to fetch us some drinks from the kitchen. Rubbing the back of my neck, I attempted to massage away all the stress knots she inflicted upon me. It was then that I felt a hand touch my back, which caused me to jump and spin around. Standing just inches away from me was Hinata, slowly retracting her hand.

"Riku," she said, her eyes sensitive and glossy, "what are all those markings you have on your back?"

A dark cloud hovered over me; the craving I walked away from just seconds ago, dulled.

"How the . . ."

"I saw them when you were still half-naked in the towel," she said, answering the missing parts of my question.

I turned away from her, not wanting her to catch my reaction. "Don't worry about it."

She didn't hesitate. "The fact that you're telling me not to worry about it only makes me worry about it all the more."

Turning back, I looked at her with narrowed eyes. "Why?"

"Again, I don't know," she answered, slightly horrified. The softness in her eyes had turned sad. "I don't understand the feelings I get when I'm around you. All I know is that I want to learn more about you."

My throat closed. I wasn't sure why she had the power to stir my emotions, but she did. She was the most straightforward person I had ever met. She scared me.

"I gotta get to work, so I think it's time for you to leave."

"I'm sorry for overstepping."

"It's fine, you didn't," I said dismissively, hoping she would drop the subject.

"Riku—"

"Thanks for coming by to drop off the school notes and worksheets, but I'm gonna be late," I said, cutting her off.

Heading toward the door, I hoped that she would take it as an invitation to follow me. Taking a seat on the raised step, I grabbed my sneakers.

"Is that why you haven't been at school, because you've been working?" She stood in the middle of the hallway, tilting her head with worry as she watched me tuck the laces into the sides of my sneakers.

"Pretty much. Gonna rat me out?"

"Why would I?"

"Dunno, just wondering."

"Well, I wouldn't," she said, surely.

"Okay," I confirmed, standing up and grabbing my backpack off the floor. "Time to go." I slipped my backpack over both shoulders, then reached for the doorknob. Trying to hurry the process along, I went back to pick up her schoolbag and handed it to her. "Here."

Meeting me at the entrance, she retrieved the bag from me hesitantly and slipped on her loafers. "Thank you."

"Yeah."

⁂

Coincidentally, we were both headed to the same station, so we ended up walking together. The walk was quiet, but not as awkward as I had anticipated. Just being with her, even without exchanging words, was oddly comforting.

This is bad.

When we arrived at the station, she tugged on my shirt. With a side glare, I stopped.

"Hinata?"

"What's your ideal type of girl?"

I met her emotion-filled eyes. "Huh?"

"You heard me."

"I almost feel like I misheard you," I stated.

"Well, you didn't."

"My ideal type, huh?" I repeated, looking up in thought.

"Mhm." She bit her lip.

I raised both sides of my lips with devilish intent. "A girl with big boobs."

She rolled her eyes. "Stop messing around."

Laughing off her irritation, I replied, "I honestly dunno anymore."

"Hmm, anymore?"

Lacing my fingers together, I tugged on the back of my neck before sighing with my whole body. "I don't have the patience to chase people or get involved in drama. And I don't like strings attached. If a girl wants to sleep with me, she should just come out and say so."

Hinata stopped and pondered what I said for a moment before opening her mouth again with a questioning glance. "But what if they want more than just sex?"

Peering down at my sneakers, I took a hindered breath. "I don't seek out those types of relationships. Hence the whole 'no strings attached' rule. Those types of relationships are too much work."

"I see," she said. Her questioning subdued for a moment.

It didn't take long for her to come up with something else to ask, though. As I was about to walk away, heading further into the station, she held out her smartphone.

"Can we exchange contact information?"

Uncertain of what relationship she hoped to create between us, I hesitated. "I'm not great at responding."

"That's fine."

With a smirk, I pulled out my phone. "D'you use LINE?"

"Yes!" She seemed more upbeat than before, and it caused my stomach to flutter.

"Pull up your code so I can scan it," I said, opening the LINE application on my phone.

Tapping her screen a few times, she brought up her code and held it out to show me. With my phone, I hovered over hers and scanned the code and immediately saw her contact ID appear on my screen.

"There."

"Thank you," she said, staring down at my name on her phone.

"Sure."

Her eyes flicked up. "Are you coming to school tomorrow?"

"Can't. I have a morning shift."

"I see," she said, with a hint of disappointment. "I'll pass by again tomorrow to drop off the stuff you miss."

"You don't gotta do that. Makoto—"

"What's the difference between me or Fujimoto doing it?"

Caught by her quick wit, I smiled. "Absolutely none."

She nodded once. "Then, I'll see you tomorrow."

"I might not be home when you swing by," I said, with a smug grin.

"That's why I acquired your contact information," she said matter-of-factly, waving her phone in my face.

Busting a gut, I tapped my rail pass on the scanner and made it through the turnstiles, then walked backwards toward my designated subway platform to wait for my train.

"Sneaky," I said, before turning around. Waving goodbye, I pressed forward. "Later."

"See you tomorrow, Riku."

Listening to her reply in the distance, I shook my head in disbelief. *I was right; she's a strange one. And I'm so fucked.*

Chapter Ten

THE FOLLOWING DAY, I opened at the convenience store. Having had a late closing shift at the restaurant the night before, and after sleeping less than four hours, to say I was exhausted was an understatement. Hoping to squeeze in a nap before another shift at the restaurant, I headed home to try and sleep for a few hours. These back-to-back shifts were killing me.

Dragging my feet up the three flights of exterior stairs of the complex, I entered my apartment and kicked off my sneakers, dropped my backpack, and practically crawled to my bed, daydreaming about how soft the pillow would feel.

I woke up about two hours later with the urge to take a piss. My phone read: 4:36 p.m. With less than two hours before my next shift, I finished my business in the bathroom and returned to bed. My phone, of course, vibrated just as I was aiming to fall back asleep. Rolling my eyes in their sockets, I debated whether to check who had sent me a message.

Caving to curiosity, I looked at my screen and was glad I made the right decision.

[LINE Hinata Tachibana]: Hello, Riku Nakajima, this is Hinata Tachibana. Are you home?

Remembering that yesterday she had said

she would message me before coming, I smiled at how overly formal her message was.

[LINE Riku Nakajima]: Hey, Hinata. Yeah, I am.

Not even a second later, there was a knock.

No fuckin' way.

Sluggishly getting out of bed, I headed to the entrance. Opening the door, a ray of unwelcomed sunshine beamed down on me and illuminated my dark, windowless hallway. Like a henchman from the underworld, I felt attacked by the light.

"Ah, what the hell," I said with irritation, as I covered my face from the sun. In between hiding from the sunlight and adjusting my eyes to the brightness, I saw Hinata standing on my doorstep, holding another bag.

"Good day, Riku," she said, with a slight bow of the head. "Sorry, did I wake you?"

Finally adjusting, I shook my head. "It's fine." Leaning against the door frame, I crossed my arms. "Diligent, aren't we?"

She saluted sloppily like a sardonic soldier. "I messaged you before knocking."

"You did indeed," I nodded condescendingly, acknowledging this new, and fairly amusing, side to her. "But you're supposed to message the person *before* you even leave your place, or else you could potentially be wasting your time if they aren't home."

She shrugged. "I'll make a mental note for next time," she said, tapping the side of her head.

I couldn't help but cackle.

"Are you going to invite me in? I *did* come all this way."

The smile I cracked turned playful. "I'm not in a towel today."

She looked to my waist, staring longer than expected, then flicked her eyes back up to mine. "Is that the only time I'm permitted to enter?"

"Depends."

"On?"

"What your intentions are once you're invited inside," I stated, intrigued to hear her response.

"I don't have an answer," she said openly, reverting to her usual direct-ness.

Tucking my chin in, I glared at her for a drawn-out moment. "Annnd why's that?"

"Because I've developed a strong urge to spend time with you," she admitted on the spot, peering into my eyes—my soul. "But since I've met you, you've barely been at school; it's hard to gain access to you. Moreover, I don't know what I want to do once I'm inside." She stopped, appearing to be lost in thought. "I keep replaying all our encounters in my head. Our conversations, embraces, kisses," she said, shifting her eyes down to my lips, then snapping them back up, "and the only obvious conclusion is the simple fact that I just want to be around you."

I sucked in hard and folded my lips. Her words clouded my judgement. She was wreaking havoc on my heart, throwing fuel onto the impure desires sprouting inside my head—inside my pants. I wanted to take her to my bed, to undress her, to see the body she hid under her clothes. Ever since the rooftop, I couldn't get the way her body felt out of my head. Her well-de-fined waist in my hands, her legs wrapped around me, the quickening of her breath each time we kissed—all of it had been ingrained in my memory.

I wanted more. I *needed* more.

Impulsively, I grabbed her hand and pulled her into the darkness of my apartment. Shutting the door, I pinned her up against it as she dropped both her schoolbag and my daily delivery on the floor. Still holding her hand in mine, I rested the forearm of my other arm on the space just above her head as she met my downward gaze.

"You're full of surprises, aren't you?" I asked, rhetorically.

She raised a brow. "What makes the things I do surprising?"

"The fact that no one, but you, would do or say the things that you do."

She placed her free hand on my chest. "Is that so?"

"Yes," I said, watching, feeling her every move.

"Is that bad?"

Bringing my face closer to hers, I moved her hair to the other side of her neck, then whispered into her ear. "Are you testing me?"

"I'm not a teacher. If anything, I'm the student," she answered, cleverly.

I felt her eyes trail down my body and back up again. "Will you be my teacher, Riku?"

She was unlike any other girl I had ever met. She was unfiltered but proper, respectful but dangerous; everything about her was extraordinarily exhilarating. I could feel my willpower waning.

Even though Hinata was a straight-A student, she didn't dress like the ones I knew. Like many others, including myself, she wore her uniform casually, which was technically against the school rules. Seeing as she hadn't done up the top two buttons of her uniform shirt, I could easily peek down her collar. She showed the slightest bit of skin tastefully.

Examining her long, slender neck, her prominent collarbone enticed me. I released her hand and tucked a small portion of hair that had fallen back into place behind her ear. With the tips of my fingers, I slowly traced the back of her ear until I made it down to her neck.

I grazed her neck until I reached the top of her bra strap. "I could be."

"I wonder how many girls have received these same, cheesy lines." I could hear the playfulness in her tone.

With a hidden smile, I snorted into the crook of her neck. "Just one; you can call me *Sensei* if you like."

"Hmm," she hummed, opening herself to my touch.

Still using my thumb, I went underneath the bra strap, guiding it down her shoulder until the strap vanished within her sleeve. I searched her piercing eyes for permission to keep going; they were narrowed and focused, but still appeared inviting. Her eyes were constantly shifting, almost like they were influenced by lust, and she was speaking through them.

How far would she allow me to take this?

Believing Hinata would stop me if she didn't like what I was doing, I began unbuttoning her shirt with one hand, pausing when I reached the portion tucked into her plaid skirt. With her chest fully exposed, I took a moment to appreciate the laced bra supporting her marvelous breasts.

Bringing my eyes to meet hers, she stared at me with the content expression she often wore. She didn't seem to hate what I was doing, but I couldn't tell if she was enjoying my advances, either. It was hard to read her, and that made it both nerve-racking and thrilling.

Hinata didn't react negatively to me undressing her, so I pressed on. I brought my index and middle finger to the edge of her neckline and slid both fingers down her chest. Carefully watching my fingers, I stopped at the start of her cleavage, just above her bra, then looked up at her once more. Again, her reaction lacked excitement.

Determined to get a heated reaction out of her, I brought my lips to the top of her left breast and placed a kiss above her bra line. As I released her skin from the suction of my lips, I felt her body tense. Before I had the chance to look up at her, she ran her fingers through my hair, swooping the longer parts of my bangs to the side until they eventually fell back into place. Glancing up, she looked at me with ravening eyes as she continued to play with my hair, twirling pieces in between her fingers.

There we go.

"D'you realize what you're doing?" I asked, ready to take her against the wall after watching her return my advances.

"Not exactly," she said, biting her bottom lip.

"Figured as much," I said, standing tall. Grabbing hold of the hand that ruffled my hair, I brought it up to my lips. "I'm at my limit."

With those words, I attacked her lips.

Asking for trouble, she slipped her tongue into my mouth; she was no stranger to this tactic. Wanting more of her, I placed my hands on her slim waist and lifted her up into my arms. She hooked her legs around me—a familiar scene. I peeled her off the door and maneuvered us down the hallway to my bed where the apartment grew brighter from the evening sun seeping in from the curtained back door and window.

Laying her down, I gently settled my weight on top of her. With my arms on either side of her head and my legs straddling her hips, I found myself tracing the curvature of her chest with my eyes. Leaning back, I placed all my weight onto my knees and grabbed the neckline of my shirt. Ripping it off as fast as possible, I tossed the shirt onto the floor. Going back on top of her, I gazed down at her and finally saw her face flush pink.

I bit back a grin.

"Are you sure you wanna go through with this? I dunno if I can stop once we start."

Calm and collected, she returned my gaze. "If we continue, will you tell me about the markings on your back?"

Her words silenced me. Pushing off the bed with my hands, I rose back onto my knees. "What . . .?"

She held herself up on her elbows. "If we have sex, I want you to tell me about the markings on your back."

Absolutely baffled, I got off her and sat at the edge of the bed with my feet planted flat on the floor. *Is this why she drilled me with questions yesterday?*

I turned to her. "D'you understand what you're saying right now?"

She sat up. "I do."

"You don't," I assured.

"But I do," she reassured.

I was captivated by her nonsense and shaken by how casually she had rattled my emotions. She was willing to trade sex for answers, and that was a problem. It was easy to see that she wanted to learn more about me, she wasn't subtle about it, but it was terrifying to be open and vulnerable. Why was it so hard to give a piece of yourself, even a small one, to someone else?

I stood. "What is this to you? Why d'you wanna know so much about me?"

"*This* is us spending time together," she stated, peering up at me from the bed. "There's something inside me that is dying to get to know you. I'm drawn to you in a way that I've never been drawn to anyone else before. Your presence offers me a sense of comfort, of understanding that I've never felt, until now. That's why I want to pursue this. I want to chase this feeling until I can't run anymore."

She was indeed incredible, but in what way? She had me confused. I couldn't figure out what her fascination with me was, specifically. What she said resonated with me; I also felt a strange sense of comfort whenever she was around. But how could she gain all that from me when I hadn't done anything to warrant it?

"Pursue what? What is there to 'pursue'? We dunno anything about each other."

"Then, let's get to know each other."

Taking a seat back on the bed, I took her hand without thinking; a first for me. "Hinata, like I've said before, I can't give you what you're looking for. I dunno how to be anything more than friends with benefits."

Interlocking our fingers, she held my hand tight. "Just because you get to know someone, doesn't mean you have an obligation to them."

She made a good point. Harming her emotionally shouldn't be something to concern myself with, she said so herself. Hinata hadn't asked for any sort of commitment from me, so why was I so scared to hurt her? She was intertwining herself in my life, and although I should hate it and put an end to it, I somehow welcomed it.

I decided to ride this out, whatever *this* was, to see how far things would go. Physical things. Because I didn't give more. I wasn't sure how.

But then, I surprised myself. I gave her what she wanted for free.

Just this one, small piece.

I let go of her hand and turned to expose my back. "They're scars."

"Scars?"

"Yeah. They're cigarette burns."

Almost immediately, I felt her warm hand caress my bare skin. The tips of her fingers were connecting the dots on my back ever so gently. "Who gave these to you?"

Hesitating, I sighed again. "My mom."

"Your mother did this?" Peering over my shoulder, I studied her face. I could see her working through her emotions. "Why?"

Looking up at the ceiling, I closed my eyes. "Anytime she caught me stealing from her, she would light a cigarette, press it into my back, and hold it there for a few seconds. It was how she 'taught me a lesson.' She would—"

Before I could finish my sentence, Hinata wrapped her arms around me. "Thank you for sharing that with me."

Opening my eyes, I looked down at her arms enveloped around my chest. Taking my hand, I placed it over top of hers. "Sure."

"Do you have work today, as well?" she asked, abruptly changing the subject.

Recalling my restaurant shift that was about to start, I suddenly lacked motivation to go. Finding comfort in her presence, I lied. "No."

"Would it be all right if I stayed longer?"

"Yeah."

Chapter Eleven

TIME ESCAPED US; close to two hours had passed. I never called the restaurant to inform them I wouldn't be coming in, so I wasn't sure if I still had a job, but I really didn't care.

We spent the whole time squished together on my tiny, single bed, without partaking in anything sexual—a first for me. Our heads shared one pillow as we exchanged stories about when we were young, one after the other.

"Makoto's mom is hella strict," I stated, sharing yet another story about my time spent with Makoto. Most of my better memories involved him and his family. "Back in junior high, whenever I'd go over after school, she'd put a hold on any goofing off until our homework was completed. When we claimed to be done, she'd make us show it to her before we could go off and play video games or go outside to kick the ball around with some friends. After checking it over, if there were any mistakes, she'd send us away to fix them."

I snorted out in laughter as I looked back on a specific memory.

"One time, I was so behind on my homework that Mrs. Fujimoto forced me to sit at the table in the living room until I was all caught up. I had been at it for hours; my brain was fried. Makoto sat with me and tried to tutor me, but he eventually fell asleep out of boredom." I

smiled to myself. "Mrs. Fujimoto came into the living room, saw Makoto sleeping, then shook her head. She left to grab a blanket to cover him, then took a seat beside me. As if it was the most natural thing to do, she jumped right in and began helping me with my homework. I was extremely bad at math, and Mrs. Fujimoto didn't go easy on me, but she had the patience to go over everything with me, as many times as it took, until I got it. It's thanks to her, and Makoto, that I was able to maintain my grades in school."

My apartment was dimly lit from the setting sun peeking its way in, allowing me to see Hinata's face clearly. She turned to me, then smiled tenderly. "She sounds lovely, Riku. You're lucky to have someone like her looking out for you."

She was right, I was undeniably lucky. "Yeah."

The smile on Hinata's face weakened. "And being strict doesn't always mean someone is doing it with malintent. Sometimes, it's the only way a person knows how to show they care. My mother operated much in the same way when it came to schooling, before she got sick."

Since I already knew Hinata was adopted, she went into greater detail about her childhood and upbringing. She vividly remembered her birth-parents, as she was eight when she was forced to leave her home. Before she was adopted by the Tachibanas, her family name was Komatsu. When she discussed the period in which she went about changing her family name, Hinata seemed a bit sad, as if she only changed it to please others. But I didn't find that to be completely true. I had a gut feeling she did it so that she could feel like she belonged. I almost changed my surname to Fujimoto for the same reason.

Hinata inherited her unusual hair colour and eyes from her mother, something she seemed happy about. When Hinata was young, her mother developed a terrible illness, one the doctors couldn't figure out, much less find a cure for, causing her to remain hospitalized until she eventually died. Her father, not strong enough to cope with the loss of his beloved wife, took his own life.

"Did you see him do it? Did you watch him die?" I asked without restraint. I was so invested in the story of her dark past that my possibly insensitive, unfiltered questions didn't register with my brain before they flew out of my mouth. "Sorry, I didn't—"

"It's fine," she said, touching my arm for reassurance. "I don't mind talking about it, especially not with you."

With . . . me?

She gave me another weak smile. "But to answer your questions, no, I didn't."

Hinata explained that she had found her father's lifeless body in his bedroom the following morning. I tucked her in even closer to me as she expanded on how her father had left her a handwritten letter about how much he loved her, but also about how weak and sorry he was.

In the span of two weeks, Hinata lost both her parents, was made to leave her home, change schools, and move in with people who were *like* family but *weren't* family.

Like me, Hinata didn't have any grandparents. Her adoptive parents were good friends of her birthparents; people she grew up with and trusted. The Tachibanas had always wanted children though had not conceived their own, and so welcomed Hinata into their home with open arms.

Hinata went on to talk further about the Tachibanas, especially her younger twin brothers, Kazumi and Izumi, who her adoptive parents miraculously conceived later on. She spoke fondly of her brothers, which gave me the impression that she truly loved them. Her brothers were still young; therefore, they had no idea that Hinata wasn't related to them by blood. She mentioned how she would often pick them up from school while her parents were at work. She didn't speak much about her adoptive parents except to say that Mr. Tachibana was a bigwig businessman who was often transferred to where he was needed most. As a result, Hinata had lived in six different cities and towns, having lost track of the number of houses altogether.

"Do you have any siblings?"

Having thought about the same question often, I continued to stare at the ceiling. "None that I'm aware of."

"I see . . . Do you know where your mother is now?"

I took a burdened breath. "Yeah, she's still in the ward of Shinjuku."

"Do you want to talk about it?" Hinata asked, hesitantly.

"Even if I talk about it, it won't change anything. In the end, she's still a shitty mom."

"Have you ever gone to visit her?" she asked, anyway.

Wondering how she was able to ask questions so rapidly without hesitation, I found myself slowing down. "I know where she frequents, but I haven't gone and approached her outta freewill."

"Why?"

"'Cause," I said, taking another deep breath before shutting my eyes. "I just go back every once in a while, to see for myself that she's still alive."

She paused for the briefest of moments, then fired another one. "What about your father?"

My eyes sprang open in anger and shifted into a hostile glare at the empty space before me. Refusing to look at her, I replied with irritation, "What about him?"

Out of the corner of my eye, I saw her head turn toward me. "Where is he?"

"How the fuck should I know?" I said, unintentionally raising my voice.

"I'm sorry," she said, dejected.

Flashing my eyes her way, I could see her body shying away from me. Taking my arm, I placed it behind my head to elevate it.

"No," I said, scratching a non-existent itch on my head, "don't be sorry. It's just . . . I dunno who my old man is."

I leaned my cheek on my bicep to look at her, hoping she could see the apologetic look on my face. In the beginning, I wouldn't have cared if she pegged me to be the asshole I was. Especially after the whole thing with Sakura, my assholeness had only increased. But things felt different now, and I couldn't explain why. They just were. I didn't want her current image of me to be painted with colours from the guy she initially met.

Hinata returned to her relaxed position beside me, but then looked at me with guilty eyes. "Sorry, I didn't know."

"It's not your fault. We've been talking about parents for a while now. It was only a matter of time before you asked about him."

"Do you have any shared memories or stories of him?"

"No. My mom refused to tell me anything about him."

"Not even his name?"

"Nah. But to be honest, I don't even think she knows what piece of shit knocked her up. Unlike your brothers, I was definitely a mistake."

"Does that mean your surname, 'Nakajima,' is your mother's maiden name?"

"I guess? I know nothing about my family. So, I can only assume she kept her family name."

Hesitating, she eventually asked, "Have you ever considered meeting your father?"

"No."

"No?"

"Yeah, you heard me. No."

"What if—"

"Why would I wanna meet a man who resorted to sleeping with the kinda woman my mom is? He's either involved in drugs or had his hands in something dirty. He's probably a man who was, or is, cheating on his wife with a bunch of easy women, like my mom."

"Riku . . .."

"It would be better for me if he's dead. This way, I don't have to be tied down to anything or anyone else."

"But Riku, your mother is alive."

"If she continues living the fucked-up life she claims to enjoy, she'll wind up dead sooner or later."

The atmosphere grew heavy. Even though those words were mine, and I meant every one of them, I felt like a hypocrite. I felt no better than the sleazy woman I was describing and had spent years hating. I was every bit as pathetic as my mother was. The apple never falls far from the tree.

I was even more of a piece of shit than I gave myself credit for, though. I knew Hinata's birthmother died unexpectedly from an illness, but I blurted out something so insensitive around her, anyway. No matter how much I despised my mother, Hinata still loved hers.

As I mulled over my words, she placed a hand on my bare skin. I watched as her slender fingers danced across my chest, feathering up and down my abs before stopping to rest on my heart. Goosebumps sprouted on my skin from where she touched.

"I don't think you were a mistake."

My eyes caught her gaze. "Sorry to say, but I most certainly was. It was made clear to me many times by my mom."

"Let me rephrase that. I *know* you weren't a mistake; because if you were, then us meeting would also be considered a mistake, and I don't believe that to be true."

"Hinata . . .."

Just as her name escaped my lips, Hinata replaced her hand with her head and rested it on my chest. She was quiet for a moment, which caused my heart rate to increase, but then, she glimpsed up at me.

"Riku, as long as you have a heartbeat, you have the right to live."

My nose flared, my throat closed, and my chest stiffened. All things I'm sure she could sense as she rested on top of me. Taking my free arm, I wrapped it around her shoulder, then took the arm behind my head and used it to hide my face, not wanting to willingly expose my vulnerability. She said the most bizarre things, but she always managed to hit me where it hurt.

Hinata lifted off my chest and forced her way through my lousy barricade by pushing my arm away. Our eyes met, and although I had been crying silent tears, she never addressed it. Instead, she brought her lips down to meet mine.

We exchanged a few kisses as she threaded her fingers through my hair, but we soon stopped when she got distracted by a specific area just above my left ear. She ran a finger over the area multiple times in discovery. Stumped, she decided to investigate by parting the hair in that section.

"It's a scar," I explained, answering her unasked question.

"What's this one from?"

"Another from my mom."

I could see sympathy floating in her eyes as she passed over my scar again. "What happened?"

"She threw a plate at me, and it shattered into a million pieces. One of the sharp edges gashed the side of my head open. She got me real good that time."

"Did you need stitches?"

"Probably, but she didn't take me to get them."

Hinata fell silent. It was as if she was taking a moment to live out the scenario that I described to her in her head. She smiled weakly. "Riku, you must be tired. I can tell by the dark circles under your eyes. I noticed them yesterday, too. You should get some rest."

"Rest?" I asked, thrown off by the way she shifted the conversation.

"Yeah," she said, just before removing her hand from my head.

With mixed feelings, I grabbed the hand she used to tousle my hair. "Where are you going?" I asked, almost desperately, lifting myself up.

Still smiling, she gently pushed me back down. "Nowhere. I'll be here when you wake up. Promise."

Nestling back into my arms, she made herself comfortable as she placed her head on my chest once more. I was terrified by the feelings that swept over me when I thought she was going to leave. Wired by her presence, and too scared to fall into a deep sleep, I kept waking to check if she was still lying next to me. As promised, she remained in my arms until I could no longer keep my eyes open.

The aroma of empty alcohol bottles was sickening; they were littered throughout our tiny apartment. Garbage was piled up near the doorway and lined the hallway leading into the kitchen.

"Mommy, what are we having for dinner?" I asked, staring into an empty refrigerator.

Sitting at our small table in the living area, smoking a cigarette and drinking a beer, my mother rolled her neck and dropped her head to glare at me. "Dinner?" she questioned, anger emerging in her tone.

"Um . . . ye-yeah, d-dinner," I said, unable to stop my voice from quivering. "I'm hungry, Mommy."

"Does it look like we got anythin' to eat, 'ya stupid brat?"

"Um . . . ."

She stubbed out her cigarette in one of the emptier ashtrays sitting in the middle of the table, then stood. Stumbling over to me, she came into the kitchen and grabbed the back of my neck, digging her nails into my skin. Shoving my face into the opened refrigerator, she asked, "Does it look like we got anythin' to eat? DOES IT?"

Terrified, tears formed in my eyes. "Mommy, stop!"

"You're hungry?" she shouted, still holding my neck. "Then, go get a job so you can buy your own fuckin' food! I can't afford to always feed you. God, you're so damn needy!"

"Mommy, please!"

Annoyed, she tossed me aside. Tripping over a few garbage bags, I hit the floor. Trying to hide my tears, in fear that seeing them would only upset her further, I lowered my head.

"What, d'ya think you're better than me? Huh, brat?"

"No," I sniffled, "I never said that."

"DON'T YOU DARE TALK BACK TO ME, 'YA FUCKIN' BRAT! I'M THE ADULT HERE!"

Wanting to get my apology across properly, I looked up. Making eye contact, my mother's eyes were wider than ever and filled with a rage I knew all too well. "I'M SORRY! Please, Mommy, forgive me! I didn't mean—"

"SHUT UP!" she screeched. Grabbing a plate off the counter, she threw it at me as hard as she could. Missing, the plate hit the cupboard, inches from my head, before I felt its impact.

"AHH!" I cried. Before the pain sank in, shock took over. Peering down at my lap, I noticed shards of the shattered plate had scattered across me and the entire floor. Finding one piece that was tainted red, my vision tunneled as I reached for a spot on my head that had begun to pulsate. Bringing my hand down to eye level, my hand was covered in blood. Looking at my shirt, I saw it saturated with blood. "AHH! I'M BLEEDING! MOMMY, I'M BLEEDING!"

As I panicked and screamed for help, my mother stared blankly at me; her eyes were cold and lifeless. After a few moments, she went to the bathroom and grabbed a towel.

"Here," she said, tossing the towel at my feet. "Clean yourself up before you stain the whole damn kitchen red."

Reaching for the towel, I looked up at her one last time, begging for help, right before she grabbed her purse and walked out of the apartment.

Chapter Twelve

W HEN I AWOKE from my nap, Hinata was no longer by my side.

In a panic, I sat up and frantically scanned my apartment. What was usually a gloomy, practically empty space, was unusually bright from the light of the replacement lamp Makoto bought me.

Looking down, I found her sitting on the floor. To my surprise, Hinata hadn't left. Instead, she was fully clothed in her uniform and sat on a cushion at my table, quietly doing homework.

She's here. She's still here.

Hinata spun around. "Riku, what's wrong?" she asked, concern sweeping her face.

Realizing she had kept her promise by staying by my side, my crazy heart rate regulated. It was somehow reassuring to have her with me.

Wiping the sweat from my collarbone, I smiled wholesomely. "Nothing. Nothing at all."

Her eyes softened. "How do you feel?"

"Rested."

"That's good."

"Yeah," I said, as I rose from my bed. "Doing homework?"

"Mhm, to pass the time."

"Speaking of time, what time is it?"

"It's just after 8:00 p.m."

"8:00 p.m.?" I repeated with wide eyes. "Don't you gotta get home? Won't your parents worry?"

"It's fine, I've already notified them."

"I see," I said, as I bent to grab my shirt off the floor. Putting it on, I reached for the pack of cigarettes and lighter on the table beside my bed, then went to the kitchen to grab a can of cold coffee. "Want one?"

Hinata turned to me. "No, thank you."

"Suit yourself." Closing the refrigerator, I walked to the sliding back door, then stopped to look over my shoulder. "I'm gonna go out for a smoke."

She got to her feet. "I'll join you."

"As you wish." *Why am I being so short with her? What the fuck is my problem?*

Outside on the tiny balcony, I leaned against the railing, as I often did, cracked open the canned coffee to take a sip, then pulled out a cigarette and placed it in between my lips. Setting the coffee down near an ashtray on a small table, I brought the lighter closer to my mouth. As I cupped the cigarette to light it, I could sense Hinata's eyes on me.

"What is it?" I asked, turning to her as I exhaled smoke.

"Aren't you going to offer me one?"

"No."

"No? Why's that?"

With a quirked lip, I said, "You shouldn't smoke; it's bad for you."

She leaned back against the railing and propped her elbows up. "Is that so?"

"Yep. A cute girl once told me that."

"Hmm, clever."

"Thank you."

"Not you, just the comment."

Chuckling under my breath, I looked away and took a puff.

"Why do you smoke, then?"

Looking out at the night illumination from streetlights, and the hundreds of apartment buildings and single-family houses in the neighbourhood, I exhaled. "Dunno. Maybe because I have nothing to lose."

"Except your life."

I smiled. "Which isn't worth all that much."

"It is to me," she said, not missing a beat.

Turning to her, she returned my look with sharp eyes. Unable to determine what she meant; I was almost too scared to find out.

Why does she say shit like that? Shit she doesn't mean or know the consequences of.

Pretending this conversation wasn't serious was the only way I could move past the growing ache in my chest. I let a laugh tumble out of me to pass the stress she burdened me with.

"Riku, I'm not—"

"Hinata," I interrupted.

"Yes?"

My eyes returned to the view in front of me, but then shifted to my hands. Watching the pieces at the end of the cigarette burn and fall off, I lost the smoker's itch to finish my cigarette.

"I'll walk you home," I said, ashing the cigarette before grabbing my coffee. "It's late, and I've kept you out long enough."

"It's fine, I've already told my parents I'd be out late."

"It's not fine," I snapped, evading the intensity I felt from the eyes I knew she had glued on me. "Let's go."

Without another word, Hinata followed me back inside where she packed her books and supplies into her schoolbag, then met me at the entrance. As she slipped on her loafers, I opened the door. Still avoiding direct eye contact, I locked the door behind us before making my way down the stairs of the apartment complex. Hinata trailed along in silence.

Reaching the station, Hinata pulled my arm back and broke the prolonged silence.

"I'm fine on my own from here."

"No, I'll take you the whole way."

"You don't have to do that. It's out of your way."

"It's the least I can do for making you bring me the stuff I missed at school. Plus, you wasted your day by staying with me as I slept."

Hinata shook her head. "I did those things because I wanted to."

"I know. And I'm doing this because *I* want to."

With a little smile, Hinata stepped in front of me and tapped her rail pass on the terminal scanner, then walked through the turnstiles and toward the numbered platforms. As we approached our platform, we stood off to the side and waited for the subway. While we waited, she spoke up once more.

"Thank you."

I tilted my head. "For what?"

"Everything."

Narrowing my brows in suspicion, I was held back from asking what she meant because the loud, screeching sound of the subway arriving on its designated line took over.

⁂

We rode the subway for five stops before getting off, and that's when I realized Hinata lived a lot closer to the school than I did.

We took a few of the main streets before entering a residential area. The houses in this area were huge; far bigger than anything I had ever lived in or could imagine living in. They were single detached, mixed between modern Western and Japanese homes with large yards and gated properties. Remembering Hinata's father was a successful businessman, this neighbourhood showed that they were better off than most.

After turning a few corners, we arrived at a house on a corner lot with the nameplate: Tachibana. The house was rectangular in shape with a flat roof and large, top-to-bottom windows that were structured all around.

"We're here."

Staring up at the enormous house, I looked back and forth between her and the mansion before me. "Man, Hinata, I didn't peg you to be *this* rich."

"I'm not. This is a company house; we don't own it."

"Makes sense, since your dad transfers a lot."

"Mhm. It's futile for us to own when we never know how long we'll be in one place for."

"That makes sense. But still, this house is amazing."

"It's bigger than we need. At times, it feels like I'm imprisoned inside a glass box, on display for all to see."

A glass box, huh?

Before I could ask Hinata to explain what she meant, the front door to her house opened and a middle-aged man stepped outside.

"Hinata?" the man called, taking a few more steps. "Is that you?"

Descending the stairs onto the walkway, he approached us at the waist-high entry gate.

"Yes, it's me. I'm home."

He smiled tenderly at Hinata. "Welcome home." Quickly taking note of my presence, his smile diminished as he looked my way. "And who might this be?"

Hinata stuck out a hand in my direction. "Father, this is my classmate, Riku Nakajima."

With an internal laugh, I could feel my lips struggling to sustain a straight face. *Father? Why's she so formal with her dad? I know he's her adoptive dad, but still.*

"Classmate, huh?" Mr. Tachibana said, looking me over.

Composing myself, I took a detailed look at Mr. Tachibana, just as he was doing of me. He fit the perfect description of a typical businessman. He was average height, clean-cut, wore glasses, had short, black hair that was groomed neatly, dull brown eyes, and wore a tie over his white, tucked in dress shirt. I suspected that inside the house he had a suit jacket that completed the outfit.

Feeling the need to show the utmost respect, I bowed. "Nice to meet you, sir."

"Raise your head, Mr. Nakajima," Mr. Tachibana said kindly.

I lifted my head.

"So, you were the one Hinata was studying with at the library," he prompted, staring at me with strong judgement. "Pretty late to be out studying, don't you agree, Mr. Nakajima?"

Though he delivered his question calmly, Mr. Tachibana worded it in a way as if he were testing me, baiting me even.

Library? I see, even the straight-edge Hinata lies to her parents. "I do. I brought forth the same concern to your daughter." Looking at Hinata, I winked at her, purposely tattling on her to see what she would say next.

Giving me the side-eye, Hinata glared at me before responding to her father. "With his grades at the bottom tier, he asked if I could tutor him after school. We got caught up in studying and lost track of time. Once we realized what time it was, Riku offered to escort me home."

I snorted a conspicuous laugh. *'Bottom tier,' huh? She sure knows how to get under someone's skin.*

Hinata was a seasoned liar, packed full of spice and surprising flavour. The lies rolled right off her tongue the moment they formed in her mind. I was both turned on and skeptical by this ability.

"Indeed, I see," Mr. Tachibana said, easing his confrontational eyes. "Well, thank you for looking out for my daughter. I appreciate the gesture, especially this late at night. I'm glad Hinata has kind classmates, such as yourself, and is making friends properly."

Not being scolded felt weird but being thanked by him felt even weirder. Maybe it was because I was introduced as a classmate that Mr. Tachibana didn't feel threatened by me. Besides Makoto's parents, Mr. Tachibana was the first parent to ever thank me.

"Enough," Hinata said, distressed. She seemed mildly embarrassed as her cheeks flushed. "I have friends."

"Yes, of course, Hinata," Mr. Tachibana said, with a reassuring smile.

Suddenly, a burst of energy came flying out of the Tachibana household. "Hina!" shouted a small boy. "Hey, Izumi," he said, looking over his shoulder. "Come quick, Hina's home!"

Just as the boy came barreling out of the house, another identical boy appeared at the doorway.

"Kazumi, wait for me!" yelled the second boy, as he chased after his double.

When both boys reached the gate, they stood beside Mr. Tachibana, bouncing up and down with excitement.

"Shh! Boys, settle down. You need to lower your voices this late at night. We don't want to bother the neighbours," Mr. Tachibana advised. "Wasn't your mother in the middle of putting you two to bed?"

Both boys covered their mouths with their hands. "Sorry, Daddy," they said simultaneously, giggling with muffled voices.

Hinata looked at me, then stuck out a hand toward the two boys. "Riku, these are my twin brothers, Kazumi and Izumi," she said, going from left to right. The boys resembled their father; they all had dark hair and eyes.

Not having ever expected to meet any of Hinata's family members, especially this many in a single night, I began to feel an unpleasant twinge in my chest. Putting on the best smile I could muster, I answered, "Nice to meet you guys."

"Mr. Riku are you Nee-san's boyfriend?" asked Kazumi.

Out of the corner of my eye, I could see that Kazumi's question had caught the attention of Mr. Tachibana.

Not wanting Hinata to respond first, since I had no idea what crazy answer she would give, I replied immediately, "No, I'm not. We're just classmates."

I took a second glance at Mr. Tachibana who instantly relaxed his tense shoulders, a reasonable response for a doting parent. With curiosity, I shifted my gaze to Hinata. Strangely, Hinata wasn't looking back.

"Aww, that sucks. You seem really cool, Mr. Riku," Kazumi said, somewhat disappointed.

"Just Riku is fine. You can drop the 'Mister.'"

"I don't want Nee-san to have a boyfriend," added Izumi, slightly upset. "Then she won't have time to play with us."

"Okay, okay, that's enough, boys," Mr. Tachibana said, taking charge of the awkward conversation. "It's time for bed." He grabbed one hand from each twin. "Come on, let's go back inside. Hinata will be in shortly. Won't you, Hinata?"

"Yes," Hinata answered respectfully.

"Aww! But I wanted to play with Riku," whined Kazumi, sulking as he was dragged inside.

"Maybe another time," Mr. Tachibana said, redirecting a possible tantrum before dipping his head in a respectful bow at me.

As the Tachibanas went back inside, Hinata finally looked at me.

"Sorry about them."

"Nah, it's fine," I said, shaking my head. "It was nice to see how much your family cares about you. Those kids adore you."

"Yeah," Hinata said with an unspeakable distance. "I adore them, too."

Not knowing how I should reply, in fear of revisiting our conversation from earlier, I decided now would be the best time to escape. "Well, I'm gonna get going. It's late and I don't wanna make your family worry more than they already have. Goodnight, Hinata."

Just as I was about to leave, Hinata grabbed my hand, forcing me to turn back around. Our eyes met, but Hinata didn't let go.

"Hinata?"

"Will I see you at school tomorrow?"

This again? When will she give up? "Maybe."

"Maybe isn't good enough."

Taken aback, I felt a ping of irritation. "'Isn't good enough'? Hinata, I'm not your boyfriend. I can do whatever I want."

"I'm aware of that."

"Then, what?" The irritation I felt quickly morphed into anger. "What d'you want from me? What is it that you think I can do for you?"

"I don't know."

Remembering where we were, and that this wasn't the best place to have this type of conversation, I tried everything in my power to calm down.

I shook off Hinata's hand. "Don't make a scene. This ain't the time or place to get into our little back and forth skits."

"That's not what this is."

"Then, what is *this*?" I raised my voice accidentally, knowing full well I needed to keep it lowered. "What're we doing?"

Hinata paused for a second and just stared at me without batting a single eye. Her gaze felt heavy, like her eyes had grown two individual shades darker. "Nothing. We're doing nothing," she answered coldly. "Goodnight, Riku. Thank you for escorting me home."

Her tone was substantially dry. It almost reminded me of our first encounter, the time Makoto introduced us. However, this time, I got the feeling that I was successfully able to shake her, possibly enough to even piss her off. Turning around once more, I half-expected her to grab me again. Taking a few steps away from the Tachibana residence, I was finally free to leave. But not in peace.

"Riku," she called out to me once more.

As she called my name, a jolt zapped through me. Stopping in my tracks, I had a hard time turning around. Staring at my feet, I paused to listen.

"I wasn't lying when I said your life is important to me. Please remember that."

The sound of a metal gate opening and closing echoed down the street. Seconds later, the click of Hinata's shoes tapping against the cement walkway could be heard as she walked up to the house, climbed the steps, and entered through the front door.

With my eyes still glued to my feet, and my feet glued to the ground, I clenched my teeth together and bunched my hands into fists.

WHAT THE FUCK, HINATA? Why d'you go outta your way to make stupid comments like that? I actually don't fuckin' get you, not one fuckin' bit. Is this all some type of twisted game to you?

Even if I were to have asked Hinata all those questions, I already knew they would remain unanswered.

It was hard to tell who knew less about themselves: me or Hinata. If there was one thing I could say about her, it was that she understood her emotions and actions far less than I did. I couldn't lie to myself; she intrigued me, she had from the moment I met her, but the question of *why* remained.

Maybe I'm sexually frustrated?

My cellphone vibrated in my pocket. Opening LINE, I cracked a diluted smile at my screen.

> [LINE Annoying Big Breasted Woman]: Hey, Riku! Sorry
> about last time. I didn't mean to freak out like that. Are you
> free tonight? I'm lonely . . .

Yeah, that must be it. I just need a quick lay.

The perfect distraction was right in front of me. All that was left for me to do was accept it.

> [LINE Riku Nakajima]: I'll be home in 45 mins.

I took out the lighter and pack of cigarettes I brought along, placed one cigarette between my lips, and lit it. Exhaling, I started my prideful walk back to the station.

This is the way shit should be.

Chapter Thirteen

O N MY WALK back from the station, the dusk sky had turned grey, and it began to drizzle. The exterior stairway of the apartment complex was well lit as I made my way up to the top floor. As I climbed the final step, the sky shifted into a heavy downpour. With the sound of the rain drowning out my surroundings, I turned the corner and the woman, whose name I couldn't remember to save my life, was waiting outside my door. Making eye contact, she smiled at me seductively.

"You're early," I said, approaching the door. "Didn't I say forty-five minutes?"

"Aww, come on, Riku," she whined annoyingly. "Don't be like that." Latching on to my arm, she pressed her giant breasts against me. "The least you could do is be more excited to see me."

"Whatever," I said, ignoring her gesture while pulling out the key to the door.

"Hmph," she grunted.

"What?"

"So, you *do* lock your door."

"Only when I leave."

"But not when you sleep?"

"Not usually."

"That doesn't make any sense."

Unlocking the door, I rolled my eyes. "Doesn't have to."

With the door wide open, we took a step inside. Unlike Hinata, this woman kicked off her heels haphazardly and left them where they landed. With fervour, she unbuttoned her blouse.

"Where did you want to do this?" she asked, turning around to face me so I could watch her slowly slip the blouse off her shoulders. With her bra exposed, she tilted her chin down and peeked up at me with lustful eyes. "The bed? The shower? Right here at the entrance?"

Without a word, I moved toward her. Unlike Hinata, this woman had extremely short hair, making it near to impossible to tuck any of it behind her ear. I slipped my fingers through the tips of her hair until I reached the back of her head, bringing her face closer to mine. Without hesitation, I kissed the lips of the nameless woman who sought me at her convenience. As we kissed, my chest pounded violently, creating an immense sensation of what could only be described as pain.

What the fuck is this feeling? It's so intense that it's practically crushing my lungs.

Kiss after kiss, the woman took charge and hurriedly led us to my bed without breaking the contact of our lips. She undid the button of my jeans before we stumbled upon the bed, then laid on her back and grabbed my neck to lower me down on her.

Pulling away from her lips, I sat up on my knees and took off my shirt. Tossing it aside, I gazed at the big breasted woman before me. Without wanting to, my head became filled with thoughts about Hinata. I recalled the way Hinata looked up at me from the exact same position, just hours ago. The way Hinata's face flushed pink felt like something only I had ever witnessed. Getting the straight-A Hinata to show some sort of emotion was a thrilling challenge that I had accomplished.

Why was I still hung up on a girl that I didn't even sleep with?

"Um, hello . . . Riku?"

Blinking a few times, I could have sworn Hinata's face flashed before me. Instead, all I really saw was a confused, half-naked woman beneath me.

"What the heck is going on?"

"Uh . . .," was all I managed to muster.

"Riku, do you want to have sex or not?" she asked, partially lifting herself up. She looked down at the non-existent bulge in my pants.

This isn't the first time I've slept with this dumb-ass woman, so what the fuck is wrong with me? Everything is the same; familiar—she hasn't changed. There's nothing physically stopping me from sleeping with her. She's already in my bed for fuck's sake! So, why can't I get it up?

"No," I answered unconsciously. "I don't."

"No? What do you mean 'no'?" Dramatically throwing her head back into the pillow, she sighed. "What the fuck do you want, Riku?"

Removing myself from what was once a casual hobby, I sat at the edge of my bed, thinking long and hard while staring into space.

There was a strong disconnect between my head and my heart, and especially my dick. The lust I harboured for the quick lay vanished instantaneously. All I could think about was Hinata. The way Hinata's breasts looked in her laced bra, the way her waist easily fit into my hands as I lifted her into my arms, and the smoothness of her skin against mine—they were all so distinct. But it wasn't just that, it was the way Hinata stayed. We hadn't even slept together, and she still chose to remain by my side, waiting. Just waiting.

That's what I truly wanted.

My thoughts rendered me speechless.

The bed rocked back and forth. Without turning my face, I lifted my eyes up at her as I watched the woman get out of my bed and stand before me.

"What's my name?"

Jerking my head back, I stared up at her in confusion. "What?"

"Do you know what my name is, Riku?"

Thrown off by her timing, I continued my stare. "Why bother asking something so trivial? Now of all times?"

Snorting out air, she shook her head. "'Trivial,' huh? Riku, are you afraid that I'll want to start some sort of serious relationship with you? You know this is just sex, right?"

Stretching my hands out behind me, I leaned back on the bed, then clicked my tongue. "Don't flatter yourself. This has never been anything more than casual sex, so learning your name is of no importance," I informed, with a mouth full of distaste.

"I see," she scorned. "Well, as long as we're on the same page, then.

Because realistically, I'm married, and you're just a high school kid I fuck around with."

She was no better than my mother—than me. But the difference between us was that now I wanted to be better. I just didn't know why. But I knew who I wanted to be better for.

"The feeling's mutual," I answered, peering up at her with a disgusted smirk.

Walking back to the entrance, she picked her blouse up off the floor and put it back on. Stepping down from the raised entryway, she hunted for her heels. Slipping them on, she cocked her head over her shoulder. "Call me once you've figured your shit out. I don't need to be disappointed with all the men who touch me."

With those final words, she stormed out.

While most would have considered this hookup a failure, I felt an odd sense of liberation.

Standing, I zipped up my jeans, grabbed my shirt off the bed, then walked to the sliding back door to have a cigarette.

Outside, the heavy rain had subsided, but water droplets were dripping from the overhang of the roof above. At the edge of the balcony, I pulled out the pack of cigarettes before hanging my arms over the wet railing. With a cigarette in between my lips, ready to light, Hinata's words circled me once more: *'I wasn't lying when I said your life is important to me. Please remember that.'*

Unable to light something I'd had no problem igniting countless times before, I took the cigarette out of my mouth and slid it back into its pack. Recalling her words only heightened my loneliness, a loneliness that could no longer be fulfilled with mere one-night stands and cigarettes.

Dammit, Hinata. God-fuckin'-dammit.

Chapter Fourteen

WITH LESS THAN an ounce of energy, I rubbed the lack of sleep from my eyes. My brain was overworked from the sleepless night; it had been racing with thoughts of Hinata. This girl shouldn't have had such an influence over me. But she did.

Pulling my phone out from underneath the pillow, I unplugged it from its charger. The time on the screen read: 5:03 a.m.

With an unexpected early start to my day, I rose from bed with displeasure to take a cold shower before work. Trying to wash the all-nighter from my face, Hinata's question about school popped into my head: *'Will I see you at school tomorrow?'*

Getting out of the shower, I left the bathroom in search of clean clothes. As I put on sweatpants, my phone vibrated on my bed. Walking over to it, Makoto's name appeared on the screen. Opening LINE, I read the message.

[LINE Makoto Fujimoto]: Hey man, I know you probably have work today, but is there any chance you can play hooky? I really need to talk to you . . . but it has to be in person.

Halfway through Makoto's message, I had unknowingly held my breath. By the end of it, my chest tightened, and my throat became dry when I read: *'[. . .] but it has to be in person.'*

Releasing the pent-up air, I slowly sat on my bed, vacantly staring at my phone.

No way. He couldn't possibly know . . . Could he?

Scared to reply, I eventually mustered the courage to formulate a mediocre response.

[LINE Riku Nakajima]: I'll see what I can do.

Guess it's your lucky day, Hinata.

Turned out that what I *could* do was quit the restaurant; having two part-time jobs was becoming difficult to manage in my current state. But I needed at least one for income. So, before heading to school, I stopped by the restaurant and left a handwritten note on my manager's desk. The restaurant didn't open until 11:00 a.m., therefore, I'd have to come back another day to hand in my key.

I travelled from one job to the next. At the convenience store, I confessed my age to the manager, who miraculously forgave me for lying after lecturing me about the importance of education and obeying school rules. Though I upheld the lie about my school allowing part-time jobs, I got to keep my job on the condition of reduced hours. Money was going to suck for a while.

It was just after 7:30 a.m. when I reached the station, and if I hurried, there was a good chance I would catch homeroom. Wanting to make sure things went as planned, I reached out to Makoto as I waited on the platform for the subway to arrive.

[LINE Riku Nakajima]: Yo, I got the day off. I'm headed to school now, but I'm gonna be late.

Within a matter of seconds, I received a reply.

[LINE Makoto Fujimoto]: It's fine. We'll talk at lunch.

After receiving his confirmation, I went to the nearest washroom at the station to quickly change into the school uniform I had in my schoolbag.

⁂

Arriving at school, I checked the time once more as I walked to the shoe lockers. It read: 8:38 a.m. As I exchanged my shoes, I laughed quietly to myself.

I think this is my best time yet. Without Makoto's help, that is.

Climbing to the fourth floor, I walked down the hall until I reached the classroom. Entering through the front door, I immediately locked eyes with Kobayashi-sensei as he was finishing up attendance.

"Mr. Nakajima, you *almost* made it on time," Kobayashi-sensei said, twitching famously. It was a pattern of behaviour that he had adopted, probably because of me.

"Almost," I said, shrugging my shoulders. "Maybe next time?"

As the class laughed at our exchange, I walked past Kobayashi-sensei to take my seat. Before sitting, I inadvertently glanced at the back of the room to my old seat where Hinata was already looking my way. I could have been mistaken, but I was pretty certain Hinata flashed me a smile.

Fuck . . . Why did my eyes automatically search for her?

While the class representative relayed all messages for the day, I took note of Sakura sitting at her desk. Catching her gaze, she glanced away as soon as we made eye contact. It was different from the usual side-eye she had defaulted to giving me lately. We never spoke after that disastrous encounter, and after the way things went down, this silence between us was for the best.

⁂

When it came time to head to the science lab, Hinata caught up to me in the hallway.

"I see you decided to come to school after all?" she said, less pompous than usual.

I felt overwhelmed by her presence, especially after thoughts of her had kept me from the easy lay I had planned last night. She had no right to suddenly show up and completely derail my life.

Trying to calm myself by putting on a façade, as I seemed to be the only one who felt awkward, a smirk crossed my face. "I had to come settle a few things."

"I bet when you say 'things,' paying attention during class isn't one of them."

Glad she was talking to me normally, I replied, "You know me well."

"I pride myself on getting to know you," she said, without skipping a beat. *The hell does that mean?*

The hall quickly emptied around us, as teachers and straggling students rushed to their classes. Taking the initiative, she stepped in front of me and taunted me with a smile over her shoulder. "We should head to our next class before you're late to that one, too."

As much as I wished to just continue as if nothing had happened, I couldn't do it.

"Hinata," I said, almost in a whisper.

Hinata turned around at the soft call of her name. "Yes?"

"We need to talk," I stressed.

Her face turned serious. "I agree, but do you wish to have this conversation right here, right now?"

"No," I answered, weight slowly easing off my shoulders. "I'm just glad you acknowledge that things aren't necessarily straight between us."

"Yesterday was quite a roller coaster," she said, shifting her weight from one foot to another. "I spent much of my night thinking about everything, with you at the centre. I believe I've finally tied together a few conclusions."

There was a charged pause in my reply when she admitted that I was at the centre of her thoughts. I was eager, but also terrified of what this conversation would cost me.

"Do you have time today?" she asked.

"I'm supposed to meet with Makoto at lunch, plus I have a feeling that Sensei is gonna wanna have words with me sometime today, as well. Raincheck?"

"Sure," she said, just as the chimes rang. Taking in the sound, she turned back around. "Now we're both late."

"I told you I was a bad influence on you," I said, catching up to her.

"When did you say that?"

"It's always been implied."

Chapter Fifteen

A T THE START of lunch, I turned in my seat and saw Makoto stand up from his. Until now, we hadn't had a chance to exchange a single word in person. Just as I was walking toward him, the front door abruptly slid open.

"Mr. Nakajima, a word, please."

Shuddering, I stopped and slowly turned around to face the annoying demon at the front.

"Sensei, can this wait until after school?" I pleaded from the middle of the classroom.

"Now, Nakajima," Kobayashi-sensei demanded.

Turning back to face Makoto, he smiled understandingly. Waving his hand, telling me to go, he mouthed, "We'll talk after school."

Nodding my head in agreement, I followed Kobayashi-sensei, leaving my classmates in whispers behind me. Sensei shut the door behind us, a likely attempt at some privacy in the open hallway.

I knew I needed to be the one who started the conversation or else my head would get chewed off before I could even get a word in. "Sensei—"

"Riku," he overpowered, as expected, "where have you been? You have been absent for more than a week! Didn't we just have a conversation about how you need to attend more days as a requirement to graduate? Do you care at all about possibly being held back? You haven't made any effort whatsoever."

I could tell Kobayashi-sensei was beyond frustrated. After all, he was right. Trying to put out the fire surrounding him, I eased off the jokes I had saved up.

"You're right, Sensei. We *did* have a conversation about this. But I've been trying—"

"Doesn't look like you have *tried* all that hard, now does it?" Sensei turned to walk down the hall. "Let's take this somewhere more private. Come with me."

"Fine," I huffed. He was testing my patience.

Leading us to an empty prep room, he shut the door behind us, then walked over to one side of the room and leaned his back against the wall. Crossing his arms, he propped up one foot and planted the sole of his shoe on the wall.

He looked at me with furrowed brows. "Go on, I'm listening."

Trying to remember where I left off, before I was rudely interrupted, I changed my approach. "To be completely honest with you, Sensei, I didn't originally plan on attending school today. I had every intention of skipping and going to work instead."

Tilting his head, he shot me a steely glare. "What stopped you?"

"Makoto."

"Ah, I see. The reliable Fujimoto."

"You could say that."

"Anything else you want to tell me?"

"Actually, there is," I stated sturdily. "I reduced my availability at the convenience store. I'll no longer have any shifts during school hours."

With a piqued interest, Kobayashi-sensei uncrossed his arms. "And, what about your other job?"

I shrugged. "I quit that one."

Dropping his foot, Kobayashi-sensei pushed off the wall with his back and took a step toward me, then placed a hand on my shoulder. "I was wrong. You have made some effort. My only question is, who are you doing it for?"

"Makoto," I answered again, without much thought. *And Hinata. And maybe a little for you. But I'd rather fuckin' DIE than ever admit that to a demon like you.*

"Wrong answer, Riku."

My face twisted. "What? Why?"

Removing his hand, he shook his head. "You should be making this type of important decision because *you* want to make the effort to change and be more present, not because *Makoto* wants you to."

As a teacher, his job was to look after his students—he had always made that very clear. Maybe he was able to help his other students, but there was something that Sensei didn't quite understand about me.

I was broken. Unfixable. It was too late in the game for me.

"Sensei," I said, with a swift smile, "I don't have much going on in my life. It's quite meaningless, actually." I wiped the smile off my face as I thought in greater detail. "But I still need to repay those who've helped me get this far. I've lived a moderately cushioned lifestyle, thanks to the Fujimoto family. I have an obligation to repay them. I need to show them that I'll be all right on my own. All I gotta do is continue balancing both school and work for a while longer. It's hard, but I'll do it. Once I'm eighteen, and I've graduated, everything will be different."

"Riku," he said, reeling from shock, "why do you think things will be so different once you turn eighteen?"

"I'll be an adult," I declared confidently. "I'll be able to live independently without being hassled and work as much as I want so I can support myself. No one will be responsible for me, except me."

He filled his lungs with air, then closed his eyes and exhaled slowly. "Riku, listen," he said, opening his eyes with a piercing gaze directed at me, "you're just a kid. You're a really smart, pain in my side, kid, but still, just a kid."

Being a *kid* meant you were naïve and knew nothing. I didn't want to be a kid anymore. I could feel the blood coursing under my skin, while on the surface, my skin itched from the heat.

"Do you know how I know you're smart?" he asked, rhetorically. "It's because you have passed all your tests and exams with average marks. Those have been the only times you have bothered to show your face at school.

It's your attendance and participation that is seriously lacking, plus all the homework assignments that you have failed to turn in."

Shrinking down, my eyes fell to the floor. That was the first time a teacher had called me 'smart,' in any shape or form. I didn't know what else to fight back with. In an angered silence, I bit my tongue and allowed him to continue with his lecturing.

Sensei sighed. "Riku," he said my name in a less strict tone, as if sensing my defeat, "I know I'm hard on you, but I'm only trying to help you. And maybe that's hard for you to accept, but it's true. I want you to be able to come to me for help with anything that's bothering you, even if it doesn't pertain to school."

My eyes flicked up. I was interested to see what expression his face wore. His eyes were soft; his brows no longer knitted in anger.

Come to him for help? Help with what? What could he possibly do to help me?

All I ever did was disappoint people, so why couldn't he just accept the disappointment I was and move on?

There was so much change happening in my life; I felt more lost than ever.

"That's enough for today," he said, taking my silence as my response. "I got off topic. What I originally came to discuss with you is that it's been decided that you will be attending supplementary lessons over the summer. Lessons begin the day after the student body is dismissed for the break. You are to attend each and every day." The harshness in his voice had returned. With a sharp, reprimanding tone, he asked, "Do I make myself clear?"

"Crystal," I answered, grinding my teeth.

"Excellent. You may go."

Asshole.

Chapter Sixteen

THE LONG-AWAITED TALK was upon us; there were finally no more distractions.

Makoto left the classroom first, and in passing, told me to meet him outside near the school's flowerbeds.

He sat off to the side on a concrete ledge that wrapped all the way around a giant tree growing in the middle of the courtyard. He was hunched over on his knees, focusing on his hands. He appeared restless as he fiddled with the tips of his fingernails.

Coming to a stop right in front of him, my sneakers entered his line of vision.

"Riku!" he exclaimed, flicking his head back in complete shock.

"Scare 'ya?"

"A bit. I didn't hear you coming."

Slipping my hands into my pockets, I smiled stiffly. "Seemed like you were deep in thought, Vice-Prez."

"I was."

His response was weird. The carefree attitude Makoto typically showcased at school was not currently present. The happy-go-lucky Makoto I knew had washed away, like chalk on the pavement after rain. This scared me.

"Sorry we had to push this to after school.

That stupid Kobayashi wouldn't let up. Hope it didn't conflict with student council stuff."

"Don't worry, I didn't have any student council duties today." Makoto chuckled, dryly. "Sensei's still on your case, eh? What did he want this time?"

"Oh, y'know, the usual. Harping on me for missing school and whatnot. He told me I gotta attend supplementary lessons over the summer break," I shared, leaving out everything else Sensei said.

"That's shitty."

"Meh, it's fine. I already expected as much."

From there, an uncomfortable silence crept upon us.

Hating this awkward tension, I decided to get straight to the point. "What did you wanna talk about? Must be important if you told me to ditch work."

Avoiding my eyes, he went back into his hunched over position. Taking a seat beside him, I patiently waited for his reply.

"I confessed to Sakura."

My eyes bulged and my stomach curdled; it felt like I had taken a direct punch to the gut. Slowly, I turned toward him. "You did, huh? What, uh, what did she say?"

Still looking downward, he twirled his index fingers in circles. "I was rejected . . ."

With his fading sentence, I held my breath, knowing there would most likely be an explanation.

"She cried as she rejected me."

Swallowing the built-up saliva trapped in my throat, I blew out the pent-up air within me. Knowing all too well what could have caused Sakura's tears, I played dumb. "Cried?"

"Yeah," he responded, dejectedly. "When I asked her why she was crying, she could barely look at me. At first, I thought my confession was a burden to her, that it was the worst thing I could've possibly done to our friendship. Then, she mentioned your name."

Sitting up straight, he pierced me with apprehensive eyes.

Continuing down the inescapable hole I created for myself, I started to sweat. "My . . . name?"

"Yeah."

"What . . . what did she say, exactly?"

"She said: *'Riku and I need to tell you something, but it's best that you hear it from him.'* So, Riku," he said, with hooded eyes, "what is it that *you* need to tell me?"

Of course, she would fuckin' leave it like that. Leaving me in an impossible situation. That bitch.

"Makoto, I—"

"Riku, if you're about to lie to me, then save it. I don't want to hear bullshit."

"Makoto." I spoke his name, in a long-suffering sigh.

"I'm serious, Riku. I know how good you are at lying through your damn teeth. Just tell it to me straight, man. What's going on? Did you do anything indecent to her?"

Makoto's eyes were dripping with mistrust; he was searching my face for answers. He was fully invested in what I would say next. Now, he wouldn't dare avert his eyes from mine, and I felt like I couldn't either.

I had nowhere to go and no one to turn to. I was the one at fault, the one to blame. But having Makoto despise me was something I wasn't sure I could handle. I had so much time to reflect upon my actions and prepare myself for this moment, so why didn't I? Did I really believe that this would all just blow over without being addressed?

"Riku," he prompted, his voice cracking. Defeated.

Fuck, fuck, fuck.

With sheer terror, I took the biggest breath of my life, one I thought my lungs couldn't possibly hold. The words felt acidic in my throat the longer I stalled. In the end, I blurted out exactly what had been eating away at me. "I slept with Sakura!"

Almost immediately, the colour drained from Makoto's face and it looked as if his soul had left his body hollow; his insides completely pitted. His eyes became big and glossy, just before his jaw dropped.

I had destroyed him.

"Makoto, I'm so fuckin' sorry, man! I wasn't in my right mind! We were at a karaoke mixer—and I got drunk—and the next thing I knew, I woke up in my apartment and Sakura was lying naked beside me—and—"

"ENOUGH!" Makoto shouted, shaking his head back and forth with watery eyes. "That's enough."

"Mako—"

"You know," he started, as he wiped the tears rimming his eyes, "I thought you were going to come here and tell me that you guys kissed. That's the extent to which I thought this conversation might go . . ."

"Mako—" I tried again.

"But, for you to stoop so low as to fucking sleep with her, when you damn well knew I liked her . . . Why am I not the least bit surprised? It's you, after all. You sleep with anything that walks. You've been this way since junior high. God!" he shouted, like he was in pain. "Is this why you were weirder than usual when I mentioned that I was ready to confess to Sakura?"

"I . . . I . . .."

I was on the verge of shattering. My throat closed and my stomach plummeted so far down inside me that I thought it would disappear. The outside air felt impossibly thin. I had disappointed Makoto so many times in the past that I had lost track. But this, this outdid everything. Nobody ever gave a damn about me, except Makoto and his family. So why, why couldn't I live up to their expectations and be better?

"I can't be around you right now," he stated, standing up. "I need some time alone to think and figure out this fucking mess."

Shifting my horrified gaze up to him, I stared at his back with disbelief as he walked away. *That's it? The conversation's over? What the fuck! How? Makoto, you can't let me off that easy!*

"Makoto, wait!"

He came to a halt. "Riku," he said, in a hushed voice, "I need to think over my words carefully. I don't want to say something that I might regret."

No, Makoto. You don't understand . . . THINGS CAN'T STAY LIKE THIS!

Jumping to my feet, I pleaded out of desperation. "GET MAD! BE HARSH! BE BRUTAL! YELL AT ME, DAMMIT! Just fuckin' hate me!" With no energy left, my knees buckled, and I fell to the ground. "Why the fuck d'you keep me around, Makoto? Why d'you constantly put up with a piece of shit like me? All I ever do is ruin shit and disappoint everyone. I dunno what I'm doing anymore. I'm fuckin' holding you back, man!"

Whipping around, Makoto marched toward me.

Tears streamed down his face, while his hands turned into fists. "The only person you're holding back is yourself, Riku! GOD DAMMIT!" he shouted angrily, running his fingers through his hair and tugging at it aggressively. "Why are you like this, man? You push away everyone who cares about you!"

Just as I had done, Makoto also fell to his knees, landing a few feet in front of me.

"I fucking love you, man—you're like a brother to me—but you make it really hard to carry out a friendship. You sleep around because you're afraid to be alone, but you insist on being alone because you're dying to be independent. How the fuck can you be independent if you don't know how to take care of yourself? There have been countless times I've turned a blind eye to the shit you've done because it never made much sense to me. But above all, through thick and thin, I stuck around because you're damn important to me, Riku. THAT'S what friends do; they stick around. Just because you think you're alone, doesn't mean you have to be lonely."

The chambers of my heart ceased to pump, and goosebumps rippled across my entire body. Speechless, I felt tears of my own drip onto my chest and soak through my uniform shirt. The tears that didn't make it onto my shirt rolled down my cheeks and fell into the palms of my hands resting on my thighs. He spoke the truth.

If I was him, I would have ditched a friend like me long ago.

Getting to his feet, Makoto wiped his face once more before patting the dirt off his uniform pants. Turning away, he spoke over his shoulder. "Think about the things I've said. I can only hope that something I've said will click."

With my knees still buried in the dirt, I was left feeling uncertain. "What's gonna happen to us?"

"I don't know, Riku. I honestly can't say. You have to give me some time, man."

"Yeah, okay," I said frantically, picking myself up.

I watched Makoto walk away from me and eventually disappear.

My head was a mess, much like my life. Even when Makoto was long gone, I found it difficult to move. Standing underneath the big tree, the rumbling sound of thunder reverberated across the sky. Peering up between the holes of the branches and leaves, grey clouds swirled across the sky. Within seconds, rain sporadically fell, then turned violent.

Chapter Seventeen

MY SOCKS SLIPPED off my feet and had gotten lost within the puddles inside my sneakers as I walked. With the intensity of the rain crashing down, I was completely drenched. The uniform I wore clung to my body; water had infiltrated everything. But at that moment, I couldn't be bothered to care. With each step forward, I gathered an unknown courage to keep going, until I lost sight of where I was or where I was headed.

Traversing along a blind path, I was led by emotion. I walked aimlessly for what felt like hours in the torrential downpour, until I reached an unforeseeable destination. I tried to figure out where I had wandered to, but my vision was hazed. Blinking numerous times, the rain made it difficult to get a clear scan of my surroundings as raindrops got caught in my eyelashes. Closing my eyes, I listened to the heavy rain I was immersed in.

The world around me was at a standstill.

"Riku?"

Unsure if what I was hearing was true, I opened my eyes and followed the ghostly voice that called my name from down the road. Squinting, I could see the figure of someone holding an umbrella getting closer. It seemed we arrived in the same place at the same time.

"Riku, what are you doing here?"

My life was in shambles, but like an angel, Hinata appeared before me. Allowing my body to guide me, I had managed to make it all the way to Hinata's house.

She sacrificed her dry state by holding out her umbrella to cover me. Just seeing her drove my sleep-deprived mind wild; it was hard to describe the reason for the unsettled throbbing inside my chest.

Hinata was the light in my eternal darkness, come to pull me out of my world painted with malice.

Without thinking, I reached out to Hinata and grabbed hold of her hand. Pulling her into me, I heard the umbrella make a thud as it hit the ground. We stayed in each other's arms for a moment, soaking wet, before Hinata backed away. She reached for my hand and intertwined our fingers as she bent down to pick up the umbrella. Then, she guided me through the gate and up the walkway to her house.

Hinata released my hand after leading us inside. When the lights flicked on, she turned around to face me.

"Riku, your expression is scary. What happened?"

Lifting my head, I caught her gaze. Feeling the need to avert my eyes, I looked past her to the unfamiliar, open space before me.

The entryway was a massive foyer where ten people could easily fit. The Tachibana's house had natural, Japanese-style wooden accents incorporated within the modern décor and structure. Giant framed pieces of artwork hung on the white walls lining the main floor hallway and leading up the stairs. Although there were plenty of pictures, none of them were family portraits.

"Riku," Hinata called out again, in a forlorn tone.

Shifting my eyes back to her, I took a moment to soak her in. Her gaze fell over me like a blanket; comfy and warm. Taking a step forward, I placed my head down on her shoulder. Grabbing her arm once more, I released a lethargic sigh.

"You win, Hinata."

"I win?"

"Yeah, you win. You always win. You have from day one."

"Riku, I don't understand what you mean?"

Closing my eyes, I tried to detach myself from what had happened with

Makoto and concentrate solely on my breathing. Everything inside of me felt jumbled and unorganized; I was seconds from going insane.

Not knowing if what I was saying made any sense, I spat out each thing that crossed my mind. "I didn't ask for any of this. My strong front crumbles around you. You bring out a different side of me, one that I've never shown anyone. You're constantly swirling around in my head; your face, your words, your actions—they all haunt me daily."

Hinata placed her hand on my head and began grooming my wet hair. I could've easily drifted off to sleep while standing if she didn't quit her scalp massage.

"It makes me happy to hear you say that, Riku," she whispered into my ear, her voice elated.

"It's true, every last fuckin' word. Hinata," I said, choking on my words, "I dunno what these feelings are; I can't make heads or tails of them. What I do know is that I'm too comfortable now to let go of them without trying to understand them. I hate how much I'm attracted to you, how enthralled I am by your presence. You're literally driving me fuckin' crazy!"

She ruffled my hair again. "Where's this all coming from? Did something happen?"

Realizing where I was and what I was doing, I shot up and backed away from her. "Sorry. This oughta look bad if your family sees."

"No one's home."

"Seriously? But it's already so late."

"Since tomorrow is Saturday, the twins don't have school like we do, so I dropped them off at a friend's house where they'll be sleeping over. My father went on a short business trip and took my mother."

"I see," I said, skeptical of the predicament I found myself in. "I should go. Sorry for the intrusion."

I turned on my heel to flee, but Hinata reached for my hand and pulled me back.

"Stay."

Without looking back, I shook my head. "I don't think that's a good idea."

"You came here for a reason, didn't you?"

Flustered, I thought long and hard about what she said. *Did I come here for a reason? If so, what is it? Why did I stop* here *of all places? What the fuck am I expecting from her?*

"Honestly, I dunno," I answered, turning around in defeat. "I just sorta . . . ended up here."

"Then, there must be a reason," she drilled.

"Trust me. If I knew what it was, I'd tell you."

With retreating eyes, she lowered her head. "Whatever it is, please don't go."

Seeing the sour look on Hinata's face strained me.

What did she mean 'stay'? Stay longer? Stay the night? Which is it?

"Hinata."

"Please, just a bit longer."

Longer it was. "Fine. I'll stay a bit longer."

She took off her wet loafers and brought them together, then flipped them around to face the front door before setting them down at the raised step of the entryway. With a step up, her wet socks made a mushy sound as they met the wooden floor. I followed suit.

Feeling obligated to properly announce my arrival in a home other than my own, I called out to the empty space. "Pardon the intrusion . . .."

"That's not necessary."

"I know, but it feels weirder not saying it. Plus, you said it when you came over to my place, too."

With laughter, Hinata headed down the hallway. "This way," she said, signaling with her head for me to follow. "We need to get out of these wet clothes."

"It's fine. I didn't bring a change of clothes," I explained, tagging along.

"You can borrow something from my father."

"No, really, it's okay."

"You'll get sick otherwise."

Not wanting to wear something belonging to Mr. Tachibana, as it oddly felt like he would be watching me, I shook my head. "I'll be fine."

"No, you won't."

She ran up the stairs, returning about a minute or so later.

"Here," she said, tossing an outfit in my direction.

I caught it with my chest. "I said I was fine."

"And I determined that you weren't."

"Hina—"

"Don't worry. My father won't even notice."

"It's not . . . that," I mumbled.

"You can change in the bathroom down here, I'll go upstairs. Make sure you bathe first, or else you'll get sick," she fussed. "After you have finished, I'll come grab your wet uniform to wash it."

Preventing a verbal brawl, I caved and agreed. Without another word, Hinata passed me and headed back upstairs, triumphantly.

Taking a guess on which door she had referred to; I found the bathroom on my first try. When I opened the door, the lights automatically turned on. The bathroom was abnormally spacious for a guest bathroom. Matching the parts I had seen of the house so far, it was extremely modern and expensive by design. This lifestyle was one I was not accustomed to.

Inside, I shut the door and locked it. Leaning my back against the door for support, I drew in a deep breath and held it, then peered down at the clothes in my hands.

What the fuck am I doing? Why'd I come here?

Contemplating my life choices, my body grew heavier as I grew more and more tired from standing still. Knowing there was no time for sleep, I pushed myself and walked toward the shower.

Peeling off my wet uniform, I tucked my wet clothes off to the side before opening the glass door to the prerinsing area. After, I turned the showerhead on and let the water run warm before stepping underneath. I rested my forehead on the shower wall and placed my hands on either side of my head. As I let the hot water run down me, I shut my eyes to think.

Fuck, man! I can't believe I came to Hinata's house of all places. What was I thinking? Why was this my first *choice of places to go? Why didn't I just wander on home? Being here, alone with her, ain't good. Definitely* not *good.*

Unsure of how long I had been in the shower for, a thick fog developed, meaning it was well past time to get out.

Spending the remainder of my time washing quickly, I reached for one of the folded towels outside the shower and tied it around my waist, then grabbed a smaller towel for my hair. The luxury of owning more than one towel was exceptional. Taking a moment to dry off, I dropped the two towels on the floor and stared into the mirror as I put on Mr. Tachibana's clothes. The outfit was a dark grey tracksuit that was a bit tight in the crotch and short in length of the arms, so I pushed up the sleeves.

With both hands stretched out on the edge of the countertop, I dropped my head. "This is so fuckin' weird."

Unsure of where to leave the wet items, I wrapped my school uniform inside the large towel and carried everything into the hall, then placed the wet bundle by the entryway.

Killing time, as Hinata was nowhere to be found, I walked toward an open room on the opposite side of the hallway. The room I entered had the massive windows I previously admired from the outside. There were also enormous built-in bookshelves full of books I had never heard of, including numerous piano books.

Skimming over the items, my eyes fixated on a piano off to the side. As if just being in its presence was enough to potentially damage it, I circled it carefully. Its basic features reminded me of the one at school, just much bigger.

"It's a semi-concert grand."

Alarmed, I spun around. "Shit, Hinata! You almost gave me a damn heart attack," I said, patting my chest in relief.

Giggling freely, like a girl I hardly recognized, she responded, "Sorry." Hinata stood directly under the archway with damp hair that might've been towel dried at best.

She wore a white, long-sleeved sweatshirt, black tights, and thick, fluffy socks. There was something about tights that drove guys wild—I was no exception. I also noticed she was wearing earrings in her double pierced earlobes, and I liked the look they gave her. Everything about the Hinata standing before me was attractive. A heat was building below my waist.

This is bad. Very fuckin' bad.

"Whatever," I brushed off, gazing back at the piano as a distraction. Genuinely infatuated with the musical instrument beside me, I changed the subject. "A grand piano, huh? I've heard of those."

"They come in different sizes, but grand pianos are pretty common."

"I see," I said, staring attentively at the piano keys. "Hey."

"Hmm?"

"Can you play for me?"

"Oh, um, I'm not very good," she said, dispassionately.

Rolling my eyes, I caught her in her lie. "C'mere."

Hesitantly, she made it over to the piano. Before anything else, she placed one hand on it and guided her fingertips elegantly across the top until she reached the seat. I was mesmerized by her.

Gently sitting on the piano's bench, she stared at the keys, then at me. "I haven't played in a few years."

"Liar. You were playing at school not that long ago."

"So, that was *you* making all that ruckus in the hall," she said, with a toothy grin.

"Yeah, sorry. I happened to stumble upon the music room in an attempt at getting away from a demon."

"Demon?"

"Yeah, the demon known as Kobayashi-sensei."

"Ah, I see." She snorted out a laugh. He's always after you, it seems."

"You're not the first to notice," I said, sighing.

Smiling at my remark, she grabbed me. "Have a seat."

Yanking at my arm, she pulled until I awkwardly tripped over my own feet and came close to falling on top of her.

"Jeez, careful!" I exclaimed, catching myself with the piano's assistance. "I'm not gonna be held responsible if this expensive looking instrument breaks from your roughhousing."

She giggled. "It's fine. Nothing broke."

"Not yet, anyway," I said, taking a proper seat beside her.

Adjusting her posture, she began cracking all her fingers and knuckles individually. When the last one cracked, she hovered her fingers over the keys of the piano, then froze.

Lifting my gaze from her hands to her face, I noticed that her eyes were closed. "Everything okay?"

She pulled back her hands and opened her eyes. "It's nerve-racking having you watch me."

"But I've already seen you play."

"That was before I knew you were watching," she stated, with a creased forehead.

"Just pretend like I'm not here," I said, trying my best to sound convincing.

She glared at me out of the corner of her eye. "Easier said than done."

"I'll be quiet. Promise."

"Fine, but don't laugh," she warned.

"I would never," I said, taking my index finger and drawing a 'X' over my heart. "Cross my heart."

Taking in a deep breath through her nose, she parted her lips ever so slightly before releasing the air. Placing her hands back over the keys, this time, she managed to press her fingers down on them.

Winded by the sound of the first few notes flowing into my ears, I was compelled to shut my eyes. Hinata's playing revealed the same troubled and unhappy tone as before. It was laced with extreme sadness.

Finding comfort in this depressing tune, I knew Hinata and I were much more alike than I wanted to admit. Even if it was for just a while, her piano playing distracted me from the problems I kept running from.

Hinata played for about fifteen minutes uninterrupted. I wasn't sure if she was playing actual known songs, or ones she had composed herself, but I listened quietly, nonetheless. As if that was all she needed me to do.

When she came to a stop, there was momentary silence.

"Riku."

Opening my eyes, I turned to her. "Hmm?"

Focusing on the piano keys, she asked, "Can I play you one more?"

Wondering why she felt the need to ask permission, I nodded. "Of course."

Hinata closed her eyes once more, but this time, when she touched the keys, the tone was shockingly different. Thinking back to when I had caught the tail end of her playing at school, right before Kobayashi-sensei interfered, the tempo of the music also transformed. What was once sad, depressing, and troubled, was now fiery, aggressive, and emotional.

Wanting to know what had changed, I searched for the explanation in her face. To my surprise, her facial expression was not what I had imagined. Hinata was crying. Tears skated down her face gracefully as she played on. At length, it seemed as if she was expressing a part of herself that she couldn't express with words. Just by listening, I could tell that the wounds she had were deep, and that the teardrops she shed would somehow never dry. She was a flower that had bloomed in the wrong season, struggling, and trying to survive. I couldn't take my eyes off of her.

Customarily, a song has some type of ending, where the listener can more or less understand when it's wrapping up. Though I couldn't tell how many songs she had played before this one, as they all started blending together, this last song Hinata played was definitely out of the ordinary.

Without warning, the music came to an abrupt stop, and Hinata was now breathing heavily. It seemed like Hinata was unaware that she was crying because she dabbed her cheeks with her fingertips, noticing the wet sensation.

"Sorry," she said, trying to hide her shaky hands, "I got a bit carried away."

I was utterly speechless.

Even without being knowledgeable of the piano, not knowing which keys created which sounds, I understood that the piano was like an extension of Hinata. Her self-confidence had blinded me to the fact that she was secretly crying on the inside.

Standing, she walked around the bench and out of my line of vision, reappearing on the other side as I twisted to locate her.

"Are you hungry, Riku? You must be, right? After all it's late, and you were completely soaked when I found you. So, I can only assume that you were walking outside in the rain for quite some time. Also, you still never told me what's wrong," she ranted, out of sorts.

Rising from the bench, I turned to face her. "Stop for a minute," I said, empathetically.

With tearful eyes, her gaze flicked away, as if to hide her face.

"Hinata?"

"I hate it here," she declared, weakly lifting her head.

I hesitated before taking a step closer to her. "Here? As in this house?"

"This house, the last house, the next house—they're all the same."

Something was wrong. I continued to slowly approach her. "What d'you mean? What's going on? Are you moving again?"

She shook her head. "That's not it."

"Then, I'm sorry, but I don't get what you mean."

She wiped the lingering tears. "Just because there are people who live here, doesn't make the house full."

This wasn't the first time Hinata used this riddle on me. Thinking back to one of our very first conversations, I tried to remember the context in which she used it.

"Hinata," I said, reaching for her hand, "you have a family who truly loves you—I've witnessed it firsthand. So, why does this house feel so empty to you?"

"Just because they *love* me, doesn't mean I feel *loved* by them."

At that moment, it hit me. Hinata and I were one in the same. We had people who cared about us, as Makoto pointed out to me, but we were still lonely, just trying to find a place in which we belonged.

"I get it." My manner softened.

She dove into my chest, burying her face and hugging me tightly, and I wrapped my arms around her. Hinata was just short enough to fit perfectly under my chin, allowing me to rest my head atop hers. We stayed in each other's arms for a while, quiet and still.

Finally feeling good about moving on from the emotional moment, I had an answer to her previous question. "Actually, I am pretty hungry."

Enveloped in my arms, she answered, "I know. Your stomach's been growling."

Chapter Eighteen

Hinata guided me to the massive kitchen and instructed me to wait at the bar-style counter, as she went to toss our wet clothes into the wash. When she returned, Hinata decided to make me her most confident dish: omurice. She bounced around the kitchen with pep as she collected what she needed, and I caught her smiling many times during preparations. She seemed to really enjoy cooking.

Other than the delicious meals Mrs. Fujimoto made for me, and had Makoto drop off, I couldn't remember the last time someone cooked for me.

Watching Hinata in the kitchen caused my stomach to flip. Maybe I was just hungry, but seeing her happy made me feel good.

The delicious smell of food soon filled the room, causing my mouth to water. Putting the finishing touches on the dish, I watched Hinata write something on it with ketchup, like most did for children. Placing the dish in front of me, she took her apron off and hung it up on one of the hooks on the wall, then sat on a stool beside me. Reading what she wrote on the fluffy omurice, it said: heart.

"Heart?" I questioned.

"Yeah."

"Why?"

Propping her elbow up on the counter, she rested her chin in her palm. "Because you make my heart feel many things, Riku. I get

this ticklish uproar that spreads like wildfire throughout my chest. But I've also noticed that my heart is the most at ease when I'm near you."

My throat rolled nervously, and my heart swelled.

She caused me to feel so many emotions that I almost felt suffocated. Hinata wasn't afraid to say anything, and that scared me.

While getting to know her, I've learned very little. She was outright crazy, but it was the kind of crazy that kindled a fire within me. She made me question who I was and what I wanted. We may have both been broken, just staunching each other's wounds, but maybe that's exactly what we needed.

"Hinata, listen . . .," I started, but was made to stop.

"I'll listen after you eat."

"Aren't you gonna eat anything?"

"I ate with the twins before dropping them off at their sleepover."

"Gotcha."

"Go on," she insisted.

Not needing to be told a third time, I dug in. Taking the first bite, my eyes lit up. "Yo! This is sooo good!"

She smiled. "I'm glad you like it."

Shoving the next spoonful into my mouth, I almost forgot to swallow. "It's above and beyond what I was expecting. How'd you get so good at cooking?"

"You don't need skill to cook, you just need will," she said, angelically.

"Looked like you were in your element while you were making this, though."

"I don't mind cooking for other people, especially if they look happy while eating something I made," Hinata said, smiling faintly. "But unlike the girls at school who talk about making bentos for fun, I've always done it because I had to. When I was younger, and still lived with my birthparents, I was often asked to make my own lunches for school. Considering my mother was in the hospital, and my father religiously stayed by her side, I was left alone to take care of myself most of the time."

Hearing Hinata bring up her birthmother again had me thinking back on mine. "Well, at least you had the will to learn. I'm not much of a cook—like at all. I can't cook worth shit. But it was hard to learn when there was never any food at home."

"Did your mother never cook for you?"

"Nah, she was barely home. I briefly remember the one time she did try to cook, and she burnt the entire thing. She was usually too busy getting drunk or high to care about stocking the house with food. Any money she had went to supporting her addictions."

Hinata's face never wavered. "What did you do for school lunches, then?"

"Any money I managed to steal from my mom I used to buy meal tickets at the school's cafeteria. But, soon after I met Makoto, it wasn't long before his mom figured out my situation and started making two bentos for Makoto to bring to school. Then, once I moved in with the Fujimotos, each morning Mrs. Fujimoto would personally hand me my own bento, as if I were her own kid. It was awesome."

"I didn't know that you lived with Fujimoto?"

"Oh, yeah . . . I did. For a little while."

"The Fujimotos sound like wonderful people."

With a snort of air, I smiled. "They really are. They've sacrificed so much for me; I owe them my life," I said, taking a moment. "Throughout my time knowing Makoto, he's constantly vouched for me. Growing up, he's always been my voice of reason, mostly when it came to teachers and other authoritative adults. He'd use his words when all I wanted to do was use my fists. If it wasn't for him, I probably would've dropped out, or been kicked outta school by now."

"I can tell that you truly love Fujimoto."

"Yeah, I truly do. He's the best damn friend a guy could ever ask for. I'd do anything for him."

I'm such a hypocrite.

"Then, how come whenever you talk about him you seem sad?"

I lowered my spoon. "What?"

"Since earlier, whenever you speak about Fujimoto, your face screams sadness. Is everything all right between you two?" She looked at me with an arched brow, her curiosity clear.

She caught me. Or maybe I *wanted* her to catch me. It was shockingly scary how well she could read me.

"Not at all," I declared, willingly.

Hinata tilted her head. "What happened?"

Looking down at my half-eaten dish, I avoided her inquisitive eyes. "I'm pretty sure I destroyed our friendship."

"What did you do?"

Picking my spoon back up, I played with the remaining oozing omurice on my plate, slowly pushing it back and forth. "I fucked up, that's what I did."

"I doubt that. I'm sure it's something that can be worked out."

"You don't get it."

"Then, make me get it," she said, with a sharp tongue.

Fuck, she has me eating out of the palm of her hand.

I turned to meet her fiery gaze. "I slept with the girl he likes," I admitted, my pulse erratic. "He welcomed me into his damn home, put a roof over my head, fed me, gave me clothes to wear, and how do I repay him? By sleeping with the only girl I've ever known him to fuckin' like."

Hinata had no reaction. She absorbed my confession like a sponge all while remaining neutral.

"Did you know that he liked her?"

"Yeah."

She continued to soak everything in without judgement. "Why did you do it, then?"

"I was drunk. I know that's no excuse, but it's the truth."

"I see," she paused. "Do I happen to know this girl?"

It was hard to tell, but it felt like she was seeking these answers for reassurance in some way. But for what? Depending on my answer, would it bring her clarity?

I wasn't sure about anything going on in my life, there was always one problem after another, but for some reason I was *sure* I didn't want to hurt her. I didn't want to hurt her, but lying to her at this point would be worse.

"It was Sakura Sato from our class. There's no use in hiding it now, I've already told you everything else."

I watched Hinata's eyes enlarge. She sat upright, then took her hands and placed them on the stool underneath her thighs to sit on them. With unwavering attention, she asked, "When did this happen?"

"Weird enough, it was the day I met you," I explained, looking into her fearless eyes. "Makoto only found out about it today, though. That's what I was doing before I came here. I had tried my best to hide it from him, but in the end, I was cornered by my lie."

Sighing, she looked aside. "That was a pretty terrible thing you did." She dug into my wounds.

"I know," I agreed, still disgusted with myself.

"I can't speak for Fujimoto, but if I were him, I would forgive you."

Shocked—again—I lowered my spoon. "Why?"

"At the end of the day, they weren't dating . . ."

"Yes, but I betrayed him!"

She brought her eyes back to meet mine. "Let me finish."

Wisely, I let her continue.

"What you did wasn't what a friend should do, but you sleeping with Sato only proves that she never liked Fujimoto to begin with. This might have been a blessing in disguise for Fujimoto."

"I don't think Makoto sees it that way. I know I sure as hell don't."

"He may not at the moment, because he's hurting, but give him some time. Fujimoto is a logical person; there's no way he could give up on your friendship so easily, not after everything you've been through together."

Listening to Hinata explain her take on the situation was shockingly uplifting. Though I still had doubts, I was somewhat reassured by her words. "I hope you're right."

The corner of her mouth curled up as she stared at me, but soon, her smile wilted away. "Can I ask you something vague?"

"It's never stopped you before," I smirked.

"Is this what you call 'dating'?"

With this unnerving question, my mind went numb. "Huh?"

She reconstructed her question. "Me and you—are we dating?"

My ears rang from the silence that filled the room, as Hinata left it up to me to break it.

These irrational feelings that emerged whenever I was around her were growing at an uncomfortable rate. My heart violently thumped within my chest, as if threatening to escape. I felt stupid by being triggered by a simple question, but I was scared to allow myself to feel anything for her.

We're not . . . right? I don't ever remember asking her out or vice versa. So, why the hell would she come out and ask that? Now, of all times!

Stuck on how to answer, I was more than positive that Hinata was a virgin, since I was her first kiss. Meaning, she probably wanted a normal relationship which was something I wasn't sure I could offer.

The only serious relationship I've ever had was in junior high when I lost my virginity to a senpai a year older than me, and it lasted no longer than a week. Other than the silly title that was placed on it, nothing was *serious* about it. And that's how I liked it. I had enjoyed my time fooling around with girls, with no strings attached.

Until now.

I felt powerless when it came to Hinata, but I was helplessly attracted; I couldn't deny that. At the same time, there was a part of me that was afraid to move forward with her in any relationship. I didn't want to tarnish such an innocent beauty.

"Hinata . . .."

"Riku, remember when you told me that you may not be able to give me what I'm looking for, and I said that I wasn't sure what it *was* that I was looking for?"

It was hard to forget our first sexual encounter. At that time, I thought she was someone experienced who spoke my language. All I wanted to do that day was have my way with her. "I remember."

"Well, I finally figured out what it is I've been looking for. I know what I want."

"And, what's that?"

"It's you, Riku. I want you," she expressed strongly, placing a comforting hand on my thigh. "I like having you by my side. It's hard to explain, but I feel a connection that I don't want severed. I may not have comprehended it at that time, as I was mostly just curious then, but you have helped me discover and understand parts about myself in many ways. I like the way you make me feel. I have fun just being around you."

My jaw tightened.

I've only ever known one way of living, which has been to take what I want and look out for myself. I was a greedy person who put himself before others, but now, when it came to her, all I wanted to do was put her first. She held a fraction of my heart within the palms of her delicate hands, and that scared me shitless.

"Hinata," I said, as I grabbed my stool and inched it closer to hers,

"I'm not good enough for you. I can't give you luxuries such as these." I fanned my hand out, highlighting the room at large. "This house, your fancy belongings, the lifestyle you live—all of it. I'll never amount to anything more than what I am now—I have nothing. I'm a womanizer; I've always been a guy who seeks casual sex by scoping out my next prey. I'm pretty sure you're confusing your feelings with infatuation."

"None of that is true," she said, shaking her head back and forth. "Where you come from doesn't define who you are. What you do with the life that you're given, that's what defines you. I know you're capable of so much more, Riku."

She lifted her hands up and out in front of her while twisting at the waist, showcasing the same space around us.

"I don't want any of this, I never have. This house is too big, and even though it's full of stuff, it's completely bare. All the houses that I've lived in are practically identical; they never feel like *home*. Every last one of them has given me the same isolated feeling. I'm tired of feeling alone in a place that's supposed to be my home, my sanctuary." Her wandering eyes returned and fixated on me. "Since I've met you, I don't feel as lonely anymore. The Riku I know now is the Riku that I've come to like and enjoy spending my time with. These feelings coursing through me *are real*."

She had my pulse racing.

I understood the comfort that Hinata was describing. Just having her around brought me a type of relief that I've never experienced before. I unquestionably came to like her, to such an extent that it was worrisome. I wanted consistency, and that was exactly what Hinata proved to be.

I grabbed her hand and gently stroked the top of it with my thumb. Staring at our connected hands, I was left deep in thought. "I dunno where this is going, I never have with you, but maybe it will lead somewhere good," I said, giving her hand a squeeze. "Since the moment we've met, I can't get you outta my mind. Fuck," I said, my voice a sigh, "I've tried, but you crossed it once and never left."

I stopped to clear my throat.

"You're like a damn roller coaster of emotions: you frustrate me, you annoy the hell outta me, you're overly persistent, but even with all that, you attract me in so many ways that it's damn exhausting. You've even stayed by my side when I needed someone. Hinata," I said, looking into her eyes while taking in a nerve-racking breath, "I dunno what this is, but what I *do* know is that there are at least a million better guys out there. With that full disclaimer, I'm willing to see where this goes . . . if you are."

Hinata leaned in and kissed me. "For the record," she started, leaning back from the kiss, "I don't think any one of those million guys would understand me the way you've come to." She brought her hand up to my cheek and I leaned into her palm. "I know we accidentally stumbled into this, but why do you make it seem like love is some formidable foe that's out to get you?"

My jaw tightened, again.

Having her use the word 'love' ultimately freaked me out. Love was such a loaded word, one that was hard to unpack. I knew the context in which she used it was justified, but hearing it still shook me. I had just come to terms with *liking* Hinata that *loving* her was something I couldn't fathom.

"I, uh, I dunno."

With a sensitive expression in her eyes, she caressed my cheek. "That's fine. There's no right answer, I guess. But if you ever want to get something off your chest, just know I'm always ready to listen. I want to be your girl-friend, not your burden."

Smiling apologetically, I yielded to her. "Fair enough."

Chapter Nineteen

WITH A LOSS of appetite, and the remainder of my food already cold, I helped tidy the kitchen while Hinata left to check on our clothes. As she flipped our clothes over to the dryer, I realized our time together was coming to an end.

When Hinata returned, I had already finished tidying everything up. Meeting her in the middle of the kitchen, she approached me slowly. Without saying anything, she stared up at me.

"What's wrong?" I asked, finding her expression to be different from what it was moments before.

"Nothing," she said, smiling delightfully. "I'm just happy that you're here."

That damn smile of hers is striking.

She hadn't shown such a wide, happy smile in front of me before. I liked it. I liked that I was the one who caused such a beautiful smile to appear on her beautiful face. With her smile alone, I'd bend to whatever she wanted.

Placing my hands into my pockets, I leaned forward and brought my lips to her forehead. "Me, too."

Returning my forehead kiss with one on the lips, she grabbed a hold of my sweatshirt and pulled me back in. Removing my hands from my pockets, I slipped my fingers through Hinata's hair and held onto the back of her head as we kissed more deeply. With the exchange of

our kisses, Hinata placed her hands gently on my wrists. Remembering to control myself, I brought our make out session to a quick end.

"Your hair's still quite wet, huh?" I said, tucking a few loose strands behind her ears.

"I have thick hair, so it takes longer to naturally dry."

"You should blow-dry it before you get sick," I said, reversing our roles.

Touching the ends of her damp hair, she grabbed my hand. "Come with me."

"Where?"

Already pulling me along, she looked back. "To my room."

Digging my heels into the floor, I brought us to a halt. "Why?"

"My hairdryer is in my room. I'll blow-dry my hair, at your request, but there's no reason for you to hang out down here by yourself. We can just hang out in my room."

Not convinced, I waged a war with myself. *Why can't she just bring the damn hairdryer down here? Y'know what—whatever—it's fine. You got this, bro. No need to lead with your dick. She ain't like that. I don't want shit to be like* that. *She'll dry her hair, we'll chill and talk some more, then hopefully our clothes will be dried, and I'll escape before anything* happens. *You can do this, man. No sweat.*

I surrendered to her pleas. "Lead the way."

Stepping inside Hinata's room, I was in awe of its size. Much like the rest of the house, everything was off-white, except for the wooden floors; the walls and the furniture—all white. She had a modern queen-sized bed with two bedside tables, a spacious vanity with a mirror and chair, a dresser, a television, a two-seater couch, a western coffee table, a bookcase with a plethora of books, a cozy reading chair—along with a walk-in closet *and* connecting bathroom.

Captivated, my jaw practically dropped to the floor. "This is literally the size of my entire apartment, maybe bigger."

"It's ridiculous, isn't it? Bigger than anyone needs, really."

I took another look around the room and paid closer attention to the finer details. Yes, her room was full of furniture, but it wasn't filled with objects that expressed who Hinata was as an individual. Aside from the bookshelf, there was nothing that resembled a hobby or a collection. Not even a single picture was out on display. Just like the main level of the house, this room also felt staged.

Walking over to her vanity, Hinata took out a hairdryer from one of its drawers. "Make yourself comfortable."

"That's impossible. I'm too stunned to even move."

Giggling under her breath, she pulled out the vanity chair. "Have a seat."

"Me? Why? My hair is basically dry."

"'Basically' doesn't mean it is. Sit."

"Tsk," I clicked my tongue, "you're so demanding." Walking over to her, I took a seat in front of the vanity mirror as instructed.

Hinata plugged in the hairdryer and turned it on. She tested the warmth of the air on her forearm first before she brought it close to my head. Then, she ran her fingers through my hair in all directions. In a matter of seconds, my hair was completely dry.

"Told 'ya. There was barely anything left to dry."

Rolling her eyes, she cracked a smile.

Reaching up, I grabbed the hairdryer out of her hand. "Your turn," I said, standing up.

Without complaining, Hinata and I changed places. Taking a seat, she peered at me through the mirror, blushing. When she took note of how red her face was, she averted her eyes.

Is she . . . being shy?

Bringing all Hinata's hair to the back, I picked up the hairbrush resting on the vanity. Brushing it thoroughly, I turned on the hairdryer. After getting rid of any knots and tangled pieces, I put the brush down and used my fingers as a comb against the heat of the hairdryer. Moving all her hair to one side of her shoulder, I lost focus when the nape of her neck became exposed.

Taking my thumb, I dragged it down the back of her neck, slowly. Mesmerized by the appealing structure of her long, slender neck, my mind drifted. Bending forward, I placed a kiss on the side of her warm neck.

Staring through my eyebrows, I looked to the mirror in search of her reflection. Hinata was staring back at me. She was flushed up to her ears— too cute to bear. Wrapping my hand around the front of her neck, I grazed her chin softly as I tilted her head up. I sought her lips desperately.

Kiss after kiss, I quickly lost my breath.

The jingle from the dryer downstairs sang throughout the quiet house. Coming to my senses, I broke free from her alluring lips.

What the fuck am I doing? I gotta put a stop to this before things escalate. I mean, I wanna go further with her—obviously—but I don't wanna ruin this good thing we got going between us. Ruining shit based on my desire to have sex with her ain't worth it.

Turning off the hairdryer, I crossed my arm in front of her and placed it down beside the hairbrush on the vanity. Standing up straight, I avoided her sensual gaze.

"Your hair's dry, our clothes are dry, that means it's time for me to go."

Twisting her upper body, she grabbed the back of the chair and looked at me. "Are you really going to leave?"

"You're killing me," I said, bringing a palm to my face and a hand to the back of my neck. I rubbed both out of stress. "D'you know what will happen if I stay?"

"That's what I'm hoping to find out."

Sliding my hand down my face, I looked at her wide-eyed. "The way you play is dangerous, Hinata. I don't think I'll be able to stop this time."

"Then, don't."

With what seemed to be resolved eyes, Hinata rose from the chair. Crossing one hand over the other, she grabbed the bottom of her white, long-sleeved sweatshirt with both hands, then slipped it up and over her head in one swift motion. Tossing it to the side, she stood before me in a similar, but different, laced bra.

My breath hitched; my mind went numb with realization. *Holy . . . fuck.*

Remembering the last time I saw her this way, I knew that Hinata cared very little about keeping her virginity, as she almost willingly gave it to me in exchange for an answer to a question.

I couldn't tell if she was fascinated with the idea of sex or if she was fascinated by having sex with me. She could experience her first time with literally anyone—I wasn't anything special. Hinata was gorgeous, in more ways than one. Any guy would be lucky to have her. But contemplating her being with someone else, having them touch her body so freely, pissed me off.

Hinata wasn't just someone I was messing around with for fun; she was important to me. She had expressed her feelings for me and stuck around in my moments of sheer weakness. I wasn't sure why I cared so much about her virginity, but because of it, she seemed a lot more fragile in my hands. Being with her made me feel guilty for all my past behaviours.

Trying to withstand temptation, I eagerly devoured her with my eyes.

She took a few steps toward me and gazed at me with the flutter of her eyelashes. "Riku," she said, her expectations blatantly obvious.

What she was doing was foul play.

Battered by the tightness inside my chest, I felt the need to exercise caution before I was left with undefinable consequences. Before we progressed, I needed to tell her about the recent activities of the older woman I no longer found pleasure in sleeping with. The one I met up with yesterday just after seeing her, the one who strictly called me upon convenience.

"Hinata, I can clearly see where this is going, but before anything happens, I need to tell you something."

"Hmm, what is it?"

Not wanting to withhold a piece of information that could possibly change her mind about wanting to give her first time to me, I reluctantly came clean. "Last night, after I walked you home, I almost slept with someone . . .."

Stoically, Hinata's eyes never flickered. "I see."

Feeling the urgency to explain, I jumped to elaborate. "She's an older woman who I casually spent nights with to kill time. She's a ruthless woman who constantly cheats on her husband without remorse. But honestly, I'm no better," I confessed knowingly, "because I knew this and chose to sleep with her anyway."

My hands grew clammy as I watched Hinata's eyes judge me.

"Why are you telling me this, Riku?"

She posed a good question. Why indeed? It's not like we knew each other's feelings this time yesterday, or had a label placed on our strange relationship. So why did I feel the need to tell her?

"Uh, to be honest . . . I dunno. I just felt like you should know before wasting your time with me."

"Riku, the time I spend with you is never a waste."

"But Hinata, this isn't just 'hanging out,' this is *sex*," I debated. "Usually, I don't take sex this seriously, it's always been a game to me, but with you . . . it's different. I've never taken someone's virginity before, and I know it's usually a bigger deal for girls. I just wanna make sure you're okay after knowing what I almost did. I don't wanna keep shit from you because I don't wanna hurt you."

Hinata smiled tenderly. "Thank you for wanting what's best for me," she said, wrapping her arms around me in a hug. "But, if what you're feeling is guilt, then you shouldn't." She lifted her head off my chest to peer up at me. "I can't count something like that as unfaithful, since we had no idea what we were to each other yesterday. Those past incidents and sexual relationships that you dabbled in, have shaped the person you are today," she explained calmly, her eyes unwavering.

Relief washed over me; I had mistaken her attentive eyes for judgement.

"I do have one question, though," she added.

My pulse quickened. "Yeah?"

"You said 'almost,' meaning that you refrained from engaging in the act. Why?"

Snorting out a gust of wind, I couldn't help but chuckle. "It was because of you."

One of her eyebrows raised higher than the other, as her forehead wrinkled with confusion. "Me?"

"Yeah," I said, turning my face. "I tried to spend the night with her, like I normally would've, but each attempt I made, your face would appear in my mind and your nagging voice rang through my ears." I smiled at the thought. "It was probably at *that* moment that I knew you had gained absolute control over me. I realized I would rather fight with you than sleep with someone else."

Shifting my eyes back to Hinata, I caught her blushing.

"What are you trying to say, Riku?"

Didn't she get what I was insinuating? Did I really need to spell it out for her? "You . . . y'know what I mean."

"Maybe. But I want to hear you say it."

My silence took the place of words.

"Say it."

Her directness was intimidating, and a bit embarrassing; the blush of her cheeks was contagious.

"Hinata, you're killing me," I said, tugging on the back of my neck.

This time, Hinata was silent. Waiting.

Each time I swallowed, the walls lining my throat burned. I knew exactly what she was looking for.

"I've never properly liked someone before," I blurted out, in awe of myself. "I'm not sure if I'm capable of returning the depth of your feelings or what the depth of my own feelings are. But I do know that I care about you. I . . . like you, Hinata."

The blush on her cheeks expanded up toward her ears. "I see," she said, turning her head and shying away. "Thank you."

I cleared my throat. "Y-yeah."

"Can I ask you one more question?" she asked, and I was grateful she didn't get hung up on my half-ass confession.

"You wouldn't be Hinata if you didn't," I laughed.

"Well, the question is more out of curiosity than anything else. The answer makes no difference."

My laughter subsided. Scared of what she could possibly ask, as it was never something easy, I grew anxious. "Just ask already."

"How many girls have you slept with?"

My throat tightened. Like I had predicted, her question was difficult to answer. Even though she said she was asking out of curiosity, I knew my answer could potentially alter Hinata's decision.

Burdened with the person I was, I groaned. "Truthfully, I dunno the answer. After many drunken nights, I've lost count."

Hinata accepted the information and processed it quietly. Her expression hardened. I had no idea what to expect; she left me with a drawstring of emotions to contemplate alone.

I shouldn't have told her. Stupid! Idiot!

"Are you *sure* you wanna experience your first time with me?" I broke, unable to take the silence. "Don'tcha wanna explore your options with someone purer? Someone who's had fewer sexual partners?"

I kept supplying her with excuses to not have sex with me, something the old me would have *never* done. I feared change out of my control, but I feared hurting her more.

Hinata stared at me head on. This time, the colour of her cheeks returned to normal. "Riku, you're special to me. You already have so many of my firsts. I can't imagine sharing *this* first with anyone other than you."

Though she was straightforward about her feelings, the thought of being *special* to her was overwhelming. Her feelings splashed colour in my grey life.

A heartfelt smile crept its way onto my face. "I hope the person you've chosen is the right one. I hope I can make you happy."

"I'm sure that the happiness I gain from here on out will be enough for a lifetime's worth."

I grinned, bringing my forehead to hers. "I guess this means I'll be in your care."

Chapter Twenty

INCHING CLOSER TO her bed, we kissed until we both ran out of breath. At full force, we removed more of our clothing, tossing pieces onto the floor in every direction until we were down to our final garments.

My eyes scoured over her body; I had never seen anything so beautiful. It was hard to tear my eyes off her. In front of me stood a gorgeous, well-sculpted woman. I marveled at the fact that she chose me, wanted me.

Her matching black laced bra and panties were exciting to look at, as if she had everything planned from the get-go.

"Ought to let y'know, what you're wearing is a bit erotic. Are you trying to kill me?"

"You wouldn't die so easily," she taunted. "But I did hope that you would see it."

Cunning. She may have been inexperienced, but she knew exactly what she was doing. The way she looked me up and down, smiling, made her hotter than any other woman I'd ever seen fully naked.

I could no longer lie to myself; I'd been aware that something had been blooming. From the moment I saw Hinata I've wanted to devour her. There was a beast living inside of me, dying to claw its way out. But it wasn't just her body that lured me, her whole being was infectiously

exquisite. She was caring and compassionate; her selfless ability to take care of others without seeking something in return was a quality I admired. She proved herself as trustworthy with more than just my secrets.

She lifted a fog that had been cast over me, clearing up more than just my vision. The muddy thoughts that consumed me during moments of lust, were now diluted and ran clear. The game had changed. The perfunctory steps of emotionless sex were no longer appealing if *she* remained in the picture.

I placed a knee down on the bed and leaned into Hinata for a kiss. Grabbing my shoulders, she pulled me along with her as she leaned back, and we tumbled onto the crisp, white sheets together. We both laughed, then I helped her move to the middle of the bed and turned our next kiss into many.

Hinata ran her fingers through my hair and gripped tight as my lips travelled over her cheeks and down her neck. Her eyes started a long, slow journey down my body—admiring the view. She grazed one of my forearms with the tips of her fingers a few times, up and down. Her touch was promise, and its softness derailed me. Who knew that a simple gesture could bring comfort more than skin deep.

I focused on other aspects of her, things I found myself craving more of. Like a scent that reminded me of blooming flowers on even the cloudiest of days; her heat that drove my own even hotter; her heartbeat that played the keys of its own piano piece. Each aspect belonged to Hinata, shaped Hinata, and I was fortunate enough to experience each magnificent part.

She trusted me with her body, and I was lucky to see this vulnerable side before anyone else. She shot an excitement through my veins that got me addicted in a whole other way. If she were to disappear now, I'd surely be at a loss.

Gazing up at me with piercing eyes, her face was flushed as she smiled at me with invitation. Her two-coloured eyes reflected two variations of me, and it drove me wild. I wondered if that's how she always saw me? Down how many layers did those colours go?

Unbelievably turned on, I engraved the image of her lying under me into my mind.

"Riku."

"Yeah?" I said, with wandering eyes.

"What should I do if I like it too much?"

She always said the most bizarre and impulsive things. Stunned, an unexplainable gawking noise emerged from my mouth. "GAH! Don't say weird things, especially now!"

"I'm just saying what's on my mind."

"That's the scary part! Most people don't say all the shit that's on their mind. Now, of all times."

"Then, most people aren't honest."

"You're right, they aren't."

With a smile that masked a hidden laugh, she reached up to ruffle my hair.

Shifting my eyes downward, I scanned her body and noticed that the kiss mark I had placed above her breast was still visible. Taking my finger, I hovered over the area. As my finger danced in the air, an inch above her bare skin, she reacted to my phantom touch with anticipation. Her eyes squinted shut as she inhaled and held a breath, stiffening her chest.

This game of temptation was quickly coming to its peak.

I slid my hand underneath her, and she arched so I could unclip her bra. She exhaled and began to relax as I guided the straps off her shoulder, down her arms, and onto the floor. There was nothing but perfection underneath her clothes. As I stared, Hinata grabbed my hand and brought it to her breast, then leaned up to kiss my cheek. I loved how forward she was, guiding my hand to the places she wanted to be touched; I was in awe of how natural it all felt between us.

I turned my lips to hers and brought my other hand up, tangling my fingers through her hair until I was cradling the back of her neck. Hinata sprang kiss upon kiss on me until my senses were intoxicated with nothing but her.

I moved from her breast, down her smooth stomach, exploring. I looked up to see what expression she had on her face and saw her staring down at me, attentively watching my hand trail further and further down her body. Her body spoke my language as it trembled at my touch. And then, it dawned on me.

Hinata was never hard to read, I just hadn't been paying attention.

Playing with the elastic band of her panties, I slipped one finger under them. She helped remove them by lifting her hips, and the movement alone unhinged me. Unable to peel my eyes from her body, I noticed a small tattoo of a bird inside an open cage near her hipbone.

Just when I thought I had come to learn everything there was about her, I knew nothing.

"Do my eyes deceive me, or does *Hinata Tachibana* have a *tattoo?*" I asked, blown away.

With the tips of her fingers, she touched the tattoo on the front of her hip. "Your eyes are working just fine."

"When the hell did 'ya get that? You trying to be part of the Yakuza now too, or what?" I mocked, referring to the rumour she spilled about me when we met.

Hinata smiled with reserve. "I got it on my sixteenth birthday. I had it done by the cousin of my friend, Neiko, without my parents' knowledge."

I came to learn just how much of a bad girl this top-ranked student really was. Having a tattoo was a big feat here in Japan. She risked a lot just by having one, especially being a young woman.

"That's pretty cool." I smiled mischievously, proud of her deviousness. "I admire you for having it. I've always wanted one."

"Why don't you get one?"

"I guess I could, I have connections, I just never got around to getting one yet. I want something big, so it'd be expensive."

"Hmm," she murmured.

"When's your birthday?"

"February 10th."

"Maaan, I'm jealous."

Puzzled, she narrowed her eyebrows inward. "Why? When's your birthday?"

"December 31st; the last day of the damn year."

"A New Year's Eve baby. How nice."

My face twisted. "Nice? How?"

"Your birthday is always a grand celebration. Everywhere you go on New Year's Eve, people are celebrating you."

Outside of Makoto's family, that was the first time anyone had ever spoken about my birthday in such a positive manner.

Each year, since meeting Makoto, I spent my birthday and New Year's with the Fujimotos, as my mother was never around. It was customary to eat cake with family and friends during the holidays, but Mrs. Fujimoto always made sure I had my own cake. She said it wasn't good to mix the two occasions together, because a birthday was a birthday and should be celebrated as such.

Smiling, I looked deep into Hinata's bright, mysterious eyes. At times, I wish I could get a glimpse into her brain, just to see how it worked.

"Your enthusiasm's infectious," I said sarcastically. "Thanks."

She tilted her head and looked genuinely perplexed. "For what?"

"For being you."

"I don't need to be thanked for that. It's kind of difficult otherwise."

Shaking my head, I reverted back to the tattoo I found to be unbelievably sexy. "Why a bird? And why's it inside a cage?"

"For freedom, and also entrapment," she said, without hesitation. "Freedom is a state of mind; it dangles in front of me, tempting me at an arms distance. While I'm technically free to do what I want, with graduation approaching and all, I also feel compelled to stay put. Caged birds are under the care of someone else, stuck in comfort, while wild birds are free to go where they want, when they want. Nothing is holding them back." She sighed with her whole body. "I don't want to fly away, but I want to at least stretch my wings."

Her eyes shone with excruciating pain, a pain I wanted to console. "Hinata?"

"It's nothing," she said with a forced smile. "Everything's fine now."

Her expression upset me, but I wasn't sure what to do. I bent down and placed a reassuring kiss upon her lips. From there, one kiss turned into two kisses, rekindling the spark that had cooled. I threw my boxer briefs on the floor and enclosed Hinata's body with my own until we were skin to skin, everywhere. I was losing what little self-control I had left. Soon the heat and softness would be all I knew.

Reminding myself of an important necessity, I leaned over the edge of the bed to grab the sweatpants from the floor where I pulled out a condom from my wallet. No matter how much I'd slept around in the past, I had vowed from the start to never be irresponsible about it. Although Hinata was someone I cherished, I could never imagine ruining her life from a stupid mistake out of horniness.

Rolling the condom on, I came back down on top of Hinata, hovering. The forced smile she had given me was gone and some of the brightness had returned.

I wanted her. Fuck, did I ever.

"Are you sure about this?" I asked, stretching out each word to make sure she heard me. "Now is your last chance to back out."

"I'm sure," she said, with a half-smile. "I won't change my mind, no matter how many times you ask."

I could sense my face reddening. "If it hurts too much, let me know, okay? Don't refrain yourself."

"Okay."

⁂

That night, I took Hinata's virginity.

For the most part, all I could hear were the laboured sounds of our breathing. Each time she whispered my name, an electric shock surged through me.

Afraid of hurting her, I checked in with her often, taking care to make adjustments for her comfort. I wanted this experience to be pleasant for her, just as it was for me. There were a few times Hinata squeezed my hand in discomfort, but eventually her hold relaxed, along with the rest of her body. I sensed her want, her need for me to continue.

It was amazing to be able to experience such a deep connection with someone, a connection far beyond just the physical. I was dying for the warmth that Hinata easily provided. A warmth that infiltrated all the dark parts of my heart. I was convinced that no one else could truly satisfy or fulfill me the way this unique woman did, with her mysterious bird tattoo and striking two-coloured eyes. There were so many layers to her, to me, and I knew that together we could help peel back those layers to discover the beauty hidden underneath.

I grew up believing I was a nobody. And after sharing all that with her, she still decided on me.

She *chose* me.

All along, I had been searching for *her*. I never want to let go of this hand, *her* hand.

It wasn't long until my heart only knew how to beat to the rhythm of one name.

Hinata Tachibana.

Chapter Twenty-One

IT WAS THE middle of the night, and we knew there were only a few hours left before we had to get up for school. Nestled in my arms, Hinata's naked body was pressed against mine. Peering down, I could only see the bridge of her nose as she rested her head and hand on my chest, prolonging the skin-on-skin contact.

After having slept with Hinata, my head and my heart felt a million times lighter. I could have never imagined that sleeping with someone who held importance to you could feel different than sleeping with someone for pleasure.

Was this what people referred to as 'true bliss'? If so, it felt like I'd be punished if I were any happier.

The thoughts floating around in my head settled as soon as Hinata shifted in bed. Using the hand on my chest, she guided herself up. With the bed sheet draped over her, the moonlight shining through her bedroom window illuminated her profile quite beautifully as she looked at me.

"Riku."

"Hmm?"

"Are you tired?"

"A bit," I fibbed, as I was going on my second all-nighter. Placing one arm behind my head for support, I looked up at her. "How're you doing? How's your body feeling? I wasn't too rough with you, was I?"

"No, I'm fine," she said, shaking her head. "Everything was perfect."

I was pegged with embarrassment from her openness. I coughed to clear my throat. "Th-that's good."

She stared at me. "Can I ask you a few more questions?"

The awkward feeling just washed away. "Why not?"

"Why did you feel the need to have so many sexual partners?"

"I guess . . . it was my cure to being lonely."

It was weird to admit such a thing out loud, but it was true. Having the Fujimotos was great, but they weren't *my* family. Not by blood, anyway.

"I became detached from my body. That's how I was able to sleep with all those women," I said, feeling shameful. "I guess I held myself hostage from love and affection, thinking that if I occupied myself with lust, it would be the same. But I was wrong. In the end, once they left, I felt lonelier than ever."

"Does that mean you've found love now?"

"Hinata, I . . . I dunno how to answer that," I stumbled.

"That's okay. If I'm being honest, I'm not sure I know what love is," she responded, as if lost in thought. "How does one determine what love for an individual is over the love for a family member or friend?"

Relief washed over me; her response was calming. She didn't force fake feelings upon me like other girls had, she was honest to the core, especially with herself. This was probably one of her most attractive qualities.

"I also dunno the answer to that question."

"That's fine. It was rhetorical." She looked up at the moonlight shining through the window.

"I have a question now," I said, sitting up in bed. Reaching over to her, I tucked the hair behind both her ears. "When'd you pierce these?"

She brought both hands up to her earlobes. "I pierced them myself during my junior year of high school."

"You pierced them yourself?" I repeated in amazement. "Did it hurt?"

"Not at all. My main concern was that they were even on both sides," she giggled.

"I bet," I said, with a crooked smile. "I've always wanted to get mine pierced, just never got around to it. Very much like the tattoo."

"Want me to do it?"

My eyes grew wide at her spontaneous request. "You? Pierce my ears?"

"Yeah. I know how to do it."

"Now?"

"Yeah."

Glancing over at the digital alarm clock on Hinata's side table, it read: 2:48 a.m. *Who needs sleep really, right?* I shrugged. "Meh, why not?"

Hinata's face lit up as she hopped off the bed to put on her sweatshirt and underwear. In the process, she found my boxer briefs on the floor and threw them my way. She walked to her vanity chair, grabbed it, and directed me to her bathroom where she placed the chair. Then, she instructed me to sit and wait for her there.

About five minutes later, Hinata returned to the bathroom with a few items in hand. She had a pair of small, hooped earrings, a sewing needle without thread, a lighter, alcohol, a cup of ice, and a single piece of cut apple.

"What's the apple for?"

"In case you get hungry."

I rolled my eyes with a smirk.

She cracked a smile. "It's to put behind your ear so that when I pierce it the needle doesn't jab into your neck."

"Oh, so she has jokes now, does she?" I said, fear tangled in my tone with the mention of 'needle' and 'jab' and 'neck' all in the same sentence.

"Everything will be fine."

"You sound pretty confident," I said, again, in fear of her eagerness.

"That's because I am."

Setting up, Hinata took the needle and sterilized it with the lighter, then she poured some alcohol over the earrings to disinfect them. Next, she grabbed a cube of ice and rubbed it on my one earlobe. Dropping the ice into the sink, she lifted the piece of apple and placed it behind my ear.

"Ready?"

"Just get it over with."

A second later, a sharp, pulsating sensation erupted from my ear, then faded. I now understood why she used the ice, because seconds after, my earlobe started burning.

Removing the needle, she took one of the earrings and pushed the sharper end through the newly created hole, then fastened the tiny hoop. "One down, one to go. You wanted to do two, right?"

"Let's do it."

In less than ten minutes, I had pierced ears.

"Good choice, by the way. I'll buy you a pair of earrings to replace these ones," I said, looking in the mirror at the tiny, black hoops hanging from my earlobes.

"Thanks, and no need. I have plenty."

"I insist."

Hinata smiled, as if giving up on a fight she knew she wouldn't win. "Let's head back to bed and try to sleep for the few remaining hours we have left."

Bringing the chair with me, I followed Hinata back into her room and returned the chair to the vanity. We regained our positions back in bed, keeping on the few clothes we had just redressed ourselves in. Hinata burrowed her face into my neck, being cautious of my newly pierced ears.

I let the atmosphere of the silent, moonlit room overtake me before sleep claimed me.

Chapter Twenty-Two

LATER THAT MORNING, I was awakened by Hinata shaking me back and forth, followed by a nasally laugh. For a split second, I was extremely confused as to why I had woken up in a room other than my own, but then I recalled the wondrous memories of the night.

Squinting at Hinata with half opened eyes, I noticed that she was already dressed in her school uniform. Swinging my feet out of bed, I stretched and looked at the clock with half-lidded eyes. It read: 6:01 a.m.

Jeez, do all flawless students get up at the same ridiculous time? Her and Makoto are like clockwork. "When the hell did you get up?"

"Good morning to you, too," she answered sarcastically. "I woke up half an hour ago but decided to let you sleep a bit longer as I prepared a few things."

"Thanks," I said, with a weary but appreciative smile.

Rubbing the sleep from my eyes, I walked toward the bathroom to make myself somewhat presentable for school while Hinata left me alone to get ready. In doing so, my earlobes grew itchy. So, without much thought, I tugged on them violently to relieve the itch. I immediately regretted that decision as my ears caught fire.

With the harsh reminder that they were freshly pierced, I winced and ran the rest of the way to the bathroom, slamming my hands down on the countertop in dramatic agony. Turning the tap on, I let the water run cold, then splashed the icy water onto my ears.

Taking a step back to breathe, I peered down at the counter at something I hadn't noticed before. Right next to the sink was a brand-new toothbrush with a sticky note that had my name on it.

Man, she thinks of everything.

Looking straight on, I gawked at the sleep-deprived person staring back at me in the mirror. Ugly as I was, I felt oddly refreshed. Even though I had slept just three, short hours, and was tired beyond belief, I could honestly say that it was the best sleep I've had in a while.

Downstairs, I found Hinata in the kitchen where she had just finished preparing breakfast. The scene that developed in my head, as I thought about the entirety of the morning, was that of us being newlyweds.

Would every morning be like this if Hinata was a constant part of my life? Would she stay by my side, like this, always? These thoughts sent shivers down my spine and up my neck, but in a good way, an exciting way. The possibility left me wondering if it was worth holding out for or if I was just kidding myself.

While I watched her confidently scurrying around, we eventually made eye contact, and she smiled at me warmly.

"Breakfast is ready," she said, placing a few bowls on the centre island.

Gazing at all the steaming food, my jaw dropped. "Wow, this is amazing. I honestly can't remember the last time I actually ate breakfast, let alone a home-cooked one."

Hinata scowled. "You need to start eating properly, Riku."

With a subtle laugh, I took a seat at the island countertop. "Yes, ma'am."

Once we were fed and ready to go, we made our way out the door. If we weren't wearing high school uniforms, it would have looked like we were a young, married couple leaving for work. It was an image my mind drew up astoundingly quick. The same thoughts from earlier continued to flourish in my head, further haunting me.

School was never something I took seriously, academically. It was a place I went to when I needed to escape from the crappy home life I lived. The way I saw it was that I could at least spend time with my friends if I went to school instead of being stuck at home with that miserable woman.

Of all days, though, today was different. Today I felt anxious.

I was scared at what expression Makoto's face would show. I worried about seeing Sakura. I thought about Kobayashi-sensei holding me back after school to dig further into my past or lecture me about my future. Lastly, I was nervous about how Hinata would act in class. All things that were undesirable to deal with on a scorching Saturday morning.

Arriving at school, we entered through the gates together, waited for each other to switch our shoes, and walked up the three flights of stairs to our classroom. In my entire life as a student, I believe this was the earliest I had ever arrived at school, even with Makoto on my ass hassling me.

Allowing Hinata to enter the front door of the classroom before me, I quickly stopped as she came to a standstill. Looking at her frame from behind, I stretched out my neck and tilted my head around her to see her face.

"What's wrong?" Following Hinata's line of sight, I saw her staring off into the half-full classroom at Sakura, who returned her stare with a sharp glare. "Hinata," I whispered, standing upright. "Leave it. Her problem is with me."

Without a word, Hinata walked into the room and made her way to the back where her desk was. I walked along the wall of the chalkboard to mine. As I took my seat, a few of my classmates approached me.

"G'morning, Nakajima! Yo, when did you pierce your ears?" an energized guy by the name of Kazue Chiba, asked.

"Last night."

"Whoa! That's badass! Kobayashi is gonna flip once he sees them."

Laughing alongside him, I pictured the demon's classic, pissed off face. "He'll hold me after class, without a doubt."

"They make you look even sexier," a girl by the name of Yuka Kinoshita, who I've slept with once in the past, commented.

Not paying her much attention, as I didn't want to wrongly insinuate anything that could potentially hurt Hinata, who I'm sure was listening from the back of the classroom, I answered with a mere, "Thanks."

Kinoshita seemed displeased with being brushed off, so she took it upon herself to make her presence known by sitting on top of my desk. Crossing her legs seductively, so her uniform skirt could intentionally ride up to expose her legs and upper thighs, she placed her hand on my shoulder.

"We should hang out again sometime, since we had SOOO much fun the last few times."

I leaned back in my chair to purposely remove her hand, then glared up at her with distaste. "Not gonna happen."

With a spiteful look, she asked, "What? Why not?"

"I don't do that anymore."

"You, Riku Nakajima, mister playboy, doesn't play around anymore? Are you joking?" Kinoshita said, with a thorny tone to her voice.

"Lay off, Kinoshita," Chiba butted in, in my defense. "The guy's obviously not interested. Take a hint."

"Whatever," she said, hopping off my desk angrily. "You'll be sorry, Riku. Don't come crying to me when you change your mind."

As Kinoshita was about to walk away, I cocked my head. "I don't cry over people with shitty personalities."

"You're a fucking asshole, you know that?" she said, storming off.

Cocking my head over my shoulder to reply to Kinoshita, my eyes unintentionally met Sakura's across the room. And hers intentionally stared back. "More than you know," I said, under my breath.

"Kinoshita is such a handful, huh? She thinks she's top shit."

I pulled my eyes away from Sakura's. "Don't worry about her," I said, looking up at Chiba. "She's all talk and no bite."

Chiba laughed while shaking his head.

Just as I was about to advise Chiba not to get involved with the likes of Kinoshita, the ultimate king of assholes made his grand appearance.

"Good morning, class. All right, everyone to their seats. Quickly now."

Without realizing it, the class had grown full of students who were now scrambling to their desks. And just like that, my mood changed. I couldn't wait for Kobayashi-sensei to see me in class, well before him.

"Do my eyes deceive me?" Kobayashi-sensei said, blinking a few times. "Mr. Nakajima, how lovely to see you on a Saturday morning, on time and seated, no less."

Peering through my eyebrows, I smirked. "Thought I'd try something new. Y'know, to keep an old man, like yourself, on his toes."

A vein bulged on the side of his neck as his eyebrow twitched. "You have a comeback for everything, don't you, Mr. Nakajima?"

With the laughter of the class backing me, my smirk grew two sizes. "I learned from the best."

Rolling his eyes and letting out a sigh of annoyance, Kobayashi-sensei picked up the attendance book from his desk in irritation. "Moving on. Let's commence roll call."

Waiting in excited anticipation for Kobayashi-sensei to notice my pierced ears, I opened my schoolbag to take out my books and a writing utensil. Feeling the material on the outside and inside of my bag, I realized that it was completely dry.

Assuming Hinata must have taken care of it, I smiled. *She really DOES think of everything. I gotta thank her later.*

"Riku Naka—" My name was next in roll call, but Kobayashi-sensei cut it short. "Mr. Nakajima, what have you done to your ears?" he asked, with stress in his voice.

The smile I already wore grew from ear to ear. "Like 'em?"

Kobayashi-sensei closed his eyes and placed the attendance book down on a stack of papers he had at the front, then stretched his arms and rested his hands on the edges of his desk. "Why? Why me?" he whispered to himself. Shaking his head, he took a deep breath and stood tall. "Take them out, Mr. Nakajima, before Principal Koga or another teacher sees you and I get reprimanded for running a class full of delinquents."

"No can do, Sensei. If I take them out now, they'll probably get infected, and the holes will close."

Kobayashi-sensei looked at me as if he was ready to rip them out himself. I could tell he was at his limit. Maybe he had an exhausting school week and was sick of our shit? It wouldn't surprise me, as no one listened to or followed the school rules to such an extent.

"We'll discuss this after class. Now," he said, picking up the attendance book and looking back toward the class, "let's continue."

Called it. As expected from the king of demons.

Chapter Twenty-Three

SCHOOL ON SATURDAYS ran a bit differently; they were half days and only happened twice a month. The workload was much lighter and there weren't as many subjects taught—it had always been the perfect day to skip.

At midday break, I was struggling to stay awake and dying to get my hands on a can of cold coffee. Kobayashi-sensei had stepped out for a bit, but before I could even make it out the same door, a small scenario started unfolding at the back of the room that gained my full attention.

Most students were up and out of their seats, forming small groups to chat or play a quick card game, but my eyes were glued to what was specifically taking place at Hinata's desk.

Hovering over Hinata was Yamada.

Continuing to watch silently from afar, everything seemed in check as it appeared that Yamada was just asking Hinata about something related to schoolwork, until Yamada placed a lingering hand on Hinata's shoulder.

And, just like that, my train of thought derailed. I felt something that resembled a punch go straight to my gut.

Doing something unimaginable, I marched to the back of the room and grabbed Yamada's hand, crushing it within mine as I pulled it away from Hinata. A rage like no other surged through me as I tossed Yamada's hand to the side and grabbed him by the collar of his uniform shirt.

"Nakajima! What the fuck, man? This again?" Yamada shouted, causing an uproar as he struggled to get free.

Red was the only colour I saw, blinding me from noticing that the eyes of all my fellow classmates were on me. I was deaf to their whispers.

My jaw ticked. "Don't touch Hinata with your filthy hands."

Yamada's eyebrows furrowed, forming a 'V.' "Bro, you're tripping! All I did was ask Tachibana about yesterday's homework! What's it to you?"

Yamada's lips were flapping, but I couldn't register a single word he was saying. Everything around me was still radiating red as I replayed the image of Yamada's hand on Hinata's shoulder in my head.

My Hinata.

"Riku, stop! Let go of him."

Automatically listening to the voice reaching out, as I had done most of my life, I broke out of my trance.

Makoto's hand tugged at my arm; the colour red dissipated and the sounds of everything and everyone around me instantly filled my ears. I hadn't noticed his sudden appearance beside me, practically out of thin air.

Releasing my hold on Yamada, I pulled my hand back, but maintained full eye contact.

"Riku?"

Catching onto another important voice that spoke my name, my eyes softened as I shifted them down to Hinata, who was still seated at her desk beside me. The two-coloured eyes that stared back at me were full of concern.

Before I could say anything, Kobayashi-sensei re-entered the room.

"All right, settle down. Break time is over. Everyone, please return to your seat. Let's get the rest of the lessons over with so we can all enjoy what's left of the weekend."

"Hai!" the class said in unison.

As everyone scurried back to their desks, I could hear faint whispers floating around the room. Yamada left our confrontation in a heap of aggravation, mumbling and swearing as he returned to his desk. I could tell he had more things he wanted to say, but couldn't, due to Kobayashi-sensei's reappearance. Makoto also left my side as quickly as he had appeared, without saying another word.

"Mr. Nakajima, is there a problem?"

With my back toward the front, and my eyes locked onto Hinata's, she gestured her head at me, signaling for me to go sit down. Unsure of what to make of the situation, I did as I was expected.

"No, Sensei," I answered, dejectedly.

⁂

The remainder of the day carried on without further disruptions. Like the shitty student I was, I didn't accomplish a single thing. I couldn't even be bothered to copy down the notes from the board.

When the end of day bell chimed, my classmates all rushed out the two doors as fast as possible, all except me. I was cursed by the evil demon, Kobayashi.

"Miss Tachibana, you may also take your leave now. Class has been dismissed."

"I have a prior engagement with Riku, so, I'll wait."

I turned around to face her. *Did we make plans for after school? I don't remember us talking about anything in particular . . .?*

"I see," Kobayashi-sensei replied, with much speculation. "As you wish, but may I ask you to step into the hall for a moment? I need to speak with Mr. Nakajima, privately."

"Yes, Sensi," she answered. Hinata lifted her already packed schoolbag and threw it onto her shoulder. "I'll meet you at the shoe lockers, Riku."

"Sure," I said, watching her leave.

"Riku," Kobayashi-sensei said, demanding my attention.

With such a stern tone, my head snapped back to him. He continued to stand at the front, as I looked up at him from my seat.

"When did you become acquainted with Tachibana?"

"Recently."

"Riku," he said, crossing his arms in front of his chest, unimpressed.

"What?"

"Just how 'acquainted' are you?"

With a raised brow, I asked, "What's it to you, Sensei?"

"Don't play coy with me. She called you by your first name, Riku. I may be a teacher, but I've heard about your track record with this school's female population."

"Just the ones from this school, eh?" I teased, attempting to lighten whatever punishment he was bound to inflict upon me.

"Riku," he warned. The many ways in which he said my name was punishment enough.

"Sensei, you call me by my first name all the time. What of it?"

"Riku, enough."

"Jeez, Sensei. Lighten up."

"What is your relationship with Tachibana?"

Not understanding why this teacher, out of all the rest, seemed to enjoy disrupting my life, I wasn't sure if I should tell him that Hinata and I were dating or if I should deny any romantic relations with her. "Does it matter?"

He sighed with immense burden. "Tachibana is at the top of your grade; she cannot afford to get distracted right now."

"What does that mean?" I asked, having known the answer.

"It means you're a distraction."

Bingo.

"For you, hanging around Tachibana would be a vast improvement. Much like Fujimoto's presence in your life, I believe Tachibana could have a positive influence on you," he said, with hints of a backhanded compliment on its way. "But unfortunately . . ."

Mhmmm.

"I believe that Tachibana's parents won't be as understanding and tolerant about their daughter hanging around with someone of your stature."

"Stature?"

"Someone who takes school lightly. Someone who doesn't care about their grades. Someone who—"

"All right," I said, cutting him off, "I get it already."

My face fell. I knew exactly what he was getting at, right from the get-go. But it still hurt hearing him say it. His words cut deeper than I had expected.

"Don'tcha think I know all that?"

Apparently, Kobayashi-sensei was not expecting that response, so he probed at this new development. "Know what, exactly?"

Things inside me were cracking, inches from shattering. These feelings were getting more and more destructive as the days carried on.

Like the child I knew I secretly was, I chose to continue to ignore the root of the problem and lash out at him instead. "Don'tcha think I know Hinata is too good for the likes of me? That she could do so much better and spend her time with someone who matters, someone who has a promising future?"

I wasn't sure if it was the fact that I didn't know where I stood with Makoto, or the fact that Hinata had entangled herself so deep within my life that I didn't know what to do with my feelings, or if it was because Kobayashi-sensei was on the receiving end of my outburst; a person so determined to dissect every aspect of my life, but I was at my limit of how much shit I could handle.

There used to be nothing about which I was passionate enough to waste my time debating over.

Nothing, until her.

Hinata was someone I knew I shouldn't have, but now that I had her, I couldn't simply let her go. Her existence was like a drug, and her presence was what I was addicted to. If not for Makoto, she was all I had left.

"I get all that, okay! I've expressed that to her so many times." Standing, I balled my hand into a fist and turned my thumb toward my chest. "But, in the end, she chose *me*. She. Still. Chose. Me," I repeated, highlighting each word. "Hinata weaseled her way into my life; she's at the centre of *everything*. I can't let her go that easily!"

Kobayashi-sensei looked shell-shocked.

"If that's all you wanted to talk about, Sensei, can I please leave?" I asked, already collecting my things. "Hinata's waiting."

Without getting an immediate response, I threw my bag over my shoulder and headed for the front door. Just as I reached the sliding door, Kobayashi-sensei called out to me.

"Riku."

With my hand ready to pull the handle, I stared blankly at it as I waited for his final biting comment.

"Take good care of yourself, and Tachibana. I'm rooting for you."

Without turning around, I absorbed Sensei's compliment.

"Yeah," I said with a suppressed smile, before clearing the doorway.

Descending the stairs to the main floor, skipping a few steps along the way, I made my way to the shoe lockers at full speed. Someone special was waiting for me.

Hinata stood formally as she waited near my shoe locker, holding a bottle of Pocari Sweat. When our eyes aligned, she smiled. Slowing to a fast walk, I came up beside her.

"Ready to go?"

"I wasn't aware of a 'prior engagement,'" I stated, opening the locker to exchange my shoes.

Dropping my sneakers on the floor, I stepped into them. As I bent down to adjust the backs of my shoes around my heels with my fingers, Hinata brought the cold bottle of Pocari Sweat to my cheek.

"That's because we didn't have one."

"Then, why'd you tell that stupid Kobayashi we did?" I asked, taking the bottle from her as I stood up and tossed my school slippers into the locker.

"Did you want to spend more time than necessary with him on a Saturday?"

"Definitely not."

"Then, stop complaining."

"I'm not," I said, grinning. I lifted the bottle. "What's this for?"

"You seem out of it," she said, the same concern from earlier presenting itself on her face. "Considering you didn't get much sleep last night; I thought you could use a pick-me-up. Hope it helps."

Feeling the condensation of the cold drink numb my hand, I cracked it open. *It's no black coffee, but it'll do.* I took a sip. "Thanks."

"Don't mention it."

Twisting the cap of the bottle back on, I gazed at her. "Hey . . .."

Walking ahead of me toward the school's entrance, she looked over her shoulder. "Hmm?"

"Um, about what happened in the classroom . . . with Yamada. Sorry, I dunno what came—"

"Like I said," she held up a hand, talking over me, "don't mention it."

My nose stung, as if the sports drink was carbonated and I had drunk it too fast, but that wasn't the case.

Hinata's words were precise and to the point, like usual. By this time, she probably knew me better than I knew myself. Small gestures like these were all it took to make me feel happy and forget about my mishaps. This girl was a well-calculated explosive, patiently waiting to go off within my chest, and she had full control of the detonator.

Reaching for her hand, I grabbed it and squeezed, then brought it up to my lips and placed a kiss on it. "Thank you."

"Yeah," she said, a light shade of pink colouring her cheeks.

Chapter Twenty-Four

ON THE WALK home, I went with Hinata to go pick up her twin brothers from the sleepover at their friend's.

Hinata rang the doorbell while I stayed back and waited out of sight. In no time, one of the twins came flying out of the property gate, while the other came hand-in-hand with Hinata a few seconds later.

When the first twin passed me, he spun around like a ball of energy, then pointed at me with excitement. "Ah! Mr. Riku is here!"

"Kazumi, stop that. It's not polite to point," Hinata scolded, as she approached him with Izumi by her side.

Kazumi's the fireball. Got it.

"Sorry, Mr. Riku!"

Laughing lightly, I replied, "Hey, didn't I say to drop the 'Mister'?"

Kazumi covered his mouth with his hands. "Sorry," he said, again, this time with a muffled voice.

As the four of us walked back to the Tachibana household, I noticed that Izumi was very attached to Hinata as he refused to let go of her hand.

Kazumi, on the other hand, talked endlessly about how much fun they had at their sleepover, never once pausing to take a breath.

Approaching the house, Kazumi pushed the front gate wide open, casually taking the lead. Turning back, he locked eyes with me.

"Hey, Rikuuu! Are you gonna come inside and play with us?"

Just as I got asked this question, my phone vibrated in my pocket. Pulling it out, I saw that it was my manager from the convenience store.

"Ah, give me a sec. My work is calling." Turning my back to them, I took a few steps to get some distance before answering. "Hey, Boss."

"Hello, yes, Riku? I'm glad I caught you!" she said, winded. "I know I said I would need some time to figure out your new work schedule, but do you think you would be able to cover a shift for this afternoon? Tarō called in sick for the mid-shift, and I don't have a replacement. If you can make it in, I should have your new schedule by the end of the shift. What do you say?"

Looking over my shoulder at the Tachibanas, I smiled softly. "Not a problem. I've finished school for the day, anyway. I'll need to stop at home to swap my uniform, though."

"Thank you so much, Riku. You're a lifesaver! See you soon. Bye-bye."

Slipping the phone back into my pocket, I looked to Kazumi. "Sorry, little man. I got called into work. Can I take a raincheck?"

"Okayyy, Kazumi said, sulking. "But next time we gotta play for reals! Promise?"

"You got it," I winked, feeding off Kazumi's contagious energy.

"Boys, head inside. I'll be there soon," Hinata chimed in.

"Okay!" Kazumi answered, joyfully running up the walkway to the house.

Izumi, on the other hand, was reluctant to let go of Hinata's hand.

Hinata took note of Izumi's hesitancy and bent to his level. Eye-to-eye Hinata asked, "What's wrong, Izumi?"

In frustrated silence, Izumi didn't answer, soon turning to follow his brother into the house.

"Hmm . . .."

"Everything okay?" I asked.

"I'm sure it's nothing, but Izumi is definitely acting weird." Hinata pondered. "Maybe something happened at the sleepover?"

"Yeah, maybe," I said, shrugging my shoulders. "Kids are strange sometimes."

"Not Izumi, though. He's hard to read, but he's usually well-behaved."

"Sounds like someone else I know," I hinted, raising a brow.

"Very amusing," she said, glaring at me.

"I'm teasing. I'm sure things are fine." Switching topics, I looked down at my wristwatch. "Sorry, Hinata, but I gotta go. Don't wanna keep my boss waiting too long."

"Of course, sorry for keeping you."

"Nah, it's fine. I've enjoyed our time together."

With a gentle smile, Hinata replied, "Me, too."

"Will your parents be coming back today?" I asked, stalling.

"They should be coming back first thing tomorrow morning."

"Ah, I see."

Before leaving, I wanted to get a few things off my chest, but I wasn't sure how to go about it. I wanted to thank Hinata for everything she did for me last night, and this morning. There were so many things I was thankful for and each one of those things involved her.

"Um, Hinata."

"Hmm?"

"I, uh, I feel weird just leaving like this. This is a first for me. I dunno what I'm supposed to do or how I'm supposed to act. Is it fine just acting normal, to carry on as if nothing happened?"

Hinata's smile turned into a frown. "I don't want you to carry on as if nothing happened, Riku. I want you to treat this relationship as something special. It would be nice if we could continue growing, together. That's what I think."

Hearing Hinata's true feelings was reassuring. She was just as involved and looking forward to our newfound relationship as I was.

"Agreed," I said, with a grateful smile. "Sorry to have imposed on you yesterday. I showed up outta the blue, a complete mess, and you took me in without question. You've helped me with so much. You washed my clothes, fed me, and let me stay the night. Honestly . . . thank you."

The smile returned to Hinata's face. "Riku, I care about you. I can confidently say that I would do anything to help you. Please don't ever forget that. If you're ever in trouble, please come to me."

"Yeah," I said, digging my hands deep into the pockets of my pants, "I will." Taking a few steps toward her, I placed a kiss on her lips, then directed my mouth to her ear. "Next time, you can come stay the night at my place." Pulling back, I smiled at her flirtatiously. "I'll message you later."

Hinata's face flushed pink. That was twice now. I had mastered the ability to make her blush—mission accomplished.

As I walked off, Hinata called out to me.

"Riku!"

Turning around to face her, I continued walking backwards down the road.

With such a serious expression, her parting words came out louder than expected. "Don't take too long to message me! I'll be waiting!"

Tripping over my feet, I caught myself before I ate shit. Standing upright, I smiled, then turned back around to avoid showing her how excited I was at a promise for a *next time*.

To shout something so boldly out in the open—yup—she's definitely crazy.

Chapter Twenty-Five

GROWING UP, NOBODY had ever given a fuck about me, except the Fujimotos. They were caring enough to take me under their wing and treat me as if I was their own son, even though they already had three children to worry about. Makoto, the youngest of his siblings, had two older sisters: Megumi, who was twenty, and Mitsuki, who was nineteen. Both sisters were in a college or university here in Tokyo, but neither of them lived at home. These two girls were also like sisters to me.

I owed my life to the entire Fujimoto family, a family upon which all I ever did was impose. I hated being their burden.

At the end of my junior year of high school, I made a deal with the Fujimotos. It entailed living alone in the studio apartment, owned by Makoto's Uncle Ito, practically rent free, as long as I accepted help from them financially. Having to accept money from them killed my pride.

I began skipping school to maintain two, sometimes three, part-time jobs, allowing my grades and attendance to slip. During my second year of high school, I became so fixated with the need to pay the Fujimotos back that I'd forgotten why I owed them in the first place.

At the end of my shift, the manager and I discussed how many hours I would be allowed to work at the convenience store per week as a student. After having everything rearranged, I grew nervous about my hours being drastically cut, considering I no longer had the job at the restaurant to compensate.

When I arrived at home, I was surprised to see someone sitting near my door. I practically froze.

"Makoto?"

I appeared to have startled him as he put his phone down and quickly jumped to his feet. "Riku!"

"How long have you been waiting here, man?"

"Not long. Like ten, maybe fifteen minutes . . . ish."

Makoto was drenched in sweat, so I could tell he was lying. He was wearing shorts and a T-shirt, but I knew that sitting outside for ten minutes, sheltered from the sun, wouldn't make someone sweat that profusely. He had been waiting there much longer.

"Makoto," I said, stressed, "you should've messaged me. I would've told 'ya I picked up a shift at work."

"It's fine," he said, with fleeting eyes. "Messaging you felt . . . weird."

With the way things were between us, I couldn't disagree, so I dropped the subject. "Wanna come in?"

"Yeah, sure."

Walking past him, I unlocked the door, then urged him to enter ahead of me. Taking off our shoes at the entryway, Makoto, of course, lined both pairs up perfectly and turned them to face the door. He then followed me into the multipurpose living area where I dropped my bag before we took a seat at opposite ends of the table.

"D'you wanna take a shower? Looks like you could use one."

"I'm good."

"You sure?"

"Maybe later."

"Suit yourself."

We sat across from each other in awkward silence; I could hear my eyes blinking.

Not knowing another way to break the thick ice, I got straight to the point. "So . . . why'd you come all this way?"

Makoto was quiet for an additional moment, then inhaled deeply. "You know, I thought a lot about what happened yesterday . . ."

I sucked in a quick breath. *The conversation between us yesterday seems so long ago.*

". . . and what happened today in class," he paused, as a new thought popped into his head. "Speaking of, what the heck was that all about?"

"What?" I said, releasing the nervous breath I held.

"Don't play dumb, idiot. You know exactly what I'm talking about. What happened between you, Yamada, and Tachibana? You had Yamada by the collar. You were pissed as hell, man."

I could see that Makoto was trying to engage in a conversation like he typically would, and that made me happy. It felt good to talk to him somewhat normally.

"A lot's happened recently," I said, in a roundabout way. "To be honest, Makoto, my life's a giant fuckin' mess."

"What else is new? It's been a mess since I've known you, but you contribute to that mess. You make things harder than they need to be, Riku."

With an agreeable smirk, I dropped my eyes. "Yeah, you're right." Lifting one knee at a time, I rose from the short table. "Want something to drink?" I asked, walking toward the kitchen.

"Riku, you're stalling."

"Right again," I said, heading to the fridge to grab a canned coffee before turning back to face him.

From across the table, Makoto straightened his back as he sat cross-legged, then peered at me with concern. "What else is going on with you?"

"You sure you don't want anything to drink?" I asked, holding my gaze, as well as the refrigerator door open. "You might be here a while."

"That bad, eh?"

"Like I said, a lot's happened."

"Give me a teaser."

"Well . . .," I started, closing the refrigerator, and cracking open the can of coffee to take a sip, "for starters, I'm dating Hinata."

Makoto's glasses slipped down the bridge of his nose as his jaw dropped. "Wuh-whaaat? Tachibana? WHEN? HOW?" he interrogated, clearly surprised.

"Yesterday, and . . . it's complicated."

"HUUUH!" he shouted, with exaggeration. "You, Riku, the infamous womanizer, are dating the new girl, Tachibana? With strings, feelings, AND attachments?"

"Yeah."

"Is the world ending?"

"C'mon, man. I'm serious here."

"So am I," he returned with a sharp tongue. "Then, the thing with Yamada was because of Tachibana?"

"Basically."

"What happened?"

"I blew a fuse," I admitted, ashamed. "He touched her and that was enough for me to see red."

Makoto's eyes twitched. "Well, colour me surprised. So, what I interfered in was *you* growing *jealous* over a girl? Man, what a rich experience! Who even are you?"

"I've been asking myself the same set of questions. It's like a piece of me has been cut out and replaced with something new, something . . . strange."

"I can't wait to hear more."

On that note, I tried again. "Final offer, d'you want something to drink? Yes, or no?"

"Yes, tea! A whole pot's worth. I will *absolutely* be here for a while."

"Told 'ya. And yo, I don't own a teapot."

"Sure, you do. I bought it myself when you first moved in. Two yunomi cups, too. It was a housewarming gift for you, but mostly for me."

Turning back around, I began searching through the two kitchen cupboards for the mysterious teapot and cups that I couldn't recall ever laying eyes on. Matching one side of my lip with a raised brow, I looked over my shoulder. "Well, I'll be damned." I grabbed the teapot out of the back of the cupboard. "I doubt you've ever used this."

"Bro, what are you talking about? I use it almost every time we hang out here. Especially if I sleep over. I have my own tea stash here and everything. Do you even live here?"

Staring at the teapot in my hand, I shrugged, then faced him completely. "Eh, news to me."

"You're mentally exhausting, you know that?"

"So I've been told."

I didn't have a kettle, so I had to boil water the old-fashioned way in the only pot I owned. Standing over the compact stovetop, drinking my coffee, I watched the still water eventually bubble.

"Hey, Makoto," I said, never taking my eyes off the burner.

From the table, he replied, "What's up?"

"Why're you being so nice to me?" Taking the pot off the burner, I placed my can down and faced him. "After everything that happened yesterday, how can you still treat me so kindly?"

"Riku," he commenced, without an ounce of hesitation, his tone stern but his voice shaky, "I've done a lot of reflecting." He laced his fingers together and placed his hands on the table. "I realized that endlessly thinking about you and Sakura, together, drove me crazy and made things worse on me. My head and heart were throbbing hysterically." He stopped to swallow. "I won't deny it, hearing that you slept with Sakura was hard to digest. A huge kick to the balls. I've liked her for so long, man—and you knew that—but you ended up sleeping with her, anyway. I know you said you were drunk, but that isn't nearly a good enough excuse."

Acid lined the walls of my throat as I tried to swallow, burning on its way down.

I fucked up. I knew it. Makoto knew it. Everyone who knew, knew it. All I did was fuck things up for those I cared about, and there was always an endless number of excuses for me to provide.

Except this time.

This time, the confrontation was unescapable. And I welcomed it, no matter how difficult.

Makoto continued as I stood quietly. "The trust I have in you is certainly broken; I know because I feel this gaping hole in my chest. But I truly believe things can be mended between us. You're like a brother to me, Riku, and I love you as such. I'm the one who knows you best, man."

Tears welled up in his eyes as he changed the direction of the conversation, and I could feel tears pricking the backs of my eyelids.

"Overall, it all comes down to the fact that Sakura didn't like me to begin with. Although she rejected me, I still had the tiniest bit of hope that maybe someday she'd change her mind, but it took you sleeping with her for me to realize that I never stood a chance. She never saw me in a romantic way; she friend-zoned me—hard."

Oh, Makoto.

"I've come to terms with it. It just wasn't meant to be. But my friendship with you *is*. When I thought about who I'd hate losing and disconnecting with the most, your face appeared in my head first. That's how I know that we'll be all right." Makoto used his bicep to wipe the individual tears that fell. "FUCK!" he cried out. "I hate feeling like this."

If I were in his shoes, I would have dropped a friend like me ages ago. It just went to show how much of a better person Makoto was.

He had every right to feel the way that he did. I was a total piece of shit, a piece of shit that never learned.

Pain pierced the back of my throat as I suppressed the tears. No amount of swallowing calmed the sting. "Makoto, I can't keep taking advantage of your kindness. People have always quit on me; throwing me away when I got too hard to handle or deal with—but not you. I dunno how you can continue to forgive me over and over, man. You've always been so compassionate; it's one of your strengths, but also one of your flaws." I hung my head. "I'm truly sorry about Sakura, and I know no amount of apologies can change the outcome. I'm a complete asshole, through and through. I don't want this to be taken lightly because I'm a thousand percent at fault. I've known that from the moment I realized what I'd done."

"There's no room for modesty amongst best friends, Riku. If we can't let this go, then we'll never move past this."

I threw my head up. "But Mako—"

"Stop, man, seriously." He rose to his feet. "I'm not messing around. I want you to let this go."

"I can't just let this shit go, Makoto," I said, raising my voice and throwing my hands up. "I'm gonna carry this shit for the rest of my life! If you can't trust me, how can you even consider me a friend?"

"That's for me to deal with, not you. How I choose my friends is on me." Makoto stepped into the cramped kitchenette and walked right up to me. He pointed a finger at me and pressed it firmly into my chest. "I will NEVER quit on you or throw you away. I never have and I won't start now.

What I need you to do right now is figure out a way to forgive yourself, so in turn, I can forgive you, too. I'm not saying this shit is going to be easy to deal with, because hell, it won't, but we have to try." He lowered his hand. "I'm willing to try, but the question is, are you, Riku?"

Taking half a step back, I internalized what Makoto was asking of me.

Here I was, getting another free pass from a Fujimoto. While Makoto spent time thinking about how to make shit better between us, I went out and got myself a girlfriend. I stole his chance at romance and replaced it with my own. So much had happened, but in the end, I still chose my own happiness over his. I hadn't learned a fucking thing. I was still a giant, selfish prick.

The pain festering inside was only growing worse with how easy Makoto was letting me off. It's like my whole life I've been on fire, with Makoto constantly putting out the flames ready to engulf me.

I felt the shittiest I had ever felt and didn't know how to make this feeling go away. What was the right thing to do? Was there even a *right thing* to do?

I couldn't take back my actions; they weren't as simple as words.

"I want to, Makoto. Believe me, I do," I said, with a shuddering breath. "But I dunno how. It baffles me how easily you're able to push this matter aside and forgive me."

"I haven't forgiven you."

"But you said—"

"I said: *'Figure out a way to forgive yourself, so in turn, I can forgive you, too.'* Don't mistake my words for anything else."

Releasing all the pent-up air held within my lungs, my shoulders slumped. "You're extremely difficult to reason with."

"That's laughable, coming from you."

We both smiled.

"Okay, I'll try," I said, doubtfully.

"That's all I ask."

After that, Makoto decided to stay the night. We didn't have school the following day, and we had loads to catch up on. He took a shower as I re-boiled the water that had cooled for his tea. After everything was ready, Makoto reclaimed his spot back at the table while I took a seat on my bed with my lukewarm coffee. We talked about what had been going on within our lives, making sure to leave nothing out. Not much had changed on his end, except for his confession to Sakura. Which I ruined.

I told Makoto about my sudden relationship with Hinata and tried to explain Hinata's bizarre personality, which kept me on my toes. With the little romantic knowledge I had, I expressed the refreshing feeling I got when I was with her. I wanted to convey how important her presence had become. And, of course, I also told Makoto that Hinata and I had slept together, which didn't surprise him in the least. He asked if I had come clean to Hinata about sleeping with Sakura, and I confirmed I had. He was concerned that Hinata might have pulled away from me if she knew my track record with women. I explained that there wasn't much Hinata didn't already know about me.

"I told her about my scars."

Stunned, he set his tea down on the table. "You—You told Tachibana about the cigarette burns on your back?"

"Yeah."

"Does that mean she knows about your mom?"

"She knows *of* her, but very little *about* her. My mom is someone I never want Hinata to meet."

"I don't disagree with that," Makoto paused, staring deeply into the cup of tea resting in between his hands on the table. "Your wounds go deeper than just flesh; the scars are embedded within you, Riku. I don't hate many people, but I *do* hate your mom for everything she's done and hasn't done for you. She's a terrible mother."

"She's a terrible human being, period. Some people shouldn't be parents—that woman is one of them."

"That, too," he said, leaning back onto his hands as he stared blankly in front of him. "I still have nightmares about that day."

"What day?"

"The day we took you from your mom," Makoto answered dryly. "I remember when we dropped you off, and my mom telling me that we were going to wait outside of your house for a little while. At that moment, I didn't understand what she meant, but I didn't need to wait long to find out."

Recalling the unforgettable day that he was referring to, I dropped my eyes to my hands. Looking down at the can, I lifted it up to my lips to take the final sip. "Yeah, me too. Though I'm grateful to have escaped from that shithole, I can't seem to burn the look of that woman's damn face from my memory. That day, your mom became like a second mother to me—a real mother to me. She's my hero. Your mom is what I picture all moms *should* be like."

"And she sees you as a son." He spoke with a smile in his voice. "A lot happened that day. I mean, you were only eleven years old. But a lot continues to happen each day that passes, too," he said poetically, as he paused before pressing forward. "It's all so crazy."

"What is?" I asked, shifting my gaze to him.

"Life, and how much you've changed, especially in these last few weeks. You went from a horny womanizer, to this relatable guy, who seems to be in a serious relationship, but can't figure out his true feelings to save his life." Makoto smiled at me with admiration. "I'm in awe of you."

"In awe of me?" I asked, cocking my head to one side.

"Yeah, and the grand transformation you've undergone unknowingly. Tachibana's turned you into a reformed playboy. She must be some girl if she's able to make such a massive change happen."

I let the wall behind me catch my fall, then rested my head against it. Looking up at the ceiling, I rolled the empty can of coffee between my hands. I fully understood what Makoto was saying. For a while now, I felt different. A good different. I felt the change taking place inside me, step-by-step, and it was all thanks to her. She was incredible.

"You have no idea."

"Don't screw this up, Riku."

I threw the pillow on my bed at him, as if I were pitching a baseball. "Thanks for the encouraging words, asshole."

He dodged the pillow, and we shared a laugh. It felt great to laugh with him.

"I'm being serious, man," he said, readjusting himself. "She seems good for you. I approve."

A smile crept its way onto my face. "Wanna know something funny?"

"What?"

"I now have something—someone—I treasure, and I don't think I can stand to live a life without her. Those women from before were nothing but distractions, predictable—but not her. She's unlike anyone I've ever met," I stated confidently. "She's a huge pain in my ass, but she's also the brightest star in my sky. I'm not sure if I know what love is quite yet, but I'm starting to see her a lot more clearly." My smile grew. "All the good things that've happened to me recently are her doing. I've learned that wanting to be around someone is different than wanting to be with them. I wanna be *around* you, but I wanna be *with* her. Does that make sense?"

Makoto smiled wholeheartedly. "It does, and I don't think it's funny at all. I'm happy for you, Riku, honestly. I'm glad Tachibana came into your life."

Having someone listen to what was on my chest felt freeing. And I'm thankful it was Makoto. "Me, too."

"You know, Riku," Makoto paused, propping his elbow on the table to rest his chin in his palm, "it's all over the moment you think everything related to her is a pain. That's called *love*, my friend." He winked.

Staring blankly at Makoto, I was at a loss for words. "'Love,' huh?" I said, under my breath.

"Yep," he taunted. "But I'm glad. I can finally relax now."

"What d'you mean you can relax?"

"It means that you've always been a giant pain in MY ass, too! A pain which causes me daily stress. Now that you have Tachibana, she can look out for you."

I crushed my empty can and threw it at him. "Y'know, you really have a way with words."

"I try," he said, with an impish grin, again, dodging my throw. Returning to his upright position, he grabbed his teacup and swirled the remainder of tea around inside. The playfulness in his eyes had diminished.

"What's with the gloomy face?"

"Not gloomy, just thinking."

"About?" I asked, pushing him to expand on his thoughts and not leave me hanging.

He brought his elbow back up onto the table to rest his chin on his hand. "Remember back in middle school when those guys in the soccer club were picking on me and you beat them up for it?"

Reflecting on my actions in the memory he was reliving, I chuckled.

"Of course, I remember. I almost got suspended because of it. Why're you bringing that up now?"

"Was just feeling a moment of nostalgia, that's all," he said, continuing to swirl his tea. He often swirled his drink whenever he was thinking hard or withholding something.

"Nah, that ain't it," I said, twisting my face in suspicion. "You brought that up for a reason."

Makoto rolled his eyes. "It's nothing, really."

Copying him, I rolled mine out of annoyance. "Wanna know why I did it?"

"Beeecause you're a delinquent?"

"Ha-ha," I said, forcing out an obnoxious laugh. "No. Dick. It's 'cause your mom told me to watch over you at school, to protect you. So, that's what I did. Might've gone overboard, but whatever." I shrugged, remembering the terrible state I left those guys in. "But honestly, I would've done it again. I regret nothing." I brought my eyes to match Makoto's. "You always have my back, figuratively, so having your back physically is one of the only ways I know how to return the favour."

Makoto returned my sincere words with an outburst of laughter. "That's too funny."

"Why's that funny?"

His laughter subsided into a calming smile. "Because my mom told me the same thing. She told me to keep an eye on you at school and help out whenever I saw you struggling."

"Really?"

"I swear," he said, while drawing an 'X' on his chest, right over his heart.

"She played us from the start," I stated, and we both broke out in laughter. "Your mom's the best, man. Sneaky, but the absolute best."

"Yep, she sure is," he said, nodding his head. "But don't tell her I said that."

"Oh, I'm definitely telling her."

"Don't." He sighed. "She'll never let me live it down."

"Exactly."

Makoto grabbed my pillow from the floor and threw it back at me. "Dickwad."

Catching the pillow in my hands like an American football, I placed it beside me on the bed. Sliding down the wall, I laid my back on the bed with the pillow under my head, peering at the ceiling once more and dwelling in many thoughts.

I inhaled until my lungs were full, then released the air slowly. "Thanks, Makoto. I dunno where I'd be without you."

"Probably dead," he answered morbidly, without holding back.

"Man, you're full of witty comebacks today, aren'tcha?"

"What can I say, I'm just too good."

We shared what felt like the hundredth laugh of today.

"Yeah, yeah," I brushed off.

"Do you know what would be really good right about now?"

"What?" I asked, still focused on the ceiling.

"Ramen."

"You're such a weirdo," I said, smiling.

"But I'm your weirdo. You're stuck with me, jerkface."

Chapter Twenty-Six

"BYE, RIKU. SEE you next time," Makoto waved, as I stepped out of the backseat of Mrs. Fujimoto's car.

"Later, Makoto," I said, hesitantly shutting the door, never knowing if there'd be a 'next time.' Each time I went over to the Fujimotos, I was taking a chance. Going to different elementary schools now made it harder for us to see each other.

"Riku," Mrs. Fujimoto called from the driver's side window.

"Yes?" I said, walking up to the lowered window.

"If you ever need anything, don't hesitate to ask, okay? Even if you don't live close by anymore, I'll always come pick you up if you need me to," she said, intuitively.

With a fake, reassuring smile, I answered, "Okay, I won't. But everything's fine, Mrs. Fujimoto. I gotta go though, or else my mom will worry."

"Hurry on inside, then," Mrs. Fujimoto said, shooing me with her hand.

Waving goodbye, I turned around and wiped the smile from my face, knowing all too well what awaited me momentarily.

It was spring, the start of a new school year, but things for me hadn't really changed. I was living with my mother, something I knew never lasted long. It was only a matter of time until shit hit the fan and I'd be taken away again. Even though

I had grown accustomed to being shifted around, I never got used to it. I didn't want to get used to it.

I dragged my feet up to the second floor of the apartment complex and placed my hand on the doorknob, twisting it. It wasn't locked; it never was. Drawing in a deep breath, I held it as I opened the door only to be faced with a familiar shadowy and gloomy entryway. Looking down, I only saw my mother's shoes. These were the days I could never guess what mood she'd be in. Walking into the dark abyss, I shut the door and slipped off my sneakers as quietly as possible. Knowing I needed to, but not wanting to, I announced my arrival.

"Mom, I'm home."

With not even a moment to spare, the lights flicked on, and my mother came charging down the hallway, fists balled.

"WHERE THE FUCK HAVE 'YA BEEN? I'VE BEEN WAITIN' HOURS FOR 'YA TO COME BACK! WHEN I CAME HOME, YOU WERE GONE!"

As she raised her voice, my shoulders grew stiff and tightened toward my neck. Afraid to answer, I remained still and quiet.

Looking me up and down, she grew more irritated. "Looks like you've gained some weight, huh? Did 'ya find a nice family to take 'ya in? Who's been feedin' 'ya, huh brat?"

She wasn't wrong; I had gained weight. Since returning to this apartment, after my mother regained custody of me, I had spent most of my time, especially the weekends, at the Fujimotos. They included me in family meals and activities. As I ate, did homework, and spent time with Makoto, Mrs. Fujimoto washed my clothes. This routine had carried on for a few months already, and I had hoped for my mother to never find out. She was barely home, so keeping this secret had been easy, until today.

"Remember the friend from my old school that I've told you about? Makoto Fujimoto? I go to his place often to hang out. While I'm there, sometimes I have dinner . . . ."

"The Fujimotos, huh? Must be nice," she said, in a condescending tone. "While I'm over here STARVIN', you're having the time of your life with your goddamn stomach full!"

I was old enough to understand that when her tone changed, and her voice elevated unevenly, bad things were about to happen. "Mom, I—"

"You ungrateful little brat! I'm your fuckin' MOTHER!" she announced, as *her eyebrows knitted together, and her tongue rolled. "How dare 'ya treat me like scum! Ever since you've come back to this fuckin' place, you've been givin' off some shitty ass attitude for a worthless brat."*

"Mom, I wasn't!" I cried, hoping to calm her down.

In these moments, I never knew what I could do to make things better. I didn't know what she wanted from me. Realistically, what could I do?

Marching up to me, she slapped me across the face, then grabbed the back of my neck. "You're lucky to have me, 'YA HEAR THAT?" she shouted into my ear, each word sharper and more piercing than the last. "YA WOULDN'T LAST ONE FUCKIN' DAY WITHOUT ME!"

Just as she dug her nails into the back of my neck, there was a knock at the door. Almost immediately, my mother threw me to the side. Catching myself before falling, I stumbled back and away from her, but remained in sight of the door. Though I was scared to see who was on the other side, a small ball of hope formed within my chest.

"Who is it?" my mother barked, her voice a level lower than before.

"Sachiko Nakajima, it's the Shinjuku CGC," a stern, male voice responded. "Open the door."

My mother froze. Watching her from behind, I could tell that she was panicked. She then booked it to the door and locked it before she spun around, her eyes set on me. Rushing toward me, she bent down on both knees and grabbed ahold of my hand. Flinching, I pulled away.

"Riku, baby, Mommy's sorry for hittin' you," she said, parting my hair to one side. Her eyes were bloodshot and extruding from their sockets. There was a thick stench of alcohol that lingered in her breath each time she spoke. "There are some bad people at the door who wanna take you away again. But you won't go with them right, baby? 'Cause Riku, y'know Mommy loves you, right?"

"Ms. Nakajima, open this door immediately," the same voice repeated, this time more assertively.

Tears immediately formed in my eyes as I stared at my mother's terrifying face. There was a knot stuck in my throat, one preventing me from speaking.

Seconds after, sounds of the door being tampered with could be heard, and moments later, it busted open.

My mother pushed me back and quickly stood in front of me. Falling on my butt, I watched the disaster unfold before me.

"What—HOW DARE YOU BARGE IN HERE!" my mother fought. "You can't break into someone's home and do as you please! I'm gonna call the cops!"

One by one people began filing into our apartment. In total, there were four people: one male and one female officer from the Shinjuku CGC, and two police officers. The man, whose voice I hadn't initially recognized from behind the door, was my case worker, the one who had taken me away and placed me with terrible foster families.

"That won't be necessary, Ms. Nakajima," my case worker said, flicking a hand in the direction of the two police officers standing next to him.

My mother stilled. From the back, I could only visualize the immense anger displayed on her face as she balled her fists, tight. Pushing off the floor, I tried distancing myself, but my socks slipped many times on the wooden floor under me.

"We received numerous calls regarding your son, Riku," my case worker continued. "It has come to our attention that after being rehabilitated and reunited with your son, you have begun using, yet again, and are deemed unfit to take care of him. As per the agreement, we will be taking your son into our custody, permanently. We will place him with a family that is better suited to take care of him and his needs."

"NO!" my mother shouted, falling to her knees. "NO, NO, NO! You can't take 'em away from me! HE'S MINE!"

"Ms. Nakajima, please, you are only making this harder on yourself and your son," said the female CGC officer, as she went to my mother's aid. "He will be in good hands."

As the female CGC officer tried calming my mother, someone else forced their way in through the front door. "Excuse me, please, let me through."

As soon as I locked eyes with the fifth adult to enter our chaotic apartment, my shoulders deflated, and the ball stuck in my throat disappeared. Faster than I could have imagined, I rose to my feet and ran toward the door. The person who had made a late appearance was none other than Mrs. Fujimoto, with Makoto hiding behind her.

I broke down crying in her arms as she slightly bent to my level.

"Oh, Riku! There, there. I'm here, everything will be fine," Mrs. Fujimoto comforted, squeezing me tight and patting me on the head.

"Ah, you must be Mrs. Fujimoto. Sorry we took so long to arrive. My name is Goro Ishida, from the Shinjuku Child Guidance Centre," my case worker said, bowing his head as he introduced himself. "We spoke on the phone. Thank you for your cooperation in helping us organize this."

"So, it was you!" my mother growled, jumping to her feet. "YOU BITCH!"

Looking over my shoulder, I saw my mother lunge at Mrs. Fujimoto, but was promptly apprehended by the two officers who quickly took her to the floor to detain her. She continued shouting and swearing at Mrs. Fujimoto, but Mrs. Fujimoto stood her ground and never batted an eye as she continued to hold me close. Everyone watched as the police held my mentally unstable mother down while she kicked and screamed the entire time.

Mrs. Fujimoto escorted Makoto and I outside of the apartment complex where she proceeded to speak with my case worker, and another police officer who arrived for backup. Makoto and I sat off to the side with a large blanket wrapped around us as the grownups spoke in private. Makoto constantly reassured me that everything would be fine, but all I could think about was where and who I would be made to live with next. Trying to listen in on what the grownups were saying, I grew more and more anxious.

"But Mrs. Fujimoto—"

Suddenly, Mrs. Fujimoto raised her voice. "But nothing. I'll foster, adopt, or whatever is needed to protect that child! That child has been crying out for someone to come and save him for far too long. I'm not about to give up on him after all this. He will not be put back into the system. I will be taking Riku back home with me, that's final."

"You hear that, Riku? My mom says you're going to come and live with us! Isn't that awesome?" Makoto said with excitement, leaning over to side hug me.

Tears poured; I couldn't wipe them away fast enough. The small ball of hope that festered within my chest had burst. There were no words to describe how happy I was.

"Yeah, awesome," I said, in between sobbing breaths.

Chapter Twenty-Seven

"LISTEN HERE," KOBAYASHI-SENSEI announced, "summer break isn't just for lazing around and sleeping all day long. You guys still have homework to complete, and as third years, you need to start studying harder for college and university entrance exams—so don't slack off! I advise that some of you look at picking up one or two reference books from a bookstore."

"Haaai," the class groaned in agreement, dragging the confirmation along their tongues.

Mid-July quickly crept upon us, and all the students had just returned to their homeroom classes from the closing ceremony held in the gym.

Makoto and Hinata had passed their exams with flying colours, while I barely slid by. Although I seemed to have patched things up with Makoto, I hadn't seen much of Hinata outside of school. I attended classes regularly, like a good boy, but didn't get a thrill from studying like Hinata did. While she studied, I picked up as many shifts as I was allowed.

Since supplementary lessons would most likely consist of just me and Kobayashi-sensei, I banked on bargaining with Sensei to let me out early. But who was I kidding, he was strict as shit.

"For those of you who've had an outstanding number of red marks on any of the past tests, and have missed countless days on end,

I'll be seeing you first thing tomorrow morning for supplementary lessons," Kobayashi-sensei announced, darting his eyes to me.

Demon.

"Everyone else, have a safe summer holiday and I'll see you all back for second semester in September. I expect everyone's homework to be on my desk first thing when you walk back into this classroom," he dictated, as the student's excitement for summer drowned out the sound of his voice. "Dismissed."

Most of my fellow classmates jumped out of their seats and flew out the doors at lightning speed, while a handful threw papers in the air to celebrate before meeting up with friends to make summer plans.

"Ready, Riku?"

To the right of my desk stood Hinata. I sighed, dismissing thoughts of tomorrow as I rose. "Yeah." Grabbing my schoolbag off the hook on my desk, I looked back at Makoto. "Hey, man, you coming?"

In the midst of packing his bag, Makoto raised his eyes to acknowledge my question. "Can't, I have to head over to cram school."

I clicked my tongue. "You suck."

Smiling, he said, "You should be thanking me. Now you have more time to spend with Tachibana."

Moving my gaze over to Hinata, I could see that she was grinning at Makoto's comment. She smiled a lot more now, and being the self-centered person I was, I hoped it was because of me.

With a smirk, I walked toward Makoto. Slapping him on the back, I leaned in close and whispered, "I only asked to be nice."

Makoto released a burdened sigh. "Oh, I know."

Laughing at how easy it was to annoy him, I headed to the back door with Hinata. "I'll make time to hang out, so you'd better, too," I said with a casual wave goodbye.

He waved back. "Will do. Later."

Before stepping out the door, I felt eyes lingering on me. Dragging my attention from Makoto to the direction I sense the presence coming from, I saw Sakura's eyes quickly dart away from mine.

Again? Jeez, if you wanna say something to me, then fuckin' say it already. If not, then piss off.

"Everything all right?"

Ignoring Sakura's irritating tactics, I brought all my attention back to Hinata. The only girl who mattered. "Sorry," I said, slipping my hand into hers. "Everything's fine." I smiled. "Let's get the hell outta here."

After switching our shoes, Hinata and I walked out of the building and off the school grounds. Knowing all too well I wasn't exactly 'free' for the break, it still felt good to be heading toward summer. Once we made it to the station and went past the turnstiles, I came to a halt while Hinata continued on ahead. Before she got out of reach, I grabbed her hand.

"Hmm?" Hinata muttered, turning around.

"Hey."

She tilted her head. "What's the matter?"

Still holding onto her hand, I met her eyes. "Spend the night at my place tonight."

Without much thought, she answered almost immediately. "But you have lessons early tomorrow morning with Sensei?"

"Doesn't matter."

She knitted her brows together. "You can't miss the first day of supplementary lessons, Riku. You promised you wouldn't."

"I won't. I'll still go. Promise," I said, holding out my pinky.

Looking at my raised pinky, she hooked hers with mine, completing the pinky promise. "Okay, but I'll have to go home and get a few things first."

"What're you gonna tell your parents?" I asked, unhooking our fingers.

"That I'm staying over at a friend's house."

"Believable," I said with a chuckle. "Well, I gotta pass by someplace first, anyway. I'll send you a message on LINE when I'm done."

"Okay, I'll wait until then."

"Sounds good," I smiled. "Later, Hinata."

"Bye-bye", she said, walking off to go catch her train.

Waving her off, I noticed a tightness within my chest that squeezed my insides with each step she took away from me.

Ugh, this is bad. I can't believe how much I've grown to like her. I know that

I'll be seeing her later, so why do I feel so depressed that we're parting? When did I become so fuckin' needy? Blah, gross. Get it together, Riku.

Shaking off my pep-talk, I headed toward the platform I needed to take. Inside the subway car, I found a place to sit, then leaned my head against the window as I doublechecked my bag for the envelope. Confirming it was still there, I shoved it deep into my pocket.

Can't wait to see the guys. I should really stop by more often, and not only when I gotta pay a visit to my landlord.

Chapter Twenty-Eight

I FOUND MYSELF WALKING down streets I hadn't been down in a while. After making a few turns, I arrived at *Fujimoto Auto Body.* Stopping to stare at the beauty of the shop's exterior, I could see that one of the garage doors was wide open. Walking up the property, I let myself in.

Once inside, I looked around for the legendary Uncle Ito.

"Oh, ho, ho, look who we've got here, fellas. If it ain't little Riku."

Quickly whirling around, I came face-to-face with someone familiar. "Long time no see, Taka."

Akio Takanishi, aka Taka, was Uncle Ito's right-hand man. He was a mechanic who was quite a few years older than Uncle Ito, working many years in the field, but Uncle Ito trumped him in knowledge when it came to anything automotive.

The shop worked on all sorts of vehicles, but they were one of the few shops in the area that specialized in motorcycles.

"Sure has, little man. What brings you to the shop?"

Just as I was about to answer, a few other mechanics came to greet me.

"Hey, Riku! What's going on, man?" one of the mechanics asked.

"Yeah, man. How've you been?" another asked.

I knew both guys well, as they had been

working at the shop for many years. Everyone here was like family. "Ah, well, I've been good. Just wanted to talk to Uncle Ito about something. Is he here?"

"'Is he here?' HA!" Taka let out a bellied laugh, then looked over his shoulder and yelled out, "Oi, Eichi!"

A second later, Eichi, another employee, rolled out from underneath a car. "What is it, Taka?"

"Do you know where Ito is? Riku's here to see him."

"Oh, hey, Riku. Didn't see you there." Eichi stood up and wiped his hands on a rag, then flicked his head toward one shoulder, indicating to the space behind him. "Yeah, he's out back looking at a bike."

"Awesome, thanks, guys," I said, bowing lightly before dashing outside.

The yard at the back of the shop was a scrap metal disaster. There were broken down cars and motorcycles huddled in different groups, car parts piled on top of each other, and scraps of unidentifiable things clumped together all over—it was heavenly.

At twenty-eight, about ten years older than me and Makoto, Ito Fujimoto was a ladies' man who owned multiple properties, dabbled in investments, ran his own auto body shop, and rode a wicked motorcycle—a true legend. When Makoto and I were in junior high, we spent most of our free time at Uncle Ito's shop. He was a motorcycle enthusiast, talking about bikes whenever he had the chance. He inspired me to one day get my heavy motorcycle license and own my own bike.

When I was sixteen, Uncle Ito trained and eventually took me to get every motorcycle license I was allowed to obtain, even the dopey moped one, getting me one step closer to my unrestricted dream.

I spotted Uncle Ito at the back in one of the corners, nose deep in a bike. Like the shit-disturber I was, I picked up a small rock from the ground and chucked it at the back of his head.

"Ow! The fu—" he started, as he looked angrily over his shoulder, bringing a hand up to his head.

With one hand in my pocket, and a huge, devilish grin on my face, I waved. "Sup?"

"Don't 'sup' me, 'ya little turd. C'mere." He rose to his feet and sprang at me, putting me into a headlock.

"Ah! What the hell!" I said playfully, fighting him off.

"Throw another rock, I dare 'ya!"

Laughing while slightly suffocating, I beat down on the arm he had around my neck with my hand. "Okay, okay, I tap!"

"Victory by submission!" he shouted, releasing me.

As we laughed together, he pulled me in for a hug.

"It's good to see 'ya, Riku. It's been a while," he said, pushing my shoulders away at arm's length to take a good look at me.

"Yeah, sorry. I had planned to stop by more often but . . . things've been busy."

"Staying outta trouble, I hope?"

"For the most part," I smirked.

"I bet my nephew has been keeping 'ya in line. He does a good job of it, so I don't usually worry."

"Yeah, Makoto's pretty strict."

"Just like my sister-in-law," he teased, shaking his head. Taking note of my ears, his voice escalated. "Yo! When'd 'ya pierce those?"

"Uh, just recently," I said, gently touching one earring.

"They look good, man. It suits 'ya. To be honest, I'm surprised 'ya didn't pierce 'em sooner."

"You aren't the first to tell me that."

With a brief chuckle, he asked the obvious. "So, Riku, what brings 'ya to the shop?"

Pulling out a sealed envelope from my pocket, I presented it to him. "Here. This month's rent."

"Ah, I see. It's that time already, eh?" he said, before pulling out a pack of cigarettes and a lighter from his mechanic jumpsuit pocket. He lifted one cigarette up with his thumb before pulling it out with his mouth, then lit it. "Want one?" he asked, holding another cigarette up, higher than the others within the pack. "Just don't go and snitch to my sister-in-law that I'm giving 'ya one. She'd kill me."

Still holding onto the envelope, I responded, "Nah, I'm good. I think I'm gonna quit."

"Reaaally?" he asked in amazement, as the cigarette dangled from his lips.

"Yeah."

"So, you're gonna give up smoking, eh?" He removed the cigarette from his mouth and arched his brow even higher. "Good for you, kid. I just remember the little boy who was dyyying to show the world that he was all grown up. A rebellious kid who got into things he wasn't supposed to because he thought he knew everything. Now look at 'cha."

It never bothered me when Uncle Ito called me a 'kid.' No one related to me better than he did. Not even Makoto could fully wrap his head around the way my brain worked. It was always easy to talk to Uncle Ito about my problems because we shared a similar lifestyle. Or, should I say, I wanted to live HIS lifestyle.

"Yeah, well, I met someone who's slowly starting to change the way I think . . .."

Placing the cigarette back in his mouth, he pressed, "You 'met someone'? As in not just a casual hookup?"

With a loose-aired chuckle, I brought my gaze down. "At first, that's all I thought this girl was gonna be. She seemed easy, but innocent; I was dying to corrupt her," I explained enthusiastically. "Every time I encounter her, I learn something new about her. The way she thinks is different; she's dark but full of hope. I get excited just thinking about the next time I can see her. It's . . . refreshing."

"Heh."

I looked up. Uncle Ito had his arms crossed with a grin on his face. "Well, I'll be."

"What?"

"Can't believe I'm gonna say this, but I'm actually jealous of a teenage kid," he said, shaking his head. "Is that what 'ya meant by 'being busy'?"

"Kinda."

"Then, I'm happy for 'ya, Riku. I'm glad that 'ya aren't turning out to be a miserable guy like me."

"You're not miserable. In fact, I've always looked up to you."

"I know 'ya have, and that's what's always scared me."

I tilted my head to one side. "Scared you?"

"Look at me, Riku," he said, the cigarette trapped in between his index and middle finger in one hand. "Why d'ya think my sister-in-law never wanted you and Makoto to hang around the shop?"

Before I could answer, he cut me off.

"I'll tell 'ya why, it's because I'm a bad influence. I've always been a bad role model for you guys. So, when 'ya started to mimic the things I've done, I got scared that I was rubbing off on 'ya."

It was upsetting to hear how negative Uncle Ito was about himself. It left a bad taste in my mouth. "You think too lowly of yourself, man," I rebutted. "You're pretty damn successful, and I look up to you in many ways. I aspire to be like you." Pausing, I decided to come clean about something. "Okay, you may be right about one thing. There were many times I fantasized about the different women you brought in and outta your life, but that doesn't make you a bad influence or role model. It just makes you human. You've been there for me so many times over the years, and that's what counts."

He placed his hand up top my head and disheveled my hair. "When'd 'ya get so smart? Must be Makoto's influence. Doesn't matter what I do, I don't think I could've ever influenced that kid in a negative way; he's too pure."

Laughing, I swatted his hand away. "You're telling me."

Turning around, Uncle Ito redirected the conversation. "Put that stupid envelope away. Y'know damn well I don't want your money."

Annoyed, I exhaled deeply. "We go through this exact same argument every month. Just take it and shut up," I said, holding it out again. "We both know you will in the end, anyway."

With a harsh glare over his shoulder, he swiped the envelope from my hand and tucked it into his pocket. "Stubborn ass kid."

Moving away from the talk about money, I looked past him to inquire about the motorcycle he was tinkering with. "What're you working on?" I asked, taking a better look at his project. "A Honda?"

"Ah, well," Uncle Ito avoided, tugging on the back of his neck as he looked at the bike. "Guess it's not much of a surprise now, but this might actually work better."

"Huh?" I said in confusion, moving forward to stand beside him.

"I received this 2011 Honda CBR250R in rough shape a little while back. She's older, but she's a good beginner bike. She's rusted, needs a new motor, and a few specific parts, plus a new paint job—preferably black." He winked. "If you help me fix 'er up, she's yours."

"Mine?" My jaw dropped. "What the hell d'you mean?"

"I mean what I said," he restated. "The rent money that I've been collecting from 'ya over this past year was always gonna go into helping 'ya with something. I know you've always been a motorcycle enthusiast, like me, so for a while now I thought about putting that money toward getting 'ya your first bike, or something of your choosing. Then, this beauty fell into my lap. My sister-in-law is gonna give me an earful about giving 'ya a bike, but it is what it is." Turning to me, he continued. "What, did 'ya think I was actually gonna spend money that some turd-ass kid's given me?"

My eyes grew three times wider than normal. "I, uh . . . I dunno what to say."

"'Ya ain't gotta say nothing." Putting an arm around my shoulder, he patted my chest with his other hand. "That's what uncles do." Casting his gaze toward the bike, he said, "I wanted to have 'er finished in time for your graduation as a present, but why not put 'ya to work and have 'ya fix 'er up yourself? It's a win-win if 'ya ask me. Your birthday ain't 'til December, so 'ya can't get your license just yet, but that leaves 'ya with plenty of time to work on 'er."

"But . . . what about Makoto? He's your *actual* nephew. I can't accept something such as this."

"Riku, listen," he said, washing away his friend-like attitude as he stood tall. "In my eyes, Makoto ain't my only nephew. If I'd do it for Makoto, I'd do it for you, too. Ever since my brother and sister-in-law took 'ya in, I've thought of you as my nephew. Watching y'all become the fine, young men that y'all are today, is a true blessing. I hope 'ya realize that 'ya have people in this family—in this world—who care about 'cha."

Smiling, tears blurred my vision. "I'm starting to."

"Good," he said sharply, as he took a step forward. Dropping his cigarette to the ground, he stepped on it to put it out, then cocked his head over his shoulder. "And don'tcha worry about Makoto. He's also gonna get something nice from good ol' Uncle Ito, but don't go telling him just yet. At least leave one thing as a surprise. I can't go picking favourites now, can I?"

I played along. "Guess not."

"So, 'ya on summer holidays now, or what?" he asked, turning around completely.

Just as I was immersed in the magical moment of the bike, his question had to go and ruin it. With a burdened sigh, I responded, "Kinda."

"What d'ya mean?" Summer break starts around this time, doesn't it?"

"It does, although it won't be much of a 'break' for me. I gotta spend my summer taking supplementary lessons."

"Sounds like an iss-*you*-e. If someone is stuck taking supplementary lessons, it means it's *their* damn fault to begin with."

Rolling my eyes, I shoved my hands into my pockets. "You're really starting to sound a lot like Makoto."

"Correction, my dear nephew, 'ya mean Makoto is starting to sound a lot like *me*. I'm older, wiser, better looking—and don'tcha forget it."

"Yeah, yeah."

⁂

Once I arrived back at my apartment, I sent Hinata a message as promised.

> [LINE Riku Nakajima]: I'm home.

> [LINE Hinata Tachibana]: Okay. Want me to head over?

> [LINE Riku Nakajima]: Everything go okay with your parents?

> [LINE Hinata Tachibana]: Yeah, they believed me. They were happy I made 'new friends.'

Blinded by the urge to see her, I felt a bit guilty that I made Hinata lie on my behalf, even if her lies were seasoned and hers to make.

> [LINE Riku Nakajima]: Then, hurry.

> [LINE Hinata Tachibana]: Everything all right?

> [LINE Riku Nakajima]: Yeah, I just wanna see you.

I was typing faster than my brain could register. Makoto was right, I was so far gone.

I was in love with Hinata.

Chapter Twenty-Nine

A S SOON AS there was a knock on the door, my heart leapt in my chest. Opening it, I saw the person I was dying to see standing right before me. Hinata, holding an abnormally large duffle bag, was dressed casually in jeans and a pink shirt, paired with pink flower earrings.

I knew we had only been apart for a few hours, but it somehow felt like I hadn't seen her in days. This clingy, irrational person that I was becoming was almost unbearable.

I pulled her into the apartment and straight into my arms; I couldn't wait a second longer to hold her. I reached past her to grab her bag and to close the door, then rested my head atop hers and wrapped my arms around her, sighing contently. In return, I felt her arms circle my waist.

"Are you sure everything is all right, Riku?"

"Yeah. Things are better now that you're here, though."

She shifted to look up at me. "Let me see your face."

"No way." I knew I was blushing.

"Please."

"Not happening."

"Oh, come on."

Smiling into her hair, I grudgingly pulled back and tilted my chin down to save myself the headache. "Happy now?"

"Very," she said whimsically, squeezing my core.

I placed a kiss on top of her head before releasing her, then bent to grab her bag off the floor. "C'mon."

Leading her into the multipurpose living area, I placed her bag down near my bed.

"Make yourself at home."

"Sorry for intruding," she said, bowing.

"Stop being so formal. You're not intruding."

"But I am. This isn't my home, so technically I'm intruding."

"Jeez, don't hit me with a technicality."

"What can I say?" she said, shrugging her shoulders.

Rolling my eyes, I dropped the argument because I knew she'd win the debate.

Passing in front of me, Hinata bent down to unzip her bag. "Are you hungry?"

"I could eat," I said, remembering that it was close to an appropriate dinner time. "I don't have much here, so wanna go out and grab something?"

"No need," she said, pulling out a grocery bag from her duffle bag. "I have it covered."

Astonished, I hovered over her to see what else she had in her ridiculously large bag. "Holy shit, how'd you fit all that in there?"

"I already had dinner in mind when you asked me to come over," she answered, standing. "Depending, of course, on what time you were ready for me to come, I made sure to grab one of my bigger travel bags to fit everything." Walking toward the kitchen, she turned back halfway. "Is it okay if I borrow your kitchen?"

In a state of shock, I continued staring down at her bag. "Uh, yeah, sure."

"Excellent."

Peeling my eyes from the mysterious Mary Poppins-like bag, I looked away from it and over at her. "Does this mean I get another home-cooked meal?"

"Yes," she answered, fully taking charge as she rummaged through my cupboards and storage areas in search of things she'd need. "Who else is around to make it for you?"

Watching her move on a mission brought a warm smile to my already flushed face. "No one, just you." *I want it to always be you.*

I followed her into the compact kitchen space.

"Can I help with something?"

"Sure, you can chop the vegetables," she said, placing a cutting board with carrots, potatoes, and onions in front of me. "But make sure to dice them."

Standing beside her at the counter, I held a knife in one hand while staring down at the vegetables presented to me. *Dice? What the fuck does that mean?*

Sensing my struggle, Hinata reformulated her instruction. "Just cut them as evenly as possible into small pieces."

"Why didn't you just say that to begin with?"

"I just assumed you knew what 'dice' meant. It's common cooking terminology."

Giving her the side-eye, I placed my hand with the knife down on the cutting board and put my other hand on my hip. "Well, sooorry if some of us are more uncultured than others."

Laughing, she shook her head and bumped me with her hip. "Come on. More dicing, less talking."

"Yes, ma'am."

We, mostly Hinata, made katsu curry. I didn't have a rice cooker, so Hinata took charge and cooked the rice separately in a regular pot. About forty-five minutes later, dinner was ready. The smell was remarkable, like nothing I had ever smelled before.

Hinata brought our plates to the table while I went to fetch us drinks. Remembering that I only had beer and canned coffee in the fridge, I began wishing that I had listened to all those times Makoto nagged me about the contents of my refrigerator.

"I'm gonna quickly run to the convenience store down the street to buy us some drinks," I said, closing the door of my embarrassingly empty refrigerator. "Any recommendations?"

"You don't need to go to the store on my account. Water is fine with me."

"Uh, I only have tap . . .."

"That's fine. Tokyo water is usually safe to drink, even if it's unfiltered."

Grabbing two cups, I filled them both. *If Makoto saw this, he'd be rolling around on the floor in laughter.* While thinking of Makoto, I recalled the teapot he generously donated to my apartment.

Turning off the tap, I placed both cups on the counter. "I just remembered that Makoto left a teapot here. D'you prefer tea, instead?" As I said those words, I began opening the cupboards and drawers impatiently, wondering where the hell he stored his tea stash.

"Riku," she said, in a tone that demanded my attention.

Turning to her, I shut the drawer I was rummaging through. "Yeah?"

She flashed me with soft, accepting eyes. "Water is fine."

With a gracious smile, I grabbed the cups of water off the counter. "Okay."

At the table, I placed both cups down near our plates, then took my seat beside her. Lifting our hands, we clapped them together. "Thanks for the food," we said, in chorus.

Grabbing a pack of disposable chopsticks that Hinata supplied us with, I broke mine apart. Diving into the curry, my mouth was in heaven.

"This is amazing, Hinata! I know I've said this before, but maaan, you're a great cook. It's hard to believe you when you say your skills aren't 'that good.'"

"Thank you, but it's true. I'm not that good of a cook. I make variations of curry at home for my brothers. Curry is simple, but they seem to like it."

"Well, they're not the only ones. This might just be my new favourite dish," I said, with a beaming smile.

"Thank you. Even if it's not true, I appreciate you saying that."

"It *is* true," I said, looking down at the delicious meal before me. "I dunno why, but a meal that's prepared by someone tastes a lot different than one bought from a store."

"Obviously. The ones bought at convenience stores are prepackaged and usually not fresh."

"It's not just that," I said, shaking my head. "It's the fact that someone took the time to prepare a meal with the hopes that I'll eat it." I held my chopsticks together and tapped the centre of the plate. "You can taste and feel the passion that went into preparing this dish. It's truly amazing."

Feeling Hinata's intense stare, I turned to look at her.

"What?"

"I'm sorry. That was inconsiderate of me," she said, her shoulders concaving.

"What d'you mean? You didn't do or say anything wrong."

"Until now, I didn't quite understand the way you saw and experienced food."

"Nah, don't worry about it. It's stupid."

Hinata placed her hand on my arm. "It's not!" she defended. "Because of your upbringing, you're much more appreciative when something is made for you to enjoy, like food, and I think that's very admirable."

I squeezed her hand tightly. "Thanks, but don't go thinking about it to the point where it ruins your mood." With a faint smile, I shifted my eyes back to my plate. "Let's not let our food get cold. It'd be a waste."

She smiled as if she understood, then picked up her chopsticks once more.

Chapter Thirty

AFTER DINNER, I washed the dishes while Hinata went to shower first, then sat back at the table. Many thoughts coursed through my horny mind as I pictured Hinata naked in my shower.

Calm down, idiot.

After about twenty or so-ish minutes, the bathroom door opened and I saw Hinata step out wearing matching pink, floral print pyjamas. Hinata's hair was also wrapped in an unfamiliar towel.

"The bathroom is free. Sorry, but I borrowed this small towel I found on the shelf. Hope that's okay?"

Rising from the table, I walked toward her and reached out to touch the damp towel with my hand. "I have no idea where this came from?"

Must be another one of Makoto's hidden 'gifts' lying around this apartment. Because, as far as I know, I only own one towel.

I realized that I didn't offer Hinata a clean towel before showering, leaving me to assume that she had used mine. "Uh, sorry," I apologized sheepishly, "I didn't have a chance to wash the towel before letting you use it."

She placed her hand over mine. "Riku, it's fine. You don't need to worry so much about me. I brought my own towel, and pretty much everything else that I'd need to spend the night."

"Except for a hair towel," I teased, still ashamed of how shitty of a boyfriend I was.

That's it. Tomorrow I'm gonna go out and buy like five new towels just for her to use whenever she's here! I gotta make it up to her somehow. And maybe I'll grab one for Makoto, too. But just one—let's not get crazy now.

She smiled. "Everything *except* that."

Noticing her wet hair poking out from the towel, I reached out to grab a few strands, rubbing the tips between my thumb and index finger. "Shit, I don't have a hairdryer."

"Like I said, I have it covered."

"Of course you do," I chuckled, letting go of her hair. "My turn, then. I'll be quick, so sit and relax." Walking past her, I headed to the steamy bathroom.

"Oh, I forgot to mention," she said, panic in her voice. "I think I used all the hot water."

Glancing back, I looked at her eyes glossed with concern.

"Toward the end of my shower, the water started losing its warmth. I'm sorry." Her voice sounded extremely apologetic. "Maybe if you wait an hour, more hot water will become available?" she said, hopeful.

With another chuckle, I continued to the bathroom. "Don't sweat it. The building's old; there's only enough hot water for one person at a time."

"Now I feel bad! Why didn't you tell me?"

I turned and held onto the edge of the door. "It's fine. I was planning on taking a cold shower, anyway. I need to clear my head."

"Clear your head? Of what? Are you *sure* everything is all right? You've been acting weird since earlier."

"That's why I need to clear my head. I'll be out soon," I said, as I shut the door.

I turned on the shower and stepped under the shock inducing, cold water. Facing the stream of water, I lowered my head and placed both hands against the tiled wall. Looking at my arms, I saw goosebumps forming faster than I could blink.

What am I doing? I invited her to stay over, but she's not like the others. I don't want her to be like the others. I want her all to myself, but I don't want her to hate me 'cause of my selfish desires. Fuuuck . . . Balling my hands into fists, I closed my eyes. *Is she nervous? Fuck, man. Why am I thinking so hard about this? It's not like it's the first night we've spent together, and besides, we're dating, right? Isn't wanting to have sex with your girlfriend normal? If so, why do I feel so fuckin' shitty?*

After my shower, I stepped into the hallway with my pathetic towel around my waist and searched for a clean pair of boxer briefs.

"This is a familiar scene."

I jerked my head up. "What is?"

"Same towel, same stance, same search for underwear," she said from where she sat, formally in seiza at the table with a bunch of schoolbooks sprawled out.

"Yeah, yeah," I smirked, as I got the reference, then went back to rummaging through my drawer.

"At least this time the clean ones are in a drawer instead of the floor," she giggled, pointedly.

"That's because the Wonderful Makoto decided to clean my room when he was over the other night." Shaking my head, I couldn't help but crack a smile. "I'd be lost without that guy."

"Oh, Fujimoto was here recently?"

"Sure was."

"Now it all makes sense," she said, bobbing her head.

"What does?"

"I noticed that you and Fujimoto were talking to each other again at school, but I wasn't sure if things were back to normal or if you two were just being civil," she explained. "Does that mean you two patched things up?"

Forgetting that I hadn't updated Hinata about the issue between me and Makoto because of how crazy things had gotten around exams, I smiled at her earnestly. "Yeah."

"That's wonderful, Riku," she said, bringing her hands together and smiling from ear to ear. "I'm really glad to hear that."

Seeing the big smile on Hinata's face stung my chest; my heart began pounding harder. I noticed it before, but Hinata truly was smiling a lot more lately, and I was happy that I had the opportunity to experience it firsthand.

"Me, too."

Finally finding a pair of boxer briefs and sports shorts, I put them on and hung my wet towel in the bathroom next to Hinata's. Returning to the hardworking Hinata at the table, I took a seat beside her and watched her intently.

Without lifting her eyes from the page, she struck up a new conversation. "I want to learn more."

I looked over her shoulder to see what subject she was working on. "Honestly, I dunno if there's much more left for you to learn. You're already at the top of our grade. What more could you possibly ask the teacher for?"

She shot me an unimpressed look. "About you."

"Me?" I asked, taken aback.

"Yes, you," she said, fully turning to face me. "Who you are now and who you were. I want to know what you like and dislike. Everything."

Absorbing the meaning of her request, I looked away. "Everything is a lot, Hinata. I'm not sure you'll ever be ready to handle *everything*."

"Try me."

"Hinata," I said turning back to her, slightly on guard. "It's not that simple."

"I know it's not. Nothing in this world is simple. But still, I want to know, to understand."

Our gazes held, as if we were tethered. My heart tightened with each beat because I knew she was about to fire a set of difficult questions my way.

"Let's start off with something easy."

Raising a brow, I had little faith that her question would be 'easy.'

"Were you ever part of a club at school?"

Would you look at that. That's probably the easiest question she's asked, yet. "Yeah. I used to be part of the soccer club with Makoto. We played soccer a bit in middle school and throughout junior high, right up until last year."

"Why did you stop?"

Taking a deep breath, I answered honestly. "I began working a lot more at my part-time jobs to make money. I didn't wanna rely on the Fujimotos for everything, like food and spending money. They had been supporting me for so long, so I felt it was time to stop using them as a crutch and to start paying them back," I admitted. "I didn't have much time for practices or club duties after that and didn't wanna let the team down by not showing up when they were expecting me to."

"I see," she said, pausing for a moment to process things before pressing on. "Does Fujimoto still play? I haven't really seen him hurry off to practices after school like others do."

"Nah," I said, looking down. "He quit shortly after I did."

"Oh, why?"

Scooting backwards, I leaned my back against my bedframe and brought my knees up to rest my arms over them. Peering up at the ceiling, I heaved a devastated sigh. "He's never given me a proper answer. He always blames it on studying and going to cram school or whatever, but I genuinely believe it was because of me."

"Because of you? Why do you think that?"

"I once overheard him talking to the coach about needing to quit the team in order to 'keep an eye on me,'" I quoted, shrugging my shoulders. "Although the coach didn't quite understand, because I never told any teachers about my home or living situation, he couldn't change Makoto's mind."

Out of my peripheral vision, I watched as Hinata relaxed from her formal seiza position by tucking her legs casually to one side. "It seems you're both very protective of each other."

I grinned. "You could say that."

"Did you spend most of your summers growing up with Fujimoto and his family, or were you always stuck doing supplementary lessons?" she pestered, teasingly.

"Ha-ha. You're hilarious," I said, lowering my head and bringing my hands together over my knees. "As a matter of fact, this is only the *second* time I've been stuck taking supplementary lessons."

"I'm surprised it's only your second."

"Ditto." We both laughed. "But, to answer your question, I spent most of my summers with the Fujimotos in Jōetsu. Makoto's mom is originally from there and his widowed grandma lived there in a big, traditional Japanese home on a huge piece of land. Makoto and I would visit for a couple of weeks to help her with chores and other things around the house."

"You, doing chores? That's hard to imagine."

I snickered at her remark. "I can do chores!"

Hinata took an extended look around the apartment. "Seems like your grossly underpaid maid does most of the work."

I sputtered laughter. "Okay, you caught me. I'm not very good at chores.

But Makoto's grandma never made them feel like chores," I explained, smiling. "She would psych us up by calling them 'missions' and then go on to describe the task with enthusiasm." Squinting my eyes, I thought for a short moment, then put two-and-two together. "Huh, looking back, she really was a sneaky, old lady. Tricking kids into doing her housework for her."

Hinata burst out laughing. "I'd call that being smart."

"Well, all is well," I said, trying to save face, "considering afterwards she'd reward us with ice-cream or watermelon when we were done. We'd sit out on the wide, wraparound engawa of the house and fill our stomachs until we passed out from exhaustion. Man, those were the days."

"Sounds to me like you and Fujimoto were just gullible fools who were easy to persuade," she jabbed.

Placing a hand over my chest, I dropped my jaw and acted devastated. "How dare you? I'll have you know that the ice-cream and watermelon in Jōetsu are outta this world. Phenomenal! Ain't comparable to anything Tokyo has to offer. I'd say it was well worth the child labour."

Hinata giggled. "Oh, really? I'll have to try it sometime."

I held onto Hinata's words, wondering what it would be like to go on a trip with her. Could we really go to Jōetsu? Just the two of us? Together?

"Yeah, you should."

Her laughter faded into a warm smile. "Fujimoto's grandmother sounds kind."

"She was," I said, jokes aside.

"'Was'?"

I brought my gaze to the floor. "Yeah. She passed away two summers ago."

"Oh," Hinata said, a bit alarmed. "I'm sorry, I didn't know."

I lifted my gaze. "Don't be. Makoto's grandma lived a long life. She died of old age; there was nothing to be done."

"I see. Well, I'm glad a remarkable woman, such as herself, was able to live a long life."

"Me, too. She deserved it," I said, dwelling on all the trouble I caused her. "It took some convincing from the Fujimotos, and Makoto's grandma, to get my mom to agree to let me spend those summers in Jōetsu."

She perked up. "Why is that?"

Not wanting to go down the uncomfortable path of another conversation about my mother, I changed the direction of where things were headed, thinking of my own correlated question. "Don'tcha have any friends from previous schools that you spent past summers with? I never hear you talk about them."

"I have one. Her name is Neiko Uchida. It was her cousin who did my tattoo. Remember?"

Interested in my new discovery, I pursued things further in hopes that Hinata would forget about my mother. "Just one?"

It was hard to judge her demeanor as she smiled somewhat sadly. "Just one," she confirmed. "With all the moving around, I stopped trying to make friends."

She spoke of her friend in high regards but continued looking dejected while doing so. I couldn't relate her expression to her explanation. There was something I was missing.

"It seems like you really adore this Uchida person."

"I do."

"Then, how come you look so sad when talking about her?"

Hinata looked at me with slight confusion on her face; her nose twitched as she pursed her lips. "It's not that I'm sad, really."

"Did you two have a falling out or something?"

"No, not particularly. We still keep in touch."

"Then . . . what is it?"

Bringing her knees up, she wrapped her arms around them and pulled them tightly into her chest. "I'm just afraid."

"Of?"

"Losing her."

"Losing her? Why would you lose her?"

"I don't know. I have this feeling in the pit of my stomach that eventually I'll lose everyone important to me. It's happened before, so how can I be so sure it won't happen again?"

This was something that crossed my mind often, as well. I was constantly scared of losing the few people who were closest to me.

"I kinda understand what you mean."

With the sides of her mouth curved up ever so slightly, she leaned her head against her bicep and rested it there, still having full view of my face. "Yeah, I've sensed that about you from the very beginning."

"Oh really, now?" I said, stretching my legs and sitting upright.

"Mhm."

"And how'd you sense that?"

"When I looked into those coffee-black eyes of yours for the first time, I saw it."

"Saw what?"

"Loneliness. The same loneliness I have."

Taken by surprise, my eyes shot open. This wasn't the first time we admitted to being lonely. We had previously discussed the loneliness we felt before meeting each other, but the fact she knew I was lonely before I did, staggered me.

"You could tell that early on, eh? Impressive," I laughed dryly under my breath. *Damaged attracts damaged, I suppose.*

"I guess so."

The weight pressing down on my shoulders seemed to be getting lighter. Dropping my guard was easier to do around her; she was thawing my ice-cold heart every chance she got.

Before having her turn this around on me again, I thought of another question. "What're your plans after graduation? With your grades, I'm sure you're gonna aim to be a doctor or something crazy smart, like Makoto."

With a weak chuckle, and a twisted face, she lifted her head and said, "Don't be foolish."

"Foolish?" I scoffed.

"Yes, foolish. I could never become a doctor."

Surprised by the way she shut the idea down so quickly, I challenged her. "Sure, you can. You have the grades for it."

"My grades aren't the problem."

"Then, what's the problem?"

"I hate hospitals," she stated without hesitation.

Analyzing what she said, I thought back on our conversations. "Because of your birth mom?" I asked, taking a shot in the dark.

"Mhm," she said quietly. "She spent a lot of time in them. Hospitals are associated with sickness and death. If avoidable, I don't want anything to do with them."

"That's fair. I probably wouldn't either," I said, crossing my legs. "What're you gonna do after graduation, then?"

Catching me off guard, a smile from ear-to-ear appeared on her face. "I know it's a bit late, since career surveys have already been handed in, but I just recently decided."

"And . . .?" I asked, waiting in suspense.

"I think I want a career in music," she stated, biting her lip. "I applied to a few college programs last minute that pertain to music and instrumental theory."

Not at all surprised with her decision, I smiled softly. "Makes perfect sense to me."

With the same beaming smile, she said, "It was thanks to you, actually."

"Me?"

"Yes," she confirmed. "As a child, I played in many recitals across Japan, and if my school had a piano, I would spend many lunch breaks playing when no one was around."

Hinata took her right hand and started tapping her fingers against her left arm, as if she were playing the piano right here and now. The movement caught my attention, so I watched her, wondering if she was playing a piece from memory.

"But," she said, adding to her explanation, "when I played for you at my house, I was encased in so much warmth; I had never been so content playing the piano before. I hadn't felt that way in a really long time. Indulging in the sound of the piano, with you sitting beside me, was an everlasting feeling of bliss."

Watching how excited Hinata got as she went on about the piano also brought me joy. "Does that mean you hope to compete professionally?"

She stopped tapping her arm. "I thought about that route, but I think I would prefer to teach piano rather than compete. I feel like teaching children, around Kazumi and Izumi's age, how to read sheet music and scores would be fun."

"Wow," I said, with admiration. "I think that's great. I'm happy I was able to help you figure that out."

"Mhm." She smiled.

I gained more insight into Hinata's newfound dreams and plans for the future as she continued to talk. She dreamt of teaching all things piano out of her own home by potentially opening her own music school where she would give one-on-one lessons or lessons in small class sizes. Her face lit up the whole time she spoke about the future; she was captivating.

With Hinata's excitement brushing off on me, I also got excited for the future. Not knowing where it would lead me, let alone us, I was hoping that our paths would align in one way or another. I wasn't ready to be left behind.

"I like it better when I'm the one asking questions."

"I'm sure you do," I said, nudging her with my foot.

"Hey!" she said, raising her voice as she almost toppled over.

I grinned, indicating I wasn't sorry.

Rolling her eyes, she didn't waste any time with her next question. "What about you? What do you want to do after graduation?"

I shrugged my shoulders. "Nothing in particular. I just wanna get into the workforce as quick as I can, so I can start making money."

"Hmm," she hummed, her mouth shifting to one side in thought. "I knew you would say something like that."

"Disappointed?"

"Why would I be disappointed?" she said, with furrowed brows and a twisted nose.

"Dunno. Maybe you were expecting more from me? Everyone else seems to."

Hinata looked at me for a solid moment, as if studying my face, then said, "Well, from what I've learned, you don't particularly like school. So, I think that it's a perfectly acceptable choice."

Hearing Hinata support the decision I made for myself about my future, brought shock to my expression. Here was someone who got to know me in such a short period of time yet was able to accept me so easily.

"Now," she said, giving me a concentrated glare, "let's get back to a more difficult topic."

With a raised brow, I looked at her.

"Don't think I didn't notice."

"Notice what?"

"That you deliberately avoided answering my prior question."

It was hard to disagree with someone who was right. Diverting my attention elsewhere, I tried to play it off. "I wasn't. I was just curious about your friend, and what you wanted to do after high school, that's all."

"Right," she said, doubtfully. Taking a moment, likely to draft her question, she took a deep breath. "If your mother is in Shinjuku, does that mean you're originally from there, too?"

"What brought that on?" I asked, not wanting Hinata to learn any more than she already had. *Why is she so fixated on my mom?*

"I was thinking back to the first time we were alone in your apartment. You spoke very little about your mother, and what you did say about her wasn't good. Though, based on what you *did* tell me, I understand why. But I'm also curious about your childhood."

The mere mention of my mother always riled my emotions. Trying to settle the resentment stirring up inside me, I answered her blandly. "Yeah. I grew up in Shinjuku, in Kabukichō, specifically."

"I see."

"Hinata," I muttered quietly, turning my head from her. "Please don't ask any more questions about my mom."

"But Riku—"

"Please. I'm begging you."

"If not now, when?"

"I dunno."

"Maybe someday soon?"

"Maybe."

Hinata went silent. I could feel her eyes on my skin. I knew she was worried, and because I didn't want to talk about it was only more cause for her concern, but she respected my wishes regardless.

Silence fell over us for a few awkward minutes, but Hinata wasn't one to sit in silence long.

"What's your blood type?"

"Huh?" I exclaimed. Whipping my head back, I needed to know what brought on *this* question. "Where the hell did that come from?"

"Not sure. Since you didn't want to continue talking about your mother, it was the next question that popped into my head."

I stared at her suspiciously. "You really are a strange one."

"I've been told."

Still not sure what she could possibly want with that knowledge, exposing such information wouldn't hurt. I caved into her nonsense. "Not like it matters, but I'm type A."

"Interesting. I'm type O."

"Why's that interesting?"

"It's just interesting that our blood types are different."

"Of course they'd be different. You're an alien."

I received a powerful kick to the side.

"Ow!"

"Serves you right," she said, scrunching her nose and eyebrows.

Finding her annoyingly cute, I grabbed Hinata by the hand and brought her into my lap. Pulling her legs around me, we sat face-to-face.

"Enough questions," I whispered, leaning into her.

She cupped my face, then searched my eyes. "But I still have more for which I want answers," she replied, her thumb skirting over my bottom lip.

Later," I said, inching my lips closer.

Falling victim to her gorgeous eyes, I went in to claim her lips, and with the response I was hoping for, she kissed me back. We kissed and kissed until the kisses turned into the urge for something more.

Chapter Thirty-One

T HE WALL-MOUNTED AIR conditioning unit that came with the apartment was old and hardly worked, leaving my apartment muggy and hot beyond belief. And it was only getting warmer the closer we got to each other; the sweat dripping off of us was a clear indication.

From the back sliding door, the setting sun filled the apartment, turning everything different shades of orange, including Hinata's soft skin. The windows were open, so one could hear the cicadas singing loudly outside if they stopped to listen. But all I could hear was our laboured breathing, as I stood with Hinata in my arms.

She wrapped her legs around me instinctively, like our bodies were custom fit for each other. With that bold move, Hinata anchored her arms around my neck like reins and took total control—control over me. She had me hooked in more than just a physical way.

Facing the bed, I lowered us down. I straddled her long legs with my own, framing her head with my arms against the pillow.

Everything in this moment was perfect.

I could feel her breath against my face as I feathered kisses down her neck and wondered if she could feel my heart beating fast against her chest. Affectionately, I gazed at her from above. Her eyes glistened up at me from below; she was gorgeous.

"We don't gotta go all the way if you don't want," I said, falling for the sparkle in her eyes. "We can just make out or fool around a bit if you're more comfortable. These moments between us don't always gotta end with sex."

"I want to, though," she said, without much hesitation. "If it's you, Riku, I want to."

I smoothed some hair off her face. "Hmm."

With her floral pyjama shirt bunched up and out of place, Hinata's exposed shoulder came into focus with her bra strap vividly showing. With my index finger, I pushed the strap out of the way and kissed her shoulder multiple times until I left a distinct mark. She lowered her shoulder and tilted her head, granting me full access. When I increased the suction, Hinata released a seductive sigh.

Moving together, I helped Hinata sit up halfway, and she tore her shirt from her body, throwing it to the side. She'd carried on with the pink theme, matching her underwear to her outfit. Her bra wasn't as flashy this time, but that didn't stop me from staring, enthralled at her chest. In all honesty, it didn't matter what she wore; everything looked good on her. But she looked even better naked, under me.

Our lips found each other many times as we undressed. Though she was close enough where I could feel her skin on mine, I wanted her closer. She had consumed everything; my head and my heart only had thoughts and feelings about her.

I moved a strand of hair that had fallen back onto her face, then separated our lips. "Are you sure this's okay?" I asked, terrified of fucking up and hurting her in any possible way. So much so that my mind wouldn't rest until I was assured. "I know this isn't our first time, but I don't wanna force you into doing something you don't wanna do. I mean, I took your virginity—"

"Correction, I *gave* you my virginity, Riku. There's a difference," she stated, with zero confliction. "You need to stop treating me like I'm a fragile piece of glass." She reached for my hand and cupped it on her cheek. "I *want* to do this, and I only ever want to do this with *you*."

I clung onto her words like a rope. She was right. I was treating her as if she were something fragile, something so delicate she'd break if I wasn't careful. But she wasn't. She was far from it.

Fuck, man. How could a heart like hers ever be satisfied with a heart like mine? I have nothing to offer.

"Why'd you seek me out?" I blurted out unintentionally, immediately regretting it.

"Because you make me feel special," she said, almost automatically. "You see me for me. You don't tip-toe around things. You don't hide things. You tell it like it is. I trust you."

My breath hitched. "You . . . trust me?"

"You haven't given me any reason not to."

She knew all the right things to say. I was acutely aware of my feelings for Hinata, of how intertwined she was in my heart, and her words only provided me with additional confirmation.

Not knowing when I looked away from her, I allowed my eyes to make the brave journey back to her face. I brought my other hand up to her cheek and held her face in between my hands as she continued to cup my hand. Brushing her cheek with the pad of my thumb, I gazed upon her beauty for a few moments before placing a gentle kiss on her lips.

I was in love with this girl, something I never dreamed possible. And I'd do everything in my power to hold on to her trust.

Reaching over to the side table, I opened the drawer and pulled out a condom. Tearing it open, I knew that there was no going back. I had already tainted her.

"It shouldn't hurt as much as last time," I said, rolling on the condom, "but let me know if it does, okay? I'll stop."

Nodding her head, Hinata shut her eyes and tilted her chin up to kiss me. Sliding one hand up her neck and into her hair, I cradled her head in my hand as I met her lips.

Slowly, I took Hinata for a second time. But, unlike last time, Hinata guided me, positioning me where she wanted. And I was here for every damn second of it.

This was by far the best sex I had ever had.

Chapter Thirty-Two

LYING ON MY back, refusing to accept it was morning, I turned to where I last remembered seeing Hinata. Searching for her with my hands, her body was missing. My eyes shot open. My bed was empty; she was gone.

Panicking, I flung my body forward and threw the sheets off me. Desperately searching the apartment, I looked toward the kitchen.

"Good morning, Riku. I hope you slept well."

My panic decreased and my breathing regulated as I stared at the magnificent woman standing in my kitchen. She was dressed in a different outfit from yesterday, and busy working away on breakfast. I was taking mental snapshots, storing the images away safely to remember this moment forever.

"I hope you're hungry," she said, bouncing back and forth between the induction stove and counter space. "It's not much, but I'm making onigiri filled with tuna mayo. I figured it was something easy to make before you head off to supplementary lessons."

At a loss for words, I grabbed the bed sheet, wrapped it around my waist, and walked into the kitchen. Coming up beside her, I looked down at the pot of cooked rice as she grabbed small handfuls of it, inserted the filling, then shaped them into triangular balls with her hands.

There was a smile that appeared on her face

as she concentrated on perfecting each ball of onigiri. Snaking my arms around her from behind, I placed my head down on her shoulder.

Lowering her hands, she placed a finished onigiri on a plate off to the side. "Is everything all right, Riku?"

Not knowing how to express how grateful I was for her existence in my life, I replied, "Everything is more than all right."

She wiped her hands on a rag, then threaded her fingers through my hair. "You're distracting me. The onigiri are going to be shaped funny."

Taking a whiff of the tuna mayo scent, I felt a smile poking through. "It smells great. I can't wait to devour them."

"They'll be ready soon. Go put your uniform on while I finish wrapping nori on these. You can't be late on the first day or Kobayashi-sensei will be furious."

"Don't remind me," I said, burying my face deeper in her shoulder. "I'm not looking forward to spending summer with that demon."

Flicking my forehead with her finger, she laughed. "Come on now, it's no one's fault but your own. Get a move on."

"Yes, yes," I said, rolling my eyes playfully while taking a few steps back. "Need help with anything?"

Waving her hand, she shooed me away. "What I *need* is for you to get ready."

I couldn't help but chuckle. "Haaai."

After throwing on a plain, black T-shirt, I put the button up, short sleeve uniform shirt over top. Adjusting my collar, I left the buttons undone and purposely forgot the tie.

I couldn't help but glance over at Hinata scurrying around every chance I had. Unlike my mother, who chose alcohol and drug addiction, Hinata was my addiction, and I was completely immersed in her.

I've thought this before, but I could definitely get used to a sight like this. Waking up each morning to her and going to bed each night with her in my arms, having someone to come home to and discuss how our days went over meals, to go on long bike rides with, and listen to the calming sound of the piano—all sounds so perfect. So perfect with her.

"It's ready," she announced, plating the final onigiri.

She was just about ready to bring the plate of onigiri out to the table when I flew into the kitchen and beat her to it. "Let me at least do something."

With a smile, she pulled back and followed me to the table.

After eating every single onigiri, Hinata and I tidied up and said goodbye. I laughed silently as I watched her head off with her big duffle bag around her shoulders. I insisted on paying for the groceries she brought over, and at first, she flat-out refused my money, but eventually agreed to allow me to pay half.

Arriving at school, I sighed dramatically before taking the first step onto the practically empty school grounds. Dragging myself up each flight of stairs to the classroom, I slid the front door open. To my unpleasant surprise, I saw the face of someone I wasn't expecting to see.

"What're you doing here?" we both said, with matching looks of disgust.

Sitting in the front row was Yamada, two desk spaces away from mine.

"It's no secret that I'd be here for supplementary lessons," I said, eyes narrowed.

"True," Yamada replied, smugly.

Just as I was about to take a step inside and wipe that smug smile off Yamada's face, a demon-like presence crept up behind me.

"Good, you've both arrived."

Behind me stood Kobayashi-sensi, trying to make his way into the room.

"Mr. Nakajima," he said, nodding. "Good morning."

"Morning," I said, giving a grunt of dismissal.

"Please find your seat so we can take attendance."

Attendance? How many people are we expecting?

Eyeing Yamada as I walked past him to my desk, I set my stuff down, begrudgingly. "How many of us are there gonna be? To be honest, I thought it was just gonna be me."

"It's just the two of you," Kobayashi-sensei replied.

"Then, why do we need to take attendance? Obviously, we're both here," I said, fanning out my hand.

"It's school policy," he said with a sigh. "Don't make this difficult, Mr. Nakajima."

"That's dumb," I said, taking my seat.

"Riku, don't start," Kobayashi-sensei said informally, already having enough of my shit. Taking a better look at me, he raised a very sharp brow. "Where's your tie?"

"I forgot it."

He shut his eyes and pinched the bridge of his nose in an attempt to calm himself. He took a deep breath, then released it. "Just because it's summer doesn't mean you can slack off with your uniform." He dropped his hand to his side. "Don't forget your tie tomorrow. Also, button up your shirt."

"Yeah, yeah," I said, rolling my eyes.

As I buttoned up my shirt, Kobayashi-sensei set up his course material for the first lesson. "Make sure you write this down. There will be a test tomorrow," he said, grabbing a piece of chalk off the chalkboard ledge.

"Tomorrow?" Yamada and I both exclaimed in unison.

"You're joking?" I added, my mouth hanging open.

"We have a lot of material to cover and have less than three weeks together," Kobayashi-sensei explained, looking at us over his shoulder. "Did you think you could miss half the semester and get away with easy summer lessons?" He turned back to the board. "Think again, Mr. Nakajima. There will be four tests per week. So, don't fall behind. That goes for you too, Mr. Yamada."

"Yes, sir," Yamada answered.

'Yes, sir.' Kiss ass . . ..

⁂

At the two-and-a-half-hour mark, I dropped my mechanical pencil in the spine of my notebook. "My brain's fried! Do we get a break from this hell?"

Kobayashi-sensei looked at the clock on the wall. "I guess we could break now. We're about halfway through the morning, anyway."

Thank, God!

"The cafeteria and school store are closed, but the vending machines are stocked. You're welcome to wander the halls to stretch your legs," Kobayashi-sensei informed, organizing his things. "I'll be in the teacher's lounge if you need me. We'll meet back in fifteen minutes."

The moment Kobayashi-sensei left the room, my head hit the desk. Hitting it a little harder than expected, I bore the pain inaudibly so Yamada wouldn't notice.

Closing my eyes, I thought about grabbing a canned coffee. *Should I go to the vending machines on the first floor to grab one? Ugh, why does it gotta be so damn far?* While deeply contemplating my coffee crisis, I was rudely interrupted.

"Yo."

Annoyed, I rolled my head on the desk to face him. "What d'you want, Yamada?"

"What the fuck is wrong with you?" he said, brows furrowed into a 'V.' He rotated in his chair to face me.

Thrown by his attitude, I lifted my head. With an arched brow, and an Elvis Presley raised lip, I stared at him. "What d'you mean?"

"I mean, we used to be good, then all of a sudden, you flipped shit on me," he explained, less aggressive. "I used to look up to you, man. What gives?"

I wasn't sure if Yamada was trying to pick a fight with me or mend a friendship, but neither interested me. More friends meant more problems, so at best, I kept acquaintances. "I dunno, man. Lately, you've just been saying and doing shit that's been pissing me off. That's all."

"Like what?"

"Butting into things that y'know nothing about."

"Like, Sato, for instance?"

This guy. "Careful what you say," I warned.

"Okay, then what about Tachibana?"

With Hinata's name mentioned, I stood abruptly. The sound of the chair's legs scraping across the classroom floor pierced my ears. "Careful," I repeated.

"Why?" he grinned. "Are you screwing both of them? Is that it?"

I knew I was at fault for his prying questions, as he only ever witnessed the parts I wished nobody was around to see. But still, I hated the way he spoke about Hinata, as if he knew her. When in fact, he knew *nothing* about her. He didn't deserve to.

Even though there was a desk between us, I flew over it and landed a punch on Yamada's cheek. He fell out of his chair and we both landed on the floor. The desks and chairs around us shuffled about noisily as we roughed each other up.

Remaining on top, I grabbed Yamada's collar and lifted him off the floor.

With his face inches from mine, I stared him right in the eye. "Wipe that smug grin off your fuckin' face, you son of a bitch. Don't you EVER sully Hinata's name like that again, d'you hear me?" I threatened, shaking him back and forth within my grasp.

"Get off me, man!" Yamada said, trying to break free. "Kobayashi-sensei is going to be back soon and then we'll both be in shit!"

Tossing him back down, I rose to my feet. "If I ever hear my girlfriend's name come outta your dirty mouth again, I'll kill you."

"Girlfriend?" he questioned, hung up on the word. "You're dating? Why would Tachibana ever date a guy as unhinged as you? It doesn't make sense." He lifted his head and rubbed his cheek. "But whatever, it was a fucking joke, man. Chill."

"Learn how to tell better jokes."

I brushed off his comment about calling me unhinged and walked to my desk, bringing the chair back so I could take a seat. I found joy in watching Yamada struggle to lift himself back into his chair.

"I can't believe there was ever a moment where I wanted to be like you," Yamada said, with another lousy attempt at hurting my ego.

"Didn't I tell you before? You don't wanna be anything like me."

"I see that now."

Things went silent. Time was ticking and our fifteen-minute break was almost up.

Guess I ain't getting that coffee, after all. Stupid prick. Why, outta all people, did I have to be stuck with him all summer? With a deep, long sigh, another thought crossed my mind. *No, no, it could be worse. I could be stuck here with Sakura.*

Moments later, Kobayashi-sensei slid the front door opened and reentered the room. Stopping, he took a look at the unorganized desks and chairs around us, then focused on Yamada's bruising face.

With a twitch of his brow, he locked eyes with me. "What happened here?"

"Why're you looking at me?" I said, my back against an invisible wall.

"Well, for starters, Yamada's face is extremely red on one side, and the area around his desk looks as if a typhoon hit it."

"And?" I said, trying to fake innocence.

"Riku. Hallway. Now," Kobayashi-sensei demanded, pointing to the door in which he came.

I clicked my tongue, as I rose from my desk forcefully. "This is bullshit! Why do I get blamed for everything?"

"Language," Kobayashi-sensei snapped, escorting me out.

Sliding the door shut behind us, Kobayashi-sensei looked at me with confusion. His angry tick was still apparent, as his eyebrow twitched uncontrollably. He looked furious.

"I can't leave you alone for fifteen minutes without you starting a fight. What's that all about?"

"Sensei, you weren't there. You dunno what really happened."

"Enlighten me," he said, crossing his arms in front of his chest.

"It's fine. It's dealt with and it won't happen again," I said, making two tight fists down at my sides. My fingernails dug into my palms as a reminder to hold my sharp tongue.

"It's *not* fine and it absolutely *won't* happen again," he declared, raising his voice. "Do you know what could happen if Yamada tells his parents about this incident and they escalate it to Principal Koga and the Board of Directors? If that happens, Riku, I can't protect you. You will be on your own. There's a strong chance you won't graduate if you get suspended, or worse, expelled. You're so close to the end, why screw things up now?"

"Protect me?" I questioned, fixating on that specific part of his reprimanding speech.

"Yes, protect you. What do you think I've been doing this entire time?"

I let the words escape under my breath. "Giving me shit."

"Riku," Kobayashi-sensei said, uncrossing his arms and shifting his weight from one foot to the other. "You make things hard for yourself, and for me. I know you think I'm constantly on your case, which may be true, but that's only because I care about your well-being. I care about what happens to you, inside and outside of my classroom. I'm hard on you because without guidance you tend to stray off course."

Hearing the stress in his voice almost made me feel bad that I was such a pain in the ass, until I recalled all those times where he targeted me specifically.

"I'm not a kid who wanders off, Sensei. I can handle myself." I dropped my gaze to my feet. "I always have."

"I know you can. Trust me when I say that I believe you can handle yourself quite well, better than half the students in this school."

"Then, why're you always singling me out?"

"I do that to check up on you," he said, earnestly. "For the most part, I see the students in my classes each and every day. I'm getting pretty good at knowing who is doing okay and who isn't, and who needs extra help. You, Riku," he paused to catch my downward gaze, "need extra help. I don't see you as often as I do the others, so I would like to do everything in my power to try and provide you with that extra bit of help when I can. Anything to help you succeed in a future with which you're satisfied. Sometimes, it only takes one gesture to save somebody."

Thinking back to the comment Hinata made when I first spoke to her up on the roof, about Sensei treating me differently, I began wondering if *this* was what she meant. Taking what Hinata said into consideration, I began seeing Kobayashi-sensei in a new light. Yes, he was annoying beyond belief, and yes, he meddled in things that didn't involve him, but he never had ill or malicious intentions behind anything he did.

I lifted my head. "I believe you," I said, the words drifting off my tongue.

I caught a quick glimpse of Kobayashi-sensei's elated face. He looked relieved.

"Do I have to separate you and Yamada for the remainder of these supplementary lessons?" he asked, with a light scoff.

"No, I'll behave."

"Can you at least tell me what the argument was about?"

It wouldn't make a difference if I told him the truth, but I caught myself hesitating. "It . . . was about Hinata."

"I see. Well, we'll leave it at that. You don't need to tell me," he said, easing off, for once. "After all, I'm a no-good teacher who meddles too much into the personal affairs of his students."

I grunted with another noticeable smirk.

We returned to the classroom to finish the rest of the morning. After Kobayashi-sensei checked on him, Yamada confirmed he was okay and willing to continue with supplementary lessons.

While Kobayashi-sensei proceeded, I daydreamed about taking Hinata to the beach and possibly attending a summer festival with her. All things I never would have considered before her.

But before her didn't matter anymore.

Chapter Thirty-Three

SUPPLEMENTARY LESSONS WITH Kobayashi-sensei and Yamada felt like they lasted a lifetime, while my free time with Hinata and Makoto felt almost non-existent.

Makoto must have been feeling the same way I was because shortly after my longing thoughts, he shot me a message, inviting me to stay over. Making time in our schedules, we were finally able to plan a much-needed guys night. Hearing that I was staying the night, Mrs. Fujimoto made a shit-ton of food, leaving us stuffed. Though we were about to burst, it didn't stop us from eating a bunch of junk food as we played video games all night long.

That same night, Makoto admitted that he was slowly starting to get over Sakura. This news brought me both joy and regret, though I knew it was still a sensitive topic for us. With everything out in the open, all three of us had grown uncomfortably awkward around each other. Makoto and I were on the mend, but Sakura still avoided us at all costs. Rightfully so. There was no doubt in my mind that Makoto could do so much better than Sakura—he deserved it. He didn't need to waste any more time on her.

In between strict studying sessions, Hinata and I attended a summer festival. She wore a floral pink yukata that her mother helped her put on, and it looked extremely cute on her. We walked around the festival grounds for a while, stopping to play games and grab food at stalls. Hinata was especially fond of octopus filled Takoyaki balls, so we had to go back a few times to get more. Her feet grew sore from the geta she regretted wearing, but said it went with the summer festival get-up, so we took frequent breaks.

While we sat, we talked about what we would do with the remainder of our summer and decided to fit in a beach day before it ended. Since I had no experience with honest dating, I found myself growing giddy with excitement as the planned date drew near. I couldn't wait to see Hinata in a swimsuit.

When the day arrived, the sun was out, making it scorching hot—perfect weather for the beach. Hinata wore a striped two-piece with a skirted bottom, causing me to overheat for a completely different reason. I was feeling all sorts of crazy emotions, temptations, and desires. If we hadn't been in public, I would have attacked her right on the sand. As the sun set, we took a walk up and down the shoreline, splashing each other along the way. Using the water as an excuse to touch her, I playfully grabbed her and tossed her into the ocean many times. All in all, it was a good day; a day I was sure to remember forever.

During the remainder of the summer, when I wasn't in supplementary lessons or hanging out with Hinata and Makoto, I was at the shop working on the bike with Uncle Ito and the gang. The guys at the shop had given me my own pair of coveralls with my name sewn onto the lefthand side chest pocket, just like theirs.

After spending many hours working on the bike, I finally decided what I wanted to do after graduation. If Uncle Ito allowed it, I wanted to be a mechanic at his shop. Of course, as a rookie under his wing.

❦

One night, as I was walking Hinata home, I told her about my decision in wanting to become a mechanic.

"That's fantastic, Riku!" she squealed, bringing her hands together as she congratulated me. "I'm thrilled you have a goal to work toward."

"Thanks," I said smiling, her encouragement fueling me.

"Will you go right into it after graduation?"

"That's the plan," I said, running my fingers through my hair and stopping to scratch the back of my head. "I'm hoping to work at Makoto's uncle's shop, if he's okay with it."

Hinata tugged on my hand to get me to tilt toward her. She planted a kiss on my cheek. "I'm so happy for you."

"You're gonna get us in shit if your parents see," I scolded, standing upright. I brought her hand up to my lips and kissed the top of it. "We're right in front of your house, y'know."

"Oh, please. You don't care about that," she scoffed, playfully.

"I do care!" I said, in a loud whisper. "Your dad is an intimidating guy."

She laughed off my concern, and even though I had said it in a teasing manner, there was truth behind my warning.

I took this moment to finally disclose the fact that Uncle Ito had gifted me a motorcycle, and that I had spent most of my days at the shop working on it. Hinata was a bit skeptical at first. She was concerned that once I got my full license and had the bike all fixed up and ready to go, I would severely hurt myself. Though I stated I was experienced in riding smaller and lighter bikes, I tried my best to assure her, and quite frankly convince her, that everything would be fine, hoping that there would eventually come a time when we could ride together.

We stayed outside her house for a while longer, chatting until she deemed it time to head inside. I let her make that decision; I would have stayed outside all night long talking to her if given the chance.

✦

On the second last day of summer break, while I was at work, Hinata sent me a LINE message asking me to call her once I had a second. On my break, I stepped out and dialed her number.

"Hi, Riku."

We didn't call each other often, so hearing her voice on the phone always excited me. "Hey, Hinata."

"Sorry to bother you. I know you're working."

"Nah, it's fine. I'm on break," I reassured. "What's up?"

"My parents want you to come over for dinner."

My eyes bulged. "Dinner? At your house?" I said, my voice going up a few octaves.

"Correct. My parents want to meet my boyfriend."

Oh shit. She told them. I swallowed the lump stuck at the back of my throat. "You told them you had a boyfriend? What did they say?"

"They said I should invite you over for dinner."

They said she should, *or did they demand it?* "Uh, w-when?"

"Tomorrow."

"TOMORROW!" I shouted into the phone, unintentionally.

"Tomorrow," she repeated. "Does that work for you?"

Again, I swallowed, trying to loosen the lump in my throat. "Tomorrow is . . . perfect," I said, reluctantly agreeing to dinner.

"Awesome," she said, her voice joyful. "I'll send you the time over LINE. See you then. Bye-bye."

"Later," I said, hanging up. I stared down at Hinata's name on my phone screen.

Holy fuck.

Chapter Thirty-Four

WHEN I ARRIVED at the Tachibana residence, I stood outside for a few minutes and gazed upon the enormous house through the gate.

It wasn't long ago that I wandered here aimlessly, not realizing what my destination was or who I was seeking.

That day, everything changed.

I buzzed the intercom, then walked up to the door where Hinata greeted me. "Welcome, Riku."

"Pardon the intrusion," I said, more nervous than usual as I stepped inside. *What am I getting so nervous for? It's just Hinata.* Looking down at the plastic bag in my hand, I remembered the gift I brought. "Here." Handing the bag to Hinata, I explained, "It's a cake. I picked it up from a bakery along the way."

"Thank you," she said, accepting the offering. "But you didn't have to bring anything."

"I've never bought a 'thanks for having me' gift before, but Makoto suggested it. I didn't want your parents to look down on me if I showed up empty-handed."

"You're putting too much thought into this," she said with a tender smile.

"Look, Izumi, Mr. Riku is here!" shouted an energetic voice from the top of the stairs.

Looking up from the entryway, as I removed

my sneakers, I saw two, identical little heads poking out from around the corner of the wall upstairs. Full of excitement, Kazumi ran down the stairs, skipping steps along the way, while Izumi came down at a normal pace, holding onto the railing for support. Once Kazumi reached the bottom, he gunned it toward us.

"Mr. Riku, are you really gonna have dinner with us?"

"Hey, how many times do I gotta tell 'ya to drop the 'Mister' bit?" I said, narrowing my brows at the thought of a six-year-old thinking I was old enough to be called 'Mister' anything. "Riku is fine. And yeah, that's the plan."

"Oops!" Kazumi said, covering his mouth with his hands, as if he had said something bad. "Sorry. But, yay! Riku is staying for dinner! Did you hear that, Izumi?" Kazumi said, turning back to his brother. "Riku is gonna eat dinner with us!"

Izumi remained silent.

Izumi definitely has a sister complex. Sorry to disappoint 'ya, little man, but I don't plan on going anywhere. Listening to my inner thoughts, I sighed internally. *Why am I arguing in my head with a little kid? I dunno who's more childish—me or a six-year-old?*

"Kazumi, settle down," Hinata said, sternly.

"What's all the fuss about?" a familiar voice asked from down the hallway. Shortly after, Mr. Tachibana rounded the corner, and within seconds, he locked eyes with me. "Mr. Nakajima, welcome."

I bowed. "Hello again, sir. Thank you for having me."

"Please, raise your head," he said, his voice still very much on guard. "Come in. My wife has finished preparing our meal for tonight."

Lifting my head, I stepped up onto the wooden floor from the raised entryway.

"Riku brought a cake for dessert," Hinata said, likely making sure to acknowledge my good efforts.

"I see," Mr. Tachibana said, shifting his eyes to the bag in his daughter's hand. "Thank you for the thoughtful gift. We'll make sure to eat it for dessert."

"Yay, cake!" Kazumi shouted all the way down the hall.

Hinata smiled at me before following Kazumi and her father. Making sure to walk in between me and Hinata was Izumi, who glared at me from the corner of his eye as he passed in front of me.

This kid hates me.

As I entered the kitchen, there was a woman, presumably in her forties, working diligently behind the counter. Her movements reminded me of Hinata, when she was cooking omurice for me in this same kitchen not that long ago.

The woman stopped shuffling around as soon as she saw me. "Oh! Hello, there," she said, with a gentle, upbeat smile. "I'm Yoko Tachibana, Hinata's mother."

Bowing again, I introduced myself. "Hello, it's nice to meet you. I'm Riku Nakajima," I said with an embarrassing voice crack. "Thank you for having me."

"The pleasure is ours, Nakajima-san," Mrs. Tachibana said, warmly. "Hinata hasn't told us much about you, so I'm eager to get to know you better."

Without much thought, I stood upright and responded with a smile of my own. "That doesn't surprise me. She tends to keep to herself."

Mrs. Tachibana appeared surprised by my comment based on her facial reaction, but also as if she agreed. Then, she smiled again. "That's true."

"Riku brought a cake for dessert," Hinata said, handing the bagged cake to her mother.

"Oh, how sweet of you! But you didn't need to do that."

"It's just something small," I said, tugging on the back of my neck. It was then that I noticed the multiple, steaming hot dishes spread out on the countertops.

I smiled to myself. *Reminds me of a Mrs. Fujimoto dinner.*

"Riku, you can sit beside me," Hinata said, grabbing my hand and directing me to the table.

With the smallest bit of contact, Izumi was quick to pull our hands apart as he cut through us to make his way to his spot at the table.

"Izumi, what's the matter?" Hinata asked, looking to her brother.

Sitting, Izumi turned his head, then grunted, "Hmph."

"NO FAIR!" Kazumi cried. "I wanna sit beside Riku!"

"Kazumi," Mr. Tachibana said firmly. "We don't raise our voices inside."

Covering his mouth again, something Kazumi often did when scolded, he apologized with a muffled voice, "Sorry, Daddy!"

"Kazumi, you can sit beside Riku during dinner, and then I'll sit beside him during dessert. How does that sound?" Hinata compromised.

Kazumi balled his hand into a small fist and pulled it in toward his waist. "Yes!"

"Kazumi," Mr. Tachibana cautioned.

Going to his default, he covered his uncontrollably loudmouth one more time. "Sorry, Daddy."

"Jeez, I didn't know I was so popular," I teased, looking at Hinata.

"Ever since I told them you were coming, Kazumi has been talking about you non-stop," Hinata explained, showing me to my seat.

"Yeah, it's been annoying," Izumi commented, almost under his breath.

"Izumi!" Mrs. Tachibana scolded, with her hands on her hips. "You are being very rude to our guest."

"It's fine. My feelings don't get hurt that easily," I reassured lightheartedly, taking a seat.

"Well, that's good," Mrs. Tachibana said, slowly lowering her hands. "But honestly, I don't know what's gotten into him lately. He's not usually like this."

"So, I've heard," I said, giving Izumi a smirky side-eye as I tucked in my chair.

"I'll help," Hinata suggested, offering her mother assistance.

"Thank you, Hinata," Mrs. Tachibana said, before turning to her husband. "Taichi dear, can I get you to place this on the table?"

"Of course, Yoko darling," Mr. Tachibana said, responding to his wife's request promptly.

Watching Hinata interact with her family brought out another fascinating side to her. At home, she spoke more than she did with anyone at school, but the distance between her and her parents was still apparent.

"Riku," Kazumi called, tugging on my arm, and snapping me back into my surroundings.

"Hmm, what's up?"

"You lied to me!"

"I did?" I said, tilting my head. "About what?"

"I heard that you ARE Nee-san's boyfriend."

"Oh, yeah?" I said, caught off guard. "Who'd 'ya hear that from?"

"Nee-san. She told us."

Looking at Hinata, I scowled at her. *Not only did she tell her parents, but she told her brothers, too.* "Did she now?"

Hinata returned my scowl, then slightly raised one corner of her mouth. "Yup! She said you're her boyfriend now."

Turning back to the table, I crossed eyes with Izumi. "Yeah, well, we are *now*. Last time you asked, we weren't . . . .."

"Is that so," Mr. Tachibana interrupted, placing a few dishes on the table.

"I already explained this," Hinata stated sharply, also placing a dish down.

"Oh, so you aren't a liar?" Kazumi said, his spirits lifted.

"Nope. I'm a truther," I said jokingly, trying to lighten the heaviness accumulating in the room.

When everything was set, everyone sat down to eat. The table was western style and rectangular in shape, so it made sense to have Mr. and Mrs. Tachibana at each end, the twins on one side, and Hinata and I on the other. But, with Kazumi so determined to sit beside me, Hinata sat with Izumi across from me and Kazumi.

Mrs. Tachibana prepared all sorts of dishes, like miso soup, meat and potato stew, ginger pork, hamburger steak, dried mackerel, and curry rice—enough to feed an army. It was exactly like a Fujimoto dinner. Not wanting to offend Mrs. Tachibana, I made an effort to try a bit of everything, though by the end, I was ready to explode and feared I would have no room for air, let alone dessert.

During dinner, light conversation was made. But during dessert, after Kazumi and Hinata had switched places, Mrs. Tachibana was first to dive into the real reason behind this organized dinner.

"So, Nakajima-san—"

"Please, call me Riku. I'm not used to such formalities," I said, unintentionally interrupting her, but wanting to get formalities out of the way.

"Riku, then. How did you and Hinata meet?"

"They're in the same class, Yoko darling," Mr. Tachibana answered for me as he sipped sake from his sakazuki cup.

"Good gracious, let the boy speak for himself," Mrs. Tachibana defended.

"I asked *him* the question, not *you*." Shaking her head, Mrs. Tachibana went on. "Sorry, Riku. So, you're in the same class? That's exciting."

"Yeah," I said gingerly, not wanting to reveal that I only recently started attending school more frequently.

Smiling earnestly, she continued. "What are your plans for after high school? Are you attending college or university?"

Knowing this was an interrogation session masked as a dinner, I'd come prepared to answer difficult questions. I didn't want Hinata's parents to disapprove of our relationship. There was no room for lies.

"I plan to go straight into the workforce, actually," I admitted. Resting my hands on top of my thighs, I straightened my back to better explain myself. "School has never been something I enjoyed. I'd like to become a mechanic, after working through an apprenticeship, that is. I wanna start earning money quickly so I can support myself and repay those who have helped me get where I am."

"Interesting," Mrs. Tachibana said, with a mildly judgmental tone. "What do your parents think of your decision?"

Hinata jumped to my defense. "Um, Mother—"

"It's okay, Hinata," I stopped her. Peering at Hinata from the corner of my eye, I grabbed her hand underneath the table. Focusing my attention back on Mrs. Tachibana, I continued. "I appreciate the concern, Mrs. Tachibana, but I don't have parents who have input in my life."

The gentle smile Mrs. Tachibana wore up until now faded and was replaced with a confounded look as she knitted her brows. "Whatever do you mean? There must be at least one parent who watches over you, no?"

Drawing a deep breath, I pressed on. "I live alone. I have for a while now. I dunno who my dad is, and my mom . . .," I said dimly, not knowing how to describe her, "well, she's alive, but she's incapable of looking after me."

"Incapable?" Mrs. Tachibana questioned, sadness lingering in her tone as the word left her lips.

"Yes," I answered vaguely, with a gloomy smile. "But I have a good support system backing me in other ways."

Mrs. Tachibana went silent for a moment, eventually continuing. "This is a topic I would like to revisit later, if you don't mind, Riku?"

"Yes, ma'am," I said, releasing Hinata's hand from my hidden, firm grip.

I could sense Hinata's gaze on me, but I couldn't bring myself to look at her. I wasn't sure if I made things worse or better. If, and when, Mr. and Mrs. Tachibana learned about my situation, would they allow me to continue dating their daughter?

That was the only thought plaguing my mind.

"I'm done my cake!" Kazumi announced, springing out of his chair. He was oblivious to the grownup conversation taking place around him. "Mommy, Daddy, can Izumi and I go play in our room?"

"That's fine, but make sure to clean up first," Mrs. Tachibana replied.

"Okay," the twins said, simultaneously.

"Riku," Kazumi called out, after tucking in his chair, "you come, too!"

"Maybe later. I'm gonna help wash the dishes first," I said standing, collecting the empty plates from the table.

"Riku, you don't need to do that. You're a guest," Mrs. Tachibana said, quickly jumping to stop me.

"It's fine," I said, signally her to remain seated. "I want to. It's the least I can do."

"I'll help him," Hinata said, rising from her chair.

"Well, if you both insist." Mrs. Tachibana smiled before reclaiming her seat. "Thank you. I appreciate and will accept your offer."

As Hinata and I brought the dirty dishes to the sink, the boys took off upstairs.

"It will be quicker if we place the dishes in the dishwasher," she suggested.

Even though I always bought food in takeout containers to avoid washing dishes, today I was excited to wash them by hand. "I know, but this gives us some time alone, away from your parents. I gotta rebuild my stamina so I can face more of their questions."

Hinata nodded. "I'm sorry about them," she said, watching me pre-rinse the dishes. "I didn't expect my mother's first round of questions to be so personal."

"I did."

"You did?"

"Yeah. I know exactly why I was invited. Your parents wanna find out what kinda guy you're dating."

After washing the first dish, I handed it to her so that she could dry it with a cloth. "I guess you could be right."

"Of course, I'm right," I said, with a spiteful grin.

Bumping me with her hip, she almost sent me flying. "Make sure you wash those dishes properly. Slacker."

"Yeah, yeah."

While Hinata and I worked on the pile of dishes, I kept tabs on Mr. and Mrs. Tachibana, who were peacefully sipping tea at the table.

"You know," Hinata commenced, attentively drying a cup, "deep down, I was excited to hear your answer to my mother's question. I, too, want to learn more about your mother."

Not taking my surroundings into consideration, I stopped washing and thoughtlessly dropped my head on Hinata's shoulder. "I know. I'm sorry."

With a damp hand, Hinata ran her fingers through my hair, pushing back my bangs. "'Someday,' right?"

"I'm pretty sure that 'someday' is gonna be today. I don't think your parents will drop that topic as easily as you."

"Hmm."

Realizing what I was doing, with Hinata's parents in the same room, I lifted my head and resumed my washing duties. "Let's finish these quickly."

Chapter Thirty-Five

AFTER DISHES, HINATA and I returned to the kitchen table where Mr. and Mrs. Tachibana were now sitting across from us in the twins' usual spots. Hinata took a moment to pour a cup of tea for me and for herself, then topped up her parents' cups.

"Sorry to put you on the spot, Riku, but now that the twins are upstairs, I can't help but fixate on where we left off regarding your mother," Mrs. Tachibana said.

Trying to smile politely, I reached for Hinata's hand under the table again. "Sorry for being vague," I said, dropping my gaze. "It's just, I don't particularly like talking about my mom or my past. But, to show you that I'm serious about your daughter, I'll answer whatever questions you have."

I felt Hinata squeeze my hand under the table. Without trying to make things obvious, I avoided looking at Hinata and instead squeezed her hand back.

Taking in a full breath, I found the courage to look up at the wondering eyes surrounding the table. I explained the type of person my mother was to Hinata's parents and anticipated what their reactions would be once I relinquished the unpleasantries of my past. Their eyes grew wide from shock while their lips pursed together, as if unsure of what to say.

Not wanting to give them the chance to

misunderstand what kind of person I was, based on my upbringing, I went on to explain my childhood, including the Fujimotos involvement.

Feeling the judgement, I rose to my feet and bowed instinctively toward Mr. and Mrs. Tachibana. "Please allow me to continue dating your daughter. I know I have, and come from, nothing, but I'm dating Hinata earnestly. Out of everything in my pathetic life, Hinata has given me purpose. I treasure her and promise to always cherish her properly."

A long silence filled the room. Still bowing, unable to see their faces, I held my stance until my actions were acknowledged by Mr. and Mrs. Tachibana.

"Riku," Mrs. Tachibana spoke first, "lift your head."

Holding my breath, I straightened up, with my arms pinned at my sides.

"Please, retake your seat," Mrs. Tachibana said, gesturing toward the chair I unintentionally pushed back during my confession.

I sat back down. Tension suffocated me as I stared blankly at the steaming cup of tea before me.

"I believe you have blown us away with your story," Mr. Tachibana said, looking to his wife who returned his empathetic glance.

Shifting her eyes back to me, Mrs. Tachibana nodded her head distractedly. "I don't believe we were expecting you to say things to such an extent."

"At any point, did your mother regain custody of you?" Mr. Tachibana inquired.

"She did, but only briefly," I explained. "She was sent to rehab, and was released after completing treatment, but she ended up relapsing shortly after I returned home."

"I see," was all Mr. Tachibana replied with.

"Was your mother ever abusive to you?" Mrs. Tachibana asked seconds after, signs of hope wavering in her glossy eyes.

"Riku has cigarette burn marks all along his back and a scar on his head," Hinata asserted in my place.

My chest and throat both tightened. Now that Hinata told her parents about the scars I had kept hidden my entire life, there wasn't really anything left to say. I wasn't upset that she told them; it was something I had planned on sharing if asked. But it felt like a Band-Aid had been ripped off, exposing a never healing wound.

The present me had already overcome so many obstacles that I feared the future me would be burdened with forever, shaping the person I *would* become, *could* become. Being involved with somebody, and not having the slightest control over the future, was insanely scary.

Mrs. Tachibana grew teary-eyed. "Oh, my goodness. You poor thing."

Not knowing how to respond, I simply said, "I'm sorry."

"Riku," Hinata said determinedly, grabbing my attention, "you have nothing to be sorry about."

"Hinata is right, Riku," Mrs. Tachibana said, wiping the tears trickling from her eyes. "You did nothing wrong."

"What about grandparents?" Mr. Tachibana cut in. "Do you have any you can rely on?"

"None that I'm aware of," I said.

Mrs. Tachibana followed suit. "That's enough for today. Thank you for answering our tough questions, Riku. We're sorry if this was painful for you to discuss."

"It's fine," I said, looking to Hinata. "It was a conversation I was prepared to have with all of you."

"We will allow you to continue seeing our daughter, but . . .," Mr. Tachibana paused to look at his wife, "we'll need to review some things before we accept you as her boyfriend."

"Dear?" Mrs. Tachibana said with a twisted face, likely confused by her husband's roundabout affirmation.

"I understand," I said, bowing my head.

"Hinata," Mr. Tachibana said.

Hinata looked at her father. "Yes?"

"Why don't you and Riku make your way to the study. Your mother and I have a few things to discuss."

"Yes, sir," Hinata said with slumped shoulders, appearing dejected as she rose from the table.

Following Hinata's lead, I excused myself.

I couldn't help but think about the outcome of what Hinata's parents' final decision would be. Their daughter had a future full of potential ahead of her, and even though I was trying to be better, I was an obstacle slowing her down.

Chapter Thirty-Six

I N THE STUDY, Hinata and I sat silently on one of the couches in the middle of the room.

My wandering eyes landed on the piano in the corner. "Hey, could you play for me?"

"Right now?"

"Yeah."

"Sure," she said, a bit uncertain as she rose to her feet.

We sat on the piano bench, shoulder-to-shoulder. I watched as Hinata straightened her back and gracefully placed her fingertips upon the tops of the keys. Before pressing down on them, she turned to me.

"Why now, all of a sudden?"

"Dunno," I said, staring at her hands. "I just feel like now's the perfect time."

Without any further questions, she cracked her knuckles, then began playing.

The sound filled my ears.

Closing my eyes, I listened to the music Hinata's fingers composed, every note more beautiful than the last. The dynamic of her playing was powerful, leaving me breathless.

I opened my eyes to find hers closed. *I wonder what she thinks about when she plays.*

Hinata's sonorous playing didn't last long, as her parents broke into the room about a minute in. Hinata pulled her hands back and turned to look at them. I glanced at Mr. and Mrs. Tachibana who froze at the archway, standing idly with their mouths hanging open.

Mr. Tachibana's eyes shifted back and forth between his daughter and the piano. "Hinata."

"Yes?"

"You haven't played the piano in years, so why . . ." Mr. Tachibana's voice trailed off.

"I thought about picking it back up again," she said, smiling as she glanced at me. "Riku also seems to enjoy my piano playing. He requested to hear me play."

"Did he now?" Mr. Tachibana said, somewhat warily.

"He did."

"How many other times has he heard you play?" Mr. Tachibana seemed to be testing his daughter, trying to figure out if she had invited me over without her parents' consent—which she had.

Sweating, I waited for Hinata's unpredictable answer. This could really go only one of two ways.

"He's overheard me playing in the music room at school. Sometimes, I play for him during our lunch break."

Liar. I said in my head, trying to hold back a tiny smirk.

"I see," Mr. Tachibana said, more relaxed.

"It was lovely to hear you play again, even if it was just for a moment," Mrs. Tachibana added. "I wish you would play more often."

"I think I just might," Hinata said, grinning joyously.

A smile was drawn on Mrs. Tachibana's face from her daughter's promising response. "Wonderful."

"Riku," Mr. Tachibana called, breaking up the happy moment.

"Yes, sir?" I answered, standing up beside the piano.

"I believe it's time for you to go," he said, turning around. "I'll walk you to the station."

"Wait, why?" Hinata broke in. "What did you two discuss in the kitchen?"

"Yes, sir," I said, again, masking her inquiry.

"Riku?" she said faintly, standing to match me.

Ashamed to look at her, I forced my gaze forward upon Mr. Tachibana's back as he left the room. "Goodnight, Hinata," I said, leaving many words lodged in my throat and a ping of pain tugging at my heart.

Shit, I really thought things went okay. Or maybe I was blindsided by hope. Either way, I fucked things up, like always.

Walking briskly to catch up with Mr. Tachibana, I made my way to the entrance to put on my shoes. Stepping down from the raised entryway, I slipped my sneakers on as quickly as possible, hastily fixing the backs of my shoes around my heel with my index finger.

Hinata raced to meet us at the door with Mrs. Tachibana following suit. This time, I couldn't avoid Hinata's eyes as they locked on mine; they were wide and conflicted.

"Thank you for having me. Dinner was lovely," I said, bowing with a straight back.

"It was our pleasure," Mrs. Tachibana answered reluctantly.

Without another word, Mr. Tachibana and I walked out the door.

Descending the steps and walking through the front gate, Mr. Tachibana took the lead as we headed down the street. He walked a few steps ahead, leaving me to watch his authoritative figure as he strolled along.

"As I'm sure you are aware by now, Riku, Hinata isn't our biological daughter," he said, without looking back to face me. "We adopted her when she was eight years old. The fact that we are not related by blood cannot be overlooked, but nevertheless, we treat and think of Hinata as our own."

I could feel the stress ensnared in his tone.

"My wife and I have known Hinata since birth; her biological father and I were good friends, you see," he stated, stopping to look both ways before using the crosswalk. "Riku," he started up again, "I know you and Hinata share similarities; understandably so, your pasts walk a similar path. The unfortunate difference is Hinata came from a household filled with unconditional love, and I'm saddened to hear that yours was not the same. Truthfully, I am, but . . .," he paused, probably trying to compile his words into a well formulated sentence, "I fear that the relationship you two have is not healthy nor sustainable."

I remained silent, but a bubble of anger festered within me from his comments.

Not healthy? Not sustainable?

"Over the years, my wife and I have tried our best to shelter Hinata from the negativity the word 'adoption' sometimes carries," he shared. "When she came to us, she was old enough to understand, so we have never had to lie to her. We have always believed that if we are able to make Hinata feel comfortable at home, then maybe she can accept that she is an important part of our family. We care for her deeply and hope that our actions reflect just that." He sighed. "Hinata tends to pull back and keep to herself, so sometimes it's hard to know what she is truly thinking or feeling. We don't want her traumatizing past to affect her bright future." Mr. Tachibana slowed his pace to match mine. With power in his voice, he turned to me. "Riku, do you understand what it is that I'm trying to say?"

His voice had an edge to it that I didn't particularly care for. I cleared my throat and stopped walking. Mr. Tachibana did the same.

"Mr. Tachibana," I said, trying to keep a cool head as the knots in my chest twisted tighter, "I understand what you're trying to get at, but I don't understand what you mean by 'unhealthy' and 'unsustainable.'"

At this point, my heart was in my throat, and no amount of swallowing would put it back in place.

"I know I'm not who you expected Hinata to be with," I said, looking away, my self-confidence diminishing. "But I've come to genuinely care for her. I can't help but be drawn to her. She entered my life at full force, taking me by storm, and I can't let go of her now." I inhaled deeply, then brought my eyes back to him. "Hinata brings out the best in me; I'm a better person with her around. I need her in my life," I confessed.

Mr. Tachibana shook his head. "That's exactly what I'm talking about."

Standing beside me, off on the side of the road, Mr. Tachibana stared at me with cold eyes. With such pressing matters at hand, I felt myself slipping, essentially losing this battle.

Waiting for a more detailed explanation, I remained quiet.

"You believe Hinata can *fix* you by healing your past; I see you grasping onto that hope in the way you speak. I can't—no—I *won't* let Hinata be used in such a manner," he declared, protectively.

His demeanor made me feel small; I cowered from the realization.

Mr. Tachibana shifted his weight from one foot to the other before placing his hand on his hips. "I'm sorry for being punitive," he said, the harshness clearing from his tone, "but Hinata has experienced so much heartache; I don't want her to be trapped in this continuous cycle of hardship."

There it was. All laid out. A clear definition of being *broken*. I always knew I was unrepairable, those who tried to fix me were just wasting their time, but deep down, I had hope.

Hinata gave me that hope.

Picking up the pace again, Mr. Tachibana continued down the street, stopping before rounding the corner. "Come on," he directed, looking over his shoulder. "The station is still a ways away, and I have one final matter to discuss with you."

I wanted to further explain myself, to show him I could do better—be better—but I didn't know what to say to change his mind. He saw me one way, and no matter what I said, his opinion would remain the same. That's how most adults functioned; they were judgmental and unforgiving. But truthfully, if I were him, I wouldn't want my daughter dating a guy like me, either.

Passing a few sets of lights, the station was in sight, but Mr. Tachibana pulled me out of the way of the heavy foot traffic.

"Listen Riku, I don't dislike you. I do believe that you are a decent, young man. Hinata sees something in you, therefore, I know you must demonstrate upstanding qualities."

I kept my eyes levelled with his. Listening. Waiting. He already shit all over me, what else could he possibly dump on me to make me feel worse?

He cleared his throat and crossed his arms over his chest. "One of the main reasons I need you to end your relationship with Hinata, before things get too serious, is because our family is moving."

"What?" Was all I could mutter as I tried to process what he confessed. My eyes froze on his lips as I tried to read them.

"We haven't told Hinata yet, so please refrain from mentioning this to her until we get the chance, but we will be leaving Tokyo at the end of October."

What?

"I received notice from work yesterday that I'll be made to transfer, again.

This is one of the main reasons why my wife and I believe it isn't wise for you and Hinata to continue your relationship. At your age, having a long-distance relationship is difficult, especially out of country. The expenses to travel from Japan to France, and vice versa, will be costly."

"FRANCE?" I spouted.

"Yes. You heard correctly," he said with conviction, jerking his head back in response to my sudden outburst. "We will be moving to France. Since my company is demanding it of me, I cannot refuse the offer."

My stomach rolled, leaving me absolutely gutted, while my ears rang loudly, blocking out all sound around me. The only thing I could sense was the vibration of the rumbling underground metro beneath my feet.

What did he mean 'France'? How could he take Hinata to France? Didn't Mr. Tachibana understand that his daughter hated moving? Didn't he understand that she could never hold onto friendships because their family was constantly uprooting? Did she even know how to speak French?

After rediscovering her love for the piano, and figuring out what she wanted to pursue after high school, how could Mr. Tachibana not see that Hinata was happy here? Here, in Tokyo.

How could he take her away from the things she liked? From *me*?

"Mr. Tachibana, you can't take Hinata to France," I said, beside myself. "Doesn't she get a say in any of this?"

"Riku, I know this is hard for you—"

"YOU CAN'T!" I snapped.

I knew it was rude to cut off Mr. Tachibana and raise my voice to him, but I had to make sure he understood what he was saying.

"For one, Hinata has two semesters of high school left. This is a crucial time in her academic career!" Not realizing my voice was gradually getting louder, I continued at the same unintentional, high level. "These two semesters will determine what college Hinata is able to attend. Entrance exams are just around the corner! Does none of that matter?" I asked, in one jumbled breath.

"Riku," he said, his voice flat.

"Yes?" I said, finally taking a breath, allowing him the chance to speak.

"These are all valid concerns; I commend you for thinking so diligently about Hinata and her future. But are those reasons fueled by your thoughtfulness toward her or by selfish emotions?"

My eyebrows narrowed and the blood in my veins coursed vigorously. There was an agonizing pain within my chest; it was heavy and constricting.

How could he be so nonchalant about something this big?

This move wouldn't be like the others; the Tachibanas would be made to relocate to Europe, not just another town or city here in Japan. This wouldn't just change my relationship with Hinata, this would change and reshape her life entirely.

Sighing, Mr. Tachibana shook his head. "I'll be taking my leave, then." Straightening out his casual, button up shirt, he readjusted his rolled-up sleeves. "I suggest you end things quickly with my daughter before either of you gets hurt. And, as I mentioned before, please do not speak of this matter with Hinata. My wife and I will find the right time to discuss it with her on our own terms."

My mind was blank. Couldn't he see it was already too late not to get hurt? Not to get too attached? Hinata had already taken the spot of the most important person in my life.

Trying to make sense of his words, I replayed them in my head.

The right time? When will that be? When's 'the right time' to talk about something like this? What am I supposed to say to Hinata when she asks what her dad and I discussed? What the fuck, man!

"Take care of yourself, Riku."

I was pulled back into the present moment as Mr. Tachibana turned his back and left. I was afraid that if I went after him, my knees would buckle.

I felt my world slowly shrinking and turning black, once again. Hinata was the one who grabbed me out of the pits of darkness, bringing me into the clarity of the light. Until I met her, all I did was survive; she allowed me to experience life by living. Now, I was forced to go back to a life without my most precious person.

I didn't want to go back to a life without Hinata. Did I even remember how?

That night, Hinata blew up my phone with messages asking me what went down with her father. I didn't know what to do. I couldn't bring myself to end things. I didn't want to. God, I didn't want to.

So, like the coward I was, I ignored Hinata's messages and calls.

What now? What do I fuckin' do now?

Chapter Thirty-Seven

SUPPLEMENTARY LESSONS WERE over and done with, and September marked the arrival of second semester. Instead of living up to everyone's expectations of me, I reverted back to my old routine of skipping school.

From the LINE messages Hinata sent, it seemed like her parents had yet to tell her about the move. Until they did, I decided not to have contact with her. Hinata was able to get information out of me easily, so I didn't want to be stuck in a situation, especially at school, where I spilled such a secret.

Makoto also sent multiple messages, nagging me about skipping the first day of second semester, even though it was just a half day.

While school was in session, I kept myself cooped up inside my humid apartment. Though I wasn't too stressed about upsetting Makoto, I was anxious about worrying Hinata with my silence. Never in my life had I been worried about upsetting a girl with my lack of communication, until now.

With my nerves taking control, I went to the fridge to grab a cold coffee, but my hand did a detour to a cold beer instead. With a beer in hand, I took the lighter and pack of cigarettes, ones I swore I'd dispose of, then headed to the back door.

Stepping out onto the balcony, I cracked open the can of beer, took a sip, then set it down on the small table. Right after, I took a cigarette out of the pack and placed it in between my lips, cupping it with my hands to light it. I inhaled and exhaled the familiar taste, as if I had never attempted to quit.

Leaning over the railing, I looked out over the active streets and neighbouring apartment complexes. Summer break was over, and I was confronted with the realism of everyday life. As I thought back to the fun summer moments that I shared with Hinata, depression settled in. Hinata quickly became important to me, and I didn't want to lose someone so significant. What I had with her, I would never have with someone else.

Stubbing out the cigarette in the ashtray as it neared its end, I couldn't deny that I missed smoking, further proving Mr. Tachibana's point. Guzzling the remainder of my now lukewarm beer, I crushed the empty can between my hands.

Dying from the heat, I ventured back inside, praying today would be one of the days the air conditioner chose to work properly.

Grabbing the air conditioner remote, I pointed it up at the wall-mounted unit. *C'mon aircon, you can do it.* Hearing the motor of the air conditioner kicking on, I held my breath with the hopes of cool air spewing out. But, like everything else in my life, I was let down and came to terms with the fact that it was, indeed, broken.

I searched Uncle Ito's name within my contacts, then put the phone to my ear.

"Oi, Riku. What's going on, little man?"

"Hey, Uncle Ito. Sorry to bother you, but the aircon in my apartment ain't working. I can hear the motor turning inside the unit, but no air's coming out. It's been finicky for the last little while, but I never got around to telling you about it."

"Ahhh, I see. That aircon *is* pretty old. I think it's the original one that came with the unit when I took over the complex," he explained. "No worries, little man. I'll get a technician out there to install a new one for 'ya. You gonna be home all day? I might be able to get someone to go check it out today."

"Yeah, that would—" I began, but got distracted by a loud knock at the door.

In that moment, my heart jumped when I thought about the possibility of it being Hinata. *It could be Makoto, though . . . The chances of that are also pretty good, right?*

Cautiously walking toward the door, I propped my phone in the crook of my neck, then reached for the handle and opened it. Like I feared, it was Hinata.

"Riku?" Uncle Ito called into my ear. "Still there, kid?"

Staring at Hinata in awe, I fumbled my words. "Uh, yeah, that's fine. Listen Uncle Ito, I, uh, gotta go."

"Oi, Riku, hold on a—"

Cutting the call short, my unwavering eyes were locked on the important woman standing in front of me.

"Hello, Riku," she said. I could tell that she was pissed by her tone alone.

"Hello, Hinata."

"May I come in?" she asked, ready to take a step forward.

I tugged on the back of my neck in anguish, reluctant to step aside. "I don't . . . think that's a good idea."

She stopped. "And why is that?"

Knowing that Hinata didn't drop things easily, I hung my head. "Please, Hinata. You shouldn't be here. You gotta leave."

"Riku, what did you and my father discuss the night of the dinner? You've been ignoring me ever since then, and I want to know why."

I continued to avoid her piercing gaze. "What has your dad said to you about that night?"

"He refuses to elaborate on the details, stating that he'll have a discussion with me later this week. All he said was that you and I should spend some time apart."

I knew I was a coward, but Mr. Tachibana was no better.

Angry about the way the situation was being handled, the urge to tell Hinata about her father's transfer was strong. I struggled to keep my lips sealed. "Then, let's wait until the end of the week. Once you and your parents talk, we'll have a talk of our own."

"No."

Flicking my head up, I immediately caught Hinata's wicked gleam. "No?"

"You heard me. No," she said, forcefully. "I'm sick of being kept in the dark. I want to know what's going on and I want *you* to tell me. Now."

"Hinata . . .."

"Now, Riku."

"Hinata, I can't."

"You can, and you will," she said, finally taking that step forward.

If things weren't bad enough, now Hinata was backing me into a corner. Finding it hard to keep everything bottled up, my temper got the better of me. "Hinata, stop!"

Looking up at me, she pursed her lips together.

"I'm not kidding around anymore," I snapped, nostrils flared. "I promised not to say anything, so I can't fuckin' tell you. It's not my place."

I could see the intense anger radiating from Hinata's eyes. The way she looked at me caused my heart rate to increase. I had never seen Hinata angry before. This was a whole new side to her, and I didn't like being on the receiving end.

Turning sharply on her heel, Hinata walked down the sheltered, outer hallway toward the stairway. Once she rounded the corner, I went back into my apartment and slammed the door behind me.

Staring at the closed door, my heart pounded aggressively. Losing control, I punched the back of the door with all my might, leaving a minor dent. But with the adrenaline and alcohol running through me, I had yet to feel the aftermath of pain in my now bleeding hand.

With my back against the door, I leaned into it for support and used it to slink down until I hit the floor. Sitting with my legs bunched up, I rested my elbows on my knees. Running my fingers through my hair, pulling it all back, I sat in the shadow of the entryway.

THIS IS FUCKIN' BULLSHIT!

Chapter Thirty-Eight

THE REST OF the day dragged on with no word from Hinata. This was the quietest my phone had been in a while.

The technician that Uncle Ito mentioned came by and installed a new air conditioning unit, leaving my small apartment fresh and cool, the only positive thing that had happened lately.

I laid shirtless and sprawled back on my bed. Drained from all the events that took place in the same day, I passed out.

When I awoke from my unplanned nap, I was faced with a moonlit apartment.

How long was I out?

Scratching my head, I sat up and checked my phone for the time. It read: 9:38 p.m.

Holy crap! I was asleep for almost five hours! Shiiit . . . Good thing I didn't have work tonight.

Reaching for the cigarettes, I clutched them in my hand as I sluggishly got up. Sticking a cigarette in my mouth, I headed to the back door. As I was about to take a step outside, there was another knock at the front. Turning to look down the darkened hallway toward the entrance, I studied the door.

There's no way it can be Hinata this time.

Changing direction, I removed the cigarette from my mouth and placed it back inside the pack, then tucked it in my pocket with the lighter. When I went to the front door, I was surprised to see who was on the other side.

"Hinata . . .?"

She was standing on my doorstep, again, but this time with her large duffle bag.

I threw my head back, rolling my neck with a sigh. "What're you doing back here?"

With no response, I took a better look at her face. Her eyes were red and puffy, all signs that she had been crying, and her hands were clenched tightly around the strap of the duffle bag.

"Hinata?" I said again, this time more softly.

"Riku, please let me stay here," she said, with a quiver in her voice.

"Hinata, wh—"

"You knew?"

I froze. "Knew . . . what?"

Tears formed behind her eyes. "Riku, I don't want to go to France."

The helpless look on her face was enough to do me in. Rubbing my hands down my face, I dropped my hostile front.

They told her.

Pulling her into my chest, I kissed the side of her head. "I also don't want you to go."

I held Hinata for a short moment before bringing her into my apartment. Once inside, I shut the door behind us, then continued embracing her. I felt Hinata's body tremble as I tried to console her. Pulling away for a second, I lifted her chin to have a full view of her tear-stained cheeks. My eyes fell onto hers; they were screaming for comfort, for familiarity. Two things I knew I could provide her with.

Wiping her eyes with my fingertips, I dried the tears from her face.

The power this woman had over me was insane. I didn't want her to just idly pass time in my arms. I loved the shit out of Hinata, and it was terrifying to admit how crazy I was about her because, at any moment, I knew how easy it could be for her to disappear.

Moving away from the entrance, I guided Hinata to my bed while I went to hunt for Makoto's tea.

While Hinata sat with her hands clasped together, I lit a cigarette from the pack in my pocket and watched the water as it came to a boil on the stovetop. Both of us remained silent, afraid to speak, but Hinata eventually broke the unbearable silence.

"I haven't seen you with a cigarette in a while."

Not sure if she was scolding me, I refrained from looking back at her. "I was trying to quit."

"Why?"

"It's a 'disgusting habit,' remember?" I joked dryly.

"Hmm," she hummed.

Peeking over my shoulder, I caught her gaze. Hinata's eyes were distant, but the distance wasn't held against me. She didn't seem to care about my smoking habit, she never once told me to quit, but I decided to do it for her. When did I decide that?

Turning back to the bubbling water, I thought about the reason I picked up smoking in the first place. "I guess it's what I immediately turn to for comfort."

Hinata didn't say anything at first, but after a moment, she replied with, "Does that mean you sought comfort in me?"

Holding the cigarette in between my lips, I removed the pot from the burner, then turned the stove off. Pouring the hot water into Makoto's teapot, I placed the tea leaves inside. Grabbing the two yunomi teacups that Makoto kept stored, I picked up the teapot and brought everything to the table.

"Yeah," I said, ashing my cigarette in the ashtray on the table beside my bed before taking my seat. From the floor, I peeked up at Hinata. "I honestly believe I do."

"You *do*? As in present tense?"

"Yeah," I answered again, unwavering. "Your presence is assuring, but things are becoming uncertain; I'm losing faith in what's in front of me. We're nobodies in the grand scheme of things. At the end of the day, adults decide what's 'best' for us without asking us what *we* want. It's always been like that, and it's fuckin' bullshit."

Hinata slipped off the bed and joined me on the floor. Adjusting the cushion beneath her, she sat in her usual straight, seiza posture.

"I stopped making friends for this exact reason," she said, her eyes glued to mine. "But when it comes to you, Riku, it's different. This time, I absolutely don't want to lose you. I can't."

There was a thump inside my chest; her words hit me, hard. But just because we felt the same, didn't mean her parents wouldn't force her to go away.

"Hinata . . ."

"Listen," she said, eliminating my chance to speak, "I've been contemplating a few things in my head. I'll be eighteen in less than half a years' time and can legally live alone. If my parents refuse to allow me to remain in Japan, then I'll run away. I just have to be on the run until I'm eighteen. Then, they can't come after me."

"Run away?" I questioned, with an arched eyebrow. "Are you nuts? You can't run away, Hinata."

"Why not?"

This was out of pocket for her character. She was having a lapse of judgement, and I could tell she hadn't really thought things through.

"You have no money, no real plan," I rebutted, being the levelheaded one for once. "I'm sorry to be the bearer of bad news, but you've had everything handed to you. The world isn't a kind place, Hinata. No one will give a shit if you're struggling on your own. If anything, people will criticize you more for it. Don't make impulsive decisions when you're upset."

As I listened to myself, I couldn't help but see Kobayashi-sensei's face pop up in the back of my mind. *It's almost as if that menacing demon is rubbing off on me. Gross.*

Remembering the tea, I took the moment to pour us each a cup.

"It sounds like you don't want me to stay, Riku," she said, turning away.

Stunned, I slammed the teapot down on the table. "Are you kidding me?" I exclaimed. "How'd you come to that messed up conclusion?"

"You're so calm about all this; it's infuriating."

My jaw dropped as my eyes grew wide. *Calm? I'm not fuckin' calm at all! I'm barely holding it together.* Even with the new air conditioning unit blasting, I could feel my temperature rising.

"What the fuck? Of course, I don't want you to leave!" With pent up anger, I exhaled one deep breath, ending in a groan. "If it were up to me, I'd take you away to a place where no one would find us and keep you all to myself."

She turned back to me. "Then, do it."

Staring into her determined eyes, I became entangled in them. This was the Hinata I initially fell for; the stubborn, fearless girl from up on the roof of the school building. She was testing me, and just like usual, she was winning.

"Hinata," I cautioned.

"Riku," she fought back.

"Don't you understand how terrified I fuckin' am?" I confessed, fear acting like a double-edged sword inside my head. "Ever since I've met you, I've been scared of losing you! You've been such a huge presence in my pathetic life that if I were to lose you now, then what would be left?" I reached out for her hand, grasping it desperately in mine. "Your existence is important to me; everything with you feels right. I know how selfish I sound, but I'm at a point where I mentally and emotionally can't anymore. I don't wanna lose this." I leaned back, slouching my shoulders. "I dunno what to do, but I don't wanna lose you, Hinata."

Hinata's eyes glossed over.

I couldn't tell what she was thinking, but I prayed she understood how much I wanted her to remain in my life, even if I couldn't physically take her away like she begged. I wanted her parents to be the ones to break her heart so that I didn't have to. After reaching this point, I would do anything for her, but I couldn't continue being the selfish prick I was. Hinata had her own life to live; I just wanted to be a part of it.

I had been walking with nothing for so long. Hinata was my everything.

Hinata inched closer to me as she gazed down at our intertwined hands. She began stroking the top of my hand with her thumb. "In the past, I've always left people behind; each move grew easier than the last. But, this time, I refuse to leave you behind, Riku." She brought her eyes to mine. "From the start, I wanted to get closer to you, to truly understand you. I'm all in. I always have been." She stopped to blink back a few tears. "I know I can't heal the wounds from your past, Riku, no matter how much I wish I could," she said, a sense of sadness present in her tone. "But I want to try and shape a brighter future with you. I want to stand by your side and face our troubles together. Please don't let this be it for us. Don't let my parents dictate what we have."

'I'm all in.' Those three, tiny words were everything I had hoped to hear from someone.

I'd rather die than be separated from someone who accepted me for me, along with all the baggage that came attached. For the longest time, that's how I felt about Makoto and his family.

But now, things were shifting. I'd become greedy.

All I ever wanted was for someone to look at me with love in their eyes. The love I had been showered with from the Fujimoto family was no longer enough. Hinata was a blessing; and although I didn't believe in any god or afterlife, her presence was almost enough for me to start believing in some greater power. I needed her, more than I ever thought.

I wanted Hinata's heart to yield to me and only me.

My mother would dangle her love for me in front of my face and use it as a threat, only saying she loved me when it was convenient. I craved those simple, affectionate words. It wasn't until I got older that I realized my mother never truly loved me; she was most likely incapable of it.

Eventually, the words: *'Riku, y'know Mommy loves you, right?'* would turn my stomach and fill my heart and head with hatred.

Love was something that took root within me like a weed. But it wasn't until now that I discovered it wasn't really a weed to begin with. It was a colourful flower in need of nourishing.

Hinata was that flower.

Squeezing Hinata's hand, I let myself fall into her. This girl, with the caged bird tattoo and two-coloured eyes, had more than just my interest, she had my heart. I felt fully exposed around her. With my forehead resting on her shoulder, I declared something I had yet to admit openly.

"I love you."

Hinata had been running her fingers through my hair, playing with the ends at the back of my neck, but immediately stopped after hearing my confession.

I sucked in a breath. My heart felt like it was going to explode. After talking it over with Makoto, I knew I loved Hinata, but did she love me?

Pushing my head off her shoulder, she cupped both hands on my face. I watched as her eyes reflected my appearance, trapping me in a fierce gaze like a siren. Her hair brushed my face as she placed a kiss upon my lips.

"I love you, too, Riku."

Chapter Thirty-Nine

HINATA SPENT THE night.

Wanting to keep her close, I wrapped her tightly in my arms, refusing to let go. Holding Hinata in my arms while sleeping was something I could easily grow accustomed to.

As we laid in bed, I couldn't help but replay Hinata's returned love confession in my head, over and over. My heart couldn't stop smiling.

Last night, I advised Hinata that it would be wise to contact her parents to let them know that she was safe. Though they weren't pleased she was with me, Hinata was given permission to stay the night since it was close to midnight when she made the call. Before she hung up, I asked Hinata to hand me her phone so I could speak to her father. I reassured Mr. Tachibana that I would make sure Hinata attended school the following day, but when school was over, I wanted to discuss a few things with him once he returned home from work.

Mr. Tachibana agreed to my request.

After school, Hinata and I went back to her place. Arriving just after 5:30 p.m., I followed Hinata into her house. As soon as the front door opened, Mrs. Tachibana came running from the kitchen with open arms and devoured her daughter in an embrace. This was probably the first time Hinata had spent the night out without permission.

Bowing out of respect, Mrs. Tachibana, in turn, bowed her head in my direction, as if to say: *'Thank you for looking after my daughter.'*

Mrs. Tachibana escorted us into the study while we waited for Mr. Tachibana. She explained the twins were at a friend's house for the evening so that we could have time to converse without being disrupted. She then dashed to the kitchen to prepare tea.

Hinata and I sat on the same couch while silence ruled the room. She noticed my eyes drifting toward the piano.

"Want me to play?"

"Only if you want to."

Hinata rose. "I'm always willing to play for you."

"I'll remember that." I smiled.

Following Hinata to the piano, we both took a seat on the bench. Like always, Hinata's hands hovered over the keys while she closed her eyes, like she was sensing energy arising from them.

"I'm going to play you something new."

I watched as she inhaled through her nose and exhaled through thinly cracked lips; her concentration was like no other. "You're surprisingly versatile," I smiled secretively. "You can play me anything you want. I'll love it all."

She hummed with a calm smile. "You're easy to please."

"Maybe so," I answered, my eyes never leaving hers, "but that's because it's you."

"Is that right?"

"Yeah."

"I'll remember that," she said, throwing shade back my way.

Shaking my head, I nudged her shoulder. "You gonna play or what?"

"Prepare yourself."

Prepare myself?

Hinata's fingers lowered onto the keys. Without further delay, she delivered a riveting opening. The sound that emerged was blasting. It was so loud, heavy, and full of emotion that I nearly jumped out of my skin when the song commenced, but shortly after, it smoothed out into a soothing tune.

The levels which this song exploited were deliberately curated. The sounds reverberated within me; I could feel suppressed memories awakening.

The melody took me back to the forsaken times of Kabukichō, where I lived with my mother in our trashy, unkempt apartment. Though those were times I wished to forget, I had inquisitive thoughts and couldn't avoid Hinata's song seeping into my heart.

Hinata knew what she was doing. Even if she never sang, I had come to realize that Hinata deliberately played songs that told a story of her life, probably knowing they also resonated with mine. Her sorrowful, combative melodies were cathartically soothing.

Hearing the noise of dishes clacking together, I glanced over my shoulder and saw Mrs. Tachibana. She held a tray with a teapot and cups while smiling from the archway. Hinata immediately stopped playing and turned to face her mother.

"Sorry to have disturbed you, Hinata," Mrs. Tachibana excused, as she entered the room to place the tray on the western coffee table in front of the couch. "You could have kept playing. I would have enjoyed hearing more."

"Maybe another time," Hinata said somberly.

Mrs. Tachibana wore a reserved smile. "Yes, of course."

Seconds later, the sound of the front door opening echoed into the study.

"I'm home," Mr. Tachibana's voice spanned throughout the house.

Mrs. Tachibana returned to the entrance to greet her husband. "Welcome home, Taichi dear. Good work today."

From the study, Hinata and I could hear whispers being exchanged between her parents. Even if we couldn't make out what was being said, we knew it was about us. Minding ourselves, we made our way back to the couch, respectfully waiting for Hinata's parents before pouring any tea.

Shortly after, Mr. and Mrs. Tachibana entered the room.

Mr. Tachibana loosened his tie and removed his suit jacket, then hung it over the arm of the chair he sat upon. Across from Mr. Tachibana sat Mrs. Tachibana on the opposing chair.

With all four of us sitting in a semicircle around the coffee table, I could feel a new tension surfacing. Mrs. Tachibana must have sensed it, too, because without missing a beat she stood up and poured tea into all four cups.

"Hinata," Mr. Tachibana called out, "I'm glad to see that you have returned home safely. You gave your mother and I quite a scare last night when you left abruptly and ignored our calls. We figured you ran off to be with Riku. You're lucky we didn't call the police and report Riku for kidnapping."

Kidnapping, really?

Hinata bowed her head. "I'm sorry. I didn't mean to worry the both of you, it's just—"

"We recognize your feelings of wanting to stay with Riku, but you also must understand, I cannot go against my company's wishes of relocating me to another branch. My job pays for everything this family has; I cannot simply deny a request of such high stature just to satisfy a teenager who believes she's in love."

Just as I was about to step in and put Mr. Tachibana in his place, Hinata put a hand on my knee and squeezed lightly. Looking from my knee to Hinata, I watched as she lifted her head. Never averting her gaze from her father's, she removed her hand from my knee and folded her hands in her lap, then stretched out her spine to sit up tall.

The Hinata of today was much more put together than the Hinata from last night.

"I *recognize* that you cannot go against your company, and I'm not expecting you to," Hinata said, her words sharp like a katana. "What I want you to *understand* is that I'm not asking to remain here in Japan simply because of Riku. I want to stay in Japan on my *own* accord, Riku is just a part of my reason to stay. I want to pursue the piano as a career and have decided to attend a college here in Tokyo that specializes in music." Hinata paused to take a breath, exhaling slowly before pressing on. "I'm tired of constantly uprooting my life to accommodate yours. As a child, you can make friends with anyone. As a teenager, it becomes difficult to make and hold on to friendships and relationships. Riku has been the only one I honestly cherish and refuse to lose. My life is here, not in France. I'm almost eighteen. Soon, I can legally live alone."

Without thinking, I piggybacked off Hinata's declaration, unintentionally raising my voice. "You don't have to live alone; you can live with me! I'll take care of you!"

"That's absurd!" Mr. Tachibana exclaimed, shaking his head furiously. With a quick glance my way, his eyebrows furrowed, and his face tensed. "Hinata will not be living with you. You're both too young to be living together."

"Taichi," Mrs. Tachibana said, giving her husband a guiding look.

Shifting his gaze to Hinata, he sighed. "Hinata, your mother and I talked things over last night. We came to the conclusion that taking you to France, at such a crucial time during your academic career, would be unwise and unfair."

The breath I was unknowingly holding onto escaped me. Hinata and I looked at each other, hopeful as to where this conversation was leading. Were the Tachibanas really agreeing to allow Hinata to remain in Tokyo?

Mr. Tachibana went on. "However . . ."

Here we go.

". . . you absolutely cannot live with Riku. Your birthparents did not entrust you to us just so that we could allow you to make inappropriate decisions," he said, leaning forward on his knees and clasping his hands together. "Until you graduate high school, you may stay in the school dormitories. This way, you will have a curfew and will be able to concentrate on your studies properly. We can discuss where you will live after high school later. This is our final decision, it's not up for discussion."

Hinata's chest collapsed, as if she had also been holding her breath, and her eyes beamed. "I accept your terms. I will stay in the school dorms."

"Then," Mr. Tachibana said, standing, "it's decided. I will make the arrangements."

Hinata jumped up to hug her father. "Thank you," she said, hugging him warmly.

Mrs. Tachibana also joined in. "Hey, I was the one who suggested the dormitory idea!"

Hinata left her father's arms and flew into her mother's. "Thank you."

Mrs. Tachibana placed a kiss upon her daughter's forehead. "It will be sad to be separated from you; the twins will be devastated," she said, brushing Hinata's hair to the side. "But this is one of the few times you have ever asked anything from us. As you were growing up, you never had any preferences, likes or dislikes when it came to food, or even an opinion on clothing when we went out shopping. I can tell how important this is to you." She pulled away to look at her daughter's face. "After you ran out last night, I convinced your father that this might be the best option for you." Mrs. Tachibana placed a hand on Hinata's cheek. "We only want what's best for you, even if it removes us from the picture."

Tears welled in Hinata's eyes as she smiled at her mother's comment. "I'll miss you all. I'll make sure to visit when I can."

"Most definitely." Mrs. Tachibana smiled brightly. "And maybe, Riku can tag along," she said, winking at me.

With the mention of my name, I rose from the couch.

"Yoko darling, that's enough," Mr. Tachibana said, clearing his throat.

"You're so uptight, Taichi," Mrs. Tachibana reprimanded, giving her husband the side eye. "You have gone and scared poor Riku with your righteous, parental attitude. I was only lightening the mood to avoid prolonged altercations. Can't you see he's smitten with our Hinata? Give him a break."

Using Mrs. Tachibana's words to my advantage, I created an opening.

"Mr. Tachibana," I said in full bow. My heart was beating at such a ridiculous pace that I almost forgot to breathe; I thought it may beat so fast that I'd bruise a rib. "Please allow me to continue dating your daughter. I promise not to hold her back, be it her grades, which school she chooses to attend after high school, or the future career path she decides for herself. Hinata makes me happy, so I wish for nothing but her happiness in return. Whatever her dreams are, I will make sure she lives them to the fullest."

At first, the room was dead silent, but then Mr. Tachibana released a noticeable sigh. "Lift your head, Riku."

I lifted my head.

"Those are some big promises," Mr. Tachibana said, hesitant. "Are you sure you can keep them? I will not leave Hinata in the care of someone incapable."

"With all due respect, sir, Hinata is plenty capable of taking care of herself," I said, looking over at Hinata.

She returned my look with a knowing smile.

"I love Hinata," I declared. Taking a moment to swish those words around in my mouth, I could feel my body tremoring. "I love her far more than I have ever loved someone in my entire life. I will not let Hinata be disappointed in the future she chooses, even if she chooses one without me in it. I'll protect her and help guide her in the best way I can. I may not have much, but I will always share what I have with her."

Taking in a deep breath, I held it. Not only could I feel it, but I could also hear my heart hammering inside my chest.

With an unwavering stare, I watched as Mr. Tachibana walked up beside me. He took one hand and cupped it around my shoulder, then gave it a good squeeze.

"That's what I wanted to hear."

Part Two:

WALKING

Chapter Forty

THE NEXT FEW months flew by.

Hinata saw her bawling twin brothers off at the airport, along with her parents, then quickly settled into the dorms on her own. There were strict rules about visitors and curfew, which came with harsh consequences. But, as we saw each other so little to begin with, Hinata would sneak me into her dorm room often, where I would spend the night wrapped around her.

Hinata, Makoto, and I became our own little study group, despite the fact I just needed to pass whereas they needed to get top marks. With each session, the three of us grew closer and formalities and honorifics were dropped. Makoto and Hinata fed off each other's intelligence, while I tagged along for the academic ride. It made me happy knowing they got along.

When they ditched me to study for their college entrance exams—Hinata for music schools in Tokyo and Makoto for medical schools all over Japan—I worked diligently on the bike. I was excited to get it on the road.

The last day of the second semester ended on December 23rd, where I passed all my term-end exams with higher-than-average marks, leaving Kobayashi-sensei's jaw on the floor.

On the morning of the 24ᵗʰ, Hinata flew to France to spend Christmas with her family while I spent it with the Fujimotos. She said she'd be back on the 31ˢᵗ because she wanted to spend part of my birthday with me.

Mrs. Fujimoto had also invited Hinata to join us for New Year's Eve, as she'd heard from Makoto that I had a girlfriend and said she absolutely *needed* to meet the one and only girl I'd given the title of 'my girlfriend.' Mrs. Fujimoto was no fool. Makoto's sisters weren't far behind; they very much involved themselves in the matter. Megumi and Mitsuki always came home for the holidays and usually stuck around until the beginning of January for the first shrine visit of the year.

With the whole Fujimoto family home for the holidays, I became weirdly anxious about introducing Hinata, in fear that they would ask her intimidating questions or tell her embarrassing stories about the past. All possibilities I would be gambling on.

⁂

On the morning of December 31ˢᵗ, my birthday, I arrived at the airport, scanning the heaps of people scurrying around in every direction, searching for Hinata. She had been gone for only a week, but I couldn't wait another second to embrace her.

[LINE Riku Nakajima]: Hey, I'm here. It's crazy busy. Where are you?

Waiting, for what seemed like forever, she eventually replied.

[LINE Hinata Tachibana]: Eyes on the prize.

Huh?

Looking up from my phone screen, my eyes caught sight of someone undeniably beautiful. There she was, standing a few feet in front of me, all bundled in her winter attire with a carry-on suitcase at her side. Without a second thought, I ran to her and lifted her up into my arms.

Stunned by my grand, public gesture, she looked down at me. "Is everything all right? Did something happen while I was gone?"

It was a question she asked me often—she was always checking in with me—but it wasn't until now that I realized how much I had missed hearing her ask it.

Peering up at her, I smiled. "Everything is perfect. Welcome back."

Sharing my smile, she replied, "I'm back."

Even though heaps of people were still around, I was looking at perfection and I couldn't help but stretch out my neck to kiss her lips. The precious lips I missed and longed for.

After sharing a kiss, she pulled away slowly. "Hey, Riku," she whispered in my ear.

"Yeah?"

"Happy Birthday."

Chapter Forty-One

I TOOK HINATA BACK to my place so that she could drop off her suitcase and rest before we went to the Fujimotos for the night.

Hinata took a shower to freshen up while I grabbed a can of coffee. Sipping away, I sat at the table and typed out a message to Makoto.

[LINE Riku Nakajima]: Yo, I just picked up Hinata. What time do you want us over at?

Waiting on a reply, I downed the rest of the can.

[LINE Makoto Fujimoto]: Come for 5:00-ish, before it gets too dark and shitty outside. My mom made all your favourites for dinner, so you better be hungry. And don't be late, jerk!

Smiling at the last part of Makoto's message, I chuckled under my breath.

[LINE Riku Nakajima]: We'll be there. Ps. I'm starving.

[LINE Makoto Fujimoto]: Good. Oh, and Happy Birthday, bro! See you guys soon.

[LINE Riku Nakajima]: Thanks, man. See 'ya.

As I sent the last message, the bathroom door opened and Hinata strolled out wearing lounge clothes with her hair wrapped in a towel. She had a hairdryer under one arm and her previously worn clothes neatly folded in her hands.

After the first shower disaster, I had immediately gone out and bought a few towels for her to use while she was here. But on a shopping trip together, Hinata had picked out a small rice cooker and a cheap hairdryer for my apartment.

Looking up, I flicked my head, signaling her to come sit beside me. Hinata knelt and joined me at the table, placing her folded clothes down beside her. I took the hairdryer from her, then plugged it into the outlet. Pulling her in front of my lap, I spun her around.

"I'll dry your hair."

"You don't have to. I'm perfectly capable of doing it myself," she said, looking over her shoulder.

I rolled my eyes. "I know."

A smile pulled on her lips. "Thank you."

Turning on the hairdryer, I tousled Hinata's hair back and forth by sections and ran my fingers through it like a comb. Her hair had grown considerably longer since I last did this at her vanity. It now reached the middle of her back.

Before I could finish drying it, Hinata's shoulders stiffened. "Oh yeah!" she exclaimed, jumping to her feet.

I turned the hairdryer off. "What's up?"

"I almost forgot."

With a raised brow, I remained seated. "Forgot what?"

Dashing to her suitcase, she unzipped it and rummaged through its contents.

"Close your eyes," she said, without looking at me.

"Why?"

"Just do it," she instructed, a hint of annoyance in her tone. "And don't peek."

"Fiiine," I groaned, putting the hairdryer off to the side.

I heard footsteps getting closer to me as she returned to the table. "Okay, you can open them."

Obeying her instruction, I opened my eyes. Sitting directly in front of me in seiza was Hinata holding a present. The present was small, just enough to fit in my palm, and was wrapped in festive wrapping paper.

Stunned into silence, I shifted my eyes from the box in her hands up to her face.

"Merry Christmas, Riku," she said, holding out the present. "Sorry it's a bit late."

"Hinata," I said, slowly reaching for the present, "you didn't have to get me anything."

"I wanted to," she said excitedly, handing me the gift.

Staring down at the box in my hands, I felt a sense of happiness stretch across my chest. "Guess I should grab yours, too."

"Mine?" she said, a look of surprise washing across her face. "I wasn't expecting anything, since we never discussed exchanging gifts."

"That's why I hid yours," I said, leaning behind me and stretching out my arm to open the drawer of the table beside my bed. "I didn't want you to get weirded out or anything."

"Why would I get weirded out?"

Shutting the drawer, I returned to my seated position and explained. "I dunno. Other than Mrs. Fujimoto, and Makoto's sisters, I've never given a girl a gift before."

With a genuine smile, Hinata's cheeks flushed. "I'm honoured, then."

Placing a small giftbox on the floor in front of her, I waited impatiently for her to open it.

"You have to open yours at the same time," she said, picking up the giftbox.

"No way."

"Why not?"

"Because I wanna see your reaction first."

Pouting, along with eyebrows drawn together, she glared up at me. "That's not fair."

"Don't care. Deal with it."

She shook her head with a grin. "Fine."

The giftbox I gave her was red with silver stripes and had a silver ribbon wrapped all the way around, securing the lid, something the shop clerk had put together for me. Slipping the ribbon off, Hinata removed the lid. Watching her eyes glow and grow wide, I received the exact reaction I was hoping for. Hinata gazed at the gift before her, then up at me.

"Riku," she whispered, almost too stunned to speak. "This gift is too extravagant. This must have cost you a fortune."

I chuckled. "How can you tell? You haven't even opened the smaller box within the box yet."

Inside the giftbox was a tiny jewelry box that contained two pairs of silver earrings, ones that I specifically picked out with Hinata in mind to replace the pair she kindly donated to me. One pair was a small hoop, while the other was a cubic zirconia, cherry blossom-shaped stud. Reaching for the jewelry box, I snapped it open and undid the backings that were fastened to the insert.

"I've never put earrings in someone's ears before, but let me give it a try," I explained, directing her to come closer.

"Earrings! But Riku—"

"But nothing," I said, cutting her short and pulling her to me. "I picked up some extra shifts at work while you were gone. Let me spoil you a bit."

Hinata sighed in defeat, then gathered her hair and held it to the side so I could take out the earrings she currently wore.

After struggling to pull apart her current studs from their backings, I finally managed to remove the earrings from her ears, then handed them to her to hold. Hinata's ears were so small it was hard to see anything I was doing. I grabbed the new hoops first. Feeling like a contortionist, as I morphed my body into many positions just to get the hoops in, I had to place Hinata in my lap with her back toward me to get the final stud in place. When I was done, I placed a kiss on the nape of her exposed neck.

Hinata touched the area I kissed with her fingertips, then turned around to face me.

"Merry Christmas, Hinata."

Sliding her fingers up to her earlobes, she immediately jumped up and ran to the bathroom to look in the mirror. A few moments later, she poked her head out into the hallway.

"I love them! I'll make sure to cherish them. Thank you."

"Please do," I said, smiling.

I saw a bashful smile cross her face. Dipping back into the bathroom once more, she took another look at her reflection before returning.

"Your turn," she said, kneeling.

Reaching for the present I'd put off to the side, I removed the bow and ripped off the wrapping paper. I was left with a little box that had a picture of earbuds on it with words written in both French and English. I was familiar with the English wording, but it was impossible to read the words in French. The style of earbuds in the picture looked expensive.

"Hinata, these look pretty pricey."

"Please," she said, shaking her head, then touching her earlobes. "Nothing compared to these luxurious earrings."

"That's completely different."

"Is it, now?" she said, with an arched brow. "Those wireless earbuds are popular in France. I saw many locals wearing that brand. When I was out shopping with my mother and the twins, we consulted a salesperson who spoke highly of their quality and features. Depending where Makoto ends up for school, I thought you could use them on the trips when you go to visit him."

I could feel a smile stretching my cheeks from one corner to the other. To have someone think so deeply about a gift they selected for me was beyond touching.

"These are great. Thank you," I said, continuing to smile widely. "I'll make sure to use them."

"I'm glad to hear that you like them," she said, smiling tenderly. "But there's one more."

"One more?" I repeated. "What d'you mean?"

Hinata reached behind her and pulled out another small present that she had kept hidden. Holding it out in front of her, she surprisingly said nothing. All she did was tilt her head and smile.

"Hinata," I stressed, "I don't want you wasting all your money on Christmas presents for me. Being able to spend this day with you is already more than enough."

"Good thing it's not a Christmas present," she said, matter-of-factly.

I reached out to receive the second present, then removed the lid of the giftbox. My chest tightened, and my relaxed breathing grew scarce.

"Happy Eighteenth Birthday, Riku."

Inside was a thin, black ID wallet. Staring down at the gift, I froze.

"Since you'll be getting your full motorcycle license soon, I thought you might need a slimmer wallet. I figured it would be easier to ride on a motorcycle with something more lightweight than a traditional wallet. It's honestly only big enough to hold one or two cards, and maybe a few yen notes, but I hope you'll find it useful."

Mesmerized, I looked up at Hinata. Smiling through tears I tried my hardest to hold back, I covered my eyes with my arm.

"Are you all right, Riku?" she asked. She placed a hand on top of the one resting on my thigh that held the giftbox.

"You're really something, y'know that?"

Hinata pushed the arm covering my face away.

"Gah," I mumbled, turning away from her. "Don't look at me."

"But I want to see your face." Placing both hands on my cheeks, she brought my head closer to hers. With our faces aligned, she stared deep into my eyes. "Do you not like the present? Is that why you're crying?"

Embarrassed to explain the weakness I showed her, I moved the gift to the side and pulled her into me. Hiding my face, I rested it on her shoulder as I often did to escape the intensity of her beautiful eyes. My ears felt like they were on fire, so there was no doubt that they were red.

"It's the opposite," I said, with a complicated sigh.

"I don't understand."

Chuckling under my breath, I closed my eyes. "I guess you wouldn't."

"Please explain. I want to understand."

Rubbing the tears that quickly dried on my cheeks, I lifted my head off her shoulder and pulled back to sit up straight. I made a resolution to stop dodging her blunt questions like a child.

"You put so much thought and effort into both these gifts that it brought me to tears. Other than you, the Fujimotos are the only ones who've ever remembered my birthday and have given me something." I sighed. "I've always hated my birthday. Like you once said, it's a day that most people celebrate, but not because of me. The fact that you remembered my birthday—and came back to spend it with me—was truly all I could've wished for. You, giving me two, extremely thoughtful gifts, was the cherry on top of this already amazing birthday." With enough courage to meet her eyes, I smiled wholeheartedly. "I feel like the luckiest guy alive right now, and honestly, I'm a bit embarrassed."

Hinata's shoulders slumped and the expression on her face was somewhat weak. The corners of her mouth drooped a little and her lips were stretched thin. She seemed a bit sad, which wasn't the response I expected.

"Hinata?"

"Riku, I'm glad you liked both presents."

"Okay. Then, what's wrong?"

Hesitating for a moment, she held my gaze. "I'm sad that you admitted to never getting a present from your mother on your birthday."

Seeing Hinata's eyes glossed over, I felt like she was about to break down and cry at my expense.

I pulled her into my lap, this time to straddle me. I brushed damp strands of hair away from her face, guiding my thumb across her cheekbone and down until I rested my hand on the back of her neck. My fingertips ran up and down her smooth skin as she broke out in goosebumps.

"Y'know, I never wanted to get involved with you," I admitted, with a thought that often crossed my mind. "I'm a bad influence with a messed-up life; I don't have any merits. I didn't wanna drag you into my shit. But, if I'm being brutally honest, I'm glad I did."

"Riku," she said softly, "you're not a bad influence. And you have merits, plenty of them. Please don't say such things about yourself."

"Heh," I replied, with a crooked smile. "Thanks."

She brushed my hair back with her fingertips. "Even if you didn't want me to get involved in your life, I think I did a pretty good job of doing it all on my own."

With uncontrollable laughter, I broke eye contact. She had me there; I couldn't deny her accuracy. But I pressed onto more serious matters. "Hinata."

"Hmm?"

"I don't want you worrying about stuff from the past. You can't go back and change anything anymore than I can. I now know I can't change my past no matter how hard I try, but I'm determined to change my future. All that's left for us to do is keep moving forward and better ourselves. Being with you has taught me that. So please, don't be troubled by a woman who isn't even around. She's not worth your time."

Hinata remained quiet for a moment, then lowered her lips onto mine.

Starting off with a simple kiss, she continued by kissing me more and more, soon instigating something further as her tongue dueled aggressively against mine. After playing with the hem of her shirt, Hinata took note of my eagerness and made haste in removing it, leaving her bra and bare skin exposed.

Silly as it was, I had missed her touch—like many other things—in the short time we were apart. I'd grown restless without her around.

Wrapping my hands around her now, my body acted on its own. Following Hinata's lead, I pulled my sweatshirt and undershirt up and over my head. We latched on to each other; our bodies fitting together perfectly.

Nibbling on her ear, I whispered, "Hinata, help me recharge."

"I'm not a charger," she said, laughing briskly.

Grinning, I whispered again, "You're the only thing that powers me, though."

From the corner of my eye, I saw a modest smile that curved her face and creased the skin around her eyes. She was adorable.

"Let me see what I can do, then," she said standing, nonchalantly inching her way up on the bed.

Eying her body with pure desire, I followed her lead, once again. I rose to my feet, never once breaking the intense eye contact that we shared.

What a birthday this has turned out to be.

Chapter Forty-Two

AFTER INDULGING IN each other's bodies, Hinata and I spent the rest of the time catching up. Nothing too exciting happened on my end. I had kept myself busy with work at the convenience store and tinkering on my bike, while Hinata's time was full of family.

She spoke about her family's new life in France and how they seemed to be settling in and adjusting nicely. Mrs. Tachibana found it challenging to learn French, while the twins had already picked up most of the language and were easily able to converse with their classmates. Mr. Tachibana had learned a bit of French from previous business trips, so he was adapting to their new life a lot quicker. Hinata went on to talk more about the twins, expressing how she had missed them dearly.

Hinata was insistent on bringing a gift to the Fujimotos out of respect. I couldn't deny her thoughtfulness because I did the exact same thing when I went over to her place for dinner.

On the way, we pushed through the snow that Tokyo was so graciously blessed with, and stopped to pick up a small box of assorted anko daifuku wagashi. I had to hold Hinata back from selecting too many confections because I knew, from experience, just how much food Mrs. Fujimoto had probably made.

Once we turned onto the Fujimoto's street, I thought it would probably be best to coach Hinata on a few things.

"Hey," I said, grabbing her hand to slow our pace. "I should probably share a few things about Makoto's family, just to make sure you're comfortable and prepared."

Matching my speed, Hinata looked to me. "Okay."

Letting go of her hand, I made a mental list, starting off with the most important. "Firstly, Makoto's dad is deaf."

Shocked, Hinata's lips parted. "Oh, that's very interesting. I never would have guessed. I'm glad you told me."

"Yeah, sorry. I probably should've mentioned something sooner. But it never came up in conversation. If you need help translating something, just let me know."

"You know how to sign?"

"Yeah," I nodded. "Makoto's family taught me."

"That's even more interesting," Hinata added, smiling. "Would you teach me?"

Impressed, I smiled. "Sure."

"Amazing. I can't wait to start lessons." She brought her hands up and clasped them together, smiling widely.

"If you talk slowly and pronounce your words clearly, Mr. Fujimoto will most likely understand you just fine. He's a pro at reading lips."

"I'll keep that in mind."

"If I had told you sooner maybe I could've taught you a few easy things to sign for today. Sorry, that's my bad."

"It's all right," she said, shaking her head. "I'm sure things will be fine for today. I'll make sure to learn for next time so that I don't fall behind in future conversations."

Next time. Future conversations.

Touched by her willingness to adapt and learn more about those important to me, I wanted to pull her into my arms and hug her tightly, but if I did, I wouldn't be able to let go.

She put her hands into her jacket pocket and looked ahead. "What's the second thing I need to learn?"

"Secondly, Makoto's older sisters, Megumi and Mitsuki, are absolute nutcases. They're probably gonna harass you and bombard you with questions, so you should prepare yourself. They mean well, but they're intrusive. Again, sorry. It's something I should've warned you about sooner."

Hinata giggled, then turned her focus back to me. "That's what you're so worried about?"

"One of the reasons, yeah," I said, trying to convince her. "You don't understand how intense they can be. If they want information outta you, they're gonna use whatever means necessary to get it."

Hinata continued to giggle. "I'm sure I can manage."

Scarred by childhood memories, I shook my head. "For your safety, I hope so."

"Anything else?"

"Lastly, be prepared for Mrs. Fujimoto."

"And why is that?"

"She's the definition of overprotective. If you think Makoto's bad with always being on my case, he's got nothing on her."

Trying to fight back laughter, Hinata nodded in acknowledgment. "I'll be sure to keep on my toes."

"Hey," I warned, throwing up my hands, trying to get my seriousness across, "I'm just trying to look out for you. Who knows what this crazy family has up their sleeves."

"Yes, yes. You've given me a heap of fair warnings," Hinata teased. Removing one hand from her pocket, she grabbed ahold of mine, then smiled again. "Now, if you're done worrying and coming up with excuses, we should hurry. We don't want to keep them waiting."

Her smile twinkled, brightening the whole winter sky with just one simple action, much like my heart. I loved her smile, a smile that could lift a person's spirits with just one glimpse. Being with Hinata was like being in a wonderful dream that lacked all sense of reality. I never wanted to wake up.

Allowing myself to be consumed with Hinata's excitement, I tightened my grip on her hand. Stepping in front of her, I took the lead once more.

Chapter Forty-Three

MAKOTO'S STREET WAS long with many bends, snaking along like a winding river. We walked for about ten more minutes before coming across the Fujimoto nameplate embedded on the outside of their property. The Fujimotos lived in an average, detached house on an average, residential street—nothing overly big or fancy, but homey, nonetheless.

Accustomed to walking through the gate that separated the house from the road without buzzing the intercom, I led Hinata up the short path until we reached the front door. For some odd reason, I hesitated before ringing the bell.

Why does this feel so awkward? It's like I'm bringing a girl home to meet my parents for the first time. Analyzing my inner thoughts, I realized that's *exactly* what this was. Why had it taken me this long to realize what I was getting myself in to?

While I contemplated my next move, my finger remained hovered over the button. Before I could press it, the door flung open and two unhinged women flew out.

"Ri-Ri!" they both shouted in sync. "Happy Birthday!"

Without having a chance to brace myself, Megumi and Mitsuki pounced on me and wrapped me in an inescapable hug.

UGGGH! How embarrassing!

Makoto's sisters knew how much I hated being called 'Ri-Ri,' so they intentionally called me by that nickname to piss me off or embarrass me, especially Mitsuki. Mitsuki came up with the name one day, and from my repulsed reaction at the time, both sisters found my response hilarious. So, it unfortunately stuck.

I hadn't heard them call me it in a while, so I had strongly hoped they had forgotten, but silly me. Why would they? Of course, they would bring it up today of all days.

"Really, guys?" I stressed, an underlying irritation growing in my chest.

"What? What did we say?" Mitsuki asked, grinning mischievously.

I rolled my eyes. Not wanting to draw attention to it, I refused to repeat the nickname. I could only pray that Hinata didn't hear it.

"Man, you sure took your sweet ass time getting here, birthday boy," Mitsuki said, moving on and playfully berating me. "We thought you'd never come."

"Jeez, Mitsuki, lay off the poor guy," Megumi said, coming to my rescue, like usual.

Megumi, the oldest, always felt the need to protect Makoto and I, even though I was fully capable of looking after myself. Mitsuki, on the other hand, was the wildest of the three. She had so much sass and energy that Makoto and I would often get tired just listening to her ramble on about useless stuff while she paced back and forth. Though they were sisters, the two differed in style. These two women shaped Makoto into the soft, annoying, little pushover he had become.

"C'mon, we're barely late," I said, struggling to lift my constricted arm to check my wristwatch. The time read: 5:08 p.m. "Eight minutes, big deal."

"Forget that," Mitsuki said, quickly changing pace and brushing off her concern about our tardiness. "Riku, notice anything different?" Mitsuki and Megumi released me from their clutches as Mitsuki twirled around in slow motion. "Huh? Huh?"

Not sure what it was that I was supposed to notice, I took the opportunity to provoke her. "Hmm . . . Did 'ya get a new personality?"

Just as I spit out my sarcastic jab, I was immediately met by Mitsuki's fist, perfectly aimed at the core of my gut. Her reflexes were crazy good. I guess taking karate and judo all those years paid off.

Blatantly ignoring my existence, Mitsuki quickly shifted her attention to focus on Hinata. "You must be the famous girlfriend," Mitsuki said point-blank, with zero repentance for what she had just done.

"Mitsuki! You're being rude," Megumi scolded, shoving Mitsuki's head down into a full bow that matched hers. "Sorry about my sister. It's nice to officially meet you," Megumi said, standing upright. "I'm Megumi Fujimoto, and this feisty one here is my younger sister, Mitsuki. We're Makoto and Riku's older sisters."

Hinata bowed respectfully, also introducing herself. "It's a pleasure to meet you both. My name is Hinata Tachibana. I'll be in your care."

"Oh, we already know who you are, Miss Girlfriend," Mitsuki declared, pushing her sister's hand away in annoyance.

"Yes, very true. We've heard so much about you, Hinata-chan. Sorry for the sense of familiarity, but it feels like we already know you. You've become a hot topic in our household," Megumi elaborated.

"GAH!" I shouted unintentionally, recovering slowly off to the side. "Enough!"

Hinata lifted her head and turned to me. With a lighthearted grin, she said, "Is that so? All good things, I hope?"

"Oh, yes. The boys haven't stopped talking about you, especially our little Riku here. It's always 'Hinata this' or 'Hinata that.' It's sickening, really," Mitsuki said, shamelessly.

"Mitsuki," I barked, barring my teeth, and balling my fists. "Those were private conversations between me and Makoto! I'm gonna kill you."

"Pfft, there's no secrets in this house; the walls are paper-thin. And I'd like to see you try. We all know your threats are empty," Mitsuki said, snickering.

My jaw ached from having it clenched; I tried my best not to snap. Mitsuki always did and said things to tease or embarrass me and Makoto, so I wasn't sure why I was getting so riled up. Hinata knew I cared for her, but I didn't really want her to know that I had been talking about her to others. I didn't want her to get turned off by it.

Feeling the need to regain control, I relaxed my hands and unclenched my jaw. Clearing my throat, I was determined to shift the conversation. "You guys gonna let us in or just keep us out in the cold?"

"Where are our manners! Please, come in," Megumi said, shoving Mitsuki out of the way to allow us through.

"Hey! Watch it!" Mitsuki exclaimed, stumbling back. It didn't take much for her to get irritated by her sister.

"After you, Hinata," I said, sticking out my hand toward the open door.

"'After you,' he says. What a gentleman," Mitsuki mimicked, poking fun with a sarcastic jab. "Who is this considerate, nice guy?"

"Can it, Mitsuki! I can be nice—to those who deserve it," I fought back.

"Ou, touchy," Mitsuki replied, snarky.

"Don't mind these two, Hinata-chan," Megumi excused. "They're always going back and forth like this. You'll get used to it."

Hinata laughed her way inside. Following suit, I leaned in and whispered into Hinata's ear. "Sorry about them."

"There's no need to apologize, Ri-Ri," she whispered back, amused. "I think they're fun. Besides, I can tell how much you all cherish each other."

Ugggh! She heard.

Internally cringing, I pushed aside the fact that Hinata now had ammo to use against me. Overall, I was pleased with how well Hinata handled the first round of harassment from the Fujimoto sister duo. I felt much more at ease with how the rest of the night would play out.

Once we were inside, and had removed our outerwear, Megumi led us toward the living room with Mitsuki following behind.

"Makooo-Makooo!" Mitsuki stopped and sang from the foot of the stairs as she passed. "Get your ass down here! Our guests of honour have arrived."

"I told you not to call me that, you rotten sister!" I heard Makoto shout back from upstairs. "I'm coming, jeez!"

I couldn't help but shake my head in laughter. *I feel you, bro.*

Stepping into the living room, Makoto's father was seated under the large, heated kotatsu in the middle of the room watching the television with subtitles. Once he caught wind of our presence, he turned and stood to greet us. With a quick custom bow, he looked up at me and Hinata, then smiled his tender, welcoming smile.

Mr. Fujimoto was a kind, gentle man. His soul was pure to its core, much like Makoto's. In looks, Makoto took after his father, while his sisters definitely took after their mother. From what I'd come to learn about him, Mr. Fujimoto never got angry or reprimanded his children. He was extremely supportive of them, including an outsider like me. He was an engineer by trade, so he excelled in building things and working with his hands.

Bringing his hands up, he began to sign. "Happy Birthday, Riku." Then, he followed with "How have you been?"

Making sure Hinata understood what Mr. Fujimoto was saying, I translated for her, and she nodded with an openly accepting smile.

Replying, I signed my response back to him, making sure to also say it verbally so that Hinata didn't feel left out. "Thank you. I'm doing fine, how about yourself?"

Mr. Fujimoto smiled again, then signed, "I'm doing great. Also, Happy New Year to you both."

I translated his reply to Hinata.

"Oh," she said, thinking up a response. "Please tell him I also wish him a Happy New Year and let him know we brought these for everyone to share." Hinata lifted up the bag of daifuku.

I signed Hinata's response, then Mr. Fujimoto reached out and grabbed Hinata's hand to thank her.

"You don't need to translate this one," Hinata stated, gripping Mr. Fujimoto's hand firmly. She placed her other hand on top of his and smiled, mouthing, "Thank you for having me," slow enough for him to read her lips.

Mr. Fujimoto smiled at Hinata, then accepted the daifuku and placed the bag on the table. Facing me, he signed, "Your girlfriend seems nice. I'm glad you found each other. I always worry about you, you know. Sometimes, your habits are risky and not good. Please treat her kindly."

Lowering my head, I avoided eye contact with him while signing in response. "I will."

"What did he say?" Hinata asked.

"Uh . . . well," I wavered, not wanting to share everything Mr. Fujimoto said.

"He said that he's constantly worrying about Riku because Riku's always messing around, so he wants Riku to treat you well," Makoto ratted, speaking up from behind his sisters as he entered the room with the family's beloved Shiba Inu in his arms.

"Makoto," I hissed, "you could've left some of what he said out . . .."

"Why? That wouldn't be fair to Hinata," Makoto said, sticking his tongue out at me as he put Shintarō, the dog, down on the floor. "Don't worry, Hinata, I'll make sure you get the *accurate* translations for the remainder of the night."

Clicking my tongue, I folded my arms across my chest. "You should be treating ME kindly, after all, it's MY birthday."

Makoto lifted his leg up high and kicked my side. "Shut up, you spoiled idiot! You practically missed my birthday back in March! You're a guest here. Act like one."

"Oh boy, here we go," Mitsuki said, rolling her eyes as she bent down to pet Shintarō who had walked over to her and Megumi.

"Brothers. Am I right?" Megumi chimed in, also bending to pet Shintarō.

"Hey! That hurt, asshole!" I said, playfully raising my fists. "I already said I was sorry for sleeping in on your birthday. What more do 'ya want from me?"

While the two of us were at it, a burst of laughter broke up our friendly match. Freezing in mid-punch, about to connect an uppercut to Makoto's stomach, I looked over at Hinata who was laughing hysterically.

"Hinata . . .?" I called out, skeptical of the person busting a gut before me. I had never seen her laugh so hard.

With Hinata's sudden outburst, Shintarō ran to greet her, as if he hadn't noticed the unfamiliar person in the house.

Calming herself, Hinata wiped a joyful tear while bending to Shintarō's level to shower him with affection. She patted his head and rubbed the back of his ears, smiling with a mouthful of teeth. "It's so lively here. This is so much fun."

Relaxing my fist, I dropped both hands to my sides and stood up straight alongside Makoto. Watching Hinata share a pleasant moment in the place that brought me the most joy, was unexpectedly soothing. This place, and these people, were all I needed.

"What's with all the commotion in here?"

Mrs. Fujimoto entered the living room while holding steaming hot dishes in each hand.

"Ah, if it isn't my favourite boy!" Mrs. Fujimoto exclaimed, with sparkling eyes. "Happy Birthday, Riku, and Happy New Year."

"'Favourite boy'? What about me?" Makoto said dumbfounded, offended by his mother's outright affirmation.

"Oh . . . you're here, too. Yes, Makoto, you're also my favourite," she said, less enthusiastically.

"What do you mean? That didn't sound sincere at all! I live here, and I came out of you!" Makoto retaliated, defensively.

Hinata broke out into yet another fit of laughter, catching Mrs. Fujimoto's interest.

"Ah! This must be Miss Hinata Tachibana," Mrs. Fujimoto expressed excitedly, frantically rushing to place the food down. After abandoning the dishes on the table, she rushed to Hinata. "My, what a beauty! It's a pleasure to meet you. I've heard such lovely things about you from the boys."

Hinata bowed her head lightly at Mrs. Fujimoto with a polite bend of her neck. "The pleasure is mine, Ma'am. Thank you for inviting me. I'm honoured to be here celebrating such an important day with you and your family."

"AHHH!" Mrs. Fujimoto squealed, piercing everyone's ears, and taking us by surprise. "You're absolutely adorable!" She looked back at her husband, then signed while also verbalizing. "Is she not adorable?"

Mr. Fujimoto smiled and nodded his head.

"The food!" Mrs. Fujimoto suddenly exclaimed, as if she had forgotten about something tremendously important. Spinning around to face me, she frantically said, "I made all your favourites, so I hope you're hungry!"

Mrs. Fujimoto's mind was always going at top speed; she had a hard time focusing on one thing. Maybe it was because she had a busy household where everyone demanded her attention all at once. Mrs. Fujimoto was a housewife who did everything efficiently, giving each task a hundred and ten percent of her effort. She was kind and loving but could raise her voice and start havoc if anyone messed with her family. If she ever got to that point, there was probably a good reason for it. She was beyond scary, but I respected and loved everything about her.

"Starving," I said, playing into her madness. I knew it wasn't an option to leave without eating everything she worked so hard to make.

"Miss Tachibana, I hope you're also hungry," Mrs. Fujimoto said with a happy expression, looking toward Hinata. "Today's a special day, after all."

"Yes, ma'am," Hinata replied.

"Excellent!" Mrs. Fujimoto shouted, clasping her hands together. Heading toward the hallway to return to the kitchen, she stopped. "You two, let's go. I need your help carrying out more food. Also, one of you can bring out the utensils to set on the kotatsu."

"Yes, Mom," both girls said in unison.

"May I help?" Hinata asked, just before Mrs. Fujimoto was out of sight.

"Nonsense," Mrs. Fujimoto fought, quickly poking her head back into the room. "You're a guest in this household. Besides, why do you think I had so many children?" Mrs. Fujimoto winked, then vanished.

"What the hell!" Mitsuki retaliated, chasing after her mother.

"Honestly," Megumi said, releasing an irritated sigh before following suit.

"Forget those ridiculous women," Makoto said, regaining our attention. "Come, let's sit under the warm kotatsu." Makoto jerked my shoulders jokingly from behind before sitting beside his father.

Taking the empty seat near Makoto, I slid under the kotatsu, then tapped the cushion on the floor next to me. "You can sit here, Hinata."

Reserved as always, Hinata sat in seiza. "Thank you."

Leaning into her, I whispered, "Y'know, you can relax a bit. No need to be so formal here."

"I am relaxed, Ri-Ri," she whispered back.

"Ugh, enough," I said, still whispering. "It's such an awful nickname."

She chuckled. "It really is."

Chapter Forty-Four

THE WINTER NIGHT was cold and brisk. From the apartment window, I saw that the snow had covered every inch of the ground.

Christmas came and went, just like every other year. It was just another regular day; there was nothing special or remarkable about it. Spending it alone was nothing new either, but it didn't make it any less lonely.

Since Christmas, my mother had only made one appearance, and that day was today, New Year's Eve—my birthday. Today, I was eleven years old. Thinking that she purposely came home to spend it with me, her son, was unbelievably stupid. She returned to the apartment to shower and get more clothes before leaving again. While she was in the shower, I grabbed her purse and rummaged through it, finding any loose change I could get my hands on.

It had been two days since I ate something.

While I raided her purse, I was tempted by something that the adults around me usually partook in. They were always in my mother's purse, so I wasn't sure why today was different, but all I knew was that I wanted one. Pulling out the pack of cigarettes, I flipped it open and stole one of her cancer sticks. We had many lighters that littered our apartment, so I knew my mother wouldn't notice if one of them went missing, as long as it wasn't the one from her purse.

Slipping the single cigarette carefully into my pocket, I returned everything to her purse the exact same way I found it, minus a few yen. Locating a lighter amongst the hundred in the kitchen drawer, I also placed one in my pocket.

Shortly after, my mother left, leaving me alone again. She said all of five words to me, none of them pertaining to my birthday. I sat on the floor, staring at the scratched to shit front door for about thirty solid minutes, hoping that she would turn around and come back.

Maybe she forgot?

That was a thought that never failed to cross my mind, but it was just a thought of idiotic faith and hope. I had no idea why I always gave her the benefit of the doubt.

Spending hours lying on my back and staring up at the cracked, smoke-stained ceiling, I eventually fled the musky apartment. I walked around the neighborhood, roaming the streets until it got dark. The main streets were littered with holiday lights, lighting up what was usually a dark, dreadful road. It was freezing; my fingers and toes felt like they were about to fall off. Luckily, my torso was warm, thanks to the jacket the Fujimotos got me for Christmas.

I was invited to spend Christmas with the Fujimotos this year, but I decided against it. I didn't want to inconvenience them during the holidays, so I lied to Makoto saying I'd be spending it with my mother. Knowing that he wouldn't see me during the break, Makoto brought a Christmas gift for me on the last day of school from him and his family. How much I wished I was at the Fujimotos, spending the holidays, and my birthday, with a kind and loving family like them.

I walked to a nearby convenience store and bought a cheap, prepackaged bento with the money I stole from my mother. After purchasing my long-anticipated birthday dinner, I continued to walk until I arrived at my elementary school. Hopping a part of the fence toward the back that I knew leaned, I snuck my way onto the school's property. The fence was falling apart, but so were pieces of the building, along with its equipment, so it was fitting.

School was closed during winter break, but that didn't stop trespassers—like me—from stepping foot onto the school grounds. I held myself up in one of the sheltered underpasses, sitting against a corner that blocked out as much of the crisp, winter wind as possible and ate my bento, savoring each and every bite.

When I finished, I snapped the container back together and put it off to the side, then reached into my pocket and pulled out the bent cigarette and lighter. Looking at the barely intact cigarette, I placed it in between my lips without much thought. Striking the lighter a few times, I couldn't get it to light. Remembering that my mother would usually cup the end of the cigarette with one hand while trying to light it with the other on windier days, I copied the action. Eventually, I got it to light. Not knowing what to do from there, I inhaled the smoke until it hit the back of my throat, causing me to lunge forward out of reflex. Immediately removing the cigarette from my mouth, I began hacking up a lung.

"How the hell does she do this so smoothly?"

Trying again, I placed the cigarette back in between my lips. This time, I was more successful. I inhaled, then released a puff of smoke from my mouth without coughing nearly as much as the first time. After a few more tries, I got the hang of it, though it made my insides feel like crap.

Each time I exhaled my breath clouded before me. I couldn't understand what the fascination with this horrible habit was, but I also had no intention of stopping until I was done.

Remembering I needed to flick off the loose ash at the end, I took the cigarette out of my mouth and tapped the top of the fragile stick with my pointer finger, exactly like my mother would have done. Watching the ashes fall from the tip of the cigarette onto the ground, burning straight through the top layer of snow, I took another hit. Looking up at the sky, I exhaled the smoke up into the night air.

"Happy Birthday to . . . me."

⁂

Having the chance to sneak out and get some fresh air during the party, I came across a blanket of snow. Nothing was spared from the cold, wet element; everything was completely covered in white.

Whenever it snowed during the holidays, I couldn't help but think back on the last winter I spent with my mother in that trashy apartment. My mother never gave me the time of day, but it was a bittersweet memory. It marked the end of a horrible era.

Growing up it felt like I was living two separate lives: one all alone, with pocketed visitations from my mother, and a second with the Fujimotos, who were always there even when they weren't.

I recalled getting into pointless fights with kids at school over my pathetic mother. I used to get beaten black and blue protecting her dignity, but she never seemed to care or applaud the beating I took on her behalf.

It was hard for rumours not to spread around school about her lifestyle; I had people in my face about it all the time. Everyone knew my mother was a loose woman addicted to drugs and alcohol. So, I eventually got tired of trying to hide it.

But that was all in the past. Things were better now; I was better now.

The remainder of the night was filled with enough food to feed an entire village. Mrs. Fujimoto never knew when too much was in fact too much. She didn't only provide us with customary New Year's Eve dishes, such as soba, she also made sure to prepare specific dishes for my birthday, like yakitori. On top of it all, we also had hot pot.

One of my favourite things to do was to sit under the kotatsu in the winter, surrounded by the Fujimoto family, while eating hot pot. It was a tradition the Fujimotos started on the first birthday I spent with them because they weren't sure what foods I liked at the time, and I hadn't known either.

I had mentioned to Makoto how much I enjoyed myself during my first winter with him and his family. He was so happy that I was so happy, that he told his parents. From there, Mr. and Mrs. Fujimoto created a new tradition just for me. On this holiday, none of the food combinations ever made sense, but that was the beauty of it. I was truly grateful and blessed to have such people in my life, and adding Hinata to the mix was the cherry on top.

Two hours before midnight the room suddenly turned dark, lit only by the glow of the television. Mrs. Fujimoto brought out a birthday cake with pre-lit candles and placed it on the table in front of me, singing in the loudest and most insufferable voice. Soon after, everyone else joined in. Mr. Fujimoto could usually sense the vibrations when it came to singing and music, so he clapped along.

Each year I grew more and more humiliated as I felt that I was too old to have others celebrate my birthday in such a manner, especially this year with Hinata present. I could feel my face growing hot from being the centre of attention, although I was genuinely touched.

Afterwards, I was presented with an envelope containing 'birthday' money, along with a small gift bag that contained a sweater made by Mrs. Fujimoto. I knew Mrs. Fujimoto was trying to pull a fast one on me, which was predictable because Mr. and Mrs. Fujimoto attempted gifting me money every year. I knew what they were actually trying to do was sneakily hand me New Year's money, because Makoto and his sisters were also given monetary envelopes shortly after. Every year I refused and every year the Fujimotos insisted.

Little did they know, the money they gave me each year went straight back into the money I was saving to eventually pay them back for my tuition, whether they liked it or not.

When the time came, we watched the New Year's countdown on the television, jumping up to celebrate once it hit zero. While those of legal drinking age indulged in some Japanese sake or beer, clacking their glasses together and wishing each other a Happy New Year, Hinata and I distributed the assortment of daifuku we brought.

Mrs. Fujimoto, a bit tipsy, clung onto Hinata and thanked her profusely for the kind and thoughtful gesture. When I mentioned I also participated in the confectionary gift, Mrs. Fujimoto clicked her tongue and went back to coddling Hinata.

Makoto rolled on the floor laughing, eventually saying, "Guess you're no longer her 'favourite.' How does it feel, birthday jerk?"

Hinata and I spent the night at the Fujimotos. Our stay was treated like a giant sleepover with all of us, minus Mr. and Mrs. Fujimoto, sleeping in the living room under the warm kotatsu.

The next day, we all got ready for hatsumode. Each year, the Fujimotos visited a nearby Shinto shrine on the first day of the New Year, and since Hinata's family was no longer in Tokyo, Mrs. Fujimoto invited her to join us.

After passing under the torii gates, we noticed the shrine's grounds were packed with people waiting in long lines to ring the bell, pay their respects, pray for a good year to come, and collect a fortune. I never thought praying to a god did much good, but I tagged along each year anyway, too afraid to go against Mrs. Fujimoto, who was a firm believer in tradition.

I will admit that this year, of all years, I did have something—someone—to pray for. I'd do anything to keep a smile on her face. So, I prayed for just that.

Much later, after stopping at my apartment to collect her things, I escorted Hinata back to her dorm. When we arrived, I could tell Hinata didn't want to go inside and part ways just yet by the way she stalled outside the entrance. And I was glad she did.

Staring at the ground, Hinata made some prints in the snow with the tip of her boot. "Well, that sure was eventful." She looked up and smiled. "The Fujimotos truly are lovely people."

"I knew you'd like them," I said, smiling back. "Even before they met you, they were already in love with you."

Hinata's smile grew wider. "Thank you for including me on your special day. I had a lot of fun."

I undeniably just had the best birthday of my entire life. With joyful memories such as these, I knew I could slowly overwrite all the terrible ones.

"Thank you for being there," I said, reaching out for her hand. "It meant a lot to have you there. I'm glad you came back when you did."

Taking a step forward, Hinata kissed me. Pulling away slowly, her words left traces on my lips. "I wouldn't miss your birthday for the world, Riku."

My chest grew tight. I knew I had become the clingy type of person I despised so much. It was shockingly disgusting, but I couldn't help it. My feelings for her were overflowing.

Pulling her into my arms, I rested my head atop hers. Exhaling, I whispered, "Fuck, I love you."

Chapter Forty-Five

DURING THE LAST few days of the winter break, I thought long and hard on how I wanted my future to take shape. So much had changed. Before meeting Hinata, thinking about my future had never been so complicated. All I had cared about was turning eighteen, getting my license, and leaving this shithole city behind.

Growing up I often dreamt about leaving Tokyo and moving somewhere else, anywhere else. Somewhere far enough away from my mother, though I wasn't sure if that was even possible. But as the years went on, and my mother's presence in my life became almost non-existent, while the Fujimoto's increased, Tokyo didn't seem so bad anymore.

Now, I had no desire to leave this grossly congested city if it meant I could be with Hinata and Makoto. I wanted a future with Hinata, but I didn't want to be a burden to her. She had so much potential and opportunity that I didn't want to slow her down. I had to figure out how to control the clingy, obnoxious boyfriend festering within me.

In the middle of January, I *finally* got my full motorcycle license, but I had to borrow a bike from Uncle Ito because mine wasn't fixed up yet. By the end of January both Makoto and Hinata had taken a majority of their college and university entrance exams. Results would be mailed out between the end of February and mid-March, so all that was left was to play the waiting game.

On February 10th, Hinata's birthday, she decided that taking a break was much needed. She had a video call with her parents extremely early in the morning, as we were eight hours ahead of them, also having one scheduled with her brothers for later at night. Even with her busy birthday schedule of video calls, Hinata made sure to save some time for the two of us to hang out in the afternoon. We didn't do anything extravagant and agreed on an at-home date at my place after grabbing coffee and bubble tea at a café near my apartment.

Between Christmas, my bike, and everyday living expenses, I was strapped for cash. I'm sure most girls with a boyfriend would be upset over not doing something entertaining for their birthday, but Hinata said she would be appreciative for the quietness my apartment offered. Though, I wasn't sure if she was lying.

On our walk from her dorm to the café, she had mentioned numerous times how tired she was from all the studying, so I wanted to be her means of escape from the realities of life.

Sitting at the table, I brought Hinata in between my legs with her back resting against my chest. Bringing my lips to her head, I took in her scent— flowers with a hint of strawberries—then kissed her temple.

"Sorry your birthday's so lame. I'm sure you were hoping for something more exciting."

Hinata shook her head. "It's not lame. It's perfect."

"Liar," I said, raising one corner of my mouth.

"I'm not lying!" she fought, her voice escalating. She was about to spin around and probably fight me some more, but I tightened my grip around her.

"All right, all right. Whatever you say, birthday girl. Just sit still and drink your tea."

"Hmph," she mumbled, slumping further into my chest. Twirling the straw of her bubble tea around, she suddenly stopped. "I don't want you to think that I'm not satisfied with spending time at your place, Riku. We haven't had many chances to see each other since your birthday, so as long as I can spend my birthday with you, that's all that matters to me. I don't care what we do or where we go, I just want you there."

Her words left me with a crazy pressure, an ache, a build in my stomach telling me I needed her—wanted her. Taking Hinata's bubble tea out of her hand, I placed it on the table along with my coffee, then spun her around. I got wrapped up in kissing her, until suddenly we were lying on the floor.

I hovered over Hinata's body and just stared down at her, admiring everything that she was. Of course, she was physically attractive, but there was so much more to her. Her *soul* was beautiful. It was hard to believe that in such a short amount of time she had warmed a part of me that no one else could come close to touching before.

"I'll always be here."

"Promise?" she said, gazing up at me.

"Promise."

"Hmm," she hummed, as she played with the fringe of my hair. "I'm going to hold you to that."

"Please do," I answered, before grabbing her hand and kissing her palm.

Hinata smiled at my gesture.

"There's one thing I haven't said yet, though."

She tilted her head. "And what would that be?"

Holding her gaze, I smiled. "Happy Birthday, Hinata."

The day carried on with the same feeling of contentment it started with. We lounged around, drank our drinks, made dinner, ate cake, caught up on each other's lives during the stressful entrance exam period, and of course, we finished off in my bed.

Before it was time for Hinata to leave, I gave her the birthday gift I picked out with the thought of her music school in mind. Confident that she would get accepted into her top choice, I'd gotten her a few school accessories: two notebooks, a pencil case, and a bookbag that all had a music note and treble clef pattern—a fitting theme for her new academic adventure. What pleased me the most was how much she loved them. Watching her face light up as she carefully looked over each item filled my heart with happiness.

It was by far one of my favourite days we had spent together. It gave me another taste at what a future with Hinata could be like. But I knew how fragile things were—people were. I could only hope that the simple life I led was enough for her.

Part Three:

FALLING

Chapter Forty-Six

BY THE BEGINNING of March, good news filled the air.

Like many others in class, Hinata got into her top school of choice in Tokyo, and I couldn't have been more proud of her. And on March 5th, Makoto's birthday, he got the news of being accepted into his second choice, which was in Kyoto. Soon, the two of them would become college and university students, leaving me behind. I was grateful that Hinata would be close by, but I was sad to lose my best friend, even if Kyoto was just under three hours away by subway.

I took this opportunity to approach Uncle Ito with my goal of becoming a mechanic and asked him if he would hire me on after graduation. With his quick acceptance, my future was also set, giving me some peace of mind.

Traces of spring teased the air as we went into the second week of March, just as the bike was officially road ready. Uncle Ito had put his two cents into the bike's restoration throughout its rejuvenation process, but I welcomed it because each one of his ideas were brilliant. Like he had suggested, I gave the body a completely fresh coat of matte black paint, finishing everything off with a wicked black trim. She was beautiful, absolute perfection in any motor enthusiast's eyes.

Uncle Ito graced me with another surprise by getting me a black leather jacket. He called it a 'congratulatory gift' for getting the bike done all on my own. Beyond thrilled by his thoughtfulness, I went out and bought two matching, black helmets with money I'd saved up on the side.

A few days later, on Saturday, when the night was still partially beautiful, I had the urge to take the bike out. It was past 10:00 p.m., but I was too excited to care. I drove straight to Hinata's dorm to surprise her with the second love of my life.

Once I arrived, I shot Hinata a LINE message, asking her to come out. She said she could sneak down in a few minutes. I killed the engine and parked around the corner of the dormitory, away from the front of the building to not draw attention.

About ten minutes later, Hinata made her appearance. I was happy to see her wearing a jacket because she was absolutely going to need it.

"Sorry it took me so long. It was hard to get past the dorm head without them noticing," she explained, a bit shaken from almost being caught. Hinata turned her attention to the bike while walking up to me. "It's fancier than I expected."

Sitting on the bike, with my helmet resting on my lap, I snorted. "That's all you got?"

"I don't know much about motorcycles," she stated, shrugging her shoulders. She looked back down at the bike; this time her eyes grew comically wide. "Oh my gosh!" she said, much louder than a whisper and extremely forced. "It's so amazing, so cool! Just like you, Riku!" She winked. "Better?"

Being careful to keep my voice down, I rubbed my face with both hands, exhaling a laugh at the end. "Ugh! You're too much, y'know that?"

"I've been told once or twice."

"Right," I said, picking up my helmet and handing it to her. "C'mon, get on."

Hinata reached for the helmet cautiously. "Get on? Me?"

"Who else?"

"Now? But it's so late," she said, looking around us. "And if I take your helmet, you won't have one to wear."

I commenced a sequence of bribes. "It's fine for just this one time. I have two helmets, but it's hard to carry a second one while driving. Next time we'll both wear one, promise."

"Riku," Hinata said, dubiously.

"Please. I've been dyyying to take you for a ride ever since I got the bike. Now that she's finally ready, I can't wait to ride with you," I said, practically begging. "Also, I'll try not to drive on the main roads as much so that we aren't spotted and get in shit."

Hinata went silent as if contemplating my argument.

"Are you scared?" I asked, sensing the worry in her expression. "I'll be right here. Nothing bad will happen."

"I'm nervous," she admitted. "I've never even sat on a motorcycle."

Thinking of what I could say to further convince her, I reached out and grabbed her hand. "What if I take you to Shinjuku?" I said, hesitant of my words. "I know it's late, but we'll make it a quick trip."

Her eyes immediately sparkled. "Will you really take me?"

I dipped my eyes and slowly nodded.

"Will we visit Kabukichō while we're there?" she asked, all hesitancy gone from her voice. "I want to see where you grew up."

"Hinata . . .."

"Please? I want to get to know you better. The Riku standing before me is the only version I know. There are still aspects of you and your life that are such a mystery to me."

She wasn't wrong—and knowing that made me feel even shittier. I hadn't completely kept her in the dark, but I hadn't fully let her into the light, either. Our relationship wasn't built on lies, which is something I was quite thankful for. I couldn't handle having something else to constantly worry about. With Hinata being so blunt all the time, asking whatever questions infiltrated her mind, a relationship built on lies would be nearly impossible. It was just easier to keep her from my past. Not easier on her, but on me.

Fuck, man.

Thinking about what I had gotten myself in to, I turned the key in the ignition and started the bike. "Make sure you hold on tight."

"I will," she said with anticipation, as she slipped the helmet over her head.

Chapter Forty-Seven

THE RIDE FROM Shibuya to Shinjuku took less than half an hour, adding a few extra minutes to get to Kabukichō. There was less traffic due to the late hour, so I knew I could've gotten us there sooner, but I didn't want to speed and scare Hinata into never riding with me again.

I took Hinata to see one of my old elementary schools, and a few other places I frequented as a kid. At her request, I drove through my old neighbourhood, stopping directly in front of my old apartment complex.

It had been about a year since I was here last. Everything had remained the exact same. The building was old, its exterior giving off a gloomy, unwelcoming presence. It was in desperate need of new paint, new windows, new doors—better yet—it would just be easier to tear the whole thing down and start from scratch. Those who rented out units from this building, and others surrounding, were usually involved in some sort of sketchy or full-out illegal business. Anyone in this area knew that all too well, even innocent little kids.

When I dropped the kickstand and turned off the bike, Hinata asked me to point out which unit I used to live in with my mother. Pointing up at the far end unit on the second floor, Hinata stared up at the old building in silence. With every fibre of my being, I prayed that this was enough for her, that she was satisfied with my little tour.

Checking the time on my phone, it read: 11:24 p.m., far past her dorm's curfew. If she was caught now, she'd be in major shit.

"We should get going. At this rate, you'll be out way past midnight," I stated, slipping my phone back into my pocket.

"Riku," she rasped, "There's one more place I want you to take me."

My heart thrashed within my chest, as if I were about to have a panic attack. I knew what she was insinuating but decided to play dumb. Veering my eyes from hers, I added a forced happiness to my voice. "Ah, right, I forgot to show you the soccer field that I used to—"

"Riku."

Dropping the act, I released a tense sigh. "Hinata, please, isn't this enough?"

"Riku, it will be all right," she said with a powerful, but comforting tone. "You haven't been back to check on her in a while, right?"

Hinata wasn't a fool. She clearly remembered that I'd come back here occasionally to check up on my mother, just to see if she was still alive. But the reason why I hadn't come back to check up on her in the last year was because I no longer yearned for her to be a part of my life. She clearly didn't need or want me, so why did I waste so much of my life wishing that one day she would change her mind and accept me?

At times, it was annoying to be romantically involved with someone so levelheaded, especially when most of the things I did were rash and uncalculated. Bending to Hinata's every will, I restarted the bike and raked my hair from my face. "I can never win against you."

Hinata smiled, but it had a sadness underneath; one I couldn't shake.

⁂

My old apartment complex had a darkness that lingered above it, but the attractions that drew people to the core of the red-light district were misjudgingly loud in both music and colour. The nightlife of the red-light district was said to be a tourist attraction here in central Tokyo, but those 'tourists' had no idea what really happened behind the scenes of it all. Most places aren't kind to foreigners who don't speak the native language, and, as a result, visitors are often shunned in the process of trying to enter. The Yakuza ran this district and weren't afraid to show it—they were practically untouchable here.

This place was full of corruption, and I wanted no part of it.

After doing a lot of reconnaissance, by following and observing my mother's patterns over the years, I'd discovered she spent over half her time in the core of the district, but not directly on the main strip. Low-grade women, such as herself, found work in areas that brushed incidents under the rug. The back alleyways and corners were filthy with sleazy men and women who preyed on helpless people for their sexual desires. Often money was the means of trade, but drugs and prostitution were also high up in the currency exchange.

Unlike standard host clubs and bars, where some type of stable wage was provided in exchange for a service, my mother got involved with people to whom she became indebted. Before long, my mother entered a world she couldn't conquer. She no longer had the means to stand on her own two feet without being at the mercy of someone to feed her addictions. In the midst of it all, near the beginning of her newfound lifestyle, I came into the picture and screwed-up my mother's life—something I was repeatedly reminded of. The fact that I wasn't born with some sort of health condition or drug withdrawal was a medical miracle, in my opinion.

Approaching the core of the flashy red-light district always made my stomach turn. Nothing good ever came from this place and I hated coming here. Just conjuring up memories was enough to make my blood boil. This entire district, and the foul, rich folk who spent their leisure time here flaunting their money were the bane of my existence.

I avoided driving through the main strip, since that's not where we'd find my mother, and darted straight into the back alleyways where those who wandered went looking for trouble. The back alleys were surprisingly well lit, considering how narrow they were, from shop signs that hung above their respective entrances. Careful not to draw too much attention, I rode through the streets slowly, hushing the engine. Toward the end, I killed the engine and pushed the bike along until we arrived at a relatively safe spot to park and observe from afar. Keeping a safe distance, I looked out ahead at the usual area, and like clockwork, she was there.

It was cold, barely five degrees Celsius, but there she was, wearing a skimpy outfit to attract the eyes of lustful, horny men. No matter how many times I saw it, the haunting image never disappeared. Doing what she called 'work,' she threw herself at whatever guy walked or rode by. Some stopped to entertain the idea, but eventually continued to the next available woman on the curb who caught their eye. One considerably younger and newer to the game.

Finding it unbearable to watch, I turned my head. *Despicable.*

"Which one is she, Riku?" Hinata asked, removing the helmet.

Crossing my arms over each other, I leaned and rested my forearms on the handlebars. With my index finger, I pointed out the woman I detested the most. "That one. The one with the dyed blonde hair and short-as-fuck, red skirt," I said, anger festering deep within me and quickly rising. "That pitiful excuse of a woman, over there selling herself without a fuckin' care in the world, is who society deems worthy of the title of 'my mother.'"

From behind, I felt Hinata press up against me. Her embrace brought warmth to more than just the surface of my skin, it encased my heart completely, easing the rage rooted within me. Of all the times I had willingly come here, this time was by far the easiest to cope with.

Just as I thought Hinata could finally put this infatuation with seeing my mother to rest, after having seen her with her own two eyes, she did something unimaginable. Hinata's hands loosened from around my torso, withdrawing the secure, calming grip she had on me, before she let go altogether and hopped off the bike. My heart stopped as I felt the weight on the bike shift. Twisting around, I quickly grabbed Hinata's wrist in sheer terror.

"What the fuck are you doing, Hinata? Get back on the bike. NOW!"

"I want to talk to her."

My heart rate increased drastically while my eyes protruded from their sockets. "What the hell are you saying? Stop playing games. This isn't a fuckin' joke."

"I'm not playing games, Riku," she confirmed, staring directly into my eyes. Her stare was so intense that I could feel it piercing straight through me. "I want to have a conversation with her."

Though it was cold, beads of sweat formed on my forehead and began to drip down the sides of my face. My body felt like it was burning, as if I were going into shock. Before I could make sense of what was happening, Hinata gained control of her wrist.

"There must be some part of her that wants to know how her child is doing. I know she wasn't the best mother, and I'm not trying to excuse or explain her actions, but I believe deep down she must be curious to know what happened to her son," Hinata said, attempting to make such a woman seem almost human. "Riku, you said you haven't approached her since you were separated. You watch her from afar, like we're doing now, but you've never gone up and spoken to her after all these years. She has no idea how you're doing. For all she knows, you could be dead . . ."

"GOOD!" I exclaimed, stopping her from spewing any more nonsense. Unaware of the powerful tone I took against her, I saw Hinata's body shudder. Shaking my head aggressively, I denied everything she was saying. "You're wrong, Hinata. My mom is incapable of remorse. You're meddling in shit you know nothing about. This part of my life has nothing to do with you. Fuck! I never should have brought you here!"

Hinata's eyes narrowed, and her face turned into a scowl. "Yes, it does! This has everything to do with me!" she snapped back. "How can I be with you if you only want to introduce me to the good parts of your life? That's not how a relationship is supposed to work, Riku. Life is messy, I'm aware of that. My life isn't picture perfect either and you, of all people, know that about me. Things are not fine this way. How can you move on if you can't face the one person holding you back?"

"Hinata—"

"Just being involved with you makes this my business. Don't you get it yet, Riku?" she said, her eyes softening. "I'm here for the long run. I'm here for you. Don't let your past destroy you."

Instantly, tears blurred my vision, and the tension in my body slowly uncoiled. She was too good for me. The validation I've wanted for so long, that I craved and sought for years, spilled from her perfect lips with so much certainty that I couldn't help but choke up. Hinata proved that she was here for me. Though I was over the moon to hear such cleansing words, the affirmation quickly faded from my mind and was replaced with immense fear.

"For fuck sakes, stop. I'm begging you, just stop," I pleaded, sucking in a lungful of air as I reached for her hand once more. Grabbing it, I held onto it in desperation, scared that if I were to let go something bad would occur. "If something were to happen to you, Hinata, I'd never forgive myself. Things are fine the way they are, so please, let it go. I don't need or want my mom in my life. Her presence means nothing to me now." The words that flew out of my mouth had surprised even me.

Intertwining Hinata's fingers with mine, I caressed the top of her hand with my thumb. I didn't want to ever let go of this hand. This was a hand I couldn't afford to lose. So, I couldn't understand or agree with her stupid and dangerous reasoning.

"Things are not fine," she repeated. Leaning into me, she placed a faint kiss upon my lips. "I can't leave things the way they are without knowing for sure that your mother wants nothing to do with you. I can't fathom the idea. If this doesn't work, I'll never bring it up again. You have my word."

And with that, she broke free of my fleeting grasp.

Chapter Forty-Eight

I HAD NEVER BEEN so petrified in my entire life. The moment she let go of my hand was the moment I truly understood how deeply I cared for her.

I watched Hinata walk away in what felt like slow motion, while the sounds of my surroundings dulled. The pain inside me was indescribably horrible; I wouldn't wish it upon my worst enemy.

My mother was an unstable person, and I had no control over her potential hysterics. All I could do was predict the worst possible outcome and try my best to prevent it and protect Hinata.

That urge to protect Hinata propelled me forward, and I abandoned the bike to chase after her, but my efforts were in vain. Hinata had approached my mother.

"Excuse me, Ms. Nakajima," Hinata called out, boldly.

Seemingly caught off guard by her own name being spoken out on the streets, my mother turned around, ending a conversation she was having with some bimbo off on the side. Looking at Hinata with confusion, she took a hit from the cigarette she was smoking, then exhaled it into Hinata's face. "Who the hell're you? How the fuck d'ya know my name?"

Hinata stood tall, never once relaxing her shoulders as she fanned the smoke away from her face. "I'm sorry for approaching you out of the blue like this. You don't know me, but my name is Hinata Tachibana."

My mother's eyes narrowed in suspicion.

"Okay, and?" she said, waiting for Hinata to elaborate. "What does a young thing like *you* want with *me*?"

"Well, I came here to ask you a—"

"Ah, I know what this is about," my mother cut in, smirking spitefully as she crossed her arms. "Listen hunny, if you're here to say that I slept with your boyfriend or some shit, then that ain't on me. He's a cheater and probably has always been one. If he came out here on his own, then he came seekin' me out, y'hear? Don't blame me for your lousy choice in men. Once a cheater, always a cheater. That's just a fact."

I was a few feet behind Hinata, but it felt like the soles of my shoes had been glued to the ground. Inside, I was fuming at the sadistic person standing before Hinata, belittling her.

"That would be quite an unjust scenario," Hinata said, responding to my mother's accusation.

"What?" my mother said with hostility, holding the cigarette in between her fingers. Marching forward, she stepped on Hinata's shoe with the tip of her high heel boot and leaned in closer to Hinata's face. "Don't sound so high and mighty just 'cause 'ya got a pretty face, bitch!"

I saw something familiar snap in my mother's eyes. Uncrossing her arms, she raised one hand at Hinata.

At that moment, a blackened rage took over. Rushing to Hinata's aid, I pushed her out of the way and stepped in between her and my mother, taking the slap across the face in her place. This sensation was one I hadn't felt in some time, but it didn't hurt nearly as much as I had remembered. I'd never considered my mother to be someone who thought about her actions in the heat of the moment. I wasn't sure if she held back because the slap was initially meant for Hinata, but it lacked strength.

"What the fuck!" my mother raised her voice in anger. "Is this the boyfriend 'ya came here to bitch about?"

Letting the impact of the slap soak in and mark my cheek, I turned my face and peered down at my mother through my eyelashes. Even with her high heel boots, I was significantly taller than her; she seemed so little in comparison. Was she always this small?

Catching a glimpse of her cold eyes, I saw devastation. I witnessed the exact moment she recognized who now stood before her.

"Ri-Riku . . .? Is that you . . . baby?"

My nostrils flared and my throat closed when my name left her chapped lips. Those same deranged eyes from when I was a kid were staring back at me with resentment. The ones I had nightmares about. How could I ever forget such terrifying eyes?

"Hey, Sachiko, who's this hunk?" the woman my mother had been chatting with before came over and asked. "My, my," she said, looking me up and down, "isn't he scrumptious."

I blindly searched for Hinata's hand behind me while locking eyes with my mother. Hinata immediately grabbed my hand, and I could feel her trembling.

"What're 'ya doin' here, Riku?" my mother asked, saying my name with disgust as she tilted her head and glared up at me.

I swallowed the saliva stuck at the back of my throat. "We were just leaving," I said with hooded eyes, tugging on Hinata's hand. "Let's go, Hinata."

"Riku," Hinata said, pulling back, "wait."

Turning to her, I saw the same set of question-filled eyes gazing up at me. The determination that shaped Hinata's character was exposed, clear as day, through her eyes.

Dammit, Hinata, not now!

"You look more and more like that good for nothin' man every goddamn day. It's repulsive," my mother said, completely ignoring the woman at her side.

Looking from Hinata's face and back to my mother's, I caught the evil grin my mother wore. She made that comment to gain my attention, but why?

"What?" I said, falling straight into her open trap.

"The resemblance y'have to your fuckin' father is nauseatin'," I heard her say through the fraction of a whisper. Then, her eyes turned murderous, and her words became violent. "WHY WOULD 'YA CHOOSE TO LOOK LIKE THAT GOD FORSAKIN' MAN, RIKU?" With that, she raised her hand again and slapped me across the face with a heavy palm.

"RIKU!" Hinata screamed from behind, gripping my hand and practically climbing my arm.

Just like last time, the slap didn't hurt like it had all those years ago. Surprisingly, my mother's strength seemed to have diminished from when I was a kid, or maybe I had grown stronger. I was finally able to stand on my own two feet and hold my ground against her.

"Whoa! Sachiko, calm down!" the woman shouted, attempting to settle my mother.

"GET YOUR FILTHY HANDS OFF ME, BITCH!" my mother exclaimed, pushing the woman away as she flailed about.

This was the woman I remembered.

This pathetic woman, who wasn't suitable to look after herself—let alone a child—was showing her true colours for all to witness. Pedestrians stopped to stare for a split second, then turned their heads, keeping their ignorance. This wasn't a place where people cared about others.

After lashing out at the woman, my mother turned back to me. Using all different tones and pitches, she lost control. "YOUR FACE—I don't wanna see it ever again! Y'hear me? GET THE HELL OUTTA HERE, 'YA FUCKIN' BRAT! Leave! Leave! LEAVE!"

She didn't give a fuck about me, and I was perfectly okay with it. Things were as they were meant to be. I had finally grown to accept the crappy hand I was dealt, just like Sensei once said.

"You don't gotta tell me twice," I said, deadpan. "I won't show my face ever again."

My mother glared at me somewhat contorted, as if what I said wasn't what she had expected. She seemed conflicted, like she didn't quite understand which expression to make.

I made sure to burn this memory into my mind. From here on, whenever I thought back to this day, I wanted to remember the exact moment I stood up to my mother, reversing the roles, turning my back on *her*.

She was dead to me.

I pulled Hinata along with force. This time I would absolutely fight her if she tried to escape me. For her own security, I could not afford to let her go. I would rather die than let that monster of a woman hurt one hair on Hinata's head. I had a responsibility to uphold, and that was to protect the one I loved.

I hated myself for showing Hinata this world.

Starting up the bike, I made sure Hinata safely wore the helmet before driving off. Everyone could hear my mother wailing in the background, profusely shouting my name like a banshee in the middle of the alleyway. Refusing to look back, even for a split second, I rode out of the back alleys and straight onto the road leading home.

Chapter Forty-Nine

THE RIDE BACK to Hinata's dorm was dead silent; there was nothing to be said. A cloud of despair and anguish loomed over us.

I was shaking from overflowing emotions. My pulse was aggressive, and I could feel heat radiating from my body as I fumed with anger. But above all, I was terrified. Terrified of what this encounter meant for me and Hinata.

It was past one in the morning when we returned to the dorm, and Hinata refused to get off the bike or let go of me. Hinata made it clear that no matter what I said, she wasn't going to let me be alone tonight. Lacking a single shred of mental strength or any capacity to argue, I took her back to my apartment.

When we arrived, I parked the bike near the complex's garbage area which resembled a small, covered carport, and took the key out of the ignition. We dragged our feet up the covered stairway until we reached the top floor of the complex building. When faced with the door of my apartment, I pulled out my key to unlock it. Taking the first step inside the dark entryway, Hinata copied every move I made like a shadow.

As soon as I shut the door, and we were alone, Hinata hugged me from behind. She squeezed me with all her might and pressed her face deep into my back, right in between my shoulder blades. Facing the door, contemplating my thoughts and feelings, I didn't know what to say to her. I knew nothing I said would make things better and that neither of us could change what we had just experienced.

My mother was nothing but pure evil, right down to her core. The false hope Hinata had of mending something unrepairable was heartbreaking. Reliving the moment, as I stood back and did nothing, was shameful on my part.

The only part I was at peace with was the fact that I had kept Hinata safe from physical harm. That thought alone was the single thing keeping me from falling apart. She was safe—here—with me.

"I'm sorry," Hinata rasped in a small voice. "I'm so unbelievably sorry."

Placing my hands on the arms Hinata had wrapped around me, I undid her hold and turned around to face her, then leaned my back against the door. The full moon shone through the back door, illuminating a path down the hallway. I stared down at Hinata's big, regret-filled eyes in the semi-darkness. She was crying as she relatched herself to me.

Bringing my hands up to her face, I ran my fingers through the strands of her hair that had become displaced from the helmet and forceful wind. After struggling to tame her hair, I brushed the pad of my thumb under Hinata's eyes to wipe away her tears.

"Hey, it's all right . . ."

"It's not all right, Riku!" she said over me, more tears accumulating. "I forced you into doing something terrible, so terrible that you got hurt in the process. It's all my fault. I just wanted to—"

"I know," I interrupted, trying to console her. "I know."

"But Riku . . ."

"Shh, it's all right now," I repeated, calmly. "Everything's all right."

Hinata's knees buckled, and she crumpled to the floor, slipping right through my arms. She curled herself into a ball, hugging her knees tightly and sobbing uncontrollably, while I bent down to rub her back to try and soothe her. I fed off of her hopelessness, and understood it quite well, but I had no idea how to remove the sadness. If I could, I would absorb every last negative thought or feeling she held within, but I was also struggling to hold things together. Times like these were when I felt the most helpless. If I couldn't help myself, how could I help her?

Seeing Hinata this way broke my heart, completely ripping it to shreds. But this girl was far more broken than I was. She wasn't used to this lifestyle.

I broke her.

Eventually, I moved us to my bed where Hinata wept in my arms for the remainder of the night until she passed out from exhaustion. Concentrating on how Hinata was holding up distracted me from how I was doing, something I was kind of grateful for. Through the course of the night, I replayed what had happened over and over in my head until the sun rose.

When the light of the sun enveloped the apartment, I peeked at the time on my cellphone, it read: 5:43 a.m. I had only been lying in bed for a few, short hours, but it felt like an eternity.

Looking down at Hinata, who hadn't shifted her position the entire night, I noticed tears had stained her cheeks and left streaks where they had dripped down her face. She was sound asleep, and I didn't want to wake her, so I slid out of the bed with caution. Quietly, I changed out of one outfit to put on another, being careful not to make any sudden or disruptive movements.

I fully intended to quit smoking, really, I did, but I couldn't help but crave a cigarette. I wanted something to ease the restlessness. Grabbing a cold canned coffee to spark some energy in me, I took the last pack of cigarettes I owned from my side table and headed out onto the balcony. Cracking open the can, I let the cold liquid drip to the back of my throat, cherishing its bitter taste as it slid past my tongue. Setting the can down near my foot, I flipped the pack of cigarettes open and noticed I only had two left.

Hmm . . . Guess I better make 'em count.

I placed one cigarette between my lips and cupped the end of it to light it. Inhaling a puff, I held it, then exhaled it into the air as I leaned over the railing of the balcony. Holding the cigarette between my fingers, I held onto the railing and stretched out my arms so I could do a deep stretch of my back and shoulders. I hadn't wanted to flip over in bed and disturb Hinata's slumber, and now my back was paying the price. After cracking it a few times and loosening my muscles, I bent to grab the coffee. Taking another sip, I looked out over the edge of the balcony.

Down below, things were quiet. It was Sunday, so there weren't many people out and about quite yet. Those who ran small businesses out of their homes, such as bakeries or fruit and vegetable stands by the roadside, were up and already hard at work. A simple life like that was admirable, maybe even desirable, but it was impossible now.

I'd fucked everything up, like usual.

My cheek pulsed each time I inhaled or exhaled. Bringing my hand up to my face, I traced the outline of my mother's handprint.

Right.

This was no comparison to the pain I had felt when I was a child. If I hadn't stepped in when I did, Hinata would have been in my shoes. Just thinking about that possibility had my blood boiling all over again. Why did I bring her into harm's way? Why?

"Coffee and cigarettes for breakfast? Yum."

Looking over my shoulder, Hinata was standing in the doorway. Her eyes were puffy and there were dark half-circles under them. The wounded sight of her tugged on my heartstrings.

She stepped out onto the balcony and took my outstretched hand. Pulling her close to me, I placed her between my arms as I remained hunched over the railing. With her back against my chest, I rested my chin on her shoulder.

"I promise I'll quit. Someday, just not today."

"It's fine," she assured. "I never asked you to quit to begin with."

"I know," I said, smirking sadly, "but I want to." After several, strained seconds of silence, I took in her scent: flowers and strawberries. "How'd you sleep?"

"Comfortably, all things considered."

"I'm glad."

"How about you, Riku?"

"I didn't," I said, fluttering my heavy eyes. "My mind wouldn't shut off."

Her cheek brushed up against my forehead as she turned to me. "There's still plenty of time."

"It's fine," I said, forcing my eyelids open. "I got work today, anyway."

"What! What time do you start?"

"I gotta be there for 8:00 a.m."

"Until when?"

"Until 5:00 p.m."

"I think you should call in sick today," she advised, raking her fingers through my hair. "You're in no shape to work."

"If you continue with the scalp massage, I just might pass out," I said, shutting my eyes.

"See, that's exactly what I'm talking about, Riku," she scolded.

"Sleep is for the weak."

"That's so stupid."

Lifting my head off her shoulder, I backed away from her and the railing, then took another puff from the disintegrating cigarette that had been shedding ashes down below. After exhaling, I put it out in the ashtray. "I'll sleep after work."

"Riku," she said with warning.

I took a large sip of coffee, then, with a fake smile, I spoke through gritted teeth. "I got caffeine to keep me going. I'll be fine. Promise."

Hinata's faced exhibited grave concern in response to my lie. She shook her head. "Please don't overexert yourself."

"I won't," I said, making my way back inside. "C'mon. We gotta get you back to the dorm before the dorm head finds out you're missing."

We got ourselves ready and made our way downstairs to the bike. This time I made sure to grab two helmets. My brain was working non-stop, and I didn't have time to even consider sleep. As long as I kept pushing forward, and kept feeding my body caffeine, I'd hold out. Right?

Though I managed to put on a façade in front of Hinata, I knew things as they were now weren't sustainable. We couldn't live in this fantasy world forever. A world where we blocked out all the bad things and pretended everything was okay. I knew this firsthand.

The ride to Hinata's dorm gave me time to think a few things through. But everything coursing through my mind was hard to swallow. Hinata wasn't going to like what I had to say, but my mind was pretty well made up.

This girl is broken, and I fuckin' broke her.

When the dorm building was in sight, I pulled off to the side of the road and turned off the bike at a fair distance to avoid being spotted or heard. With the kickstand dropped, I took off my helmet and placed it on my lap.

"How are you going to ride back with an extra helmet?" Hinata asked, removing the helmet from her head while hopping off the back of the bike. "Didn't you say it was difficult to do?"

We had been engaging in normal conversation all morning, and I appreciated her ability to try and separate last night from today. But we couldn't keep this up forever.

I cocked back my head and laughed. "Yeah, it's not the easiest to ride with an extra helmet because it bounces around on the back of the bike, but it's manageable. I just gotta strap it down," I said, demonstrating the task. "Just means I can't ride freely."

"'Freely'?"

"Yeah, y'know, *fast*."

Hinata rolled her eyes. "Maybe it's better for you to always ride with the spare helmet attached, then. You just might drive appropriately in accordance with the law."

I shook my head. "That wouldn't be any fun."

"I see," Hinata said with a fierce look. Peering up at the dorm building behind her, she took a step away from the bike. "I believe we made it in time."

"Did we, though?" I joked, trying to lighten the mood.

"Somewhat, I guess," she played in return. "I better get going. I'll see you tomorrow, Riku."

Right before Hinata was out of reach, I leaned forward and grabbed her hand. "Hold on a sec."

Looking back at me with an outstretched arm, she asked, "Hmm? Everything all right?" Accepting my hand, she took a few steps back and returned to my side.

'Everything all right?' There's' those words again.

With the downcast of my gaze, I held her hand in mine. Stroking the tops of her knuckles with my thumb, I inhaled one of the heaviest breaths of my life.

We can't pretend forever.

"I haven't been able to stop thinking about what happened last night. All night I was listless; I kept replaying the incident in my head, regretting that I ever took you to Kabukichō. It's a regret I'll carry for the rest of my life."

Hinata glowered. "Last night wasn't your fault, Riku. It was mine."

Lifting my head, my eyes met hers. Smiling briskly, I bit my lip. "But it was. Things could've gone much worse than they did. I put you in grave danger, Hinata. You're not used to that lifestyle, and I don't ever want it to be something you get accustomed to."

"Ri—"

"Hinata," I overpowered, "this isn't working. We've fooled ourselves long enough, don't'cha think?"

Hinata's eyes bulged. "What are you implying?"

"Y'know what I'm implying. It's been implied from the start," I smiled dryly, masking my emotions. "You're much too smart not to grasp the truth of the situation."

"Well, I must have turned dumb overnight because I don't understand what you're saying."

"Hinata."

Tears welled up in her already swollen eyes. "Stop speaking lies," she snapped, flaring her nostrils. "Things are working out just fine. Last night . . . last night was a misjudgment on my part." Fighting back the tears, she swallowed hard, leaving her voice hoarse. "Regarding your mother, you were right. I admit that I shouldn't have gotten involved the way that I did. I should have listened to you. I won't ever cross your warning again when it comes to her. So please, please don't say things you don't mean." She squeezed my hand. "We're good together."

"We're not, though," I fought back, letting go of her hand. A vicious storm brewed inside me. "You're good for me, but I'm not good for you." Hearing the words that I never wanted to say spill from my mouth made me sick. They made me want to hurl. "Shit, Hinata. You're the best fuckin' thing that's ever happened to me, but I can't drag you into my mess. Not anymore."

Her voice quivered as my name came out in a whisper from her lips. "Riku."

"I'll see 'ya at school," I said, attempting to end the conversation.

"Don't do this," she said, anger spiking her words. "What gives you the right to decide what I want?"

"Stop being so unreasonable. It's what's best for you."

"That's bullshit, Riku!"

Turning the key, I started the bike back up and slipped the helmet over my head. Kicking up the kickstand, I revved the engine. "See 'ya around."

"RIKU, WAIT!" I heard her yell with all her might as I rode off. "RIII-KUUU!"

That was twice in less than twenty-four hours where my name had been called out at the top of someone's lungs as I rode off in the opposite direction. Except this time, I wasn't sure if I was making the right decision. This time, my heart felt like it had been split in two.

I had too much baggage; no one deserved to have that unnecessary weight thrown on them. It wasn't anyone's responsibility but mine. It was better this way. Who was I to think that I could find happiness in a world that didn't want me to begin with?

Chapter Fifty

AFTER WORK I crashed pretty hard. I barely survived my shift, almost falling asleep while attending the register. Hinata had been right, I should have taken the day off.

All day I avoided checking my phone, fearing that Hinata's name would appear across my screen. It took everything I had to drive home safely without nodding off and losing control of the bike. Sleeping my stress away was the best, temporary cure, but the hardest part about going to bed was knowing that it was empty, and she would never again accompany me.

All I wanted was to forget. Forget about her, forget about my mother, forget about everything, but it was easier said than done.

Hinata wasn't just someone I could forget.

When it came time for school the following day, my body felt a bit more rejuvenated, but my mind and heart were far from being at ease. How bad I wanted to revert to my old self, skip school, and push my problems away, but with a handful of days left, I knew I shouldn't. Not only would I worry Hinata and stress out Kobayashi-sensei, but I would also put a heavy strain on Makoto, and he didn't deserve that, not so close to graduation. Putting on my big boy pants, I dragged my sorry ass out the door.

Arriving late, I parked the bike, then walked into the building, eventually making my way up to the fourth floor. Before entering, I held the handle of the sliding door and took a deep breath.

Here we go.

Sliding the door open, I immediately locked eyes with Kobayashi-sensei.

"Mr. Nakajima," Kobayashi-sensei said, his voice clipped. "You have less than a week before graduation. Do you understand how crucial these days are? The least you can do is show up on time."

"Yes, sir. Sorry."

I could tell that my sincere apology threw him off because of how sudden his expression changed. Passing in front of him with my head down, I made my way to my seat, avoiding the back of the classroom like the plague. I couldn't bear seeing Hinata.

"Yes, well, as I was saying . . ."

Kobayashi-sensei picked up where he left off before being interrupted. He was in the middle of another repetitive speech about how the final days of school would run before the ceremony.

All the third-year students had been preparing endlessly for graduation for the last two weeks by running through formal ceremonial rehearsals of the big day, while the second and first years continued with regular classes, helping when needed. In between rehearsals, representatives from each graduating class gathered and worked diligently on writing a thank you speech to the principal, administrative staff, teachers, and student body on behalf of all the third years. Meanwhile, the rest of the third-year students had been doing other boring, labour-intensive tasks to make sure the entire school was clean, inside and out, from top to bottom. Such tasks involved: washing windows and floors, weeding the gardens, and setting up the gymnasium by lining up chairs and various things perfectly.

These last few days were said to be the most important, but all I wanted to do was run away from this place.

Submerged in my thoughts, I tuned out the rest of what Kobayashi-sensei was saying. I vacantly stared at the scratches on the surface of my desk, any little thing to distract me. For the remainder of homeroom, I kept my head down and avoided everyone.

When the period was over, I bolted out of the classroom like a track star and raced down to the entrance. Just being in the loop of how the final days of school would play out, with more practices and rehearsals, was good enough for me, especially in my shitty mood. There was no way in hell I was going to spend the entirety of my day cleaning the school more than I already had the previous week.

I had heard Makoto call my name before I gunned it, but I couldn't face him just yet. I needed some time to think shit through. Since I had ignored him, Makoto followed up by sending me a message asking where the hell I'd wandered off to. Sitting on my bike in the school parking lot, not necessarily trying to keep my location a secret, I told him I was dipping early.

After reading his long, lecturing message, I replied with:

[LINE Riku Nakajima]: When you get home from school later, let me know. I need to talk to you.

Makoto eased off the strict attitude after my message, as if me skipping school was no longer a big deal.

[LINE Makoto Fujimoto]: You good, bro?

[LINE Riku Nakajima]: Honestly, not really. Just need to vent about some shit.

[LINE Makoto Fujimoto]: You're kind of scaring me, man. You don't speak up unless it's something important. Did you already talk to Hinata about it?

[LINE Riku Nakajima]: No. Leave her out of it. Whatever you do, don't tell her that we're meeting up.

[LINE Makoto Fujimoto]: I'm starting to get worried here. Things okay between you two?

Not wanting to get into this over LINE, I wrapped up our conversation.

[LINE Riku Nakajima]: I'll swing by your place later.

Makoto knew me well enough to drop shit when I didn't want to get into it. So, after my message, he didn't pry any further.

[LINE Makoto Fujimoto]: Got it.

After reading Makoto's last message, I checked to see if I had gotten any messages from Hinata. Feeling both relieved and depressed that I hadn't, I tucked my phone away and took off. A long bike ride on a nice, pre-spring day was exactly what I needed to calm down and figure out my shit before speaking with Makoto.

Work would have also been a good way to keep busy and avoid my problems, but unfortunately, I didn't have that means of escape. The manager from my part-time job had said I wasn't allowed to work any additional shifts this week because of graduation, so she gave me the rest of the week off.

I rode aimlessly, roaming the streets for a few hours, driving as far as Yokosuka and back, riding alongside Tokyo Bay the best I could. I pulled off to the side of the road to check a few breathtaking views and took out the pack of cigarettes I'd held on to. I thought about lighting the last cigarette a hundred times, but never went through with it. The temptation of having one final cigarette in my possession, that I could light at any given time, weighed on my mind, more than it should have. It would be so easy to smoke it, but I wanted to save it for something urgent, something that a simple bike ride couldn't fix. But truthfully, what was the point of quitting now? Why did I need to give it up? The person I was doing it for was no longer a part of my life.

By the end of my ride, I went to a place of comfort to kill time.

As usual, Uncle Ito and the guys were working away on cars and bikes, taking bodies apart and putting them back together again. I was allowed to work on my bike out back at any time, which led to constant tinkering and tune-ups. I had even started making a small tool collection that Uncle Ito let me store at the shop in my very own toolbox, a hand-me-down from him.

Another hour passed, and Makoto finally sent me a message saying he was on his way home from school. Tiding up my workstation, I replied with:

[LINE Riku Nakajima]: On my way.

Chapter Fifty-One

WHEN I PULLED up, Makoto was already waiting for me outside. Placing the kickstand down, I killed the engine and removed my helmet. Scared to look him in the eyes, I lowered my gaze.

"Man, you look like shit."

Caught off guard by his punitive jab, I felt forced to look up.

"I don't even need to see your entire face to know that you look like shit." Makoto smirked. "In all fairness, you came to school already looking like shit."

He was having fun at my expense, and I couldn't help but chuckle under my breath. "I feel like shit."

Just like through our messages, Makoto's tone quickly changed. Approaching my bike, he tilted his head and asked, "What happened? Did you and Hinata have a fight or something?"

With an evasive grin, I carried my gaze downward again. "We broke up."

"What?" I could hear shock in Makoto's voice as he pressed me. "What do you mean you guys 'broke up'?"

"It's just as I said. We broke up—we're no longer together," I repeated. "I dunno how else to say it."

Makoto was wary, but eager to know the full story. I could sense the difficulty he felt trying to contain his concern. "Why? When?"

I swung my leg over and got off the bike, then hung my helmet off a foot peg. Defeated by the whole situation, I stood before Makoto, barely able to flick my eyes up at him. "A lotta stuff happened . . . Can we go inside?"

Without further questioning, Makoto walked to the gate and held it open for me. "Let's go to my room. Luckily, no one's home, so we have plenty of time to talk without my family getting in the way."

Passing in front of him, I smiled lifelessly as I walked through the gate.

I went up to Makoto's room ahead of him while he went to the kitchen to prepare tea. As I waited, I plopped myself down on Makoto's bed, then flung back with great force. Sighing heavily, I placed an arm over my eyes as I thought of what to bring up first. As far as Makoto knew, things were shaping up for me; I was happy. Considering all the events that had taken place in such a short period of time, I wondered where to even begin. Everything had been going so well. How did things come to this?

Makoto entered the room shortly after, carrying a tray with a steaming hot teapot and two yunomi cups. He placed the tray on the table, then sat to pour tea into both cups. Meeting him at the table, I sat cross-legged and fixated on the steam leaving my cup as it moved up through the air and evaporated.

We sat in silence for a bit, Makoto having taken a few sips from his cup while I waited for mine to cool. The silence must have been eating away at him because soon he cut it with a direct question.

"Why did you and Hinata breakup?"

I didn't want to skirt around the issue, but his question wasn't simple to answer. For him to understand, I would have to tell him about the encounter with my mother. While I was trying to figure out where to start, Makoto jumped into another question.

"Did she breakup with you because you did something stupid that pissed her off?" he asked, raising a brow.

Eyeing him, I grumbled, "She isn't that kinda girl. Even if I had pissed her off, she would've confronted me about it and nagged me until we resolved shit."

"Then, how come you guys didn't resolve this before calling it quits?"

I clicked my tongue. "You don't understand. It ain't that simple, okay? It's not an issue that can be resolved."

Makoto rested his hands on the table around his cup, encompassing it, then stared at me. "Help me understand, then. You're being so wishy-washy about this whole thing that it's hard to decipher."

Leaning back on my hands, I looked up to the ceiling. "I know," I sighed. "I'm sorry. I just . . . I dunno where to start."

"From the beginning?" Makoto said, in question.

"The beginning, huh?"

"The last I knew, you and Hinata were fine. You were so excited about getting your license and taking her for a ride. That's all you ever talked about lately. What happened since then? Did you end up taking her for a ride or what?"

"Yeah . . . I took her."

"And?"

Reliving the happy moment with Hinata from a couple of days ago left a lump wedged in my throat. At the time, that excitement had embodied me entirely, but the feeling attached to it had long dissipated. I couldn't recall the way that toe-curling experience made me feel anymore; that happiness was replaced with fear and sadness. How could I convey such an experience in words?

"Riku?"

"Sorry," I said, dropping my eyes. Sliding backwards, I fell onto the wall that was a short distance behind me.

Makoto sighed. "Come on, man. You're giving me nothing to work with."

"Hinata met her," I finally blurted out, lifting my knees, and resting my forearms on top.

"'Met her'? Met who?"

I brought my gaze up to match his. "My mom."

Makoto's mouth dropped. It looked like his soul had left his body. "She . . . WHAT?"

"You heard me."

"Not correctly!" he said, raising his voice. "You've got to be joking."

"I wish I was," I said, my voice dying off toward the end.

Makoto took his glasses off and threw them on the table. I watched as the plastic frames glided across the table's surface, stopping in the middle. He brought his elbows up and lowered his head into his hands, pushing back his hair with full palms.

"I'm speechless. Stunned, actually."

Not knowing how to respond, I remained quiet.

"How did that even happen?"

"I took Hinata to Kabukichō."

Makoto glared at me. "On the bike? As your first ride? What the hell— Why would you do such a dumb thing?"

I propped one elbow up on my knee and rested my cheek in my hand. "I'm still asking myself the same question, because after that, everything went to shit."

"Did your mom do anything to her?" Makoto asked, on edge. He was obviously bothered by the possible outcome of events.

"I stopped her from doing anything physical to Hinata, but I couldn't deflect the emotional damage she inflicted upon her." Tears stung my eyes as I thought back on how broken Hinata had appeared yesterday. I slipped my fingers through my hair, then dug my nails into my scalp and tugged on the strands of hair with a full fist. "I couldn't protect Hinata like I promised I would. I fucked up, Makoto. I really fucked up."

"Riku . . ."

"I promised her parents I'd take care of her, and what did I do instead?" I asked rhetorically, cutting Makoto short. "I purposely placed her in the centre of danger!"

"Riku," Makoto said again, this time with a stern tone. "Why did you take Hinata to Kabukichō? You told me that you never wanted her to meet your mom. What changed?"

Discreetly wiping away the unfallen tears from my clouded eyes with the edge of my palm, I explained what happened, and Makoto held on to every word. His eyes became gloomy as if he were recreating the image inside his head.

After my explanation, he swallowed hard. "You said your mom almost hurt Hinata *physically*. Go back to that."

Stretching out my back and shoulders against the wall, I dropped my knees and returned them into the cross-legged position I was in before. "She was about to slap her across the face, but I stood in the way and got hit instead."

"Well, that explains the bruise on your face," he stated, his eyes dodging to my cheek.

"I fucked up, Makoto," I said, again, with a raspy voice, biting my lip to stop myself from crying. "Why do I always fuck everything up, man? My life was finally getting on track, I was getting my shit together! Hinata . . . she helped me get my shit together. She gave me a sense of purpose." Realizing that I was being insensitive, considering Makoto always stood by me and helped me more times than I could count, I hung my head. "I'm sorry, I take back what I said. Hinata isn't the only one who's helped me stay on the right track. You've always looked out for me, even when you should've cut all ties."

Before Hinata, the way I went about life left little room for Makoto's advice, even when I knew he was right. I used to hate when he lectured me because he often came across as superior. The choices I made were unethical and wrong, and Makoto never failed to remind me of such. Even after I betrayed him, Makoto forgave me and treated me no differently than he had before. I couldn't compete with an upstanding guy like him.

So, maybe, just maybe, I deserved this level of suffering.

"I take no offense to what you said, Riku." He lifted his cup and took a sip. "Having Hinata around has actually brought me some relief. She's another person who honestly cares about you and your well-being, wanting nothing but the best for you." Makoto stared at me with heavy eyes. "The issue with Sakura is behind us. I don't want you dwelling on that forever. That's not what I want for you. You're my best friend, man."

"Makoto, I know," I said, trying to reason with him, "but it's hard to move past something like that. It's seared into my memory; I can't just forget about it. You only live once. Your friends should have your back, especially your best friend, and what I did—"

"You only die once, too," Makoto said, quick to shut me down.

"I know that . . .," I said, warily.

"Do you?" he barked, slamming the teacup down on the table, and knitting his brows. "Open your eyes and look around you, man! You live your life as if you aren't afraid of dying. As if dying isn't scary. But let me tell you something, Riku—death is terrifying! If you were to suddenly die, I wouldn't know how to carry on." Makoto stopped to catch his breath, tears filling his unwavering eyes. "Do you know how many times I thought

I'd never see you again? Those times, where you would up and disappear, without so much as a call or message to let me know you were okay, always left me anxious. You've always been careless, doing as you please without thinking about the consequences or how your actions affect others." He took another breath, swallowing deeply. "You put Hinata in danger—there's no denying that—and I can see how upset you are with yourself, but that doesn't mean you can just abandon her. You, of all people, should know how devastating it is to be a part of such an extreme world, especially if you aren't accustomed to its harshness. So why? Why do you insist on pushing away the people who care about you once the going gets tough?"

"I haven't pushed you away," I said, halfheartedly.

"You've tried, I just don't let you."

Looking at Makoto's demeanor, I knew his explosion of unforgiving words was something he had held onto for a long time. This wasn't just about Hinata anymore. Makoto's hands were balled into fists and his face morphed into shades of red the angrier he got.

With caved in shoulders, I couldn't hold back my tears any longer, so I released them. I felt the warm water land on the backs of my hands with a small splash.

"Riku," he said, still uptight, "I can see why you broke things off with Hinata."

From the way he spoke, I could tell that he had finished putting the pieces together.

"You're scared to put Hinata in harm's way, more than you already have. The stuff you've both had to endure isn't ideal or easy to get over. Trust me, I know how traumatizing situations involving your mom are. I experienced it firsthand, remember?" He tilted his head as if waiting for me to agree. "Unfortunately," he sighed, "the family you're born into is a part of your life you can't change. In that, Hinata can somewhat relate to you. Don't forget, she's also alone now," he said with great emphasis. "Is separating yourself from Hinata really what you want? Are you okay with that decision, a decision that could possibly impact the rest of your life? If so, then there's nothing else to talk about. But," he paused, lingering on the word and watching me squirm, "since you're here, with the appearance of being emotionally bruised and worn out, I don't think you're okay with your decision at all."

Makoto had the answers to every question I had. He knew me better than I knew myself.

"I know what you're saying," I said, looking away, "but I can't let her get hurt because of me. I don't want her to live an unhappy life. All I've done since I met her is cause her problems. She gave me the energy to stand up and face forward, while I came into her life and tore her down. Hinata deserves so much more, man. She doesn't need a piece of trash like me."

"You aren't trash, Riku," he said, defensively.

"I am, though!" I argued, staring directly at him. "I'm a nobody going nowhere. Hinata, she's a somebody going everywhere. Both of you are. You both have an amazing future ahead of you, and I don't wanna get in the way. Your reason for keeping me around is questionable; I'm baffled by how caring and forgiving you both are. You—"

Before I could finish, Makoto shot straight up and walked around the table. Bending, he grabbed the collar of my shirt and pulled me up to my feet. We were practically the same height, the difference of about six centimeters in my favour, but Makoto felt much taller in this moment.

"Are you fucking listening to yourself?" he said, his face inches from mine. I could tell how pissed Makoto was by the way he rolled his tongue against his teeth through a mouth practically wired shut. Glaring at me, his nostrils flared. "Get a grip, bro. Stop self-loathing and make yourself worthy of her. Own your shit and admit that you love Hinata and want to be with her. Nothing else matters right now. Life is messy; you'll figure things out along the way. There's good and bad in every relationship, that's how they work. You can't protect her from everything. No one can. No one knows what will happen in the future, but you can't let every bad thing that happens deter you from what makes you happy."

Peering obediently into Makoto's eyes, I saw the corner of his eyebrows lower in pity. His body language had changed immensely, shifting through many emotions in a short period. His eyes, though filled with tears, were soft, and his face no longer harboured or expressed anger. I, on the other hand, had completely broken down; things were just as he had described. Dropping my shoulders in resignation, I placed my one arm over my eyes while the other hung at my side. Without a second to spare, I sobbed like a child.

"Makoto," I whispered in between sobs, "I'm lost."

Makoto's grip on my shirt loosened. "It's okay, Riku." He swallowed apprehensively. "Despite how many times you get lost, I'll come find you. Me and my entire family, we'll all come find you. Always. Even Hinata," he added choked up, his words flowing with urgency, "she definitely won't let you wander off."

Curious as to what expression he wore while saying all that, I removed my arm from my eyes to catch a glimpse. Makoto's cheeks were flushed, and his eyes were puffy. Both of us were crying like sappy children, undoubtedly an ugly sight.

I hung my head reflexively, this time with a light heart. Makoto was like a purifier, cleansing the air of the polluted world around me. In every low point in my life, whenever I was beaten and broken, Makoto was there to pick me up and put me back together—over and over—no matter the situation. "Thanks, man . . . I really needed to hear that."

Makoto released me from his clutches, then quickly threw a punch targeting the centre of my chest. "That's for saying dumb shit and making me say even dumber shit."

Catching myself from his punch, I cracked a smile, then wiped the tears from my face. "Yeah."

"Now," he said, clearing his throat, "this isn't some fairytale in a book; things won't resolve themselves. Go find Hinata and explain things properly. She's a big girl, I'm sure she's more than capable of holding it together, unlike us. Don't let her get away because of stuff out of your control." With a curled lip he went on to say, "Besides, there isn't any other girl out there who can put up with your shitty personality."

Lunging at him, I drew him into a headlock. "Watch it."

Laughing through his tears, he coughed forcefully as he used his hand to drum my arm a few times. "Bro, I tap! I tap!"

Letting him out of the headlock, I backed away to give him some air, joining in on the laughter and playful atmosphere.

Makoto grabbed his glasses from the table, fixing them to his face before massaging the back of his neck to try and ease it. Then, he swiftly jumped into a fighting stance, ready to attack. "You got lucky with that headlock, but don't let it go to your head," he teased.

A smile the size of a hairline crack broke its way through. "Whatever you say, bro. Also, you should really look into getting contacts."

"You'd like that, wouldn't you?" he said, tauntingly. "That would make me an even easier target." Makoto threw another punch, this time much slower and beelining toward my face. Catching his punch in midair, I grasped his balled fist securely.

"Thanks, Makoto." The thinning smile I held spread. "You always know how to make a guy feel better."

"You'd do the same for me if the roles were reversed," he said with a tender smile, as he stood upright and retracted his hand. "Now, get out of here and go fix this giant mess you've created. Go unbreakup—if you can even call it a breakup to begin with. Usually, breakups last longer than a day, but who am I to judge." Makoto shrugged. "I'm just glad you came to your senses."

Cracking another smile, I nodded at him in understanding, then brushed past him and sprinted to the door.

"Riku, before you go . . ."

Holding onto the door's frame, I stopped and looked over my shoulder.

With Makoto's back facing me, he scrunched his shoulders and tucked in his chin, then slipped his hands into his front pockets. "Make sure you come over for dinner more often. My mom keeps asking when you'll come by next."

"Got it," I said, the corners of my mouth turning upward. Thinking for an additional moment, I asked, "Do me a favour, will 'ya?"

"Jeez, how many favours can someone possibly ask for?" he joked, continuing to stare at the wall.

"Don't tell your family I was here today. I don't wanna disappoint them."

"I wouldn't dream of it."

"Thanks, man."

At top speed, I ran down the stairs, skipping a few steps along the way. Being careful not to eat shit and fall flat on my face, I reached the bottom of the staircase in no time and determinedly stepped into my sneakers before bolting it out the front door and taking off in the direction of Hinata's dorm.

My heart drummed through my body. *I'm sorry, Hinata. Wait for me. I'm coming.*

Chapter Fifty-Two

SITTING OUTSIDE THE complex with Makoto, it was impossible not to hear my mother screaming her head off inside our apartment, shouting every curse word in the book. Though I was able to hear her, I couldn't see her, and I wasn't allowed any further contact. Not like I wanted to be around my mother in such a delusional state, anyway.

On site, a police officer and CGC officer questioned me for hours on end, and while they did, Mrs. Fujimoto refused to leave my side. My case worker drilled me with hard, pressing questions, some of which I had no idea how to answer, but Mrs. Fujimoto came to my rescue by taking control of the conversation. She was scolded many times for talking out of turn, but that didn't stop her. Although Mrs. Fujimoto was terrifyingly assertive, I felt the safest when she was near. She looked at me with only kindness and love in her eyes, something that was hard for me to understand.

The car door swung open, and I was kindly ushered out by Mrs. Fujimoto. After what happened at the apartment complex, I was so incoherent that I didn't realize we had already arrived back at the Fujimoto residence.

Dazed, I stumbled up the walkway, keeping a few steps behind Makoto who eventually grabbed my hand so I wouldn't fall behind. Usually, I would have swatted away his clammy hand, but this time I held onto it for dear life.

Entering the house, many familiar faces awaited our arrival.

"Riku!" Megumi and Mitsuki shouted, running toward me. "You're back!"

Makoto's sisters, along with Mr. Fujimoto, were at the entrance waiting for us to return. I had left this house only a few hours ago, but they welcomed me back as if I had been absent for months. This led me to believe that the whole family had known ahead of time on what would take place today.

Makoto slipped out of his shoes and pulled me further inside. "Come on, Riku. Let's put your stuff away in our room."

Stuck on his word choice, my eyes widened, and my heart stopped. "'Our'...?"

Mrs. Fujimoto stepped inside and stood behind me, then placed her hands on my shoulders and said, "Yes, Riku. Makoto's right. This is your home now; therefore, you have a room here. Although you'll be made to share with Makoto, just like Megumi and Mitsuki share, we'll soon get you your very own bed. How does that sound?"

My face was already in so much pain from crying all day, but the tears wouldn't stop flowing. My tear-filled eyes shifted from Mrs. Fujimoto to Mr. Fujimoto, who smiled from ear-to-ear.

Looking upon Mr. Fujimoto's kind, heartwarming face, he signed, "Welcome home, Riku."

I managed to get to the dorms in less than an hour before visitors would be turned away, only to have a security guard inform me that Hinata had left about an hour earlier.

"Does she have a cellphone? Have you tried calling it?" the security guard suggested.

"Her phone!" I shouted, facepalming my forehead. I hadn't even tried to contact her; I rushed to the dorm on impulse.

Pulling out my phone, I scrolled until I came across Hinata's name in my contacts. *Man, I'm such an idiot!*

"Thanks, sir," I said bowing, while quickly making my way back out the doors.

Outside, I tapped on Hinata's name and listened to the hum of the dial tone. Looking up at the darkening sky, I grew antsy.

Pick up! Pick up! Pick—

"Riku?"

"Hinata!" I shouted into the phone, unrehearsed. "Where are you? I'm at your dorm, but the security guard said you left."

There was a brief silence, but before I could even give Hinata the chance to respond properly, I spoke into the phone again. "You there?"

"I'm here."

"Where are you right now?" I asked again.

"You went to the dorm?"

"Yeah, I'm standing outside the building as we speak." I paced the walkway in front of the dorm, not knowing which way to turn.

"Why are you there, Riku?"

"Why?" I repeated, absentmindedly. "Well, I—I wanted to say I was sorry . . . Please, we need to talk. I wanna discuss some things with you and apologize in person."

Hinata stalled for a moment before replying. "I'm surprised you don't know where I am."

"What . . . d'you mean?" I asked warily, listening carefully to any background noise for hints.

"Riku," she spoke into the phone softly. "I want to go home."

"Hina—"

Before her name could leave my lips, she hung up. Looking at my phone, I stared blankly at Hinata's name across my screen.

'I want to go home.'

I replayed those last words over and over again, trying to decipher what she meant.

Home.

A lightbulb went off in my brain.

I knew exactly where she was.

⁂

Makoto was right. I sabotaged everything good that came into my life with my skewed perception; I was the centre of all my problems. And I hadn't fully comprehended his words until this very moment. But this time, I wanted things to be different.

They *needed* to be different.

I had no resolve when it came to Hinata; nothing mattered or made sense except for her. I no longer knew how to live a life without her in it. She was my *home*. All I knew was that I wanted to be with her, we could figure out the details later, just like Makoto said.

I parked the bike and dashed up the exterior stairway of my apartment complex. I was out of breath by the time I reached the top floor. Flying around the corner, I stopped dead in my tracks as soon as I saw who awaited me. Heaving and huffing uncontrollably, I felt the pressure in my chest amplify.

"Hinata."

She was crouched down in front of my door like a lost kitten. A lifeless smile plagued her lips. "Welcome home, Riku."

There was a thickness in my throat and a joy in my chest that made my head spin when she said that simple sentence.

How did I ever come to think that I could get by without her? The thought alone was baffling. It had only been a day, and it was one of the most miserable days of my life—*I* was lost without *her*. How could I push away the person who taught me how to love? Why did I selfishly repress my feelings from her? From myself?

At first, I could only muster up enough courage to take a few steps forward until the need to hold her consumed me. Drawing inspiration from Makoto's words, I hurried down the underpass and approached her with full force. She stood to meet me, and I caught a glint of tears rimming her eyes. Her gaze was hesitant, and her cheeks were tinged red.

Coming to a complete stop in front of her, I took my thumb and brushed her tears away. "I'm sorry."

She bunched her hands into fists and drummed them gently against my chest, repeatedly. "Don't EVER do that again," she said, her voice trembling. "Don't ever decide something so important on your own. How dare you try to tell *me* the depth of *my* feelings for you!"

I held her face in my hands. "I know. I'm sorry."

"Do you think I'm that shallow of a person, someone who would judge you solely based on what type of family you came from? You can't just make statements and determine things on your own, as if you know what's best for me! I know what's best for ME, dammit!"

"You're right. I'm sorry." All I could do was acknowledge her words, for she spoke the truth.

I had pushed my insecurities on her without allowing her to share hers in return. It took me too long to understand and accept that. I made decisions that weren't mine to make alone, ones I thought benefitted the both of us.

But I was wrong, so very wrong.

With one final hit, she collapsed into me. "You can't make me fall in love with you, then leave once things get hard . . . You're truly the worst."

Hinata's feelings were pouring into my heart. To console her, I wrapped my arms around her tightly. Holding the back of her head, I pressed her further into me. With a hushed voice, I spoke into her ear, "I truly am. I'm so sorry, Hinata. For everything."

"As long as you know," she mumbled, her voice muffled from speaking into my chest.

"I do."

We held each other for a while longer, each afraid to let the other go. It wasn't until one of my neighbours stepped out of their apartment that we broke our embrace. Keeping my head low, I bowed at my neighbour respectfully, then pulled out the keys to my door and unlocked it. Reaching down, I made haste in grabbing the bag Hinata had brought with her before inviting her into the apartment.

Once inside, I dropped Hinata's bag by the entrance, then turned around to face her again. Her cheeks were wet from crying, something that I regretfully caused. Watching her shed countless tears over the last few days had destroyed me; above all, she was suffering because of the things I had said and done.

Could we really move past this?

"Riku."

"Hmm?"

"Do you love me?"

Taken aback by her blunt question, my heart thumped. Dropping my eyes, I replied, "You know I do."

Taking a step toward me, she reached out and grabbed hold of my shirt, clinging to it desperately. "I want a future with you. You and only you. It *has* to be you. Please . . . say that you want that, too. A future with me."

Staring down at her docile frame, my heart did a somersault. Our feelings were one and the same. Words alone could not describe how happy I was. I felt a devotion to her.

I can't believe I thought I could kill my feelings for her. I'm such a fuckin' idiot.

By the hand, I drew her in close once again. This hand, this body, this person, this love—I wanted all of it for myself, for the rest of my life. That, I was sure of. "I want it."

"Want what?" she asked, testing me.

"A future."

She pressed. "With whom?"

"With you," I said in a whisper. "I want a future with you, Hinata."

She hugged me with all her might as I pushed back her hair to place a kiss on her forehead.

My lips outlined her face and traced her entire neck; I couldn't wait to place many more on other parts of her body. One thing led to the next and soon we found ourselves shedding clothing onto the floor. I lifted her up in my arms and continued kissing her lips urgently. She wrapped her legs around me as I redirected us to the bed.

Laying her down gently, Hinata took charge by flipping us over and getting on top, all while we slipped out of the clothes that remained. Breaking our sequence of kisses, I stopped to look up at Hinata and gazed upon her beauty as she hovered above me. She was the epitome of perfection; and she wanted me—loved me—and I loved her.

Focusing my gaze on her face, she smiled at me lovingly as she stroked my chest with the tips of her fingers. This rush of heat on my skin, I only felt it when I was with her; I was enchanted by her touch. I soaked in the tenderness she exposed me to. Just when I thought I didn't have a shred of confidence in love, the reassurance I acquired in her smile was spellbinding.

Before we progressed further, I wanted to express my thoughts and feelings to Hinata. The feelings I kept hidden. I needed her to know that my love for her was impossible to shake, no matter how easy I thought it would be to forget about her and everything we had.

"Hinata."

"Hmm?" she hummed, her fingers still trailing up and down my chest.

"My understanding and perception of love has always been distorted," I started, swallowing aggressively while holding the intense gaze of our eyes. "But these feelings I have for you are scary as hell and are growing at an uncontrollable rate." I brought my hand up to caress her cheek. "The whole incident with my mom scared the fuckin' shit outta me. I've never been so afraid in my entire life like I was then. That's why I thought it was better to separate myself from you. To protect you. But no matter how scary these feelings I have for you are, they're also amazing."

I made my heart transparent, and even though I was terrified by doing so, I wanted to convey to Hinata that I could do it.

"Riku . . ."

"Hold up, let me finish," I said, not wanting to ruin my momentum.

And to that, she smiled and nodded.

I dragged out an exhaled breath. "I'm sorry it took me a moment to figure all that out. It's crazy to think that I tried to deny these feelings by simply tossing them away. Dramatic as it may be, considering it wasn't even a full day since I broke things off, I surprisingly learned a lot about myself. About my feelings."

"And what feelings are those, Riku?" she piped up, knowingly.

She was never afraid to ask the hard, embarrassing questions; I don't know how she could bypass the cringe factor that came attached. And I don't know why admitting such feelings was so hard for me, especially when I was only admitting them to her. But I did notice a change in me. A change she had instilled.

One corner of my mouth pulled back. "You're enjoying this, aren't you?"

"I really am."

I shook my head. "Of love—for you—Hinata Tachibana," I expressed, my face surprisingly holding its temperature. "I know I've said it before, but I don't want you to ever forget it, especially because of my mistakes. I love you, Hinata, and I don't think I'll ever stop."

Hinata lowered herself down to my lips with hurry. We exchanged multiple, deep kisses, and I took each kiss as her response.

Why did I ever assume that distancing myself from her was the best route, as if my feelings for her would dissolve overnight? Obviously, they hadn't. They wouldn't. How could they?

From the start, these feelings crept up on me, and before I knew it, I was hooked.

Hinata informed me that she had made previous arrangements to stay the night. Even if she hadn't, I wasn't going to let her go back to the dorm, not tonight anyway. Tonight, all I cared about was spending time with her, safe in my arms, and returning things to the way they were.

Chapter Fifty-Three

WITH ONLY THREE days left of high school, Hinata forced me out of bed so that we could head out early. We left the bike behind and decided to walk, as it would most likely be the last opportunity we had as high schoolers. We walked hand-in-hand for the first time, like an ordinary, stupid couple. And I was all for it.

Bringing our joined hands up to my mouth, I placed several kisses on the back of Hinata's hand. Things had definitely shifted between us. Hinata accepted all of me, the good with the bad. We were changing, growing, and we were doing it together.

Along our walk, we noticed the streets and local parks were lined with a multitude of fully bloomed cherry blossom trees. Never paying much attention before, I noticed areas of Tokyo's streets were flowing with many shades of pink. Loose petals fell from the branches above, dancing in the spring breeze before kissing the ground or shoulders of those who walked by.

Taking in the city view around me, I thought out loud. "After the graduation ceremony, d'you wanna go cherry blossom viewing?"

She looked at me, a bit taken aback. "Sure, but why the sudden interest?"

"Dunno, just thought it'd be a nice idea for a date. We could take the bike and go for a ride until we find a place that's not crowded with people. Somewhere outside the city, where hundreds of trees are blooming."

A grin happily made its way onto her face. "That sounds lovely."

Her smile caused my ears to burn, as if they had caught fire and gone up in flames. *She* was lovely. "It's a date."

At school, Hinata and I commenced our climb up the stairs to the classroom. There, we came across Makoto climbing the last set of steps ahead of us.

Wanting to grab his attention, I shouted, "Makoto!"

Makoto turned and stopped midway on the staircase before pulling off to one side, waiting for us to catch up.

"Go on ahead," I said to Hinata. "I'll meet you in class. I gotta talk to Makoto for a sec."

She looked at me gingerly.

I smiled. "Everything's all right, don't worry."

Hinata nodded. "Then, I'll meet you in the classroom," she said, continuing up the stairs. "Make sure you both get there before the final bell chimes."

"Yes, yes," I said, laughing at her teacher-like demands.

Hinata bowed her head and said good morning to Makoto as she passed him before continuing on her way. In return, Makoto did the same. He then looked down at me from the few steps above with a knowing smile.

"I'm glad to see you guys together."

"She spent the night," I said, landing on his step.

Makoto's face flushed. "Jeez, you sure don't waste any time. But, like I said, it wasn't much of a breakup."

Finding his virgin mind amusing, I chuckled, then slapped his back before pulling him into a headlock. "Wasting time is for those who have nothing to lose. I have nothing to gain but everything to lose."

We almost fell down the stairs when Makoto pushed me away trying to escape, but once he realized what I'd said, he stopped. Staggered, he gazed up at my face while remaining in a loose, half-ass headlock.

"I'm surprised to hear you say that so openly, Riku," he said with wide, bewildered eyes. "Yesterday, you were in a much different headspace. What happened to make you change your outlook so quickly?"

"Hinata happened," I expressed, letting go of him. "She's incredible . . . I dunno what I did to deserve her."

Correcting his posture and flattening out his pristine uniform, Makoto fixed his hair and glasses, then let out an annoyed sigh. "Now you're just bragging about your girlfriend."

We both shared a moment of laughter.

"Your words lit a fire under my ass, man," I said, bringing the conversation back. "So, thank you. I also dunno what I'd do without you."

"Don't mention it." Makoto smiled embarrassedly. "We're friends, after all," he said, holding onto his words. "Actually, scratch that. We're family. You've always been the brother I never had."

I tore my eyes from his as a tickle formed in my throat. "Stop saying dumb shit."

"Whatever, jerk," he said, lightheartedly.

Just then the first bell chimed, and as promised, we headed to class.

⁂

The day carried on without much effort on my part; I did as I was instructed but fooled around when opportunities arose. The cleaning portion of graduation preparations was practically out of the way, so most students were sent to do the final touchups on the gymnasium setup. Hinata and I were separated from Makoto, who had student council duties to attend to relating to the upcoming ceremony. Such an important guy didn't have time to goof off.

When the teachers weren't watching, I would often go over and distract Hinata until I was caught and harshly scolded, most often by Kobayashi-sensei. I could tell that Sensei was growing tired of my shenanigans, but this was what made the final days of high school remotely bearable. It's not like I was going to get suspended this late into the game, so why not make the most of it? Watching Sensei lose his patience with me was something I took shameless pride in. Somewhere inside him, I knew Sensei was going to miss me, there was no sense in him trying to deny it. Oddly enough, there was a slight chance that I might even miss my quarrels with him.

Keyword being 'slight.'

I didn't get away scot-free, though. Nearing the end of the day,

Kobayashi-sensei instructed me to take a few boxes to one of the prep-rooms located on the second-year's floor as punishment.

Just as I finished, and was returning to the gym, I caught Sakura on one of the stair landings. Trying my best to avoid her, my efforts were put to shame.

"Riku, do you have a moment?"

I knitted my brows and sighed with irritation. "What d'you want, Sakura? I gotta get back to the gym. Someone's waiting for me."

"Tachibana, right?" she asked, a frown flicking across her face before forcing a smile. "You two are officially dating, huh? With strings and every-thing attached?"

"That's right," I confirmed, leaving no room for misinterpretation.

Judging by Sakura's conflicted demeanor, I could tell she was working up the courage to say something, but I couldn't figure out what.

Over the past month, there had been subtle moments throughout the day where I'd caught Sakura staring at me, only to deflect eye contact once I'd met her gaze. Nothing had ever come about it, so I had paid her no mind. Until now.

"I won't keep you long, then," she said, taking a deep breath.

Before whatever this was went any further, I wanted to make one thing clear to her. "Listen, if you're looking for forgiveness or some half-baked apology on my end, then don't hold your breath," I said, crossing my arms over my chest. "Let me save you the trouble by laying out the plain fact that things will never be the same between us. We'll never be good. I'll live with the guilt of betraying Makoto forever; there's no coming back from some-thing like this." I lowered the voice I found myself raising unintentionally. "The friendship we once had isn't salvageable, Sakura. Anyone with a brain would understand that."

"I know," she said with a stern tone, absorbing all the harsh truths and insults I threw her way. "But I still want to apologize, anyway, even if it only makes *me* feel better." She blinked back a few tears. "I'm tired of walking on eggshells around you guys. We were friends—good friends—and although we can't turn back time, I can't keep carrying this heavy feeling around anymore. But, if I must carry it, I just want the regret in my chest to lighten so I can better manage it until I make peace with it." Avoiding my eyes, she brought her arms up and hugged herself, rubbing the outer parts of her arms up and down. "I don't expect you to forgive me for coming in between you and Makoto, because I know you won't, but I didn't want to graduate without having tried to at least apologize to you. No matter how much it pains me, I've already come to terms with us no longer being friends. After waking up beside you that morning, I knew our friendship was over. You became unreachable as soon as I saw the desperation and disappointment in your face."

I took Sakura's words into consideration, even if I had to fight against my better judgement.

I get it now.

I couldn't forgive Sakura because I wanted her to be better, better than me. I needed her to be. For Makoto's sake. I had unknowingly put expectations on her, and when she didn't live up to those expectations, I got upset and lashed out at her.

Reminiscing back to the beginning of high school, when life was much simpler, I think I subconsciously started sleeping around more once Sakura came into the picture. When she started hanging out with Makoto and me on a regular basis, and Makoto admitted to having had a crush on her, I made sure I was never available to her. If I was being honest, I think I did that to convince Makoto, but mostly myself, that I wouldn't go after Sakura. That she was off limits. I had kept that mentality going for a couple of years, only to throw my hard work away on a single, drunken night.

Truth was, Makoto deserved better than both of us.

"Well," she said, interrupting my thoughts, "that's all I wanted to say. I'm really glad I got all that off my chest. I feel like I can graduate with a better conscience knowing I had the chance to talk to you one final time before probably never seeing you again." Sakura wiped away a lingering tear with the palm of her hand before it had the chance to drop, then tilted her head and smiled timidly. "Sorry I couldn't be the girl you wanted for Makoto, but I guess it's better this way, right?" Leaving that as a rhetorical question, she pressed on with no room for an answer. "I'll admit, I miss having you guys around. I have a lot of regrets about how things went down, but I don't regret the three of us being friends, or the love that I felt for you, Riku. If you didn't grant me this moment, then I'd probably look back on high school with bitterness. So, thanks for hearing me out. Make sure to take good care of Tachibana, got that?"

I knew I owed Sakura an apology, but I couldn't bring myself to give her one. She wasn't the only one in the wrong; I was just as much to blame. But all I could do was nod my head.

Sakura wasn't expecting a response from me, I could tell by the way she quickly walked past me after saying her piece. All she wanted was to vent about what was eating away at her, to clear the cloudiness surrounding her mind and heart.

So, I let her do just that.

"Bye, Riku."

"Bye, Sato."

I spoke my parting words with intent, drawing a definite line of where I stood. Sakura got my message loud and clear, as she fronted me with a thin-lipped smile before descending the stairs ahead of me.

Chapter Fifty-Four

I WAS STANDING BY the shoe lockers at the end of the day, Hinata by my side, moments away from sweet freedom when my name was called out by an annoying demon.

"Mr. Nakajima," Kobayashi-sensei said. "A word, please."

Rolling my eyes, Hinata giggled as I left her side to follow Sensei to the teacher's lounge. I had planned to walk Hinata back to the school dorms, so she said she'd wait for me to finish so that we could leave together.

Tailing Sensei with audible footsteps, I followed him to his desk at the back of the teacher's lounge. His desk was in complete disarray, even more so than usual. There were piles of notebooks, textbooks, and file folders with sheets of paper sticking out at each and every end stacked higher than my head.

"Excuse the mess," he said, pulling up a chair for me to sit on before sitting down on his. "The end of the year is chaotic for us teachers."

"If that's the excuse you wanna go with," I said mockingly, taking my seat.

His brow twitched. "We're going to do this right to the bitter end, I see."

"Would you want it any other way?" I antagonized.

"Actually, yes," he said annoyed, crossing one leg over the other. Then, he crossed his arms over his chest and brought one hand up to his face, his index finger stretched up along the side of his cheek toward his temple. "ANY other way would be better."

My lips tipped in amusement at our exchange as I leaned back in my chair. "So, why am I here this time?"

Sensei broke character with a smile that curved his lips. "What's with the hostility, Riku?" he paused, judging my expression. "Relax, this is just an informative session. At this point, I'm sure you're well aware that there's really nothing you could do that can prevent you from graduating."

"How sweet," I said, grinning mischievously. "Did you pull me aside to personally congratulate me? Aww, does this mean I'm your favourite student?"

Expecting to rile him up with my comment, I prematurely laughed at my own cleverness.

"For once, you're correct."

My laughter dwindled. "I'm what . . .?"

Now having the upper hand, Sensei uncrossed his arms and continued smiling warmly. "I pulled you aside to congratulate you. It's always difficult to gauge when you'll be at school, even your attendance at the graduation ceremony is uncertain, so I thought I would do it now while I have the chance. So, here it comes." Kobayashi-sensei stood from his chair and reached out his hand formally. "Congratulations, Riku. You did it."

Staring up at him and his extended hand in disbelief, I was rendered speechless.

Besides the Fujimotos, never in a million years did I think I would hear someone personally congratulate me for graduating high school, especially not him. Though I knew the end of the year was only days away, and my final marks were submitted and were suitable to withstand scolding from the demon lord himself, I was still shocked.

After graduation, I would never be made to wear this uniform and step foot into this building again. Never be made to sit through one of Kobayashi-sensei's boring class lectures ever again.

I . . . did it? I really . . . did it, didn't I?

Rising onto shaky legs, I reached out my hand cautiously to accept Sensei's congratulatory handshake. He met me more than halfway before pulling me into a strong embrace, patting me on the back. Not knowing how to react, I remained limp.

"I'm proud of you, Riku," he said close to my ear. "You've come a long way since the day we first met. Though we've had our ups and downs over the years, maybe more downs than ups, I wish you all the best in your future." Sensei pulled back and placed a hand on each of my shoulders, his thumbs encompassing my neckline. "I have no doubt that you'll work hard to obtain the things you desire. You have amazing people looking out for you, myself included. If you ever need anything, please don't hesitate to seek me out. All right?"

My eyes were dry from the lack of blinking; I was beyond stunned.

Who was this unfamiliar, solid guy standing in front of me? Was this really the demon that had made my time in this school so insufferable? Thinking back on the last three years, was my time here actually *that* awful?

Every time Kobayashi-sensei dragged me into the hallway or to the teacher's lounge, he rarely acted upon his threats. They were more or less empty; I was more of a disappointment to him than anything. All he ever did was warn me about the things that could happen if I didn't change course, if I didn't smarten up.

Why did I believe that I hated him so much? What was there to hate? All he ever did was look out for me, far more than my non-existent father ever did. Sensei's overbearing attitude and actions were equivalent to those of Mr. and Mrs. Fujimoto, so why did I shit on him so much? Why did I give him such a hard time? Was it because I wanted to worry him? To have someone pay so much attention to me—did I secretly enjoy it?

How twisted.

Repulsed with myself and my behaviour, I hung my head. It gradually became harder to swallow the saliva that lingered; I felt my throat constricting. There was a burning sensation nesting in my esophagus, as if acid was sizzling a hole in it. Why was I such a dick? Over these last three years, I didn't learn a damn thing. Was I really ready to be out in the world on my own, without any guidance? All I wanted was to be an independent adult— so, so bad—but how could one tell if they were mature enough?

"How unlike you to be so quiet," he said, dropping his hands. "Did you happen to swallow your tongue, Riku?"

Sensei's voice broke through my spiraling thoughts. He spoke his words in a joking manner, one befitting our combative relationship. But this time, instead of a quick-witted comeback, I bit my lip to hold back tears. Unsuccessful, teardrops rolled down my cheeks and landed on the tops of my school slippers.

Trying to hide the falling tears, I quickly bowed. "I'm sorry, Sensei."

Leaning to one side, I watched as Sensei shifted his weight. "'Sorry'?" he repeated. "Sorry for what?"

"I'm sorry I was such a dick over these last three years," I stated, powering through the tears. Still bowing, I squinted my eyes shut in an attempt to stop the endless river flowing from them. "I see now that you were only looking out for me. You were always trying to help me, but I never listened. You had my best interests in mind, and I didn't care to see that. I'm sorry for making your job unnecessarily harder."

"Riku," he said, softly, "everyone you're involved with has been looking out for you. Take Mrs. Fujimoto for example." He took in a strong, profound breath. "She and I have been in constant contact over the years in regard to you, even though her biological son is also one of my students. She cares for you deeply, just as I do. As per my last phone call with her, we both came to a mutual understanding that, from here on out, you are going to be okay on your own. You've finally chosen a path for yourself, and we're very proud of you for it. So," he paused, briefly, "that's enough of that. Lift your head."

Listening to his heartwarming, behind-the-scenes justification, I made sure to wipe away the lingering tears before standing upright. With watery, reddened eyes that burned from rubbing them, I straightened out and rolled my shoulders back to appear taller. Presenting a fake sense of confidence, I looked at Sensei's composed face. "Mrs. Fujimoto, huh? She's a force not to be messed with."

"Yes," he agreed. "She's an upstanding woman, who happens to be very involved."

"I see," I said, with a smile that only reached my lips. "I'm always causing her trouble."

"You cause everyone around you trouble," he said with a scoff. "It's strange to see you get so emotional; I didn't expect such a reaction from you." Sensei reached out to tousle my hair. "You've grown, Riku." He grinned. "And not just in height."

Moving to keep him from further trashing my unkempt hair, I pushed his hand away with embarrassment.

"I'm glad I got to help shape the fine, young man you are today. Being put through the wringer with you these past three years was well worth it if it led you to become someone so strong and determined. It's water under the bridge now."

After failing to compose myself in front of Sensei, again, I crumbled at his mercy. Comforting me by messing up my hair once more, this time I let him. Though I still felt humiliated from showing him such a weak moment, afraid he'd tease me for it later, I suppressed the awkwardness I felt.

I had been unaware of the amount of people who cared about me, leading me to believe I was alone in this ruthless world. How could one be so candidly blind without having lost their ability to see?

That was a question for which I knew I didn't have an answer.

I returned to the shoe lockers where Hinata waited and found her leaning against them reading a book. Once I was in her line of sight, she placed a bookmark in her book, then shut it and stood up straight.

"How did it go?" she asked, before considering my face. "Well, I take it?"

Pondering her question for a moment, I smiled shamelessly. "Maybe he isn't such a demon, after all."

Hinata looked at me sideways. "Takes one to know one, huh?"

I narrowed my eyes. "What's that supposed to mean?"

She smiled angelically. "Oh, nothing." Unclipping the straps on her schoolbag, she tucked her book inside, then pulled out a can of coffee. "Here," she said, handing it to me.

"When'd you get this?"

"I got it while I waited for you. It's your reward."

"What am I, a dog?" I asked, grabbing the can.

She rolled her eyes. "If you don't want it, I can take it back."

Quickly cracking it open, I shook my head theatrically. "Thank you for your patronage."

Hinata guffawed. "Mhmmm."

Chapter Fifty-Five

GRADUATION DAY FINALLY arrived, and the school was prepared and presented in high accord for its annual graduation ceremony. All the graduating students were sharp and made to look their best, as we were instructed to wear our uniform blazers to present ourselves formally. It was an exceptionally hot spring day, so luckily the ceremony was held inside or else we all would have sweated our asses off.

Students filed into the transformed gymnasium in straight lines and sat in their designated seats by name, just like rehearsed. Third years sat at the front near the stage while the second years, first years, and families of the graduating students sat behind in an organized fashion. All homeroom teachers and faculty members sat on the sidelines in accordance with their respected classes.

Both Makoto and Hinata's families made it. Makoto's sisters had taken the day off to attend, saying they wouldn't miss us graduating for the world. Hinata's family had flown in from France and were staying in a hotel for a few weeks to help Hinata move out of her high school dorm and into her new college one.

During the Tachibanas visit to Tokyo, I had hoped to organize a one-on-one conversation with them to discuss a few things regarding my relationship with Hinata.

With the way the seating arrangement

worked, I sat in one of the middle rows and was coincidentally placed second-in from the end near the teachers. Out of boredom, I had been surveying the gym to pass the time, hoping to zone out long enough to bypass all the speeches. My eyes roamed the large area before I narrowed in on Kobayashi-sensei, who was now standing and whispering loudly in conversation with the principal's secretary. As if sensing my attention on him, Kobayashi-sensei locked eyes with me. Immediately, his face went pale, and his eyes screamed an unexplainable sorrow.

Fuck. Something was about to go down.

Instructing me to meet with him and the principal's secretary with a flick of his head, I rose from my chair quietly and glanced back at Hinata, who was sitting a couple of rows behind me. Hinata returned my stare with concern, as if asking me if she should follow. Subtly shaking my head, urging her to stay seated, I turned to the person sitting next to me on the end and excused myself before passing in front of them. Makoto, who was sitting closer to the front, had yet to notice the disturbance taking place behind him.

Out in the hallway there were two police officers waiting patiently to speak with me. Once the doors of the gymnasium were closed, Kobayashi-sensei stood in front of them like a guard, while the principal's secretary stood off to the side with her hands folded together.

Finding their silence daunting, my composure weakened.

"Riku Nakajima?" one of the officers asked.

"Yes, that's me," I answered, stammering tersely.

"Mr. Nakajima, sorry to disturb you at such an important time," the other officer chimed in, apologetically. He bowed. "I'm the commanding officer, Officer Yoshida, and this is my partner, Officer Kanata. We are aware that you are currently busy with your graduation ceremony; however, we cannot delay this matter any further."

Trying to recall all the bad or illegal things I took part in recently that could possibly cause police involvement left me clueless. I couldn't figure out if their appearance today would be the deciding factor in whether I graduated. I thought I had been doing a good job at turning shit in my life around. What obstacle was possibly left for me to overcome?

"Mr. Nakajima, there isn't any easy way to say this," Officer Yoshida commenced, taking in a burdened breath before continuing, "but we were called to do an anonymous wellness check on your mother, Sachiko Nakajima, this morning. We are assuming the phone call was made by a concerned neighbour."

My . . . mom?

"When we arrived on scene, your mother was found on the floor of her apartment and was presumed dead upon arrival. After further investigation, it is apparent that she had in fact been deceased for a couple of days prior to our wellness check. The cause of death is reported as a drug overdose."

My heart ceased in my chest and my eyes widened until my vision pixelated and I saw double. The officers standing before me became fuzzy shadows that bounced around the harder I focused.

She's dead?

"Mr. Nakajima, we are incredibly sorry to be delivering you this news, especially on such a joyous occasion. As per our records, we understand you were not currently living with your mother, but instead have been under the supervision and care of a Mr. Yuuto and Mrs. Aoi Fujimoto. We are unable to contact or locate your father at this time to inform him of your mother's passing, as he is not listed on any official documentation. We—"

Still trying to piece everything together, I blinked at the mention of my father. Before I could correct the officer, a hand was placed on my shoulder.

"The father is not listed because he is absent in Riku's life," Kobayashi-sensei interrupted, jumping to my rescue. "There is no need to investigate his whereabouts any further."

"And who might you be, sir?" Officer Kanata spoke up, jotting notes down on a pad of paper.

Sensei bowed his head in apology. "Sorry, my name is Jun Kobayashi. I'm Riku's homeroom teacher."

"I see," Officer Yoshida said, in response to Kobayashi-sensei. Sighing regretfully, he redirected his attention back to me. "Mr. Nakajima, we are going to need to go over a few things with you down at the station. It will be more private there, as well. We will get in contact with the Fujimotos to—"

"The Fujimotos are actually present on the school grounds," Kobayashi-sensei informed, cutting the officer off once again. "Their biological son is also a graduate today, so they are seated guests inside the gymnasium." With one hand still cupping my shoulder, he brought the other up to push back his hair. "With all due respect officers, can this not be dealt with after the ceremony? This is a very important day for Riku. I would hate for Riku's hard work to go unnoticed and his efforts to be for nothing if he were to leave partway through."

Kobayashi-sensei was extremely uneasy; his hand on my shoulder trembled. Sensei was putting up a strong front on my behalf, and though I had no words, I welcomed his touch. After having listened to everything unfolding before me, the news of my mother's death still hadn't registered. I stared motionlessly into space.

Officer Yoshida seemed perplexed, as if he didn't know the right way to go about resolving the issue at hand. Heaving another long sigh, he pressed on. "I know this is a difficult matter to discuss. I also know that I cannot be the one to decide what is best for Mr. Nakajima." Looking to me, he tilted his head to catch my eyes. "The choice is ultimately yours. What would you like to do, Mr. Nakajima?"

"Mine?" I mimicked, lifelessly.

"Yes," Officer Yoshida confirmed.

I wasn't able to create enough saliva to swallow before speaking and it left my tongue feeling like sandpaper. I wanted to speak, to answer the officer, but what was the right thing to do? Based on my decision, who would I disappoint the least?

Everything inside me was growing more and more uncomfortable. My head was spinning to the point I felt sick, like I was trapped on a constantly looping roller coaster. I was placed in an impossible position; one I didn't know how to handle. She was gone, and as sickening as it was, I wasn't the least bit sad.

"I'll leave the ceremony and go to the station."

"Riku," Kobayashi-sensei said, his voice full of surprise. "Are you sure? We can always head to the station afterwards. I can even drive you there myself."

Just as Sensei left me with another possibility to consider, I heard my name faintly being called over the microphone by Principal Koga inside the gym, most likely to go up to the stage and receive my diploma. With my lack of participation, Principal Koga's voiced could be heard repeating my name over the microphone one final time.

This became my deciding factor.

Rolling my shoulder, I slipped from Kobayashi-sensei's hold and took a step forward toward the two officers. "It's fine, Sensei."

"Riku . . .," Kobayashi-sensei said, the strength in his voice withering.

"Could you please let Makoto's family know where I snuck off to? I don't want my disappearance to worry them," I said, my back to him. "But make sure to only tell them after the ceremony is over. I don't wanna ruin the day for Makoto. That goes for Hinata, too."

"Very well," Kobayashi-sensei said, gloominess shadowing his tone. "I'll make the arrangements for the Fujimotos to meet you at the station, and I'll fill in Miss Tachibana once there's a chance."

"Promise me you'll only tell them after the ceremony," I said sternly, unwilling to budge.

"Riku . . .."

"Sensei, you gotta promise me, all right?" I said, over my shoulder.

He paused for a moment. I'm certain it was never his intention to keep that promise. "Okay, Riku . . . I promise."

Chapter Fifty-Six

"*R*IKU," SHE SAID, *holding the door open for me, "things'll be different this time, you'll see. Mommy is better now. We can finally be a family again."*

Even with the door being held for me, there was a hesitation festering inside me, keeping me from entering. Looking through the open door, things inside seemed different—brighter. The lights in the apartment were on, something that rarely happened, and the hallway was decluttered of garbage.

Taking note of my reluctancy, she went on to say, "Riku, baby, y'know Mommy loves you, right?"

My shoulders tensed and my mind went blank. This phrase hung over me like a gloomy cloud during a rainy day. Why did she have to say that? Anything other than that would have been fine.

With a light nudge, she pushed me inside. "C'mon now, don't be shy. This is your home."

Taking a few forced steps, I dropped my bag on the floor of the entryway. It had been eight months since I was taken from my home and made to live with an awful foster family. The entire time I was gone I had cried endlessly with hope to return here, to return to her. But now that I was here, I wasn't so sure. This heavy feeling inside me was troubling and hard to explain.

Before being dropped off at the apartment

complex by my case worker, I was told that my mother was 'better,' allowing me the ability to return home safely. Before, everyone around me kept saying things like my home was unsafe or unfit for me, and that's why I needed to leave for a while so that my mother could get better and make our home safe again.

Walking through the kitchen and stepping into the living area, I went over to the corner in which I slept and spent most of my time. It was there that I noticed a brand-new futon laid out on the floor.

"Surprise!" she shouted from behind, making the hairs on the back of my neck rise. "It's a futon, ta-da! Mommy got it especially for you. I saved up enough money to get it for you before your return home. Mommy was given a list of stuff to get for you before you could come back home—this was one of them. Do you like it?"

Gazing down at the soft-looking, warm futon brought tears to my eyes. "Yes . . . thank you."

"I'm glad you like it, baby," she said, hugging me from behind. "It cost Mommy a lot of money, but no worries because Mommy has a job now! Aren't you proud of me?"

Still blown away after seeing the new futon, my eyes grew wide. Tilting my head up to look at her, I said with excitement, "Wow, really, Mom?"

"It's true!" she said, sharing that excitement. Squeezing me tighter, she continued to explain. "Mommy is a waitress and has been working hard, all so that she could get her precious baby back."

"Congratulations, Mom. I'm really glad you're better."

"Yes, and now that you're home, Mommy is feeling even better!" Letting go of me, she ran to the kitchen. "Are you hungry? Mommy can make you something—anything! You name it! Mommy has been learning how to cook from the line cook at work."

Never having tasted my mother's home cooking before, I took a small step toward the kitchen. "Is it really okay, Mom? Can I really ask for anything?"

"Yep! Ask and Mommy will try her best to make it. Though, there's no guarantees that it'll taste very good," she said, tittering nervously.

"That's okay," I said, reassuringly. "Anything you make will be good. I'm sure of it."

"Then, what'll it be?"

"What about . . . hamburger steak?"

"Coming right up."

That night, for the first time inside those four walls, I went to bed with my stomach full. The hamburger steak was completely burnt, but it was the best thing I had ever tasted, because she made it for me.

But, as the days went on, the meals became less and less extravagant until they eventually phased out altogether. She missed dinner often and didn't leave me money to buy anything from the convenience store, either. Her attitude toward me also grew colder the more I forced interactions or affection. Just like before, a familiar pattern was taking shape.

One night, there was a mysterious knock at our door. Startled, I turned to the small clock near my futon to check the time. It was just after 3:00 a.m.

My mother, who hadn't slept a wink, rushed to answer the door. Peeking at the entryway from my futon, I listened to the hushed conversation.

"Don't knock so goddamn loud, you idiot! You'll wake my damn kid," my mother whispered loudly, her voice harshening with each word.

"Sorryyy," a recognizable voice said, exaggeratedly.

Trying to get a better look at the man, I squinted my eyes. To my surprise, it was the man named Daigo *that my mother used to frequently spend time with, back before I was taken away.*

"Don't 'sorry' me, asshole. I can't let 'em, or anyone, find out this time. Do y'know how hard it's been puttin' on a fake smile all the goddamn time? If I don't got this stupid brat in my possession, then I don't get government fundin'," she barked. "Whatever, you got my shit, or what?"

"Yeah, yeah. Damn, Sachiko, you're even bitchier than usual."

"Shut up," she said aggressively, ripping something out of the man's hand. "I'll pay 'ya tomorrow."

"Tomorrow?" The man raised his voice. "What the fuck? That wasn't part of the deal!"

"I don't got the money right now. But relax, Daigo. I get paid tomorrow. Swing by my work and I'll pay 'ya on my break."

"You better make good on your word, Sachiko. You know what my boss'll do if you don't."

"I know," she said, tucking something into her back pocket. "Now, get the hell outta here before my brat wakes up."

As the door slammed shut, I closed my eyes and hid inside the futon.

It wasn't long after that night that my mother was fired from her waitressing job, and the case worker reappeared at our apartment.

⁂

A feeling of liberation swept over me during my ride in the back of the police cruiser to the station. My mother's pitiful existence no longer held me back. Her meaningless life was over, and the fact that she was no longer causing herself, or those around her, harm brought me peace.

Not a single tear came to my eyes when the officers told me of my mother's passing, therefore, not a single tear was shed on her behalf. If I wasn't able to shed them, I doubt anyone else would. I won't deny the fact that I was momentarily shaken to learn the news, since I'd recently encountered my mother face-to-face and nothing about her had changed, indicating that she would soon die.

Death at a young age was a long time coming; it was inevitable for her. In hindsight, I'm surprised she lasted as long as she did. Any other ending to her pathetic life would have been a true shocker.

The black, miserable cloud that had loomed over me my entire life evaporated into a bright, clear sky in mere moments. I was free, free from her. My troubled past was vanishing from my memory, as if the memories were fragments sketched in sand, only to be washed away by the rippling tide of the ocean.

Though I envisioned it and wished death upon her many times, I can't say I ever felt remorseful for thinking those dark thoughts. There were many times that I killed my mother inside my head; I'd beat the shit out of her until she was black and blue, on the verge of death and gasping for air, imploring me to stop. But I didn't have the stomach to go through with something like that in real life. I don't think I could bring myself to actually kill someone, no matter what hardships they bestowed upon me. Though—in saying that—even if the memories faded, the pain attached to them would forever remain.

A million questions crossed my mind: Did I kill her? Did seeing my face one final time push her over the edge, causing her to end her own life? Did she ever care about me in my absence from her life? Did she overdose on purpose, or did she do it accidentally?

These, along with many more, were all questions that would forever be left unanswered.

We were all brought into this world without a choice, and I think that's undoubtedly unfair. People who don't know how to take care of themselves, let alone an innocent child, should not be given the opportunity to procreate and become a parent. Those who toss children aside, as if they are nothing more than dolls, should burn in the depths of hell. Same goes for any type of child protection system—no matter what fancy name it's given. Children are innocent participants, never asking to be placed in an unloving home situation, but the majority of people in power turn a blind eye or take their sweet-ass time to intervene. And usually by that point, it's far too late. Not everyone is blessed with a kind, caring family to come and save them.

I was lucky.

Life never stopped dangling impossibilities in front of me, and deep down I was terrified of ending up with nothing and no one to hold on to. But with each passing year, I grew less attached and learned how to be strong alone. I had to. Because my mother wasn't able to grasp her society-deemed title for long.

The more my mother pushed me away, the easier life became. She was a manipulative, self-destructive monster; not afraid to drag those close to her down with her. She was ruthless, much like my unmasked feelings toward her. By the end, we were complete strangers.

She couldn't be the mother I needed, and I couldn't be the son she wanted.

Ever since I was a kid, barely old enough to understand, I knew my mother was *different* from those of my friends at school. Whenever I went to a friend's house, they would have multiple family pictures around their homes, something which caught my attention each time because I never had a single one in mine.

My mother became an empty vessel, immersed in a lifestyle full of drugs and alcohol. It completely destroyed her, along with the few people who could tolerate her without being paid to do so. Though many tried, no one could save her; you can't help somebody who doesn't want to be helped.

For most, sadness would have been guaranteed. So, why did I feel a sense of relief and sovereignty? The air that now entered my lungs was thin but full, clean but crisp.

Before long, the Fujimotos arrived at the police station, along with Hinata and her father. I was seated in the police chief's office, which was encased with large, glass windows that allowed anyone inside to see when new faces entered through the front doors of the station. Everyone startled as Mr. and Mrs. Fujimoto came bursting through the doors, with their children filing in right behind them. Once Mrs. Fujimoto located me, she met my eyes and stormed into the chief's office without invitation.

As Mrs. Fujimoto abruptly entered, demanding to be filled in, I shifted my eyes to those who remained out in the waiting area. Gazing upon Makoto and Hinata's distraught faces, I noticed they were both huffing and puffing, most likely out of breath from hurrying over to the station after hearing the news. Tears flooded both their eyes, but I knew those tears weren't for my mother's sake, they were for mine. I could see the pity written all over their faces.

Not knowing what face to show them, I turned away, biting my bottom lip to suppress the strain of emotions in my chest. I hadn't cried yet, because truthfully, I wasn't sad that my mother was gone—never to be seen again—but I couldn't stand to see the upset faces of those closest to me, hurting on my behalf.

The day had been long and tiring, and because nothing else was required or could be done, Mr. Fujimoto was instructed to take his daughters home while Mrs. Fujimoto and Makoto remained.

Mr. Tachibana tried his best to get Hinata to leave but was unsuccessful. She wailed and made a scene, refusing to leave the station. With pleading eyes, Mr. Tachibana looked my way. Understanding that I was probably the only one who could calm her, I took Hinata into my arms. I attempted to console and convince her that everything would be okay, and that I'd contact her as soon as I could. But before agreeing to leave, Hinata did something concerningly strange.

Clinging onto me, sobbing into my chest, Hinata cried out, "It's all my fault! I'm so sorry, Riku!"

She recited this many times in between sobs. The Hinata in that moment reminded me of the Hinata who broke down in my apartment after encountering my mother. I was afraid to leave her in such a state, but for the time being, I had no choice.

"Hey, hey," I said assertively, tilting her chin up to look at me, "it's not your fault, okay?" I couldn't stand seeing her this way. It pained me. My throat rolled as I swallowed the lump that was stuck in it. "None of this is your fault, so stop apologizing. Do you hear me?" I was raising my voice now. "I don't want you to think for a second that any of this has to do with you."

Hinata nodded her head silently, but I don't think she truly believed my words. Guiding her into the arms of her father, I let her go with a heavy heart, and watched her leave the station without me.

Mrs. Fujimoto helped during the police chief's interrogation regarding my mother and family history. Because of the way my mother died, and because of my upbringing, things were much more complicated than a natural or accidental death. Now that I was an adult, Mrs. Fujimoto was not allowed to sign any documentation for me but guided me through each and every step.

From pictures taken at the scene, I was easily able to identify my mother's body. I refused to hold a funeral or create any sort of memorial in my mother's honour; there would be no grave to remember her by. No preparations would be constructed by me; I would not spend money or time on a woman, such as her, by laying her to rest.

The chief said that according to Commanding Officer Yoshida and Officer Kanata's report, my mother's body was sent to be cremated after the photos were taken as it could not last in its current condition much longer. Mrs. Fujimoto remained relatively quiet during this time, only asking me once if I was sure of my decision to not hold a funeral. Feeling no remorse about the outcome, I confirmed without a second thought, not wanting to dwell on it any further.

The interrogation session concluded, and I was released from all questioning and paperwork. I walked out of the station, a couple of steps behind Makoto and Mrs. Fujimoto, feeling like I'd been set free. With my head held high, it truly felt like things were over. The string attached to the past that bound me, broke. I was no longer a prisoner of the evil that was my mother.

Chapter Fifty-Seven

FOR THE REMAINDER of graduation night, I spent a lot of time in my head.

Mrs. Fujimoto refused to let me be alone in my apartment, so I was forced to stay at the Fujimotos for a while. I could tell that Mrs. Fujimoto found my lack of mourning extremely concerning, and a part of me figured she was afraid of what I'd do in closed quarters.

All I wanted was for things to get back to normal, but I couldn't blame everyone for worrying about me. If I was an outsider, I'd be worried, too. The probability of my mother dying from her addiction was something I had shamelessly spoken often of while growing up, so I didn't understand why Mrs. Fujimoto, specifically, was so surprised by the predictable outcome.

I messaged Hinata a few times, but she never messaged back. After waiting a few hours, I decided to call her, but also got no answer. Makoto advised me to give her some space and try again tomorrow, that her family would take good care of her. He also suggested that I get some rest after everything that happened, but it was hard to shut my brain off. Knowing Makoto was right, in both aspects, I eased off. But the memory of how Hinata reacted at the station, and the words she spoke into my chest, left me nervous.

The following day, Kobayashi-sensei appeared at the Fujimoto residence with my diploma. He proceeded to ask me if I would accompany him for a walk. Accepting his request, we headed out toward the neighbourhood park. Never having experienced the demon so quiet, like he was now, I thought of ways to break the silence during our travels.

"Sensei—Ah, guess I shouldn't call you that anymore," I smirked. "After all, you're no longer my teacher. Would *Mr. Kobayashi* be better?"

Ignoring my attempt at lightening the mood, he replied in a low voice, "You can keep calling me 'Sensei' if you want, Riku. I don't mind."

Not expecting such a deadpan reaction from him, I stopped in my tracks. We had just come off the pedestrian bridge and were now faced with the park benches that lined the main entrance. Getting annoyed by everyone's pitiful attitudes toward me, I scrunched my shoulders and balled my fists.

Noticing my disappearance from his side, Sensei stopped and turned around. "Riku? What's the matter?"

"Stop it. Just . . . stop it," I said, seething with bared teeth.

"What—" he started to say, but I cut his sentence short.

"STOP FEELING SORRY FOR ME, DAMMIT!" The sound of coursing blood pulsated in my ears.

With the afternoon sun on his back, Sensei stared at me bleakly, saying nothing. He just stood, gawking at me. Then, with fretting eyes, he spoke. "Honestly, I don't know what to say or feel on your behalf. I'm worried about you. Up until this point, you've been doing so well. I would hate to see you enter a place that could derail all your progress." He inhaled deeply. "I don't want to regret doing nothing this time."

Understanding what he was referring to, I dropped my tense shoulders. He was speaking of the past and the little girl in his class who had taken her own life.

"Last time, I sat back and waited for others to jump in and take action, but no one ever did. No one did anything. This time, I'll do everything in my power to make sure my student is okay."

He left me dubiously tongue-tied. Conjuring up a response, I couldn't bear to look at him directly. "W-why Sensei . . . .."

"Why what?"

"Why would someone like you . . . give a shit about me? Why would you go to such lengths for me?"

From the corner of my eye, I saw Kobayashi-sensei run his fingers through his styled hair. His eyebrows rose, and his eyes were round and glossy. "You don't seem to get it, Riku," he said, stressed. "Like I've told you plenty before, I care about you. Many people do, you just have to accept the help and love they offer." He stopped to clear his throat. "Sometimes I see my teenaged self in you, not as extreme, but there are similarities."

I lifted a brow. "You do?"

"I do," he confirmed, grinning. "I was so impatient to grow up and didn't want to accept help from anyone. I had too much pride." His smile faded. "But in the end, it cost me. I ended up crashing and burning, begging for the help once offered to me when it was too late."

"What happened?" I asked, thoroughly invested.

Sensei rolled his eyes, then removed his hand from his hair to tug on the back of his neck. "Long story short, I had a great family support system, but we didn't have much money growing up. I'm one of five children, and the first of my siblings to go to university and get a career outside of the family business. My family owns a few flower shops," he stated, as if knowing that I was short of asking. "My siblings have expanded it into a small franchise. It's become very successful and I'm proud of my siblings for living out and expanding on my parents' dream, but that life wasn't for me. I loved teaching and helping others learn; that lightbulb moment when someone understands what I've taught them, sends an electrical current through me." He took in a big, burden filled breath. "My siblings knew my parents couldn't afford to send me to university, after having already put five children through high school, so collectively they saved their hard-earned money to pay for my university tuition."

"Wow," I said, truly blown away. I was shocked to learn so much about Sensei and his upbringing. Just went to show that I knew nothing about him.

"Wow, indeed," he said. "I went through a lot of emotions. At first, I was ecstatic—who wouldn't be? But the more I thought about it, the more upset I got." He shook his head, but it seemed to be directed at himself. "I was mad that my siblings wasted their money on me; I didn't want to have to owe them anything. Everyone pitched in and it felt like I needed to pay everyone back. I felt like a disappointment to my family because I was the only one who didn't want to fall into routine; I didn't want to chain my life to the family business."

I considered his story for a moment. It wasn't the same as mine, but he was right, there were definitely similarities. For instance, an overbearing, caring family who wished nothing but the best for you. Ones we felt monetarily indebted to. "So, what did you do?"

"I distanced myself," he answered sadly. "I moved out and any money I made on the side from tutoring gigs went to paying my family back. I drove myself crazy. Meanwhile, my family continued to support me, no matter how many quarrels I created out of thin air. I was mad at myself and took it out on them." Sensei swallowed while looking away. It appeared that he was trying to hold back tears. "It wasn't until my oldest brother got sick and eventually passed away that I realized I wasted time on being angry for no reason. Even on his deathbed, my brother was happy and proud of me, never once mentioning the money I believed I owed him. To him, he was selflessly helping me. He never expected anything in return. And I'm mad at myself for realizing that too late." Sensei turned back to me. "Riku, let the people who love you and want to help you, help you. It makes them—us—me, happy." He cleared his throat of this sappy moment. "I guess what I'm trying to say is that maybe I favour you more than the rest of my students, something a teacher should never do or admit. Don't go telling the others, okay?" he finished, a hint of good humour in his tone.

A sharp ping stabbed my chest; Sensei's words struck me like a dagger through the heart. It was hard to wrap my brain around what he was saying, mostly because I found it hard to trust people who spoke their emotions so openly. But he was vulnerable with me, something no teacher, or adult in general, had ever been.

"I'm sorry about your brother, Sensei."

"Thank you, Riku."

Throughout my life, words like the ones he'd spoken got my hopes up, and I was tired of false hope. But he gave me a reason to trust him, time and time again, and hadn't let me down. His words laid comfort in my heart.

With a slight smirk, and tears clouding my vision, I unclenched my fists and took one step toward the blurred figure before me. "Okay, Sensei. You win."

In the end, we never made it to the park. We stepped back onto the pedestrian bridge and leaned on the railing, hanging our arms over the edge as we carried on in conversation.

With the sun reflecting off the small river flowing below us, I slowly opened up to Sensei about my dark thoughts regarding my mother. He never stopped me or offered his advice on the matter; he simply listened. Without the need to look at each other, our conversation carried on that way for well over two hours. Though I had expressed some of these dark feelings to Hinata and Makoto in the past, neither of them knew what was currently going on inside my head. Sensei was the first person to hear me convey such harsh words about my mother and her death, and how I didn't feel an ounce of remorse.

Each time I opened my mouth, I feared Sensei would judge me and start seeing me differently, but the words wouldn't stop spewing out, and he didn't react negatively in the slightest. I was angry. I lived my whole life in anger, and I didn't know how to stop. With my mother gone, who could I blame for my shitty life?

This time, the answer was simple—no one but myself.

Chapter Fifty-Eight

SENSEI AND I parted ways, and just as I was about to head back to the Fujimotos, I got a message from Hinata. Ignoring the contents of my previous messages, she said:

[LINE Hinata Tachibana]: I'm outside your apartment.

My apartment? What's she doing there?

[LINE Riku Nakajima]: I'm not home. I spent the night at Makoto's. You okay?

[LINE Hinata Tachibana]: I see.

Something seems off. Her reply is weird.

[LINE Riku Nakajima]: Are you okay?

[LINE Hinata Tachibana]: How fast can you get here?

Worried by her responses, I bypassed messaging and went straight to calling her.

"Hinata," I said into the phone when she

answered. "Are you okay? What's wrong?" Changing course, I sprinted toward the closest subway terminal.

"How fast can you get here?" she asked once more, again, avoiding my same question.

Her voice sounded distant, and that scared me. I accelerated my sprint into a full-fledged run. "I'm already on my way. Wait there for me."

"Okay," she replied, before hanging up.

Clenching my phone, I ran the fastest I'd ever run, even during my time playing soccer. Wishing I had the bike, I ran the whole way to the subway without stopping, bumping into people left and right as I went. Luckily, my train had just arrived on its platform, making it convenient to fly through the doors without having to wait. Once inside, I was finally made to stop and catch my breath, but my one leg wouldn't quit jittering as I held onto the handle above my head.

C'mon, c'mon. Faster, faster.

I positioned myself right in front of the subway car doors so I could run out and jump onto the next transfer. Gunning it out of the final subway car, I booked it up the stairwell and back up to the surface, continuing my star track run all the way through the busy streets.

Slowing, I sent Makoto a quick message saying that I was stopping by my apartment to grab some stuff and to not expect me back for a bit. I told him to tell his parents not to worry about my absence.

Knowing very well that I was pushing my cardio capabilities, I refused to stop until my apartment complex was in sight. Coming to a halt, I bent down and put my hands on my knees, taking a moment to breathe, then shot right back up to tackle the final set of stairs. Skipping every other step as I climbed, I made it to the top floor in no time. And, just like last time, she was there on the ground, leaning against the wall and hugging her legs. Waiting.

"Hinata," I said, out of breath.

Unlike last time, she didn't fake a smile. Her face was drenched with tears, and her eyes were red and swollen; she looked terrible. Red blood vessels were prominent in her eyes from the lack of sleep she must have tortured herself with. How could someone's face change so much in a day?

Walking toward her, I crouched down to her level and grabbed one of the hands wrapped around her legs. "Hinata . . .?"

"Riku," she said ghostly, accepting my hand, "I'm not okay."

My eyes grew heavy as I stared at her; it killed me to see her this way.

I let go of her hand for a split second to unlock my apartment door, then bent back down and lifted her limp body up into my arms before carrying her inside. Kicking off my shoes at the entryway, I brought her to my bed and lowered her down to sit on the edge. With a tearstained face, she looked up at me desperately. Kneeling, I took off her shoes, then crossed my arms and rested them on her lap. Her eyes followed each of my movements.

"Hinata," I spoke softly, "what happened?"

With a lick of hesitation, she lowered her gaze.

"Hinata?"

A warm teardrop fell onto my exposed arm and rolled off. Her eyes were shut tight, but that didn't stop the tears from escaping. In fact, they fell even harder. Reaching up, I cradled her cheek in my hand.

"Hinata, please."

Opening her flooded eyes, she gripped her hand around my wrist. "It's all my fault, Riku. I'm so . . .," she tried to express, but was overwhelmed by her emotions. "I'm so unbelievably sorry."

She was crying in earnest now and could barely look me in the eye. She didn't have to explain for me to understand what she was apologizing for. It was the same thing as yesterday. She was blaming herself for my mother's death, and that destroyed me. All I ever did was cause her pain.

"Hinata, look at me," I said assertively, bringing both hands up to her cheeks and supporting her face to look at me straight on. "None of this is your fault."

"But it is. I killed her, Riku! Me! I KILLED YOUR MOTHER JUST LIKE I KILLED MY FATHER!"

"STOP THAT!" I shouted over her. "Stop saying dumb shit like that! You didn't kill anyone!"

She broke free from me and pushed me away. Bringing her hands up to her face, she sobbed into them. In a muffled, tearful voice, she pressed on. "She would still be alive if I hadn't forced you to take me to see her. I made you take me to the red-light district. I made you point her out to me.

I got off the bike. I approached her, even after you warned me not to. ME! IT WAS ALL ME! You both weren't ready to see each other again, to talk to each other again, but I made you both do it! I did this—ME! Just like my father! If I'd only done better, been a better daughter, then maybe he wouldn't have killed himself!"

Lifting to my knees, I wrapped my arms around her entire head and pressed her face deep into my chest. "You didn't do this. I took you to Shinjuku—to Kabukichō—and I showed you things that I never should've. You should've never met my mom. Even if I had no idea that things would turn out like this, I knew my mom was unstable and that nothing good would come of it. I wanted to take you on a ride so badly that I jeopardized your safety." I paused to swallow my guilt; the feeling of barbed wire wrapped around my throat. "My mom overdosing was her choice—her mistake. SHE refused help and continued down that path all on her own. Just like your dad taking HIS life was HIS mistake. He never should've left you behind. He should've sought out help instead. But it was THEIR lives and THEIR choice. They chose the wrong paths. So," I said, brushing the top of her head with my hand, "that's enough, Hinata. It's enough."

Hinata didn't reply. Instead, she bunched my shirt within her hands and expelled tears into my chest. We stayed like that for a few hours, only changing our position once to lie down next to each other on the bed.

To get Hinata to ride with me on the motorcycle, I made decisions that led to mistakes. I manipulated her. And now I was faced with the consequences.

Hinata had spent the previous night convincing herself that she was responsible for my mother's death, just like she blamed herself for her father's, which was a new discovery. She had never even hinted at blaming herself for her father's death when we spoke about it in the past, but the pieces of the puzzle were finally connecting.

I held the broken Hinata in my arms as she cried, rubbing her back consistently until she passed out from exhaustion. After she was sound asleep, I slid my arm out from underneath her and pulled out my phone to notify Makoto of the sudden change in plans.

[LINE Riku Nakajima]: Yo, I'm gonna stay at my place tonight. Hinata's with me and she ain't doing too good. Let your folks

know that I won't be coming back to your place. Tell your
mom not to worry. I'm fine, promise.

After hitting send, I looked back at the sleeping Hinata on my bed. With the residue of tears dampening her eyelashes, her complexion looked awful, like she hadn't slept in days. Even in her sleep, she didn't look peaceful. I desperately wanted to expel the daunting thoughts swirling around in her head, the thoughts she had of my mother and the ones of her father, but I knew I couldn't. I was powerless.

Watching her chest elevate and collapse choppily, I wondered if she was having a nightmare. My heart drummed angrily as I gazed upon her struggling face. It took a special kind of screwed-up person—like myself—to be fine with how things turned out. Life was always shitting on me, very little left me surprised. I just learned to shut up and deal with it.

As sad as it was, I was growing content with how things were playing out, while Hinata was falling apart. I knew she was going through immense heartache, and though I wanted to help her, I also didn't want to lose her this time—I couldn't. After a failed attempt at trying to put distance between us, there was a reason we couldn't part. Hinata needed me just as much as I needed her.

It was egotistical of me, but that's what I wanted to believe.

Stepping out onto the balcony, I moved into my usual spot, resting my arms on the railing. I gazed out into the open space before me: the darkening sky, the buildings, the city lights, taking it all in as I reflected on my life and my poor decisions.

It wasn't wise for Hinata to be wasting her short break between high school and college with me. There was only a week for the transition, and her parents had travelled back to Japan to help her move and settle into her new dorm. I'm sure the Tachibanas were burdened with everything that's happened since the graduation ceremony, and I felt like shit knowing that I was the cause for the delay. Hinata should have been filled with overflowing joy and excitement to start her college life; instead, she spent the duration of her free time crying over me and the events shaping my life. Nobody ever wants the person they love to cry and hurt because of them.

I loved Hinata, but my love was suffocating her.

Peering down at the ashtray beside me, I thought of the crumpled cigarette pack in my pocket. Though the packaging looked destroyed when I pulled it out, the single cigarette that I meaninglessly held onto was slightly bent but intact. Bending down to grab a lighter I kept near the ashtray, I placed the mangled cigarette in between my lips, then lit it. Taking in that first hit for the last time, I cherished each moment I had with the poison I welcomed into my body.

Finishing the cigarette right until the bitter end, I stubbed it out in the ashtray, then went back inside to check on Hinata.

Allowing her to sleep for a few more hours, I regretfully woke her up once it hit 9:00 p.m. Groggy from being woken, I helped her get ready so I could give her a ride back to the dorms. Her phone had been going off non-stop, so I could only assume it was Mr. or Mrs. Tachibana, but I didn't want to invade her privacy by checking. After a quick phone call to her parents, explaining her disappearance and that she was all right, Hinata hung up and asked if I could take her to her parents' hotel.

Securing her helmet before my own, I started the bike and threw up the kickstand. Once we arrived, I left the bike idling as I remained seated on it. Removing our helmets, Hinata hopped off and walked to the front of the bike with sagging shoulders, holding the helmet down in front of her.

"Thank you for the ride, Riku," she said, with a bit of hesitation.

Her eyebrows were angled downward while her eyes radiated pain. I couldn't stand to see her like this. Reaching for her hand, I rubbed the top of it back and forth with my thumb. I didn't know what I could say or do to make things better, to fix her. If I did, I would have done it as many times as needed, until she felt better, over and over, until a smile was drawn on her beautiful face.

"Let me know if you need help packing or moving things into your new dorm. I'm just a phone call or message away."

"I finished packing everything into boxes before graduation," she explained with a hushed voice. "All that's left is to move it from one location to another. My father hired a moving company to take care of it since he sold his car before moving to France."

"I see," I said, with a faltering smile. Not knowing what else was left to discuss, I pulled Hinata in closer and placed a kiss upon her lips. "Goodnight, then."

Handing me the helmet in her hands, I pushed it back toward her. "Keep it."

Her eyes turned into slits as she looked at me with confusion. "'Keep it'?"

"That's right."

"I don't understand, Riku. I couldn't possibly keep one of your helmets."

"I only bought it with you in mind. I don't plan on riding with anyone else. If you keep it, it saves me from having to ride with it back and forth. Think of it as a gift." Smiling up at her tenderly, I attempted a lighthearted joke. "Sorry, looks like you'll have something else to pack."

"Riku . . .."

"Also, I don't want you to think I'm going anywhere this time," I explained, acting on her hesitation from earlier.

The sadness trapped in her eyes dissipated and was infiltrated with an ounce of what looked like hope. Her eyes twinkled. "Okay," she said, with a smiley nod.

Chapter Fifty-Nine

I T WASN'T LONG before Makoto and Hinata settled into their new lives. I helped Makoto move into his new apartment in Kyoto, all while transitioning to start at Uncle Ito's shop full-time. When I was done with Makoto, I squeezed in time to visit Hinata at her new campus. It was when we were hanging out in her new dorm room that I noticed she still wasn't back to her usual self.

Not only did I miss the opportunity to take Hinata on our cherry blossom viewing date, but I missed the chance to speak with Mr. Tachibana privately about a certain matter. Before the Tachibanas returned to France, Mr. and Mrs. Tachibana found a moment to assure me that we all just had to give Hinata time. They guessed, as I had come to understand, that my mother's death had triggered Hinata's grief for her birthparents.

Though everyone kept reassuring me that time would heal, I struggled with leaving Hinata alone. I felt like a useless, shitty boyfriend; I didn't want to abandon her emotionally or physically. The only thing I could come up with was to try and make Hinata a meal that brought her some comfort, something familiar.

Reaching out to Mrs. Fujimoto for some cooking lessons, I successfully made omurice, but only after a bunch of failed attempts. When I delivered the home-cooked meal to Hinata at her dorm, she was beyond surprised by my unexpected gift. Her facial reaction was priceless, one I wished I'd captured on camera. Though it was subtle, the smile I was able to bring to her face, with such a simple gesture, was beyond rewarding.

⁂

I was ecstatic to be working at the auto body shop; the job gave me fulfilment. Working alongside Uncle Ito and the gang, as an apprentice, was a dream. But something was missing. Even though I was progressing incredibly fast, according to Uncle Ito, I felt incredibly alone. I missed having my best friend around more than I expected, and I missed the presence of the girl I loved even more.

With Hinata being close by, we thought we'd be seeing each other often during our weekends off, but things didn't go quite as planned. She quickly grew busy with school, joining programs pertaining to the piano, and clubs like choir. Though I was lonely, I was extremely proud of her.

To suppress the absence of seeing each other, we tried to call each other as often as possible. During one of our calls, Hinata told me she reunited with her old friend, Neiko Uchida, who coincidentally got accepted into the same music school.

"It was so weird, Riku! We practically live in the same building and have been attending the same school for a while now, but only saw each other for the first time today."

I could hear the excitement in Hinata's voice as she talked about her long-lost friend, and that brought a smile to my face. "You guys probably kept missing each other in passing, then."

"That's what we were saying, too. What are the odds?" Hinata giggled.

That was the first time I had heard Hinata truly laugh since the morning of our high school graduation, and I couldn't have been happier. Finally, the tightness in my heart eased.

⁂

When summer break hit, I rode over to Hinata's dorm to take her out for a ride, knowing the day would end with her coming back to my place. Hinata and I had known each other for over a year now and had been dating just as long.

It was a Saturday, and Hinata didn't have any school clubs or activities to take care of. She was free for the entire weekend, and we planned to spend the entirety of it together.

Once I arrived at the dorm building, I flew past the new, now familiar security guard, bowing to greet him along the way, then ran up to Hinata's floor to get her. Knocking on the door, I was hardly surprised when Neiko opened it.

"Well, well, if it isn't the infamous boyfriend, Mr. Nakajima."

Hinata was in a joint room with someone from her program who she quickly became friends with, and you could often find Neiko hanging out in their room, too. Hinata's ability to open herself up to people was broadening since she knew she wasn't going to be made to move away, and I loved it.

"Ugh, don't say it like that. You sound like a Sensei that Hinata and I had in high school."

Neiko laughed as she stepped aside, allowing me to enter. "She's almost ready."

Taking a few steps inside, I asked, "Neiko, you're not going home for summer vacation?"

"I am. I leave tomorrow. I still have a few things to catch up on here before I go back home," she answered, walking further into the room, and sitting on top of Hinata's unusually messy and unmade bed.

"Gotcha."

"Too bad Hinata can't go visit her family in France. That girl is sooo damn busy! She takes on way too much."

I rolled my eyes. "Tell me about it." Looking around for the girl in question, the one that still gave me butterflies, I turned to Neiko and gave her a look as if to ask where Hinata was.

"She went to the bathroom down the hall. She'll be right back."

Nodding in understanding, I continued to look around the typically tidy room only to find it entirely upside down. The mess was solely contained to Hinata's side. There were bins upon bins of music books and scores out in the open, clothes piled up everywhere from the floor to the bed to the shared computer chair and desk, and other various items left out in the open. This unorderly Hinata was suspicious.

"What's going on here?" I asked, swiping my hand through the air to showcase the mess at large.

Neiko rolled her eyes and giggled. "She's been looking for something since last night. Turning up every inch of her room in a panic to find it before you showed up."

Raising a brow, I tilted my head. "What's she looking for?"

Neiko smiled devilishly. "Not telling," she sang.

With narrowed eyes, I shot good-humoured kunai at her.

"Riku!" Hinata entered the room and said with surprise. "You're already here?"

Turning around to face her, I wasn't sure if she was happy or disappointed to see me. "Is that a problem?" I asked, judging the shift in her facial expressions. I looked at my wristwatch. "We agreed to meet around noon, didn't we? It's okay if you're not ready yet. I can help you get your stuff together."

Hinata shook her head. "It's not that . . .." She looked a little disheartened.

"Then, what's up?"

Hinata let out a pent-up sigh. "I can't find it."

"Find what?"

"The helmet."

My confusion came to a halt. "Ah, so that's what's going on." I relaxed my eyes. "It's gotta be around here somewhere. You used it a few weeks ago on our last ride."

"Honestly, Hina, you're hopeless," Neiko said shaking her head, as she made herself more comfortable on the bed by sitting cross-legged. "How do you lose something as big as a motorcycle helmet?"

Hinata shrugged her shoulders in disappointment. "I don't even know."

"Well, it won't be in the bathroom, that's for sure," I teased.

"I went to get my toiletries," Hinata stated, shooting me a glare. "I've been so preoccupied with the helmet that I almost forgot to pack for my weekend away."

I took another look around the room, then walked over to the desk which had a blanket draped over a pile of random items. The blanket reached all the way to the floor and looked as if it had been tossed at the desk without a care. Lifting the blanket off the hidden items scattered on and beside the desk, the helmet appeared. It had been lodged in the corner between the desk and a laundry basket.

"That was easy," I said, peering over my shoulder.

Neiko flew back on the bed in a fit of uncontrollable laughter while Hinata's eyes enlarged.

"I swear I checked the area around the desk!" Hinata said, trying to defend herself.

"I'm sure you did," I said, smirking. I bent down to grab the helmet and carried it over to the door, placing it on the floor in plain sight so we could remember to take it with us. Then, I began picking things up at random to help get the room back into its original state before stealing Hinata. "Now, let's get this room in order before your roommate gets back and has a heart attack from the bomb that went off in here."

"Annnd that's my cue to leave," Neiko said, jumping off the bed and rushing toward the door. She hugged Hinata on her way out. "Have fun on your weekend away." She winked at Hinata indiscreetly. "I'll see you after the break. Have a good summer vacation. Bye-bye!"

Hinata shook her head dismissively but smiled. "Bye, Neiko. Have fun going back home."

After the whirlwind called *Neiko* left, I helped Hinata get the remainder of her stuff ready for our weekend together. Once we were good to go, I grabbed Hinata's bag and tossed her the helmet.

"Don't lose it from now until we get outside. You can't ride on the back of the bike without it."

Hinata clicked her tongue in annoyance. "I'm never going to live this down, am I?"

"Nope," I snickered.

She elbowed me in the stomach to shut me up.

"That's a foul!" I refereed. "Elbows to the gut aren't allowed when someone is holding something."

"I hardly touched you," she said, cracking a smile. "Don't be a baby."

"Ouch," I said, placing a hand over my heart. "I didn't realize I was dating such a tank. Those elegant piano hands are actually quite deadly, but not as deadly as that sharp tongue."

She rolled her eyes before shoving me out the door so that she could lock it behind us. "Enough. Let's go already."

"Yes, ma'am."

Chapter Sixty

I ADVISED HINATA TO pack all her stuff for the weekend into a single backpack, since we'd be taking the bike. Not wanting to rush back to my apartment so soon, I decided to take a bit of a scenic route.

The night before, I instructed Hinata to pack a swimsuit since I had planned for us to stop at the beach. We spent countless hours swimming and playing like children in the ocean, annoying all those who swam past, then eventually got out of the water and sat on the sand to dry off. Neither of us remembered to pack a towel, but with the scorching sun beaming directly from above, we didn't need one. Within fifteen minutes, we were practically dry and ready to put our clothes back on but decided to laze around in our swimsuits.

In search of a shady area to sit and avoid burning our asses on the hot sand, we found a quiet spot at the edge of the beach near a bunch of large, bordering rocks. The rocks had cast enough of a shadow for the two of us to sit comfortably, but I sat Hinata in between my legs so that I could lean my head against her. The summer heat was zapping my energy, and I needed her touch to reenergize. Shutting my eyes, I took in a deep, fulfilling breath, then released it with ease. This tranquil moment with her was perfect. If only all days could be as fun and carefree as this one.

"It's so hot, and your breath is making my

back sweatier than it already is," she said, leaning forward to avoid me. "Don't get too close; I'm sure I stink."

Pulling her in closer, I wrapped my arms around her and placed a kiss upon her shoulder. "Nah, you don't. But your skin is crazy salty," I said, licking the ocean residue off my lips.

Hinata leaned into me and ran her fingers up through my disheveled hair. "I can smell the salt lingering on our skin."

"We'll need to take a shower once we get back to the apartment," I replied with a crooked smile.

Hinata rolled her eyes while nuzzling herself deeper into my chest.

We loitered in silence for a moment, appreciating the ocean breeze that swept across our skin and tossed our hair in all directions. As Hinata tamed her wild hair, I twirled the damp ends of it in between my fingers.

When the wind settled, Hinata, without reluctance, asked, "Riku, do you want children?"

My stomach dropped with her absurdly random, and mood-killing, question.

I knew this would branch off into a topic I never thought I'd discuss seriously with a girl. Children were something I had known I absolutely didn't want. In the past, I was always extremely careful whenever I fooled around, making sure to use protection to avoid getting any girl pregnant. The last thing I wanted to do was procreate.

My family situation was beyond fucked; I refused to bring a child into a world surrounded by people like my mother or absentee father. Bringing an innocent child into a world where they were doomed before they could even take their first breath was selfish and reckless.

I couldn't possibly father a child—I didn't know the first thing about being a father—and I most certainly wouldn't be good at it. What child would even want a piece of shit like me as their father?

The answer was simple: none.

Hinata sensed my hesitation as the joy was sucked from my expression. "Riku?" she said, lifting her head off my chest.

With unwavering eyes, I answered, "No."

"Hmm," she hummed, returning my gaze as she pondered in thought.

Waves came crashing onto the rocks beside us, enough to spray water droplets up into the air and land on our skin before being pulled back into the ocean. There was a colder breeze in the air now as the sun was no longer directly above us.

Looking into Hinata's eyes, I was surprised that I wasn't faced with an ounce of resentment. Never dreaming that having a future with someone could be possible, where the topic of children would be brought up casually in conversation, I was out of my element.

If I want a future with Hinata, is children something she wants? Needs? Would having them make her happy? Why're we even talking about this? We're still so young!

"In the future, I would love to have a big family," she said after a long pause. She deviated her eyes, then smiled to herself. "Before the twins came along, life was grim. Being an only child wasn't much fun. In fact, it was downright lonely." She paused again, this time tucking a piece of hair behind her ear. "When I have children, I don't want them to ever feel lonely."

I took Hinata's words into account; we were both *technically* only children. "How many kids d'you want?"

"Two or three, maybe more."

I felt my eyes grow two sizes in their sockets. *Holy fuck! That's a lotta kids!*

"Riku, I didn't ask you this question to fluster you," she said, turning back to face me. Folding her legs to one side, she buried her feet in the sand. "I was just curious as to what your thoughts about the topic were. I believe I understand your reasoning."

Bringing one knee up, I propped my elbow on it and rested my chin in my palm. "Your questions always freak me out. Why would this one be any different?" I said, with a laugh that escaped me.

"I didn't mean to freak you out. Honest. I was just curious."

"Yes, yes. You wouldn't be the Hinata I love if your curiosity didn't control you."

With that comment, Hinata scrunched up her nose and flicked some sand at me. Instead of flicking sand back at her, I grabbed her wrist and pulled her into me, landing a kiss on her lips as punishment. During our kiss, I could see Hinata's eyes scanning the area around us. We were in a somewhat secluded area of the beach, so I figured we were in the clear from people's wandering eyes. But, even if people were watching, I didn't care.

I would kiss this girl in front of millions.

Lowering my head down on her shoulder, I exhaled with stress. "Can we revisit this topic in the future? Like, waaay into the future. I'm not in the right headspace to be answering questions like that right now."

Hinata stalled for a moment, then poised her mouth next to my ear. "Does this mean you want a future with me, Riku?"

I dug my face into her neck, placing numerous kisses all the way down her neckline. "You already know I do."

I could feel Hinata's cheek against mine tighten into a knowing smile. "Is this what one would call a marriage proposal?"

Stopping my trail of kisses, I looked up into her gorgeous eyes. They were beaming with mystery and wonder as to what my answer would be. She was testing me.

I had intended on having this type of conversation with Mr. and Mrs. Tachibana before jumping to the next step of asking Hinata directly. But it seemed like we always did things out of order. So, after everything, what was stopping us now?

"I had a plan, y'know."

"A plan?" she repeated, knitting her brows quizzically.

"Yes, a plan," I said dramatically, shaking my head. "I was gonna ask you to marry me after you were done with school, and we both had our shit figured out. As I am now, I can barely support myself, let alone you. I gotta take care of a few things before I can commit myself to giving you the best life I possibly can, a life you deserve. I wanna better establish myself as a mechanic at the shop and eventually pay back the Fujimoto family for everything they've done for me. I owe the Fujimotos more than I could ever give back." I swallowed. "I was gonna get a ring and ask your parents' permission before going ahead with a proposal." Wrapping my arms around her, I threaded my fingers together behind her back, securing her. "You just had to go and ask all your ridiculous questions and ruin it, didn'tcha?"

"Riku . . .."

"I know, I know—it's a lot," I said worriedly, bringing my forehead to hers. "But that's been my plan for a little while now. Ever since you and Makoto started preparing and packing for college and university, I've had a lot of time to reflect. The thought of no longer having you in my life, standing by my side, scares the fuck outta me. You've become a necessity. I honestly don't think I could manage a life without you in it."

Pulling my head back, I looked into Hinata's beautiful tearful eyes as a single tear rolled down her cheek. With my thumb, I caught the runaway tear before it dripped from her chin.

"Marry me, Hinata."

We shared a surreal moment of gazing into each other's eyes before I shook my head and held up my hand.

"I don't want a reply just yet." Falling back onto the warm sand, I crossed my arms and rested them under my head. "You'll meet many people in your life as new opportunities arise and your horizon broadens. Who knows," I tilted my chin down to peer at her, "you might meet someone better than me. But there's no way he'd be better looking."

Hinata came down on top of me, leaning against my chest and keeping her face aligned with mine. "That may be true."

Her comeback caused my eyebrows to join together.

With vexing eyes, she grinned. "But that doesn't mean I would fall for them."

"Cunning," I said, with the rise of my lip. "Should've known you'd say something along those lines."

She smiled before turning on a more serious face. "You're right about one thing, Riku. There are going to be a lot of different people that I'll encounter in my life, but none of them will compare to you. I've known you were special from the moment I laid eyes on you."

Removing one hand from behind my head, I lifted it up to Hinata's cheek to caress it. Bringing my thumb around to Hinata's lips, I traced her bottom lip. "Promise?"

"Don't insult me," she said, her eyes pointed. "Don't you know, Riku? You can't get rid of me that easily. After everything, I was finally able to understand my desire enough to catch you."

⁂

The whole weekend with Hinata was amazing; we barely left each other's side. With it being the first full weekend that we had to ourselves, the uninterrupted time allowed us to bond in a completely new way. There were times we couldn't get enough of each other, or the worn, single bed in my apartment.

Being with Hinata was comforting; she made everything better. Things made sense with her. But I still worried that I wouldn't live up to her expectations.

Me, with children of my own? I couldn't even begin to envision it.

Chapter Sixty-One

SUMMER BREAK CAME to an end, and before we knew it things had returned to normal; Hinata to regular classes while I worked hard at the shop.

Mr. and Mrs. Tachibana were scheduled to return to Tokyo come September for a few days for one of Mr. Tachibana's business trips, so I was determined to have *the talk* with them then. Having this type of conversation with them was something I wanted to do in person and not over the phone.

As the days passed, I grew more and more anxious. Hinata was aware of my plan and would now be a part of my overwhelming conversation with her parents.

When the Tachibanas landed in Tokyo, Hinata notified me that I had coincidentally been invited out to dinner with her and her parents, saving me the ask. After receiving her message, I went out and immediately bought a black dress shirt for the occasion, making sure to have my best foot forward.

Arriving at the restaurant ahead of the scheduled time, I parked my bike and noticed a small flower shop a few doors down alongside a bakery. Realizing that I was coming to a very important dinner empty handed, I decided to

grab a bouquet for both Hinata and Mrs. Tachibana, along with a few pastries since I wasn't legally allowed to buy alcohol to gift to Mr. Tachibana.

With each passing minute, I turned into a nervous wreck the closer the time on my watch got to 7:00 p.m. Tonight was important. I knew Mr. Tachibana was a man I needed to impress and have on my side, or else things could go terribly wrong.

Entering the restaurant, I felt under dressed as hell.

Even with my new dress shirt, I didn't have any dress pants or shoes to accompany it. Just a pair of my best black jeans, ones without any holes in them. I didn't own anything fancy; my wardrobe lately consisted of jeans, t-shirts, and mechanic overalls.

While being escorted to the table, I noticed that everyone had already arrived and was seated. I wasn't late, but by being the last one to make an appearance, it sure felt like it. Everyone was also much dressier than I was, adding extra embarrassment to my already unconfident appearance.

Mr. and Mrs. Tachibana sat on one side together, across from Hinata and an empty chair. Thanking the hostess for ushering me, I lightly bowed when greeting everyone at the table. Holding two bouquets and a box of pastries in my hands, I handed them out to their respectable new owners.

"Oh, Riku, you shouldn't have!" Mrs. Tachibana exclaimed, happily.

"Yes, Riku, you didn't have to go to the trouble of getting us anything," Mr. Tachibana added, accepting the box.

"It's the least I could do," I said, brushing off their concern. "Sorry that I couldn't bring a bottle of alcohol. I'm just a year shy of being legal."

"Nonsense," Mr. Tachibana said. "This is more than enough."

Taking a seat, I looked over at Hinata who was smiling as she smelled her flowers.

Mental note: buy flowers more often.

As we browsed through the menu, each deciding what to order, Mr. Tachibana informed us that we could order whatever we wanted because he would be paying for dinner with his company card. Feeling a small sense of relief brush over me, I gave myself an invisible pat on the back for bringing gifts, though it was not nearly enough to be considered a suitable method of payment in return. The prices here were outrageous.

After everyone finished their meal, Mrs. Tachibana spoke about the twins and how easily they had adapted to their new life in France. The twins were practically fluent in French, surpassing both Mr. and Mrs. Tachibana. They had weirdly become their parents' teachers.

With conversation topics thinning, I took this opportunity to speak my piece. Clearing my throat, I steeled my nerves and placed my head in a full bow while seated. I waited for everyone's undivided attention before squinting my eyes shut.

"Mr. Tachibana, Mrs. Tachibana, I have something important I'd like to discuss with you."

"Riku, what's all this about? My goodness, lift your—" Mrs. Tachibana commenced but was cut short by her husband.

"Yoko darling, let him finish," Mr. Tachibana stated, with a strict, iron-clad voice.

Wincing at his unidentifiable tone, I took a deep breath. Normally, Mr. Tachibana would be the one to tell me to lift my head, but this time he refrained from doing so, as if he knew whatever I was about to say called for a formal gesture.

Hinata placed a hand on my thigh from under the table, causing me to open my eyes. I could tell she was trying to comfort me by showing her support.

Releasing the pent-up breath that I held on to, I swallowed hard and lifted my head. I pulled my shoulders slightly behind me to puff out my chest before proceeding.

"This is a conversation that I'd much rather have in person than over the phone. What I'm about to say is a bit premature, but I wanna get my intentions out in the open and make myself clear," I warned, avoiding direct eye contact with either Mr. or Mrs. Tachibana. "In the future, after Hinata has completed college, I'd like to ask for her hand in marriage. There is no rush, of course, as I want Hinata to accomplish everything she desires before making such a decision. But I also want both of you to know where I stand as a man. Hinata and I have talked several things over, including moving in together. We want to share an apartment in the near future."

I shifted my eyes to Mr. Tachibana first as he was the one that I feared the most. His eyes were dark and narrow, as if throwing shuriken at me. I could tell he didn't like the idea of me talking about marriage and moving in with his daughter.

Flashing my eyes to Mrs. Tachibana for some reassurance, I could see she was just as stunned. She was most certainly not expecting such words to leave my mouth, but she also didn't look like she wanted to murder me for them.

Thinking about how much I cared for Hinata, and about all the shit we'd gone through, I knew my feelings wouldn't change. Be it a year, two, five, ten, or more, I knew Hinata was the one I wanted to spend the rest of my days with. Someone I could grow old with.

I set my gaze forward to both of them. "I understand that Hinata and I are both young, and that she just started college and still has much to discover. I understand all aspects of the situation our relationship is in, but that still won't change the way I feel in the future. I'm certain." Sensing Hinata's eyes on me, I turned my head to her and smiled confidently. "I love your daughter. She's unlike any girl I've ever met before. She's stubborn, pushy, curious, overbearing, straightforward, meddling . . ." I began listing, as Hinata's eyes slowly narrowed into a glare. Chuckling under my breath from the reaction I was expecting, I carried on, ". . . loving, caring, attentive, and most of all, accepting." I stopped and watched Hinata's eyes soften. "There aren't enough words to describe how amazing she truly is, and how amazing she makes me feel. I lose all sense of rational thought when it comes to her. She's one of a kind."

"Riku," Hinata whispered, looking up at me with tears rimming her eyes.

"Riku," Mr. Tachibana said sharply, requiring my attention.

Shooting my eyes back to him, I sucked in air and bit the insides of my cheeks. I was ready to hear his outright refusal of my future proposal.

"I appreciate you discussing this with us in person. I agree, this would not have been a topic that would have transcended well over the phone. However," he said, sitting upright with a determined expression, "I cannot accept or agree to such a request at this time. You are much too young to be making promises such as these. Careful on how you conduct your words, Riku. Marriage is not something to take lightly. It's not a baseless claim you should make."

Mr. Tachibana's words were like thorns; I could feel my insides pricking with malice. Not only was he refusing my proposal, but he was also challenging my feelings for Hinata—again. Feelings I had never been more certain of in my entire life.

Before I could offer a rebuttal, Hinata jumped in.

"Riku's claims are not baseless."

"Hinata, please," Mr. Tachibana said, trying to calm her before things escalated in public and our table caused a scene.

"No. I will not be silenced when it pertains to my life," Hinata retorted, anger entangled in her tone. "I also feel the same way Riku does. I want a future with him, but that doesn't mean that he's the entirety of my world. I have many things I want to do and accomplish before settling down. All Riku intended to do today was present you with his plan so that you're knowledgeable in our desired future together. Even though it won't be something that we'll act upon for years to come, he wanted to show that he respects the both of you by giving you some insight into what we've discussed. In the end, nothing is set in stone, so this adamant refusal is uncalled for." Hinata's eyes were like flames.

Though I had prepared to take control of this conversation, making sure that I had the upper hand and held the reins, Hinata one-upped me. She had me beat. Sometimes I questioned who was leading who. She said everything with confidence, not a lick of uncertainty in her tone. She was a force to be reckoned with, like someone else I knew.

Bouncing back and forth between Hinata and her father, I couldn't gauge what Mr. Tachibana's reaction would be. He often displayed undecipherable emotions across his face.

"Taichi dear," Mrs. Tachibana spoke up for the first time since things got heated, placing a gentle hand on his arm. "You worry too much."

"But Yoko darling," he said, glancing at her in a more modulated manner, "they're so young . . ."

"You worry about Hinata too much," Mrs. Tachibana declared again, disrupting her husband's train of thought before he could speak it. "Hinata's always done her best in whatever she's set her mind to and has shown us time and time again that she's more than capable of making wise decisions for herself. If this is something Hinata has decided on her own, then who are we to stop her from pursuing something she's obviously serious about?"

Shooing her husband's overbearing parental ideology to the side, she went on. "I think it's also quite admirable of you, Riku," she said, smiling in my direction. "As you are now, even with the hardships you've encountered, you were able to overcome everything and present yourself in a dignified manner. In a way all its own, it makes me happy that Hinata's chosen such a fine person. I agree with my husband on one thing, though. You both are very young to be considering marriage, and your feelings may change as you grow, but I'm glad you are both mature enough to acknowledge that."

"Mark my words," I said, straightening my back to its fullest, "I fully intend on waiting until Hinata is ready, but I do not intend on giving Hinata away to just anyone. If down the road Hinata has a change of heart, I'll do everything in my power to win her back."

Hinata nudged me. "Didn't I already tell you not to insult me? Don't take my feelings lightly, Riku."

Mrs. Tachibana smiled tenderly at her daughter, then looked at me with the same warmth. "Then, that settles it. You have my blessing for a *future* marriage. Anything before Hinata graduates will be immediately dismissed. As for moving in together, as long as it doesn't interfere with Hinata's studies, I don't see why not. Sharing an apartment will lower the cost of living and expenses, so I'm all for it," she said with a wink.

"Yoko!" Mr. Tachibana hissed, raising his voice unintentionally. Shaking his head in defeat, knowing he couldn't compete with his wife, he sighed. "Riku, get ready to have your hands full for the rest of your days."

With Mr. Tachibana's headstrong demeanour diminishing, my shoulders began to cave into a comfortable slouch all on their own. Not wanting to assume anything, I looked over at Hinata and saw her return my internal excitement with a smile.

"Now, was that so hard?" Mrs. Tachibana said, directing mild disappointment at her husband. "Jeez, you had these two terrified and shaking in their seats. You should be thankful to have such a respectful, future son-in-law who takes your feelings into consideration. A lot of young couples these days run away and get married without even notifying their parents, let alone asking for approval."

Mr. Tachibana tensed in his seat. "Let's not get ahead of ourselves."

Mrs. Tachibana rolled her eyes, as if to say she was done with her husband's negativity and the basis of this conversation.

"Mr. Tachibana, sir," I said, sitting tall and stretching out my slouched shoulders, once again, for I had one last thing to say. He looked back toward me with concern etched into his eyes, as if I were about to drop another bomb on him that he may or may not be able to handle. "In the future, when I come to ask you again, please give your precious daughter to me," I requested, my eyes never averting from his.

"When the time comes, and you're of legal age, you'll present me with the finest bottle of sake that Japan has to offer," he explained in detail. "When you do, I'll let you ask me again."

Chapter Sixty-Two

THE NEXT FEW months, Hinata and I began searching diligently for an apartment close to her campus. With Uncle Ito's shop central to everything, and me having the bike, it didn't matter where the apartment was situated. As long as it was accessible and simple for Hinata to get to and from school, then it worked for me. Making things easy for her was my top priority. I was also ecstatic to finally stop receiving a handout from the Fujimoto family and be freed from the guilt attached to it.

Amid apartment hunting, and living through everyday life, I took a break to go and visit Makoto in Kyoto. We didn't visit each other nearly as often as we had hoped because life got in the way, but we tried to make an effort whenever we could.

Makoto was the busiest of everyone I knew; he always had something going on. On top of school, extracurricular activities, and working on case studies, he also did volunteer work at the hospital. He was an obnoxiously good person through and through. It was pleasantly sickening.

The weather was on the chillier side as it was now the beginning of December. I took the bullet train to Kyoto and brought a backpack with me as I planned on staying the night at Makoto's.

Pulling into the platform at Kyoto Station, I shot Makoto a message over LINE to let him know I had arrived. He met me at the station so we could head back to his place together on foot. It was about a twenty-minute walk to Makoto's apartment, so we killed time by catching up along the way. I decided to withhold a few conversation topics until we were relaxed and seated, saving my dramatic best friend from a public display of cardiac arrest.

Makoto went on and on about all the things he had been involved in since we last saw each other. He spoke so fast that it was hard to fully grasp everything he was talking about, but I could see how excited he was with his new life in Kyoto just by watching his mannerisms and expressions.

Stepping foot into Makoto's apartment, I noticed nothing had changed since I last visited. Toeing off my shoes at the raised entryway, I took a step up and walked further into the apartment, tossing my backpack onto Makoto's two-seater futon couch in the corner of the multipurpose living area.

Makoto's place had a lot more furniture than mine did, making the apartment feel tinier than it actually was, but also a lot homier. He had the futon couch, a TV on a stand, and a bookcase. Grinning to myself at how jampacked his bookcase was with textbooks, I couldn't help but shake my head and hold back a laugh.

Nerd.

Looking over my shoulder, I watched as Makoto lined my sneakers at the bottom of the step.

"Bro, seriously?"

"What? Just because you live like a slob doesn't mean I have to," he said, snickering as he walked toward me.

Narrowing my eyes, I shot him a grimacing glare. "I ain't no slob."

In response, Makoto cocked his head back and laughed, then placed a hand on my shoulder. "You really *did* turn stupid. You're the king of mess."

Rolling my shoulder, his hand slipped off, and I quickly grabbed him and threw him in a headlock. "Shut up, nerd! Ain't so funny now, huh?"

"Hey, man, watch my glasses!" Tapping my arm repeatedly in submission, he shouted, "All right, all right! I tap, I tap!"

Loosening my grip on the headlock, he pushed his way out, readjusted his glasses, then jumped back into a fighting stance while pumping his feet swiftly back and forth across the floor.

"Round two! And no cheap shots this time!"

"You're just a sore loser," I said with a smirk.

"Am not," he whined.

Pausing, we stared at each other for a solid five seconds before hugging our sides in laughter.

"Man, I'm stoked that you're spending the night. As sad as it is to admit, I've missed hanging out with you and your stupid ass," Makoto expressed, smiling foolishly like a child participating in their first sleepover.

"Asshole," I said, giving a forlorn chuckle. "Why're you sad to admit that?"

"Because you're a jerk. I was getting sentimental over our friendship, and you're laughing?" He crossed his arms. "But fine, whatever. Guess you don't appreciate how caring of a friend I truly am. I can see that my affection is wasted on the likes of you," he expressed, sticking out his tongue.

Rolling my eyes, I shook my head. "What're you, six?"

"And a half, actually."

Busting a gut at his quick retort, I smacked his back. "I missed you too, bro."

Once settled, Makoto made himself a pot of tea while handing me a canned coffee out of the fridge. He made sure to state that he had only bought two cans of this 'disgusting black sludge,' enough to last me my overnight visit.

Taking our seats beside each other on the couch, Makoto turned on the TV and set up his video game console for us to play. Handing me a controller, we engaged in a head-to-head combative game where we both demonstrated just how competitive we really were by fighting each other to the death. After playing a few rounds, and Makoto acting like the sore loser he was when I won, we paused the game and dived deep into some pressing conversations. We filled the other in on the challenges life presented, getting the scoop on how we spent our days since we hung out last.

Saving my piece for last, I let Makoto go first.

"So . . . I kind of started seeing this girl."

Spitting out my coffee just as I had taken a sip, some even shooting out of my nose, I whipped my eyes around to face him. "YOU'RE WHAT?"

"Gah, disgusting! Don't dirty my place, asshole! And don't act so surprised," he hissed. "Girls are interested in me too, you know."

Wiping the coffee from my lips and nose with the cuff of my long-sleeved shirt, my eyes remained wide. "That's not it!" I said with an elevated voice, ignoring the mess but wanting to reassure him. "Of course, girls can be interested in you. Why wouldn't they be? It's just . . . this is the first I'm hearing of it, so I'm kinda shocked, is all."

Running his fingers through his slick backed hair, he brought one leg up onto the couch and hung his arm over his knee. With a thinned-out grin, he looked at me bashfully. "Well, you know, I'm still not one hundred percent sure what we are to each other yet, so I didn't want to mention it prematurely and jinx it. But since we're finally hanging out in person, I couldn't hold it in any longer. I had to tell you."

Happy that Sato was finally a thing of the past, I felt a smile cross my face. "Shit, that's awesome, man! What's her name? Did 'ya meet her at nerd school?"

"Ha-ha." He lit up with a giant smile. "Her name is Nanami Ishikawa, but she lets me call her 'Nana-chan.' And yeah, we met at *regular* school on the first day of orientation. She's in a few of my classes and is also participating in one of the case studies I'm partaking in. She's super cute, extremely nice, soft spoken, always willing to help others, and is also crazy smart—she scores near to perfect on everything. After talking about our studies and what we want to major in, I found out that she wants to be an oncologist so she can study and work alongside cancer patients."

Seeing how elated Makoto was, as he spoke about this girl, was heartwarming. I was thrilled to see him look so happy. This Ishikawa girl seemed like a good match for Makoto, someone worth encouraging him to pursue.

"Bro, that's so good to hear. I'm happy for you," I said with a tender smile. "She sounds great."

"She is," he answered surely, with a lovestruck smile plastered on his face that reached from ear-to-ear. "She's amazing."

"Then, what's the holdup? If she's already letting you call her by her first name, in short form no less, why haven't you asked her out yet?"

Tugging on the back of his neck, he looked up at the ceiling and sighed. "I don't know, man. What if she doesn't like me like *that*? I know she at least thinks of me as a friend, but what if she doesn't feel the same way I do and I make a fool of myself? She seems to enjoy spending time with me, but what if it's all in my head? What if she rejects my feelings when I go to confess?

Then, what?" he asked, stress and anxiety seeping into his voice. "Could we ever go back to being friends like we are now? If she rejects me . . . I'd still like her to be a part of my life. Even if I'm left in the friend-zone."

Thinking this extensively about such a thing was a *very* Makoto way to go about things. He always stressed himself out for no reason on scenarios he fabricated within his head. Though he wasn't shy when it came to meeting and talking with new people, thinking this way about girls always held him back from engaging in romantic relationships.

Taking his concerns into consideration, I patted him on the back. "You won't know until you try, bro. That's really all the advice I can give you. I know it ain't great advice, but unless you take that first step and trust your gut, you won't ever know. I guess, if there was the slightest chance that *she* were to approach *you* instead, then you'd know. But, from the sounds of it, she seems shier than you," I said with a crooked smile. "So, I doubt you wanna wait around long enough to test that theory out. Someone else might swoop in and take her from right under your nose."

Makoto sighed again, this time adding a disheartened grunt to the end. "Ugh, I know you're right. But it's such a scary thing not knowing how the other person feels."

"That's just the way it is." I shrugged. "The mind of a girl is a mysterious place. I've been dating Hinata for over a year and a half now, and I still don't fully understand how she thinks."

Makoto chuckled. "How's Hinata doing, by the way?"

With Makoto giving me the perfect segue, I decided this would be the best time to transition into what I had been withholding from him. "I'm glad you asked."

Makoto looked confused. With his brow raised, and his mouth quirked up at one side, he waited for me to continue.

"Hinata and I have decided to move in together."

Makoto's jaw dropped. "She's going to move into your apartment?"

"Nah. And since I'm not allowed to move into her dorm, we're gonna find a place near her school campus to ease her commute."

Makoto hadn't blinked in almost thirty seconds. His big mouth remained wide open. "What did her parents say? I bet they freaked out."

"Hinata's mom was cool with it," I acknowledged, side-gazing as I bit my lip. "Her dad, on the other hand, needed a bit more convincing. But he eventually agreed."

Makoto placed a hand on his chest and exhaled excessively. "Jeez, how stressful. I wasn't even there, and I was already stressing out on your behalf—like secondhand stress. I couldn't imagine being in your shoes during that conversation. I commend you, bro."

Laughing under my breath, I leaned back and stretched out against the back of the couch, my body morphing into it. With my neck resting on the top of the couch and the crown of my head touching the wall, I stared up at the white ceiling and used its tedium as a focus point. "Thanks . . . but not gonna lie, it wasn't nearly as stressful as it was when I started the conversation off by asking for Hinata's hand in marriage."

Darting my eyes to catch Makoto's reaction, I wish I could have taken a picture of his face to commemorate it for all eternity. Not only was he beyond speechless, but he also didn't blink or breathe.

"I'm sorry . . . what?" he said with a delayed reaction, glasses sliding down the bridge of his nose. "I don't believe I heard you correctly."

"Nah, you heard just fine. Trust me."

Finally, he took a breath and blinked, batting his lashes a handful of times as he stared at me intensely with a blank expression. "You—Riku Naka-jima—MARRIAGE? WHAT THE ACTUAL FUCK IS GOING ON?"

I let out an explosion of laughter, almost psychotic, at Makoto's unexpected outburst. I had to physically wipe tears from my eyes so I could see him clearly. "Weird, right?"

"No way, man. You're messing with me."

"Cross my heart and hope to die," I said childishly, making a giant 'X' across my chest.

"Shut up, bro. The joke has gone on long enough."

"Makoto, it's no joke. I wanna marry Hinata," I expressed with seriousness. "It won't be for some time, but I properly discussed it with the Tachibanas. I gave them my word that I'd protect and cherish Hinata for the rest of my days, and in return, they gave me their blessing." Turning away from him, I smiled. "A life without Hinata isn't worth living anymore. After meeting her, I realized that my readiness to die, since I had nothing, was entirely senseless. Now, all I want is for Hinata to keep on smiling. I'll continue to love her selfishly with everything I have."

"Riku . . .," he said, my name gliding like wind through his lips. "I, uh, I don't even know what to say."

"That's a first," I snickered, meeting his eyes again.

Makoto contorted his leg back and heel-kicked me in the shin.

"Ah, shit! What the fuck, Makoto?" I shouted, bending over to check the damage done to my leg. "That hurt like hell, bro. Shit."

"You always crack jokes during serious moments," he stated, uncaring of the pain he inflicted. "Can't you be serious for once?"

"I've been serious this entire time," I replied, rubbing my shin in an attempt to relieve the shooting pain.

"I can't believe you're actually considering marriage!"

Lifting my eyes back to his, I smiled. "Calm down, I ain't gonna get married tomorrow or anything. Marriage isn't an uncommon thing for people to desire."

"I know it's not. Hell, I know I definitely want to get married someday. But the fact that *you*, mister playboy, mister uninterested in commitment, mister one-night stands, wants to, is astonishing."

"I'm not the same guy as before, Makoto . . . .."

"I know you're not," he said, lifting both legs onto the couch and crossing them. "You're like an entirely different person; this version of you is the best, by far. It's just . . . I can't believe how much influence Hinata's had over you in such a short period of time. Its awe-inspiring."

Shying away, I could feel the heat rising to my face. "Yeah. Thanks, man."

"You better have a proper wedding and invite me, got that? No eloping of any sorts, you hear me?"

"Are you kidding?" I snorted, an underlying smile filtering through as I eyed him. "You're gonna be my best man."

Makoto's eyes glossed over. "Aww, Riku."

I rolled my eyes with regret. "Don't make it weird."

⁓⁂⁓

The next day, Makoto saw me to the station. Just as my train was arriving, I adjusted my backpack over my shoulders and turned to him with a question I had forgotten to ask the previous night.

"Hey, you gonna be able to make it back home for Christmas and New Year's?"

"Duh. My mom would have a fit, otherwise."

I nodded with a laugh. We both knew how important it was for his mother to have everyone home for the winter holidays, Megumi and Mitsuki included. Every year, all of us made sure to gather at the Fujimoto residence for Christmas festivities.

"Don't worry, Riku," Makoto said, landing a soft jab on my pec. "I wouldn't miss your birthday for the world."

I was annoyed with how embarrassingly happy his comment made me, but I was more annoyed with how he made note of it. Holding out my hand, I said, "Make sure you ask out that Ishikawa girl. I want a progress report by Christmas."

Makoto clasped my hand in his and chortled. "Until Christmas, then."

"Until then."

Part Four:

EVERYTHING

Chapter Sixty-Three

CHRISTMAS AND NEW Year's came and went in a blur. Everyone made it to the Fujimoto household for the holidays and, as was tradition, we all rang in the new year together.

On Christmas day, both Megumi and Mitsuki brought home men for the first time, and like the protective younger brothers we never thought we'd be, Makoto and I grilled both guys with a plethora of questions. The girls seemed serious about these new relationships, even the carefree Mitsuki, who brought the biggest surprise as she came home engaged after only knowing the guy for six months. She had kept the relationship a secret from everyone.

On top of it all, Makoto presented me with his own surprise. Though he didn't bring her home because he said it was still too early for his parents to know, Makoto and Nanami had started dating.

With December 31st also marking my birthday, I was officially nineteen and feeling more like an adult than ever before. As promised, Makoto, along with Hinata and the rest of the Fujimoto family, as well as the two new additions, celebrated my birthday with me. It was just as memorable as the last and I wondered if all my future birthdays would continue to be as joyous.

This was a family worth cherishing.

Hinata and I found an apartment a week

before Christmas but were only able to carry over a few small items to start during the craziness of the fast-approaching holidays. We decided that it would be best to move in everything after the first shrine visit of the new year when things settled down.

Not wanting to overwhelm Hinata, as school would be starting back up around the same time, I took it upon myself and offered to move everything in for the both of us. Neither of us had a bed that could comfortably accommodate two people, so Hinata had recommended we make a quick trip to a furniture store to pick one out and have it shipped to the apartment at a later date.

Asking a few of the shop guys for help, especially Taka, since he owned a truck, the gang graciously offered their manpower to help me move some furniture into the new apartment. I didn't own very much, so moving my stuff was easy.

Hinata also took on a part-time job tutoring first-year high school students a couple of nights per week without consulting me. Not that she had to run it by me necessarily, as she was free to do whatever she wanted, but I feared that taking on too many responsibilities would put a negative strain on her. I wanted to give her the opportunity to focus on her studies, just as I had promised her parents, but with Hinata being Hinata, she refused.

Once everything was moved in and ready to go, Hinata and I finally spent our first night in our very own bed, in our very first home together. Waking up to her face next to mine for the first time in our new home, knowing that this was going to be my reality from here onward, was incredible. Things were shaping up, and I felt fortunate to have had everything that I did up until this point.

Days filled with Hinata, from morning to night, were ones to look forward to.

Now that matters had settled down, and I had grown accustomed to my new life with Hinata, I was finally financially stable enough to start paying back the Fujimotos for my high school tuition—in installments. Though I did consider Kobayashi-sensei's life story many times and understood the teachings he offered, this was a life goal of mine, one I couldn't let go. Maybe I was making the same mistake as he once did, but I wanted to see things through.

This repayment was part of what fueled me.

After fighting back and forth with Mrs. Fujimoto for numerous months, as she usually spoke on behalf of her and her husband when it came to the touchy subject of money, I eventually wore her down and she caved unwillingly, very unwillingly. She was bitter for quite some time. When it came to tuition, she said that if the money they gave was put to good use, for education with the completion of a diploma or degree, then they were more than content with the outcome and expected nothing in return.

Even if I commended this point-of-view when it came to the Fujimoto's biological children, I couldn't accept this reasoning when it came to me. And I think that small fact was the difference I held onto when it came to Kobayashi-sensei's life versus mine.

No matter how much I wished it were true, I wasn't a child of the Fujimoto family by blood, and I didn't want to burden them any further. Though I always felt loved and cared for in the Fujimoto household, and was given a better chance at life by being placed in their care, a part of me knew I couldn't take their kindness for granted.

I couldn't and wouldn't.

Growing up, I unconsciously harboured a hidden set of feelings toward Makoto that I never fully comprehended. There was a part of me that always resented him for the family he was blessed with from birth. It never felt fair that he was given parents who loved and cherished him with everything they had, while I had a single, shitty ass mother who couldn't be bothered to come home half the time.

Now, I finally understood that it wasn't resentment I felt toward Makoto, but jealousy.

When I was young, home wasn't a comfortable place to be. It was a reoccurring nightmare that I couldn't wake up from. There was no love whatsoever within those apartment walls. I didn't have two parents like most kids at school did, especially ones that attended career days or came to watch sports games. So, I always wondered why I couldn't have been just as lucky to have had parents like Makoto's. Or even half as lucky; I would have settled for one, actively attentive parent.

He had the perfect life, and I wanted it.

I wanted to feel a part of something bigger, something sustainable. Mr.

and Mrs. Fujimoto would literally give the shirts off their backs for their children, and I desperately wanted to be one of those clothed children.

It took me about a decade, but I finally grasped the concept that I was *indeed* one of those children who were loved unconditionally, even if I had to be adopted in. I was blind to so many things, but slowly, things were clearly filtering through.

I was born into a world where I wasn't wanted, wasn't needed—or so I thought. It took me a while to accept that those who I cherished, loved me in return, because that wasn't my 'normal.'

I really had been fortunate all along; I just hadn't realized it.

Epilogue

OVER THE COURSE of eleven years, a lot has happened, and many things have changed. One of the major changes being that Hinata and I finally got married.

A few months after Hinata turned twenty-one, I searched far and wide for the best sake, as promised, and presented myself for a second time in front of Mr. and Mrs. Tachibana before they were scheduled to return to France. Making my intentions clear, I restated everything I had said a few years prior to make sure both Mr. and Mrs. Tachibana understood how serious I was about their daughter and that my feelings and determination had not wavered.

A year later, after Hinata completed school, we were married.

Something I also came to discover was the identity of my biological father. Prior to discovering who he was, I had never met him, but from a young age, I had been trained to hate him.

So, that's what I did. I grew up hating him.

He was absent from my life, a figment of my imagination at times. It was easier to hate someone I didn't *know*, even though I *knew* of him.

My mother constantly reminded me of how much she hated men because she said they were all 'pieces of shit' and 'good-for-nothings,' and since I was a boy, I strongly believe she hated me from the get-go. Maybe if I had been born a girl, things would have been different for her—for me.

But holding onto *what-ifs* doesn't get anyone anywhere.

It took a few years, and a lot of reassurance from Hinata, but after the passing of my mother, an aggravating itch eventually grew inside me to know who my father was and where my mother came from.

It wasn't easy to detach myself from the hatred I felt toward my parents because that anger ultimately fueled my core. But the older I got, the more the curiosity ate away at me. When I was a teenager, I was firm on not wanting to know about who and where I came from—as the years went on—it was something that wouldn't leave my mind.

During this period of soul-searching and contemplating, I picked up smoking again. I had quit for about a year, but quickly fell back into the old habit with hopes that it would alleviate some of the self-inflicted stress I carried. It also didn't help that most of the guys at work smoked, so I was around it all the time.

At first, I tried to hide it from Hinata, but the smell of cigarettes sticks to one's body and clothing like paint sticks to freshly primed walls. It wasn't long before Hinata figured it out, and although she had always called it a 'disgusting habit,' she never once got mad or forced me to quit. In fact, she said cigarettes reminded her of me and our first kiss.

I hired a private investigator and found out that, like myself, my mother grew up in and out of the system. She had been adopted at an early age but was soon abandoned because of her troubled personality and poor behaviour. From there, she bounced from home to home until she was of legal age, leaving her out on the streets to fend for herself, unwanted.

This is when everything went to shit for her.

Without guidance, my mother found herself in the red-light district where she began selling her body. Continuing that lifestyle for a couple of years, she sold herself to a random man one night, a normal business transaction, and happened to get pregnant at the age of twenty. She never contacted the man or tracked him down to inform him of the predicament she found herself in. And, for some unknown reason, she chose to keep the baby. That's when I came into the picture and was given the surname of my mother's once adopted family: Nakajima.

When I informed Mrs. Fujimoto that I had hired a PI, she confessed to me that she was the one who had called in for the wellness check on my mother all those years ago. She revealed to me that every so often she would call one in as a means of checking-in on my mother. If it wasn't for Mrs. Fujimoto, I wonder how long my mother's body would have remained on the floor of her apartment.

As for my father, the PI had to do some deeper digging into him, since his name wasn't listed on my birth certificate. It's unusual for the father not to be listed on a child's birth certificate, but my life was anything but usual. I'm sure my mother had something to do with it.

The data the PI discovered was disturbing in more ways than one, as my father ended up being someone I wasn't expecting. I had half expected him to be a part of the same lifestyle that my mother indulged in, into sex, drugs, and alcohol—an addict, a nobody. Instead, my father, Yatsu Higurashi, who was fourteen years older than my mother, was a regular, white-collar worker with an average office job and was married to his wife of over thirty years—a scumbag.

The PI presented me with a series of pictures of my father. Most of them were from recent years, but one from when he was a teenager caught my eye. I was stunned, but that reaction quickly morphed into disgust. Turns out my mother was correct about one thing; I really did look like the bastard.

My father had lived in Tokyo his entire life and had three children with his wife. What my father had no knowledge of was that he, in fact, had four children. It was as if overnight I had gained a whole family, picking up three new half-siblings: two older brothers and a younger sister.

Yatsu Higurashi lived a quiet, content life with his family, and that's the way I intended to leave things. After all this time, my father's family didn't deserve to have a bomb dropped on them and live a life of misery, even if their peaceful life was a lie. So, I kept my distance and went back to pretending like Yatsu Higurashi, and his family, never existed.

My family registry is nothing to brag about; my father's name isn't even registered on it. I have nothing to show or offer, but adding Hinata's name to the registry makes it special. Since having it added, I don't mind being a 'Naka-jima' as much. My surname isn't such a burden anymore.

After we registered our marriage, I was content with not partaking in any of the formalities a wedding entailed, but because Hinata wanted it, I went along with whatever. Hinata desired a traditional ceremony, so we had one. I didn't care how or where we got married, so long as I could have her by my side and call her my wife. The Tachibanas, the Fujimotos, a few friends, and, oddly enough, Kobayashi-sensei, all attended. Though the wedding was small, it was everything we could have asked for.

Kobayashi-sensei has stuck around throughout the years, popping in and out of my life when I need him the most, his presence now a regular occurrence. Without wanting to admit it, Sensei has become somewhat of a father-figure in my life, a little-known fact I was apparently blind to, according to Hinata. She informed me that her and Makoto had noticed a father-son relationship developing between Sensei and I since senior high school.

After a lifetime of schooling, Makoto is a doctor and works alongside his wife, Nanami. Makoto and Nanami are newly married but are already doing great things together. They transferred to Tokyo and work at the same hospital, often side-by-side. Nanami is an oncologist specializing in children with cancer, while Makoto is a pediatrician subspecializing in cancer among children, consulting Dr. Nanami Fujimoto on cases and patients when required.

Last year, Nanami gave birth to their first child, a girl named Maki. Both Makoto's parents are overjoyed at becoming grandparents for the sixth time, as Megumi and Mitsuki started families and brought forth many children of their own.

The apartment with Hinata was getting cramped, as we needed to make room to welcome a little one of our own. We hadn't planned on starting a family so soon after getting married, but accidents happen when you aren't careful on your honeymoon.

I will admit, at first, I was panicked by Hinata getting pregnant, mainly by the fact that she was so adamant about keeping the baby I deemed as a mistake. All my fears and insecurities were piling up to the point where I asked Hinata to abort the baby because I wasn't ready to be a father, and that I may never be. Thankfully, Hinata has a better head on her shoulders than I do and didn't listen to what I had to say. Instead, she helped me out of the darkness I surrounded myself in. I felt it was selfish of me to ask such a thing, and I know it must have been difficult to hear such a request come from her husband.

A request born from a moment of weakness.

After my meltdown, and after coming to terms with the fact that Hinata was pregnant and we were going to be parents, I gave up smoking for good. I quit cold turkey and never looked back. To this day, I haven't touched a single cigarette, let alone experienced a craving. It's amazing what the power of parenthood and newfound responsibilities has done to me. An instinct kicked in, and everything I thought I knew about the world, and myself, changed in the blink of an eye. This little family was my unit, and I would kill for them.

Having had enough of Tokyo and all it had to offer, Hinata and I decided that moving to a quieter place with more space would be beneficial to raise a family. I did have hopes that Hinata would take a liking to Jōetsu, after having our honeymoon there, because I had my heart set on it after revisiting its wonderous landscape. Recollections of my time in Jōetsu, with Makoto and the Fujimotos, immediately came flying back. Those are some of my most cherished memories.

⚘

"I always forget how far away you live until I'm already on the bullet train here. Remind me to never embark on this journey in the winter. I hear the amount of snow you all get out here is outrageous," he says, dropping his bags on the engawa and loosening the Windsor knot of his tie.

I chuckle while nodding my head. "You aren't wrong. It's a bit of a trip from Tokyo, no matter what method of transportation you take. Sorry to make you come all the way out here during your vacation time." Bending down, I grab his bags and place them inside the entryway of the house before escorting him to the backside of the wraparound engawa.

"Don't worry about it, Riku," he says, waving his hand dismissively. "You know I'll always come and visit when I can."

I smile. "Thanks, Sensei."

"Anytime," he says, returning my smile.

"I trust that Akari is doing well," I inquire, as we make it around back, walking side-by-side and matching each other's pace. "She didn't wanna tag along?"

"She's fine," he assures. "She couldn't take time off from work to come this time. The summer is usually busy for her, oddly enough."

Reaching the edge of the wooden engawa, I sit down and swing my feet off the ledge, hovering them a few inches off the ground below to avoid getting them dirty. Hinata always gets upset whenever dirt is tracked into the house.

Turning my head, I place my hands on my thighs and look up at Sensei as he stands next to me. "That's too bad. Guess it's hard to take time off when you're the only pastry chef, huh?"

Sensei sighs. "Yeah. She's incredibly talented, but also incredibly busy. Running your own bakery isn't easy; she complains about how stressed out she is all the time. But she never ceases to amaze me," he says, bending down to take out a bottle of sake and two sakazuki cups from a bag he brought with him. "She wakes up around 3:00 a.m. each morning to start her day. She's up and out the door long before my alarm is even set to go off." He chortles under his breath before shaking his head. "But her motivation and hardworking personality is what made me fall head over heels for her."

"Don't lie," I say, elbowing his leg, indicating him to sit. "You fell in love with her pastries."

"Those, too."

We both share a laugh.

"How's everything going at *Nakajima Auto Body*, Riku?" he asks, finally taking a seat beside me. "Business still on the uprise? I bet you're just as busy as Akari."

"Things are good, actually. Just overwhelmingly busy." I tug on the back of my neck, huffing in dissatisfaction. "Like Akari, my only problem is that whenever I take time off, all hell breaks loose. The shop is small, so I don't have many mechanics working under me, but my head mechanic is a giant stress ball anytime I'm not around. When I leave him in charge, he panics. He's only twenty-one, but he's already a fantastic mechanic, so I'm hoping he grows out of it." Loosening my grip, I let out a weighted sigh. "My goal is to recreate the same atmosphere Uncle Ito has at his shop. Disbanding from the shop gang is one of the few regrets I have from moving out here to Jōetsu. Those guys were like a second family to me; they taught me everything I know. I'm grateful Uncle Ito took me under his wing when he did. Working at his shop was the best thing for me. I can only hope to teach the same skillset and knowledge to my own crew."

"Your shop will get there some day, Riku," Sensei says optimistically. "I'm sure it took Ito Fujimoto a long time to create the family-like atmosphere that you describe. You have the passion and grit, so I know great things will come of it. Plus, Ito Fujimoto is child-free. His priorities have always differed from yours. And that's not a bad thing."

The anxiety roaring inside me lessens after hearing Sensei's reassuring words. That's what Sensei is good for, boosting up a person's morale and reducing their apprehensions. He always thought I was more than I believed I was. After experiencing it with Uncle Ito, I also strive to be a boss that my subordinates can look up to. So, if Sensei believes I can do it, then I want to prove him right.

"You always know what to say, huh Sensei?" I say with a short laugh.

He smirks. "It's a perk that comes with being a wise teacher."

I roll my eyes. "Don't flatter yourself too much, old man."

"'Old man'?" he repeats, pinching his brows inward. "Careful who you go calling an *old man*. Your time will come soon enough."

"Thirty is still young. I've got time."

"Forty is just around the corner."

"Whatever," I brush off, egotistically.

Shaking his head, he fills both cups with sake, then hands me one before changing topics. "How far along is Hinata now? Eight months?"

"Nine," I correct, accepting the cup, and taking a sip of the same sake he always graciously brings over. It's one I introduced him to, after having received high praise for it from Mr. Tachibana. "She's due any day now."

Kobayashi-sensei's eyes protrude out of their sockets. He spills half the sake from his cup before having the opportunity to taste it. "NINE? But she's non-stop! Didn't you tell me that she was just holding a class here last week? Shouldn't she be resting?"

"Try telling her that," I say, draining the remainder of my sake in a hurry. Insinuating for Sensei to pour me another, I lift my cup at him. "I've already told her to stay off her feet, but she won't listen to anything I say. Her stubbornness gets worse after each pregnancy. She's teaching a lesson inside as we speak." Shutting my eyes for a split second, I shake my head. "Right after giving birth to our first, she jumped right back into teaching outta her music room in the house and kept that mentality going. She never takes a break; the growth of her students is always weighing on her mind. She's constantly suggesting that her students *need* her, no matter if they're preparing for an upcoming competition or just having a simple one-on-one lesson. Her students are important to her." I turn to him. "I'm sure you can relate."

Refilling both our cups, his eyes fill with awe; he is genuinely amazed. "She's quite remarkable. With her skills, she has the potential to become a brilliant piano player. I have heard her solo pieces and she's notably outstanding, but I can see her heart lies in teaching. I can absolutely relate," he says, nodding. "Hinata definitely deserves credit. Teaching students is no easy feat, especially if they're anything like a certain someone." He hints, twitching famously.

Taking a sip from my second cup, I reveal a crooked smile. "I dunno what you're talking about."

"Right." He smiles and brings the cup to his lips, holding it for a moment. "But isn't that the norm for you two?"

"Norm?"

Sensei grins after taking a full sip. "Isn't it normal for Hinata not to listen to you and for you to bend to her every will? For as long as I've known you two, she tends to do whatever she wants, and you let her."

Putting my cup down, I lean back and stretch out my arms. "I can't say no to her. She has me wrapped around her gorgeous finger." The one side of my mouth quirks up. "She just keeps getting more stunning after each pregnancy; I'm at her mercy." Thinking some more, I shake my head and release a dragged-out sigh. "It's not just Hinata I gotta worry about. No one in this damn house listens to me."

Sensei chokes on another sip of sake as it attempts to go down. "I will admit, Riku, you did get yourself into quite a predicament. Your hands are most certainly full."

"You're telling me," I say, looking up at the blue sky that is partially blocked from view by the taruki rafter of the house. "A house of women is terrifying. Each day, I barely make it out alive. It's all about surviving at this point. Sensei," I say, shooting him a death glare, "don't have kids."

Splitting his sides in laughter, he places his cup down beside him in fear of wasting all the sake, having not been able to keep a single cup full. "I've already coparented one troublemaker, that's enough for me." He winks. "Speaking of which, where are the girls?"

With another dramatic, stretched out sigh, I fall back onto the engawa. "Don't jinx this rare moment." Crossing both arms, I place them behind my head as a means of support. "Those rascals are around here somewhere. Quite honestly, I'm surprised they haven't made their grand appearance yet. The amount of free, uninterrupted time I've had in this short moment with you is more than I've had in months."

Sensei jabs my side with two fingers, almost hard enough to bruise my ribs.

"Ow!" I flinch. "What the fu—"

"Don't pretend like you don't love being a father," he says, as he glances down at me, sadistically.

Before I could reply with a snarky comment, a herd of wild animal's stampedes down the boards of the engawa. Rounding the corner of the house, they beeline straight for us.

"SENSEI! KOBAYASHI-SENSEI! YOU'RE HERE!" two little voices squeal eagerly.

"Damn you, you demon. You jinxed it," I whisper, clicking my tongue.

Sensei cocks his head back to laugh at the coincidence, then stands to greet the children running his way. "Hello, girls. How have you been?"

"Gooood!" Hitomi sings, unable to contain her excitement. "We saw your bags inside."

"Sensei, Sensei! Guess what?" Hanako chimes in, jumping up and down, overpowering her older sister. She sidesteps around Hitomi to get closer to Sensei, making sure she has his full attention.

"Hey, Hanakooo! No fair! I was talking to Sensei firssst," Hitomi whines, lightly shoving her sister out of the way.

"Nuh uuuh!" Hanako fights back, bumping Hitomi with her hip.

"Yeah huuuh!" Hitomi returns, her face scrunching and turning red with seething anger.

"Girls," I warn, propping myself up with my elbows. I try to cut in but am unable to get a word in edgewise, as if I don't exist. *Reminds me of another sister duo.*

"You only do this 'cause I'm smaller," Hanako states, stomping her foot and crossing her arms over her chest.

"Do not," Hitomi defends, squinting her eyes while sticking out her tongue.

"Yeah huuuh!" Hanako says, further initiating the childish, back and forth banter between her and her sister.

"Nuh uuuh! It's 'cause you're a dummy!" Hitomi eggs on.

"ENOUGH!" I say, raising my voice above the girls to silence them. Standing, I position myself between the girls and Sensei to settle them before a headache is inflicted.

From over my shoulder, I can see Sensei cynically giggling to himself from the situation at hand.

Bastard.

"Girls, stop bombarding Sensei," I discipline, returning my stern glare down at them with knitted brows. "He's gonna be here for a few days. You'll all have plenty of time with him before he goes."

"But Daddyyy!" they both moan.

"But nothing," I say firmly. Rubbing my temples in irritation, I realize someone is missing from the trio. "Where's Haruna?"

"Dunno," Hitomi answers, shrugging uninterestedly. "Prolly reading a stupid book somewheres."

"Yep!" Hanako says, confirming Hitomi's assumption. "She's reading in the corner of Mommy's classroom while Mommy is teaching, Daddy. She said she likes reading while listening to Mommy and the other kids play the pee-no."

"Piano," I correct. Now that all children are accounted for, I release a sigh of relief. "Okay, good." I pat Hanako's head in appreciation for her information. "Thanks for letting Daddy know."

"Welcome, Daddy," she says, beaming brightly from ear-to-ear.

"Hmph." Hitomi snickers. "I knew that, too," she says, in a curt tone.

Shutting my eyes, I take a deep breath, knowing well enough that another annoying fight is on the verge of breaking out. Opening my eyes, I release my pent-up irritation slowly through my nose, then shoo the girls further outside before round two starts.

"Why don't the two of you go out and play. Seems like you've got loooads of energy to burn."

"But Daaaddy, I don't wanna play with Hanako. She's a babyyy. I wanna spend time with Sensei," Hitomi whines again, in her same little high-pitched, spiteful voice. It's the voice she uses to try and get whatever she wants, and it works more often than I'd like to admit.

Hanako's mouth drops, taking major offense to her older sister's rude testimony. "Am not! I'm four!"

"Now girls," Sensei breaks in, "your Daddy and I are in the middle of a conversation. Why don't you both go and play for now, then at dinnertime we can all sit together, and you can catch me up on all the things I've missed since my last visit. How does that sound?"

"Okay, Sensei!" the girls sing simultaneously, changing their tune awfully quick.

They jump like wild monkeys off the engawa and right into the dirt around the perimeter of the house without a care in the world, as if they weren't just fighting with each other. Then, they slip on their dirt-covered sandals, ones I didn't notice had been left unattended just below.

"GAH! You better not come back in this house with those dirty, little feet!" I exclaim, stressed by the wrath that would befall me later on by a very angry wife. "Don't come crying to me when Mommy gets mad."

"We wooon't!" they chant with carefree attitudes, running off into the forest that accounts for a large part of the land surrounding our house.

"No respect," I growl, my nostrils flaring.

Sensei howls as he stands beside me, smiling nonchalantly as he waves the girls off.

"It's because you're a teacher that they listen to you. Don't get too cocky," I hiss. "If you lived with them, they'd come to hate you soon enough."

"Hmm, I wonder," he says mystically, with a wink directed at me. "But now I know who Hitomi reminds me of."

"Shaddap, you child-free demon."

Hinata dreamt of a huge family, one full of undivided, inseparable love, and after we got engaged, she spoke of children often. The topic of adoption and fostering was brought to the table several times, because Hinata took our personal experiences into consideration, but was never revisited after she got pregnant with Haruna.

Even though I was skeptical of having children to begin with, always second-guessing if a person like me should really be bringing a life into this world, I wanted to give Hinata what she desired the most. While pregnant, Haruna's unborn existence ultimately allowed me to accept the fact that I was going to be a father, and I will forever be grateful that I took the terrifying leap into fatherhood.

Once Haruna arrived, everything was different; my world changed for a second time, and everything was put into perspective. My eyes were finally open to the possibilities this child could bring; I could go against the odds and make a difference. I vowed to never behave in a manner that resembled the parents I resented.

Currently, Hinata and I have three children—all girls, all born at home—with a fourth on the way. With Hinata's hatred for hospitals, she wanted to have natural births in the comfort of our own home. And although I was nervous for her, who was I to stop her?

Our fourth child is said to be a boy, and as soon as we found out the gender of the baby, I jumped up and fist pumped the air in excitement. An embarrassing act when I look back on it now, especially whenever Hinata tells the story. But I couldn't conceal the joy I felt in that moment. Don't get me wrong, I love all my children—some days more than others—but living in a house filled with strong females, who all have different personalities, is exhausting to say the least. Spending time with them takes everything out of me; I'm drained by the end of the day. So I'm hoping a boy will shift things.

Haruna, the oldest of our children, is eight years old, Hitomi, the middle child, is six, and Hanako, the youngest, is four. Each one of the girls is two years apart, a structure that Hinata thought out and planned strategically in advance. And after our third, we were content with where we were. Then, just over three years later, another 'blessing' was bestowed upon us.

When learning that Hanako would be another girl, adding three girls to the mix that was set to outnumber us, I couldn't bring myself to consider having a fourth. I feared a fourth would be yet another girl because it seemed like that's all we were cursed with reproducing. But the gods were on my side this time and would soon grace me with a son to help level out the diminishing testosterone.

Haruna is an identical copy of Hinata, right down to the two-coloured eyes and upfront, blunt personality with an unceasing sequence of questions. Some of the things Haruna says or asks us has left me speechless on numerous occasions. Hitomi is one hundred percent my child. She has piercing, dark features, as well as the attitude and witty comebacks to prove it. For this reason, we butt heads often. Hanako is a mixture of us both, but she is unquestionably our most delicate child. She bruises easily; internally and externally—like a peach. It doesn't take much to offend Hanako or hurt her feelings, mainly things said or done by her sisters. She's also already had more broken bones and stitches than both her sisters combined.

Hinata is by far better at handling the children than I am, and I take no shame in admitting it.

"This old house sure has come a long way," Sensei remarks, reclaiming his spot back down on the edge of the engawa after taking credit for redirecting the children's attention. He takes an appreciative look all around him before his eyes land back on me. "I'm sure the Fujimotos are thrilled to have you living here and maintaining a house filled with so many unforgettable memories."

Also returning to my seat beside him, I think back to when Hinata and I first moved in. "I won't lie. At the beginning, this house was in rough shape, and it was hard to upkeep. It was in dire need of a facelift to restore it to its original beauty. With the customary Japanese-style architecture, like the wooden beams running along the ceiling, shoji partition doors and windows on all sides of the house, and tatami floors sprawled throughout the rooms, we wanted to keep and refine its traditional integrity." I inhale a deep breath, then release it. "Since Hinata had just given birth to Haruna, I didn't want her doing any heavy lifting or labour-intensive duties, so I sloppily managed the renovations on my own for some time."

"Ah, that's right," he says, crossing his arms and placing a hand on his chin in thought. "Didn't you say that Makoto and a few of the neighbours collectively came over and offered their help?"

"Sure did. After seeing the mess that I managed to get myself into, the neighbours jumped on board to help with the renovations. Everyone here is always ready to drop everything to help. They all beam rays of kindness outta their asses—the complete opposite of Tokyo. It's amazing."

Sensei coughs, clearing his throat. "Riku," he cautions, in a low, stern tone, "careful of the words you openly say outside. You wouldn't want your *kind* neighbours to hear you now, would you?"

I let out a belly laugh. "I guess not."

"You're hopeless."

"You sound like Makoto," I say, with an insincere grin.

Sensei's face lightens. "How's the doctor doing? Have you heard from him recently?"

"Uncle Mako is doing just fine," I sneer. "He and his family were here visiting just a few weeks ago."

"'Uncle Mako,' is it?" Sensei follows up, intrigued.

"It's the nickname the girls have graced him with," I say maliciously, leaning back on the palms of my hands. "'Mako' is a nickname he's always hated, but as soon as the girls started calling him that, he didn't seem bothered by it one bit. He even refers to himself as 'Uncle Mako' when he's around them. Kids get away with everything, I tell 'ya."

"That's too funny," Sensei responds, smiling softly. "How's your relationship with Mrs. Fujimoto? Last we spoke, you guys were still butting heads."

"Gah!" I scoff, my voice flying out of my mouth as if something is stuck in my throat. There is a relentless scream locked inside my head that I feel no one will come to hear or understand. Flinging myself forward, I face Sensei as I sit and cross my legs before initiating my rant. "That woman is impossible, y'know that? Just as I finally got her to accept the money for my high school tuition, she goes and offers me and Hinata this ginormous house to grow our family. Don't get me wrong, I'm beyond grateful for this once in a lifetime opportunity because there is no way in hell Hinata and I could've afforded a house of this magnitude on our own so early on, but she refuses to set up a payment plan so we can pay her back. I know Makoto's grandmother paid off the house well before she passed, but c'mon!" My hands flail about, speaking a dramatized language of their own. "A person can't go gifting houses to those who they aren't even blood related to. I feel like I took a part of someone's inheritance. Be it Makoto or one of his sisters, this house shouldn't have fallen into my lap the way that it did. It should've gone to one of them."

"Are you done?"

"The whole Fujimoto family is so meddlesome," I resume, barely taking in a new breath while managing to ignore Sensei's remark. "Makoto went and opened his damn mouth to his parents about Hinata and I wanting to move into a bigger place in the countryside. The next thing I know, Hinata and I get offered this castle." Pausing, I suck in a quick breath of air, then shoot it straight back out. "Will I ever stop receiving help from these disgustingly nice people?" I sigh. "I'll forever be indebted to them."

Sensei sits and listens to me quietly, saving anything he wants to say for the end, or what he presumes to be the end. Once I'm done, I take in a much-needed, deep breath and exhale it, causing my shoulders to deflate.

"Done now?"

I tear my gaze away from his, then click my tongue. "For now. But honestly, I could go on forever about how much that family irks me sometimes."

"The Fujimotos see you as more than just 'their son's friend.' You know that, Riku."

My heart and head are constantly at war with each other over accepting help from the Fujimotos; grappling with such emotions is difficult. This was a slow burn that charred at me. Coming from nothing and having no one to lean on, to unexpectedly acquiring a huge support system, was a hard thing to wrap my head around—even after so many years.

"I know. I'm just being dumb." I stare into the never-ending forest ahead of me, keeping a quiet eye on the girls poking in and out of my line of sight from a distance. "What I struggle with is how I keep accepting all these luxuries from them with nothing to give in return. It just doesn't sit right with me. This should be a give and take relationship. I can't just be the one who keeps taking without giving something in return."

"I can't tell you how or what to feel, Riku. All I can do is guide you and offer advice."

"I know. Still . . .."

"But, I think, the Fujimotos wouldn't give you what they didn't have to give," he picks up, smiling with reassurance. "Down the line, there may be something only you can do or offer them. And when that time comes, I'm sure you'll jump at the opportunity to provide them with everything and anything you have."

He's right.

I have been carrying around so much unnecessary baggage because I don't know how to give back to the Fujimotos, but that is only due to the simple fact that it isn't my turn to give back yet. When the time presents itself, I will surely be first in line to assist Mr. and Mrs. Fujimoto.

"I will," I say promptly, feeling the lightest I had in years.

Just then, I feel a set of heavy footsteps on the wooden planks approaching us, trailed by the pitter-patter of small feet against the hollow structure. Looking over my shoulder, I wait until I see someone turn the corner from the other side of the house. Walking with a mission, Hinata pokes her head out from around the exterior wall, making a late appearance.

"Riku, I thought I'd find you here," Hinata exerts, huffing tiredly. Acknowledging that I wasn't alone, she bows lightly. "Hello, Sensei. Welcome. I'm sorry for not greeting you upon your arrival. I hope your journey here went with ease."

"Hello, Hinata," Sensei says, dipping his head in a brief bow to return her mannered gesture. "Don't worry about it. Riku has kept me plenty company. Thank you for having me." He winks at me, then looks back to Hinata. "Finished with your lesson?"

"Not exactly," Hinata says, panting incessantly. "I had to send my student home early."

"Oh?" Sensei questions, tilting his head.

Noticing Hinata is breathless and more exhausted than usual, I uncross my legs and rise to my feet in concern, swiftly making it to her side. "Hinata, are you okay?" I ask, reaching out my arms and hovering them before her in caution.

"Riku," she says, placing a firm hold on my outreached arm, "it's time."

"Time?" I repeat, loose lipped.

"For the baby to come, Dad," Haruna speaks up delicately, popping out from behind Hinata. "Mom's water broke in the middle of her lesson. Water went everywhere."

My eyes bulge. "WHAT?" Shifting between the informative Haruna and the slightly hunched and laboured Hinata, panic pounds deep within my ears as I stutter nervously. "N-NOW? ARE YOU SURE?"

"Yes, now," Hinata confirms calmly, breathing full breaths in and out while squeezing my arm at different intensities.

"HOLY SHIT!"

"Dad, language," Haruna scolds in the background.

"HOW ARE YOU FEELING?" I shout hysterically, brushing Haruna off.

"Riku, I'm fine. Settle down," Hinata says, wincing through what I assume is a contraction. Her calm eyes unsettle me more than the sudden turn of events. "But we need to call the doctor. Now. This baby is coming, and *fast*."

Within mere seconds, both Sensei and I are running back and forth like chickens with their heads cut off, rushing from one end of the engawa to the other. Sensei rallies up all the children and keeps them occupied while I make a desperate phone call to the doctor.

Even though I have experienced three other pregnancies alongside Hinata, and should have been a professional by now, my mind is a clean slate and I'm rendered useless.

After the doctor arrives, and Hinata is situated comfortably inside, everything happens so fast. I blink, and when I lift my eyelids, I'm met with one of the most precious little humans I've ever laid eyes on. Within an hours' time, our son, Rei Nakajima, is born.

Life challenged us, broke us, and ultimately healed us. Even though we went through so much shit, I can honestly say my life is better because I got to meet Hinata. We persevered through all of it together. Now, I can confidently say I no longer walk a life of nothing. Now, I have everything, and more.

So much more.

ABOUT THE AUTHOR

LINDSEY-ANNE PONTES (DESOUSA) was born in Cambridge, Ontario, and although she has moved around a bit over the last few years, her Cambridge roots still run strong as she continues to participate locally in Cambridge author-related events.

Growing up with an IEP (Individual Education Plan) for reading and writing in elementary school, Lindsey found it hard to read books when instructed to during class. After stumbling across some manga that her elementary school librarian brought in, Lindsey found her reading passion. Picking up a book of interest, and finally being able to understand what she was reading by using the pictures as a reference tool, Lindsey learned how to read.

Lindsey is a mom to two lop-eared bunnies, Willow and Baloo, who are constantly finding new ways to keep her on her toes when it comes to bunny-proofing her home.

Things she loves include: reading manga and watching anime, hanging out in cafés (especially Café O), reading novels (romance—obviously), indoor plants, playing Pokémon, and riding her motorcycle when the weather's nice.

Make sure to follow Lindsey on Instagram (@lindseyannedesousa).

www.petalpublishing.com

Check out **Lindsey-Anne Pontes'** other work.